RECEIVED

JUN 23 2022

BY:_____

NO LONGER PROPERTY OF
SEATTLE PUBLIC LIBRARY

D1053387

LAKESEDGE

LYNDALL CLIPSTONE

HENRY HOLT AND COMPANY
New York

To SKC

I promise all the plants at
Lakesedge are endemic species.

Henry Holt and Company, *Publishers since 1866*
Henry Holt® is a registered trademark of Macmillan Publishing Group, LLC
120 Broadway, New York, New York 10271 • fiercereads.com

Copyright © 2021 by Lyndall Clipstone. All rights reserved.

Our books may be purchased in bulk for promotional, educational,
or business use. Please contact your local bookseller or the Macmillan Corporate
and Premium Sales Department at (800) 221-7945 ext. 5442 or by email at
MacmillanSpecialMarkets@macmillan.com.

Library of Congress Cataloging-in-Publication Data is available.

First edition, 2021
Book design by Michelle Gengaro-Kokmen
Printed in the United States of America

ISBN 978-1-250-75339-7 (hardcover)
1   3   5   7   9   10   8   6   4   2

ISBN 978-1-250-84340-1 (special edition)
1   3   5   7   9   10   8   6   4   2

You should be out by the orchard, where
    violets secretly darken the earth,
Or there in the woods of the twilight, with
    northern wind–flowers shaken astir.
Think of me here in the library, trying and
    trying a song that is worth
Tears and swords to my heart, arrows no
    armour will turn or deter.

—D. H. Lawrence, *Letter from
Town: On a Grey Morning in March*

Chapter One

There are monsters in the world.

There are monsters in the woods.

They slip inside at night. Crawl through the walls of our cottage. They find their way into my brother's dreams.

It's been weeks, longer, since Arien's last nightmare, but I knew they would come tonight. All day it's followed me, that familiar heaviness in the air. I can feel them coming even before he does.

I'm still awake. Curled up on my narrow bed in the small, plain room we share. Watching him. Waiting. It's past midnight. A hot night, airless, even with our window wide open.

"Violeta?"

He calls my name and reaches out as the darkness rises through him. Shadows spill from his hands like unfurled ribbons, shrouding the floor with an inky mist. He looks at me with eyes gone solid black; they change when he dreams, and those blank eyes in his frightened face are so *wrong*. Arien is gentle and sweet. This darkness shouldn't be in him. It shouldn't *be* him, and yet—

I move toward him as the shadows cloud over us, filling the room. At first they're smoke, a haze that thickens. Then they build and build, until all the light is gone, and there's only me and Arien and the gathering dark.

"Leta?" He calls for me again, sounding frightened. Then his voice changes to a drawn-out snarl. "Leta, *Leta*."

I take his hand, starting to tremble, hating myself for it but unable to stop. Darkness pours through our clasped fingers, blotting out the moonlight. The shadows are like midwinter frost against my skin, a cold that *burns*.

I cling tight to Arien, whispering to him, "I'm here, I'm here," not letting go even when he growls viciously and starts to claw me. He scrapes my face, my throat, my arms. I bite back a cry at the pain, grabbing his other hand before he makes the scratches worse.

He'll hurt me more than this. I push the thought away, swallow it down until my mouth tastes of copper and salt. He's my brother. He would never, he won't—

More shadows come, faster now, violent, and I hold Arien close against me as they wreathe us, winding tighter and tighter. They're like vines, like thorns. I feel the darkness all over me, feel it slip and slither inside my skin. Panic knots my stomach and there's a scream caught in my throat. I take a deep breath and try to speak calmly.

"Arien, my love, you're safe, you're safe." The same words I've spoken over countless nights. Ever since the dreams began. Ever since we came to live here.

This is my seventeenth summer, Arien's thirteenth. Mother found us on the road beside the Vair Woods. Arien was a baby, and I was old enough to tell her our names—Arien and Violeta Graceling—and that our parents were dead, but little else. Whatever happened to send us into the forest at midwinter . . . I don't let those thoughts in too closely.

Fire to burn out the infection. Sparks that cut through the night sky. The scent of ash. Trees outlined against the moonlight. A whisper through the branches.

I still remember the way Mother's hand cupped my cheek for the first time, her fingers streaked with paint from the icons she made. The way the winter sun gleamed over her corn-silk hair as she bent toward me. The smell of linseed oil.

She picked up Arien and took my hand and brought us back to her cottage.

The Lady sent you to me, Mother told us once. At first it didn't sound like a threat. But we have spent our entire lives here, almost. Things are different now.

Now all I know is that I can't let my brother be overtaken by this terrible darkness. No matter how much it frightens me, I have to protect him. "It's a dream, Arien."

"You can't make it stop, Leta. You can't—"

He spits the words between bared teeth. I want to flinch away, but I force myself to be still. Arien's voice, the way he fights me . . . it's not him. It can't be him. I have to help him through this. He has to come back. I won't let him stay lost in the dark.

"It's a dream, Arien. This isn't real."

"You can't make it stop."

Shadows fill my mouth and lungs, tasting of smoke and ash. I wrap my arms tighter around my brother and cling to him. I shove aside my fear and imagine we are somewhere else, outside in our small garden. I think of sun and flowers. My hands sunk into the earth. The baskets of Summerbloom cherries I've harvested all week. I hold the picture vivid in my mind.

There's a single, insistent pull from deep in my chest. Like there's a string tied to me, the other end anchored to Arien. Warmth begins to hum beneath my skin. I think of gardens and sunlight. Not darkness, not shadows, not my brother with those blank, inhuman eyes.

Slowly, slowly, the shadows stop coming from his hands. The darkness settles and softens into the corners of the room. I hold my breath until the final traces clear, then sink against Arien with a heavy sigh.

He touches my wrist, quickly pulling back when he feels the raised welts. "Did I hurt you again?"

I close my hand over the marks. "You didn't. I'm fine."

Outside the window, the moon is low, pocketed between the thickened clouds. It glows dimly across the collection of stones I keep on the sill. I trail my finger over the one with a ripple that looks like gold, the one so smooth and heavy it fits perfectly into the curve of my palm.

4

I force myself to breathe steadily, willing my still-racing heartbeat to slow. "You didn't hurt me," I say again, trying to reassure Arien, trying to reassure myself. "It's over, my love. You're safe now."

He starts to cry. Loud, angry sobs that echo through the room, through the house. "I'm sorry, Leta."

I put my arms around him. "You have nothing to be sorry for." Then, knowing I have to say it: "But you have to be quiet."

He buries his head against me, trying to muffle the sound of his tears. His hair, red like mine, falls across his face. I brush it back from his cheek.

He swallows down a sob as I murmur gently into his ear. "Please, Arien, you have to stop. She'll hear you. Mother will hear you. Please—"

I cut off sharply as he grabs my hand, his fingers crushing mine. We both fall silent as footsteps echo from the hallway and our door is shoved open, so hard it bangs against the wall. Mother storms into the room.

Lit by the lantern flame, she's fair and golden, skin dusted with pale freckles, hair that glints as it catches the light. But it's a cut-glass prettiness, all hard edges. Whatever softness was in her when she first saw us—two lost children in the road—it's long vanished. Ever since the shadows began.

She snatches Arien's wrist, wrenches open his fingers. His hands are stained black. The shadows have clung to his skin, the way they always do. The marks are slow to fade, darkening again whenever he dreams. They can't be scrubbed away, though Mother has made him try countless times.

5

"Arien." With her other hand, she catches his chin, holds it tight until he looks into her eyes. There's a flicker across her face that might be sadness; then the light shifts, and she's cold. "Not again."

He twists against her grasp as she drags him forward, out of the room. I rush after them. "Let him go! He can't help it, you know he can't!"

"Go back to bed, Violeta," Mother snaps at me over her shoulder.

She tightens her grip on Arien's arm, pulling him through the hall as he struggles against her. I'm right behind them. When we reach the kitchen, his eyes dart frantically between the cellar and the outside door. Last time this happened, she forced him down beneath the house. The time before, she locked him out and made him spend the whole night in the orchard.

She thinks if she keeps him in the dark, the shadows will go—as if one darkness will cancel the other. She's tried so many ways to scour him clean, but none have ever worked. She's convinced his shadows are evidence of dark alchemy.

But all I know of dark alchemy—that it's dangerous and poisonous and wrong—doesn't fit with Arien. He's not the sinister gloom deep in the forest, or the creeping poison in a blighted field. He's my brother, and I'll go with Arien wherever she takes him. I'll go into the dark with him beneath the house; I'll go out to the moonlit orchard. I'll stay with him and keep him safe.

But instead of reaching for the door or the cellar, Mother

drags Arien over to the altar of the Lady. She twists his arm until he kneels, then sets a sparklight to the candles on the shelf. They flare bright, one by one.

The Lady made the world. She *is* the world. In all of Mother's paintings, she looks the same: golden and brilliant, with bronze skin and long, flowing hair. This icon shows the Lady with her fingers pressed against the earth, dissolving into the light that flows through all existence. The scene is beautiful, but as Arien falls down beneath the icon, a shadow crosses the painting and for a moment, the Lady's golden fingers seem like claws. The edges of her smile turn sharp.

Mother forces Arien's stained fingers over the candles. I grab her arm, trying to pull her back. "Stop! You can't do this!"

Everything happens fast, like a spark on a wick. She turns on me, her face tensed, and slaps me. The sound fractures the air, and the world turns white from sudden pain. I fall against the table, my hand pressed to my throbbing cheek.

As I try to shake the ringing from my ears, Mother shows me the blackened marks on Arien's skin. "You know what this darkness is, Violeta. The Lord Under will claim him."

"He won't. He *won't*."

The candle flares. She shoves Arien forward. He bites back a cry as his fingertips glow bright, haloed by flames.

Mother thinks the darkness in him belongs to the Lord Under—the lord of the dead. That the shadows will call him to us the way he'd be drawn to a dying soul. But Arien is kind and *good*. The shadows are only dreams. He isn't the same as the darkness of the Lord Under, or the magic in the world Below.

7

I grab her arm again. "He's not some blighted field to be burned down!"

"Leta," Arien whispers, quiet and desperate. "Leta, don't."

But I ignore him. Let Mother hurt me—I don't care; at least then she'll leave Arien alone. I brace myself, ready to be struck again, almost *hoping* for it, but instead she shakes me off and pushes Arien's hands back over the flames. He scrunches his eyes closed, hisses a breath through his teeth. I stare at them, feeling so powerless, so angry.

I have to do something. She's going to burn him until his hands are clean. She'll keep hurting him, unless I make her stop.

On the table is a glass idol, a candle burning at the center. I snatch it up and throw it—hard—onto the floor. It shatters into a jagged star. The sound stills the air.

Mother goes pale and her mouth draws into a sharp, furious line. Incandescent anger sparks through her eyes as she steps over the glass and grabs my wrist. Her fingers bite into my arm, marking fresh bruises over ones left from the last time she hurt me. I let the pain wash over me, glad for it, glad that it's me and not Arien.

She wrenches me toward the floor. "Kneel down."

"What—?"

"Kneel. Down."

I look at the jagged glass, the splattered wax, the smoke from the ruined candle. Arien shakes his head, his expression helpless and furious all at once. There are tears on his cheeks, and his burned fingers are tucked into a twist of his sleeve.

"Mother, stop!" He falters, eyeing the candles, steeling himself to reach back into the flames again. "I'll do it, I'll do it."

How can Mother think that hurting him, hurting me, will keep us safe? At this moment, if there's anything we need to be saved from it's not the Lord Under. Not the dark. It's *her*.

I feel as fractured and ruined as the shattered glass beneath our feet. But I keep my gaze fixed on Mother's face. Before she can speak again, before Arien can move, I kneel down. One knee, then the other.

The first cut is a bright shock. I put my hands on the floor, trying not to make a sound as I hover above the shards.

I can't do this.

I have to.

The glass pierces my knees with a hideous pain that stings all over: my fingertips, my scalp, the soles of my feet. I flinch, but some scrap of pride holds me still. Arien is safe—safe from the candles, from being locked in the dark, from everything. For now.

Mother's hurt us before, but never like this.

She crouches down and cups her hand against my cheek, her palm incongruously gentle over the place where she hit me. "I'm trying to protect him, Violeta. I'm trying to protect you."

Her expression and her voice are soft, as though she's truly sorry to see me like this. And there's a horrible, treacherous part of me that *wants* to lean against her hand, to let her comfort me. Tears prickle my eyes, but I blink them away. I stare at Mother, clench my teeth and let more of the glass cut deeper into my knees.

She watches me, unmoving, then she stands up and brushes her hands over her skirts. She crosses the kitchen, and her steps go hollowly along the hall, back to her room. The latch scrapes as she locks the door closed.

Once we're alone, Arien extinguishes the altar candles with a swift breath. Smoke wisps the air. He helps me move away from the shards, and I curl up on the floor near the hearth with my back against the wall. The room smells bittersweet from the pot on the stove, full of the cherry preserves I've made. On the shelf above are empty jars, ready to be filled once the preserves cool, our contribution for the village tithe tomorrow.

Arien crouches beside me. He's uncertain, like he wants to touch me but he's afraid. The dark has faded from his eyes now. They're the same silver gray as my own. "Leta, I'm sorry," he says in a rush. "I should have stopped her. I should—"

I fold back the hem of my nightdress. "Can you get me a cloth?"

While he's gone, I bend forward to see the cuts. I take a breath and begin to pick out the splinters embedded in my skin. I put the shards one by one onto the floor. Through the blood, the glass shines, a grim mirror to my collection of polished stones.

Arien brings me some scraps of linen. He takes the kettle from the back of the stove and fills a bowl with warm water and salt. He dampens a cloth and presses it to my knee. It quickly turns crimson and his forehead creases with a worried frown. He rinses the cloth, folds it over to cover the stain, and presses it down again.

I sit very still as he wipes away the blood. Outside the kitchen window, the leaves of the apple tree shift and shiver like splotches of paint against the gloomy night sky, black over black. I feel so cold, even though it's hot beside the stove, with warmth radiating from the banked embers.

A thought tugs, unwelcome. I wish for something stronger than me, strong enough to take away all my fear and my hurt. Something immovable, like an enormous tree that will scratch my cheek with rough bark as I lean against its trunk.

I want my mother. I want my father.

I remember my father's large hand, warm around mine. His fingers, careful, as they swept my hair back from my forehead. My mother humming to Arien as he slept in his cradle.

I miss them with a terrible ache.

But now there is only me, numb and sad and scoured clear, like the windswept mud after a storm. And if I'm not strong enough to protect Arien, then nobody will.

Arien starts to wrap two longer strips of cloth around my knees, bandaging the cuts.

"Don't fight her again." His voice is small in the quiet of the room. "It only makes things worse."

I take his hand and gently inspect his fingers. They're blistered with raised, pale welts. I blow a soft breath over his skin and he manages a faint smile. "I'll not let her hurt you, Arien. Not like this. Not at all. It doesn't matter what she does to me."

"Please, Leta."

I put my arms around him. "I'll try."

He rests his cheek against my shoulder and sighs, despondent.

Until tonight, I knew how to protect him from Mother's anger. Now the nights ahead are full of dreams and shadows and flames. I try to think of a way out, somewhere we could go to escape this. But there's our cottage and Mother, and there's the world—vast and unknown, and no safer than here. Here, at least, I can learn the new shape of our lives.

I close my eyes and try to map how things will be from this point onward, picturing a hallway full of locked doors, the walls lined with endless altars where candles burn and burn and burn. Me at the center, my arms outspread, as Arien stands behind me.

I will take everything—Mother's fear, her anger, the fire, and the blood. Let it all come down on me. No matter what I have to do, I'll never let Arien be hurt like this again.

"I'm going to keep you safe," I tell him. "I promise."

Chapter Two

Greymere on tithe day hums like a hive. The air is pollen bright. The townspeople's voices are as loud as a chanted litany. Arien and I walk through the crowd toward the village square. Everyone waits, their arms laden heavily with sacks of grain, baskets of fruit, bolts of neat-hemmed linen cloth.

We take our place at the end of the line, and I bend to set our basket onto the ground beside my feet. When I straighten, my knees give a sharp, fierce ache. I hiss between my teeth, and Arien looks at me, concerned.

"It's fine." I stare down into the basket at the jars of preserves. "I'm fine."

The cuts still seeped fresh blood this morning. There were so many pieces of glass, and they went so deep that I don't know if I've picked out all the splinters. I rewrapped my knees, then put on my thickest wool stockings to hide the bandages.

I notice Mother on the opposite side of the square. She and the village keeper are beside the altar. A canvas cloth is spread on the ground with all her paints and brushes set out neatly. She runs her hands over the icon, her touch reverent, as she checks for wear. She'll work the whole day to repair it, a chore she does every season. Add more color, then smooth and varnish the wooden frame.

Later, when the sun is lower, we'll all gather in a circle at the altar with our hands pressed to the earth to make observance to the Lady.

Arien touches my arm, drawing my attention back to him. "Leta? I—I've been thinking." He leans in and softens his voice. "What if, after the tithe, we didn't go home? What if we didn't go back, *ever*? You know Mother wouldn't stop us."

He rubs at his blistered fingers, then his gaze drops to my covered knees. I force a smile. "Should we build a house in the tallest tree of the forest? I'll make us a quilt from dandelions and cook toadstool stew for our dinner. The birds can comb our hair."

Arien scrunches his nose, the way he always does when I tease him. "I'm serious."

"Where would we go, if we did leave?" The word feels strange in my mouth. It's the first time either of us has spoken it aloud.

"We could stay here. We could stay in the village."

The thought is vivid, threaded with gold. I look at the

buildings surrounding the square. The healer's thatch-roofed cottage with flower beds beneath the front windows. The store with barrels of flour and bolts of cloth. We could work in the store. I'd weigh sugar while Arien measured lengths of cloth. Or help in the healer's garden. Tend her flowers, gather the petals and leaves she turns to medicine.

When I think of how I felt last night as I watched Arien's hands in the flames, I want to stay in the village. I do. But everyone here already treats us suspiciously. They know how Mother took us in, how our lives have been brushed by death. *Once marked, the Lord Under knows your name.* That's what people believe. And if they found out about Arien, about the shadows . . .

Arien's dreams aren't like the magic worked by alchemists, who draw on the golden power the Lady has threaded through the world. Their magic is light. His nightmares, full of shadows that come alive, are more like the power that comes from the Lord Under. Arien is not like that, not dark and *wrong* and terrible . . . But as soon as someone heard his cries, or saw his eyes turn black, they'd think he was. They'd call him corrupted. They'd fear him.

"I promised to keep you safe." I stare down at my boots, scuffed by dust. I can't look at Arien, at the tentative hope in his eyes. "I don't know if you'd be safe in the village."

"Then we'll go somewhere else, somewhere far away."

"I don't know. Maybe."

Arien sighs, frustrated. The line starts to move, and I bend down to pick up the basket as we shift forward.

15

Across the square, a woman steps out of her cottage. Her eyes flicker over the crowd—and us—before narrowing at the ground. She takes something from a jar. A handful of salt. She throws it heavily into the street, then draws her salt-crumbed fingers across her chest. Two fingers, left to right, a line across her heart. The symbol of the Lady: a protection against darkness.

"Why did she do that?" Arien asks warily.

I look more closely at the crowd. But they aren't focused on us, or anything that I can see. There's just a vague, nervous crackle of restlessness, like the air before a storm.

Everyone is dressed in their nicest clothes. Polished boots, crisp linen shirts, pinned-up braids, delicately embroidered dresses. We've gathered like this is a celebration. And it is. At least, it should be. But in the line where we wait with our tithes, people murmur to one another anxiously. Around the square, more doors open. More villagers scatter salt over their thresholds. The healer has strung garlands of rosemary and sage across her windows.

"Have you heard?" A girl comes along the line, a pen and square of parchment in her hands. She has oak-brown skin and a cloud of beautiful curled hair, which she pushes out of her face before she scans the nearby people, unsettled. Her voice dampens to a whisper. "Lord Sylvanan is here. He's come to claim the tithe."

"Lord Sylvanan?" A nervous shudder runs through me. "Here? He never comes to tithe days."

It was six years ago that we last gathered in Greymere, when it was our turn to pay the tithe to the Sylvanans, who own all the land in the valley. Then, there was nothing to fear.

The lord who came to the tithe day was older than Mother. He was tall and handsome, and wore his dark hair tied neatly back. He helped the villagers pack the wagon he'd brought to take everything back to his estate. Afterward he walked slowly through the square and looked appreciatively at the village. His eyes crinkled up when he smiled at Arien and me, running past amid a tangle of children.

But there's a new lord now. His son. Because just after our last tithe day, the whole Sylvanan family died. All except for him, the new lord.

Because he murdered them.

His parents, his brother, his whole family. He drowned them one by one in the lake behind their estate.

They said his father was found laid out on the shore, white and still, as though all his blood had been drained. That his mother's throat was snared in sedge grass, drawn so tight it cut her skin.

"Yes, he might already be here." The girl pauses and scans the crowd around us, then drags her fingers across her chest. "My village is next to his estate. We have a name for him there."

"Calathea?" A man comes through the crowd, crossing the distance in an easy stride. He has the same oak-brown skin and features, though he's pulled his curls back into a knot, without even a single strand escaping. "Thea, what did I tell you?"

"Mark off the list. Don't get distracted." Thea ducks her head, chagrined. She peers into our basket and quickly scratches a few lines on the parchment with her pen. "Sorry, Father. They were the last ones."

He sighs heavily. "You should have been finished already instead of wasting time. We still have to prepare all the tithes for transport back to Lakesedge." He takes hold of her arm and draws her closer, his voice lowering. "I don't want to be here any longer than necessary, not with *him* around."

"I didn't mean to take so long. I'll help you load the baskets when they're ready."

"No. You can stay over there, out of trouble." Her father starts to direct Thea away from us, toward a wagon.

"Wait," I call after her as she leaves. "The name they have for Lord Sylvanan in your village, what is it?"

Thea turns back to us. "The Monster of Lakesedge."

The sun is still high above the tree line. Sweat has beaded on the back of my neck, and there's a stripe of sunburn across my nose. I'm hot and itchy, prickled by my woolen stockings. But when I hear that name, I start to shiver.

"Thea. Enough." Her father mutters a warning in her ear, his expression tense. She walks over to the wagon with her eyes downcast, but when she settles herself in the seat, he pats her knee, comforting her.

A strange, sore ache fills my chest as I watch Thea and her father, remembering *my* father. His strong hands, weathered from work in the garden, but still gentle when he touched me. If he were here, he would keep us safe.

"The Monster of Lakesedge." I say it softly, only a whisper, but the words taste like smoke and darkness.

Arien steps closer to me. "Can you see him?"

I stand on tiptoe to see past the people ahead. There's a table set up near the altar, shaded by two tall pine trees, where the tithe goods will be laid out. A woman in a long, embroidered dress stands behind it. Her silvery hair is swept back from her tanned face in a braid that loosens to waves, cascading down her back.

"He isn't waiting for the tithes."

"Maybe he's like a woods wolf." Arien points at the forest, where the shadows are thick between the trees. "And he can't come out in the daylight."

"Those aren't real. That was just a story I made up."

But what happened at Lakesedge Estate sounds like a story, too. A house locked up and almost empty. A whole family murdered.

There's a knot in my stomach. It tightens with each moment that passes. I can't stop searching the crowd. As the sun dips, shadows from the pine trees at the edges of the square lengthen over the ground. Every shift of light and shade makes me jump. I expect to turn and see the monster right there, as if I summoned him when I spoke his name.

Beside me, Arien has stayed still and quiet. His face has started to turn pale.

"What's wrong? Are you worried about Lord Sylvanan? I can't see him. Maybe he's not even here."

"No." He wraps his arms around himself. "It's fine. I'm fine."

His skin looks bloodless, almost completely white. "Arien. What's the matter?"

"I—I don't—" He shakes his head, then turns and walks swiftly away without another word.

I blink, stunned. It only takes me a moment to gather myself, to follow. But when I step out into the square, I've already lost sight of him.

I slip between a row of buildings. Heat radiates against my face from afternoon sun baked into the rough stone walls. I rush past the store. Past the healer's cottage. There are footprints in the dust, about the size of Arien's boots. Smudged and smeared, like he was running. The noise of the crowd dwindles away, smaller and smaller. I'm outside the village now, in a flower field. Bees circle a white line of hives. Trees rise up beyond.

The woods. Arien has gone into the woods.

The Vair Woods stretch from Greymere all the way to our cottage. I know these woods. I see them every day. But I've never liked to go inside. Not far from here is where Mother found us all those years ago.

When I step past the border of the forest, my boots sink into the dense undergrowth. Air drifts through the leaves like a whispered voice.

"Arien?" I look ahead but there are only trees, then more trees, then dark. The afternoon sun is blocked out by thickly woven branches. "Arien, are you here?"

Finally my eyes adjust, and I see him—pale skin,

flame-bright hair—in the distance, past a line of close-set cedar trees. He's wide eyed and white, stilled by a wordless terror.

The shadows have already begun to curl at his palms.

I run toward him. Branches snag my skirts and scratch my cheeks. Darkness creeps across his eyes, and his pupils widen. His gaze turns to solid black.

"Leta?"

I grasp his hands. They're already so cold. I don't understand. Never before have the shadows come like this. It's always at night. Not at the center of the village in the Summerbloom daylight, all brightness and green leaves. Not like this.

Terror sweeps over me. *Not now, not here. He can't, he can't.* It doesn't take much to picture what would happen if someone saw us right now. His blank, dark eyes. The shadows. They would think he's a monster.

I take hold of his wrist, and he flinches. I've gripped him too hard, in the same place where Mother bruised him last night. I quickly loosen my fingers but don't let go.

I thought I'd mapped the limits of this thing that haunts my brother. It had borders of time and space: only at night, only in our room. But now everything has changed. This is all new. This is all *wrong*.

The shadows rise and wrap around us. The darkened forest turns darker still. I try to think of warm things. Sunlight. Bees in the wisteria vines. How it feels to make observance, when we put our hands into the earth and feel the golden light that weaves through the whole world. But it's too cold, too dark.

It's only a dream—but it's not, it's not. We're in the woods, in the day, and the shadows are all around us.

"Arien!" I dig my fingers into his arm. He makes a sharp, hurt sound. "Arien, call them back, you have to call them back."

It's the first time I've spoken this terrible thought aloud: that the shadows might be something he can *control*. I've kept it locked away and pushed far down for such a long time. But now it's spilled out.

I feel the tendons in his wrist go taut. The shadows wash across my face and into my mouth. My throat burns with the taste of them. I'm so cold it aches; I'm lost in the darkness. There's only the sound of our breathing. The steady throb of pain from my cut knees. A damp heat where fresh blood has seeped through the bandages.

Slowly, I uncurl my fingers from Arien's wrists. I take his face in my hands. I try to think of something to say to reassure him, but I can't. So I just hold him. I picture the sunlight in the clearing. I breathe in the baked-earth scent that drifts from the overgrown grass beside the forest. Smooth my thumbs across his cheeks.

"Call them back, Arien," I whisper. "Make them stop."

He goes very still. After a long while the shadows soften; he flexes his hands as the last wisps dissolve. The darkness fades from his eyes, and they turn gray again. We step apart. He tips his head back and lets out a shaky breath.

Everything feels wrong and fractured. Like the ground is about to crack apart beneath me. "What was that? Arien, why did it happen *now*?"

"I don't know." He kicks at the ground, scattering leaves. Then he pushes past me, headed for the path. "Come on. It will be our turn for the tithe soon."

We walk back to the village in silence. When we reach the square, the line of people has cleared away. Everyone else has given their tithes. I take our basket from the ground where I left it and go quickly toward the table. The silver-haired woman has gone. Arien and I are here alone.

The pines that flank the table are dark, with burnished light behind them. Then a shadow peels away from beneath the trees. It takes on the shape of a man. Stripes of variegated shade cut him—gray, black, gray, black—as he crosses the distance between us. I recognize him instantly.

Monster. My mouth shapes the word, but I don't make a sound. He's not a woods wolf. Not one of the fierce and terrible creatures from my stories, with claws and fangs and too many eyes.

The Monster of Lakesedge is a boy with long dark hair and a sharp, beautiful face. And somehow that makes all of this so much worse.

He's young—older than me, but not by much. His hair is past his shoulders. The waves are swept back loosely, the top half tied up into a knot with a length of black cord. Even with the summer heat, he wears a heavy cloak draped across one shoulder. There are scars on his face. A scatter of jagged marks from his brow to his jaw.

He looks me up and down, his expression unreadable. "What do you offer?"

I feel his words like midwinter, cold and sharp. The light

flickers, and for just a heartbeat, there's something *there* at the corner of my vision.

I remember a long-ago voice in a frost-laden forest. The question it whispered close against my ear.

What will you offer me?

I bite my lip, hard, and pull myself back to the present. "Nothing. I—I don't—"

Arien takes the basket from me and puts it onto the table. "Sour cherries. That's our offering. And the altar, mended."

The monster looks over to where Mother is packing away her paints. The wooden altar frame is glossed with new varnish. On the shelf below, the candles have been lit, bathing the icon in light.

I take hold of Arien's arm, about to lead him away.

"Wait." The monster's boots crush against the ground. He steps closer. "Stay a moment."

I move in front of Arien. Damp, tense sweat is slick on my palms, but I square my shoulders and meet the monster's dark gaze evenly. "We don't have anything else for you."

"Oh?" There's something feral in the way he moves, like a fox stalking a hare. "Oh, I think you do."

"No, we don't."

The monster holds out his hands. He's wearing black gloves, and the cuffs of his shirt are laced tightly all the way down his wrists. He motions to Arien, then waits expectantly. "Go on, show me."

Arien lifts his own hands in an echo of the monster's

gesture. My brother's fingers, burned clean last night by the altar candles, are now stained dark.

The monster flicks me a glance. "That isn't quite *nothing*, is it?"

"It's—"

He turns back to Arien, and the feral look on his face intensifies. "Tell me: How did you get those marks?"

Arien looks at me helplessly. This is all my fault. I promised to protect him.

Fear and fury rise through me in a hot, wavery rush. I shove my way between them until I'm right up against the monster, the scuffed toes of my boots against his polished ones. "Our mother is a painter. They're stains from the paint."

He stares coldly down at me. He's beautiful, but wrongness clings to him. It's as cloying as the bittersweet scent of sugar in the kitchen last night. Between the laces of his shirt collar, I catch a glimpse of something dark on his throat. I watch, horrified, as all the veins along his neck turn vivid, like streaks of ink drawn under the surface of his skin.

Then I blink, and whatever I saw—whatever I *thought* I saw—is gone.

The monster's mouth curves into a faint smile.

"I'm sorry." He doesn't sound sorry at all. "Clearly I was mistaken."

All I want to do is grab Arien and run away, but I force myself to be still. I scrunch my fingers into the edges of my skirts. "You were."

He takes off his gloves roughly and throws them onto the ground at Arien's feet. "Keep them."

He walks away without sparing either of us another glance, his newly bared hands shoved deep into the pockets of his cloak.

Arien bends down to pick up the gloves. He pulls them on quickly. No matter how hard I stare at him, he won't look at me. Together, we go across the square to join the crowd that's gathered at the altar. We kneel down and put our hands against the earth.

"Arien," I murmur. "Before, in the forest—"

"Please forget about it. About the forest. About leaving." He turns his face toward the icon, the bank of golden candles. "About everything."

We start to chant the summer litany. I close my eyes and press my fingers into the dirt. As the light washes over me, I try to lose myself in warmth and song. But all I can think is there might be nowhere in this world, now, where I can keep my brother safe.

Chapter Three

It's almost sunset when we reach home. Mother goes into the cottage, but Arien and I stay outside in the garden. The evening sky is cloudless, endless. Wind stirs through the branches of our orchard, and the air is heavy with lingering heat. I walk through the rows of summer plants, breathe the scent of sage and nettle as my skirts brush past the leaves. Arien follows me.

We go into the well house. It's dim inside, lit only by faint palings of light that come through the cracks in the walls. I lift the heavy wooden cover and pull the bucket up from the water beneath. There's always something eerie in this moment. That space between surface and water. The deep, silent well with the blur of ripples far below.

I wash my sweat-grimed face with a handful of water. Arien takes off the gloves and holds them, crumpled in his fist.

He looks wrung out. His face is pale, and his eyes are circled with fatigue. I put my hand on the back of his neck, and he sighs as he leans against the cold of my palm.

"We could still leave." My whisper echoes down through the darkness. The sound lingers. *Leave. Leave. Leave.*

He shakes his head, then scoops up some water and splashes it over his face. He wipes his hands against his trousers and pulls the gloves back on. "I told you to forget about it."

I fill the bucket again with a sigh and unhook it from the rope so I can carry it to the kitchen. We walk back through the garden in silence, Arien ahead of me. He's grown so much in the past few months. His shirt is tight across his shoulders though I only just let out the seams for him. He looks so much like our father did, tall and lean, while I've taken after our mother, curved and small.

A memory comes to me, blurred as the fading sunlight. Our father at work in the garden. His sleeves rolled to his elbows, his hands in the earth. Our mother with a basket of cut flowers in her arms. It's the strangest feeling whenever I think of them like this: both a comfort and a hurt.

I close my eyes for a moment and let the image linger before I go into the house.

Inside the kitchen, Mother is standing behind the table. Her hands are curled tight over the back of a chair, as though she's waiting for someone to sit down. Our eyes meet, and she grips the chair until her knuckles turn white. Her expression is wild with a mix of fear and anger. "Violeta. Arien. What happened in the village today?"

My boots catch on the floorboards as I come to a sharp, sudden stop. The bucket tilts. Water sloshes out and soaks my skirts. Arien takes it from me and sets it down carefully. We look at each other. He opens his mouth, but I answer quickly before he can speak. "Nothing. Nothing happened."

"Really?" A voice comes from the other side of the room. A voice that is newly, terribly familiar. "That's not how I remember it."

Instinctively, I push Arien behind me. The monster stands against the far wall, out of reach from even the faint glow of the stovelight. Behind him, the altar with its unlit candles is thrown dark by his shadow. He's just a silhouette, with his face hidden by the drawn-down hood of his cloak.

The monster is here.

"We didn't do anything. I already told you—"

He holds up a hand. "Don't bother to lie. I saw the two of you in the Vair Woods. I saw your brother with the shadows."

The world seems to lurch until everything is off-kilter. *He saw. He knows.*

Mother looks at Arien, her eyes wide. "What have you done?" Her face blanches as she turns to the monster. "I'm sorry. I've tried to mend him. But there's so much darkness in him. It's too strong."

"That's why I'm here," the monster says acidly. "I want him because of the darkness."

"You want him to go with you, to Lakesedge Estate?"

29

Mother's voice wavers, more nervous than I've ever heard her sound.

"Yes."

I dig my fingernails against my palms. "Arien is not going *anywhere* with you."

Arien cuts a warning glance toward me. "Leta, he's our lord."

Anger rushes up, the same way it did in the village when the monster first saw Arien's hands. Sparks dance across my vision. "You want him to go with you, to that place where you murdered your whole family?"

The monster lets out a terse growl. "Enough! Listen—I'll make this plain. Either Arien comes with me, or I'll go back to Greymere and report what I saw. By the time the sun sets, your whole village will know about him."

Everyone will know. Cold sweat beads my skin as I picture Arien dragged before the altar in Greymere, the bank of candles all alight, his fingers held above the flames.

Arien looks down at his hands, at the gloves the monster gave him. He hadn't done it out of kindness. He'd just wanted to give Arien time to get away from the crowded village, so he could make these threats where no one would hear. So he could *claim* him.

"You've hidden it for a long time, haven't you?" The monster's voice is a veiled blade. "You've been so frightened. You won't have to hide, not with me. I can help you."

Arien chews the edge of his mouth. There's a crimson

mark where his teeth have scraped his lip. "You'd help me? How?"

"He doesn't need your help!" I scan the room for an escape, for anything that will stop this, but there's no way out, nowhere for us to go. Even worse is the expression on Arien's face. He's afraid. But alongside that fear is the briefest flash of longing. There's a part of him that wants this. That's drawn by the monster's offer of help.

Arien takes a deep breath, as though he's gathering courage. "If I go with you, then what about Leta?"

Silence ticks by. When the monster finally answers, it sounds as though he's bitten out each word. "I don't want her. Only you."

I take a step toward him, my hands clenched at my sides. I'm afraid, but I can't let Arien face this alone. "He's my brother. Where he goes, I go."

He doesn't move, but stays so still that I could almost believe him another shadow.

Here I am with my work-roughened hands and my dress soaked with well water. With nothing to offer and nothing to endear me. For a moment I wonder if I should be softer while I ask him for this. But there's nothing soft about me—not the bluntness of my voice, not my hands that are still curled into fists.

I move forward. The monster turns his face away from me, the sharp edge of his mouth cut into a tight scowl. He wants to take Arien away, and he won't even look at me. I grab hold of his cloak where it falls across his shoulder, knot the fabric around my fist and give it a hard pull.

"You ash-damned *creature*! I won't let you do this!"

"Violeta!" Mother steps forward, her cheeks bright with fury. Arien pushes past, knocking the chair over with a clatter. He looks desperately between Mother and the monster. "No, please! Don't hurt her!"

Roughly, the monster unpeels my fingers from his cloak. His hands circle tight around my wrists. We're so close together that I can hear the unsteady rhythm of his breath.

I stare up into his dark eyes. "I want to go with you."

"You are the absolute *last* person I want anywhere near me."

Then he looks down at my arms, and goes quiet. My sleeves are rolled back, baring the bruises on my pale skin, smeared like they were painted with a brush. Some are fresh, blooming like dark petals. Others are faded, just the barest hints of fingers that dug and pinched.

His grip loosens, but he doesn't let go of me. We stand together—both silent, my eyes pinned on his face. *Take me with you.*

The faint *tap tap tap* of the apple tree against the window is the only sound in the quiet room. The monster releases my wrists and brushes past me without a word, his footsteps heavy as he strides across the kitchen floor. He sweeps off his hood and leans down, so his face is level with Mother's. She flinches.

"They'll both come with me," he says quietly, then straightens and turns his back to her. He tips his chin toward the doorway that leads to the rest of the house. "Go and pack your things. I'll wait outside. Hurry up."

Then he's gone, his cloak a billow of midnight as he storms out through the back door. He slams it shut behind him, the heavy bang harsh and final. My heart is pounding, and everything is drowned out by the rush of blood in my ears.

Arien looks at me fearfully. "Leta, you shouldn't have done that."

A disbelieving laugh catches in my throat. "No, I shouldn't have."

Arien starts to twist at his sleeve. I put my hand over his, but his fingers still move anxiously. "I won't let him hurt you, Arien. No matter what."

Mother stalks toward us, the air carrying a whisper of linseed oil. I think of the way she took my hand and held Arien cradled in her arms. The way she brought us back here to the cottage. She had been kind at first, but her care for us has dwindled away, like a banked fire turned to gray ashes.

"I'm sorry," I tell her.

She lifts a hand, as though she means to touch me. My knees throb, and for a single, hideous moment I think I'm going to cry.

Then her hand drops back, and her expression hardens.

"You don't know what you've done, do you?" She glances at the closed door and smiles coldly. "That monster—he deserves you both. And you deserve him."

Arien and I hurriedly pack our clothes into satchels, then go outside. The monster is waiting for us, but he isn't alone—the silver-haired woman from the village is there as well, holding the reins of two horses.

She must work for him, that's why she was in Greymere, helping to collect the tithes. I notice now that she wears a set of keys and a silver sparklight on a long chain around her neck. The same as our keeper does, in the village.

The monster stands beside her. The two of them are immersed in a hushed, urgent conversation, but when they notice Arien and me, they fall silent. The monster starts to pace a restless circle on the road, his boots scraping angrily through the dust.

The woman turns toward us slowly, her face knit into a frown. "Really? This is him? He's just a kid."

"I'm *thirteen*." Arien folds his arms. "I'm not a kid."

The monster pauses in his pacing and sighs. "Yes, Florence. This is him."

He spreads his hands, as if challenging her to argue. She stays silent, but her eyes linger on Arien, and she shakes her head, clearly uncertain. Then she glances at me and looks even more confused. "What about her, then?"

I hitch the strap of my satchel higher up on my shoulder. They're talking about Arien and me like we're not even here. "I'm his sister."

Her pale green eyes narrow. "Are you also—?"

The monster cuts in. "Never mind about her. She's no one."

He goes over to one of the horses, unbuckles the pack strapped onto the saddle, and takes out another pair of gloves. He pulls them on, fastening them tight at his wrists. "Let's go. I've wasted enough time here already."

Florence puts her arm around Arien's shoulders and guides him toward one of the horses. She helps him up before deftly climbing into the saddle behind him. Neither of us has ridden before, and Arien looks very small, so far up on the horse's back.

Then Florence flicks the reins, and she and Arien are gone, a cloud of dust on the road that grows rapidly smaller. I'm left alone. Alone—with the monster. His sharp features twist as he looks me over. The way he described me—*no one*—still stings.

"I'm to ride with you?"

He shoves back the hood of his cloak, drags a gloved hand through his long hair. "Unless you'd prefer to stay behind."

I shake my head quickly. I look up at the horse. It's enormous, with immeasurably deep, liquid eyes. It shifts restlessly on silver-shod hooves. I can see the ends of the nails, where they've been driven through its feet to hold the shoes in place.

Shakily, I touch its side. Muscles and ribs and heat move against my fingers as it takes a long, hollow breath.

The monster looks at me pointedly. Dread creeps over me at the thought of the two of us, pressed close together as we ride. "You'll have to help me up."

He puts out a hand. I fold up my skirts and he looks disdainfully at my dirt-grimed boots. Beneath the cloak, his dark linen shirt doesn't have a single crease. His own boots are polished to a dull gleam. I step hard against his hand as he helps me, hoping I smudge as much of the dust onto him as I can.

He looks at me askance, and then he laughs—a dark, incredulous sound. "Why are you wearing woolen stockings in the middle of Summerbloom?"

I grab for my skirts and pull the hem down to cover my knees. "Why are *you* wearing a winter cloak?"

He ignores my question, but he reaches absently for the collar of his cloak, adjusting the clasp where it ties at his shoulder. Then he gets onto the horse behind me. Clasping the reins in one hand, he wraps his arm around my waist. I suck in an involuntary breath and lean away from him as much as possible. He kicks the horse into motion. Grit from the road comes up, and I'm choked by the dust.

Each movement of the horse, each jolt and hoofbeat over the road, feels as though it will throw me loose. It's only the monster's arm, so tight around me, that holds me in place. I feel the dense heat of his chest against my back, his rough breath stirring my hair.

Trees flash by, streaked crimson as the sun sets. Twilight spreads through the forest with glowing brilliance and umber shadows. We round a bend in the road, and I can see Arien and Florence, far up ahead.

"What did you mean, that you could help my brother?" I ask the monster. "What do you want with him?"

I turn, trying to see his face, and flinch. His skin is washed red by the last flare of sunlight, as though he's been drenched with blood.

"You really don't know?" He waits, but I don't answer. With a scowl, he goes on. "I want his shadows."

"They're not *his*. They're only dreams. Arien has nothing for you."

I won't think of what happened in the village, in the woods, in the daylight. Everything Mother feared—that there's darkness inside Arien, that the Lord Under has a claim on him—it can't be true. It *can't* be.

The monster shakes his head derisively. "Only dreams."

And then, before I can stop myself, the question spills loose. "Is it true what they say about you, what you did to your family?"

I gasp as he twists my hair into a knot and leans closer, until his mouth is almost touching my ear.

"Yes." His breath traces over my cheek. "*Everything* they say about me is true."

A shudder runs through me. I open my mouth, but no sounds come out. All I can hear is the echo of his voice. He loosens his grip and my wind-tangled curls spill free. His arm tightens around my waist, and he urges the horse to go faster. I look to either side of us, scanning the sides of the road in search of a path, a house, anything. But there's no escape. Only the forest and the sky and the night. The monster, holding me close.

We pass through a clearing, the earth on either side of the road barren except for a fallen tree. The roots are upturned, twisted against the empty air. Outlined by the sunset behind them, they look like claws.

I turn cold all over.

Finally, we reach a wayside, where a cottage is encircled by a grove of olive trees. It's dark now, the night sky silvered by an almost-full moon.

The monster gathers up the reins and dismounts swiftly. "There's still another full day of travel until we're at Lakesedge. We'll sleep here and start out again in the morning."

I look at the cottage. It's so small—only one room. I've been so caught up in worry for Arien that I haven't even thought how we'll have to spend the night so close to the monster. How we'll be with him every night from now on, at the cursed estate.

He holds out a hand and I let him help me down from the horse. I stumble as my feet touch the ground and, without thinking, grab hold of his cloak to steady myself. He looks at me intently. I start to shiver, and his mouth tilts into a sharp smile. "Don't tell me you're cold, even with those woolen stockings?"

"I'm fine." I shove him away and go quickly to where Arien stands, dazed, beside the other horse. I pull him into an embrace.

"Are you okay?" I touch his cheek; he's pallid in the moonlight, tired and worried, but not hurt.

He nods, wincing as he rubs at a cramp in his thigh. "Everything *aches*."

The wayside cottage is dark, the windows closed up and tightly shuttered. The roof is tangled with a wisteria vine and the heavy perfume from the flowers chokes the air.

I reach for Arien, take his hand, and hold it tightly as we step inside.

Chapter Four

The room is hot, and illuminated only by a single lantern set on the table. On the wall opposite the shuttered windows is an altar. The icon shows the Lady with her head bowed and palms upturned, twin vines uncoiling between her fingers. A row of guttered-out candles sits underneath.

The monster kneels by the hearth, coaxing alight a small fire. His hair is knotted from the wind, and there's a smudge of dust on his cheek. The firelight dances over him, paints his tanned skin with amber and orange. But even like this—golden and beautiful—I can't forget what he truly is. The wrongness clings to him. Even the darkness that pools in the corners of the room seems to stretch out and gather at his feet.

He takes a fistful of twigs from the wood box and throws

them into the reluctant flames. I look at his hands and picture his fingers wrapped around a throat. When I close my eyes, the image stays. A white face, blurred beneath water, a rush of bubbles that spills out in a terrible, silent cry.

He gets to his feet when he hears us come in. He sweeps the hood of his cloak back over his hair and tilts his head toward the door. "Arien. A word."

He puts his hand on Arien's shoulder and guides him outside. Florence catches my arm when I move to follow them. "No. That isn't your concern."

"He's my brother."

"Yes, he is." She's nearly as tall as the monster, and the way she looks at me is almost as frightening. "And he's right outside. He'll be perfectly safe."

Outside the open door, Arien and the monster stand in a circle of lamplight. The monster is speaking rapidly, his voice low and indistinct. I strain to listen, but I can only catch scraps of his words.

"Two days . . . the full moon . . ."

"Here." Florence pushes a tin kettle into my hands and nods to the corner, where there's a sink. "Go and fill this for me."

I clutch the kettle against my chest and go over to the sink. I shove the kettle under the spout, hard. The edge catches with a loud clang. The bowl of the sink is filled with dried leaves and the crumbled bodies of dead moths. The pump handle is stiff. I grip it tightly and lean all of my strength into it. The water spills loose, rust tinged, splashing the front of my dress and washing the dust of wings and leaves into the drain.

I fill the kettle, my eyes fixed on the door. The monster leans closer to Arien. His mouth shapes the same word over and over. Arien shakes his head and tries to back away. He darts a nervous glance toward me, his teeth dug into his lip.

I hand the kettle to Florence, who has started to unpack a makeshift dinner from one of the bags she brought with her. I cross the room quickly, and the monster cuts to a sudden silence when he sees me approach. He turns and walks away, farther outside, until he's almost completely swallowed up by the night.

I put my hand on Arien's cheek. "What was he asking you?"

He closes his eyes and leans his face against my palm. "Nothing."

"Arien. Tell me."

He looks warily to where the monster has gone, far off in the dark. "He said—"

"Nothing," the monster calls. His boots crunch against the ground as he comes back into the room. He folds his arms, leans his shoulder against the doorframe. His eyes narrow at me coldly. "It was nothing."

The darkness behind him is like the depths of a well, but his face is lit by the lamp. He has more scars around his throat. Sharp, blackened marks that wreathe his skin like a necklace of thorns. My fingers rise, unbidden, to trace across my own throat.

What hurt him? What made those terrible marks?

And then, for just a moment, the veins in his throat turn . . .

42

dark. Just like they did in the village. The light reflected in his eyes turns crimson.

Anxiously, I look around the room, from the shuttered windows to the opened door. The olive grove is a wall of shadows beneath the moonlit sky. How many steps would it take us to run from the wayside to the trees? My mind races as I try to calculate if we could get there fast enough. If we could reach the forest before the monster caught us.

The kettle begins to steam with a piercing whistle. I jolt, my breath stuck, as blotches of white close across my vision. I fight to drag air through my tightened lungs as Florence moves the kettle from the heat. She puts it heavily onto the iron stand, then takes down a stack of enamelware cups from the shelf above the benchtop.

She fills a pot and starts to spoon in leaves from a small hand-labeled jar, making tea. The monster watches her from the doorway as she finishes, then comes forward to take a cup when she holds it out to him.

There's no table, nowhere to sit except for the folded blankets that have been laid out into four makeshift beds. They're all together in a neat row. I take the endmost two and drag them away to the opposite side of the room. Arien and I huddle together, so close that our shoulders touch.

Florence passes us each a cup of tea and a plate with a square of almas cake, spiced and sweet, made of dried apples and brown sugar.

"We'll have a long ride tomorrow." She takes a sip from her own cup. "Finish that, then try and get some sleep."

I can't remember the last time I ate, but there's only a numb hollowness in my stomach. I pick at the cake until it crumbles apart under my fingers, then drink a wary mouthful of the tea. It's bitter, with a faint sweetness that stays on my tongue. I put the cup aside and lie down on top of the blankets as Arien stretches out beside me.

There's a scrape from the stove drafts as Florence banks the fire, then the rustle of blankets. The room lulls into a tense silence.

Arien lies on his back and stares up at the thatched ceiling. His face is creased with worry, and there are tired, leaden shadows beneath his eyes. "I'm sorry, Leta. I've really messed everything up."

"Arien. This isn't your fault, not at all."

He sighs. I reach across and touch his hand, trying to think of a way to comfort him. "Do you want me to tell you a story?"

The stories are my clearest memory of our life before. And now, whenever I tell them to Arien, I hear the low rumble of my father's voice as he read aloud to me. I feel my mother's hand as we went to the village, how she promised another tale if I'd walk just a little farther.

"Mm?" Arien rolls over to face me. His mouth curls into a faint smile. "Yes, please."

"Which would you like? The knight and the prince?"

It's his favorite: a forgotten prince, rescued by a clever knight. I've never asked if he imagines himself knight or prince, rescued or rescuer. But I've seen the pleased, secretive

44

glow on his face when I tell stories that end with two boys falling in love. I know that some things are close kept, too precious to share.

"No." He rubs tiredly at his cheek. "Tell me your favorite one instead."

I wriggle closer to him and put my arm around his shoulders. The words of the story rise easily, making me feel warm and pleased as I speak them. "Beyond seven forests, beyond seven lakes, there was a labyrinth. Inside, there lived a monster. And one day, a brave maiden went in search of a wondrous treasure . . ."

I've loved this story for as long as I can remember. My parents would both tell it to me, over and over, as many times as I could convince them.

The labyrinth is deep beneath the earth, with walls that are made of trees. And at the center, a terrible monster sleeps on a bed made from bones. No one who enters has ever come out. But the maiden—when she goes inside—has a ball of twine hidden in her pocket. And as she walks, she unravels the twine behind her.

"The monster chased her, but she was fast. She followed the twine back through the trees . . ."

Arien smiles drowsily as I go on with the story. And for a moment it's like we are back in the cottage, with the walls around us and the world far away. When it still felt almost safe, before everything changed.

Then I look past him. Across the room, Florence lies still,

her breath drawn out in sleep. But the monster . . . he's awake. Reflections of the flames dance in his eyes as he watches me. As he *listens*.

I cut off abruptly. When he realizes I've noticed him, he turns over swiftly and drags the blanket up around his shoulders. My cheeks burn. I feel peeled bare. Could he tell, from my voice, how I long to be as unafraid as the girl in the labyrinth? Does he know how much I wish I had my own safe path, clasped tight in my hands?

I stay close by Arien as he falls asleep. The door has been left open to let a breeze through the room, but the night air is dense, motionless. I look out through the doorway at the unmoving branches of the olive trees. Suddenly I'm aware of how quiet the room is, how still. The monster is a darkened shape, his breath slow and heavy.

"Arien." I put my mouth against his ear. Shake him quietly awake. "We can't stay here. We can't stay with him."

He stirs with a groan. I sit up slowly, hardly daring to breathe. Understanding lights his face as he looks toward the open door. We stand up. Each shuffle of cloth and creak of floorboards is endlessly loud. I keep my eyes pinned to the monster, but he doesn't move.

On tiptoe, we cross the room. Outside the doorway, we pause. Arien spares the monster one wary glance, then nods at me, resolute. We run, together, into the barren, moonlit forest.

We run for a long time, on and on through the tight rows of the olive groves. I don't know where we're going, only *away*. I have to put as much distance between the monster and my brother as I can. I let the woods close round me, until finally the spindle-leafed branches part and give way to the wilder forest.

Arien stumbles as he tries to keep up with my swift pace. "Leta, why didn't you run to the road?"

"He'd see us there. We can circle back once we're out of the trees."

My feet catch on a fallen branch, and I stumble forward. My knees hit the ground, and I'm stunned by the pain. I dig my fingers into the detritus of leaves beneath me and let out a frustrated hiss. "*Ash*. This damned forest."

Arien crouches beside me, his frightened eyes shifting from ground to trees to sky. "Are you hurt?"

I stand up, groaning at how much I ache. "I'm fine."

We go on. I keep my gaze fixed on the path ahead, searching for a way through the trees. Every now and then I pause, straining to listen, all my muscles wound up into an ever-tightening coil with each moment that passes. The woods are full of strange noises: night birds, the creak of wood, the rustle of leaves.

And beyond that—indistinct and angry—comes a voice. The monster, calling Arien's name.

Behind me, Arien falters, staring back toward the sound. I pull at his arm. "Don't stop!"

We go farther and farther. The forest is endless. Our breath becomes labored, and my lungs burn. The light starts to fade from gray, to soot, to pitch-black as the trees close in. Even the faint moonlight that illuminates the pale branches has gone.

Arien trips, then catches himself against me. "You should have stolen a torch," he whispers, irritated.

A feverish laugh snags in my throat. "I'll remember that next time we're running away from a monster."

Then the monster's voice, harsh and furious, echoes through the trees, and we fall into a desperate silence. I tug on Arien's arm, guiding him forward between two pale trunks. We go on swiftly through the dark.

The air is hot, the summer heat trapped by the latticed branches. Sweat soaks my dress and tracks down my spine. I swipe my sleeve over my forehead and lift the heavy weight of my hair from my neck. Surrounded by the trees and the heat and the dark, I can't see, can't catch my breath. But we have to keep moving.

I run with my hand outstretched, grasping at the air in front of me. There's a crunch of leaves, a wrench on my arm. Arien staggers back, his hand torn loose from mine as I fall forward.

"Arien?" I turn in a circle, searching. "Where are you?"

"I'm here!" He sounds muffled, far away. "Leta? I can't see anything!"

Then his voice is cut off, an absence that's filled with the night. I hold my breath, trying to listen for him through the dark. "Arien!"

My fingers strike against another trunk. But rather than

cold and smooth, the bark is wet, smeared with a thick, oozing liquid. I snatch my hand back and scrub it against my skirts. The ground is damp, too. Mud catches my boots as cold moisture seeps in through my stockings and over my feet.

I'm in a clear space, ringed by trees. Skeletal roots jut from the forest floor. In the canopy above there's a bare piece of sky—star specked, lit by the moon.

And at the center of the clearing is a single, tall tree. Its bark isn't pale but an oily, midnight black.

The grove is blighted. The magic in the earth—the Lady's light that flows through the world—is poisoned with darkness from the world Below, and it's spread through the ground, the roots, the trees. It happened in the almond orchard near Greymere once, but never as bad as this. Here, even the air feels wrong.

My feet cut through the sodden earth as I pace the clearing, but whatever path led me here has now vanished. I'm caged by trees. Arien weaves back and forth on the other side, trying to find a way through. He looks at me, his face a frightened sliver between the trunks, before he's swallowed up by the gloom.

Then a low growl cuts through the air.

"Arien?"

He doesn't answer. Everything is still. I can't even hear the monster.

The growl comes again.

I press back against the edge of the grove, my pulse thudding hard. Behind the poisoned tree there's a blurred movement. A creature comes out from the darkness, hunched close to the ground.

It takes form. Long legs, a tail, pointed ears.

Sharp teeth.

A wolf.

Head lowered, it stalks forward. I'm frozen by fear, captured by the intent sharpness of its eyes. It gathers itself, teeth bared, a growl in the depths of its throat.

I shout over my shoulder. "Run, Arien! You have to run, you—"

The wolf leaps. I throw myself down and curl forward, closing my eyes as I wait for those teeth to tear through my skin.

Then a bright wave of heat flares past my face. I look up hurriedly. The monster is there, tall and dark and *furious*, with a pine torch clutched in one hand. Arien is behind him, wielding a broken branch.

The monster rushes between me and the wolf. They collide in a blur of cloak and claws and teeth. He feints, then the wolf is on him, snapping ferociously. There's a sickening bite, and the monster cries out as the wolf catches his arm. He wrenches himself free with a snarl, the sound spat through his teeth. He looks just as fearsome as the wolf, just as dangerous.

He thrusts the torch forward. Sparks fill the air, and the wolf writhes. Then everything happens in a blur, so fast I can hardly parse together what I'm seeing. There's the sound, a slice, a splatter of dark blood over the ground.

The monster shoves his hand against the earth where the soil is wet and black and blighted. The air gives a tremor, and the sense of wrongness from before builds and builds.

I can feel it in my chest. I can taste it, sour, on my tongue. Tendrils of darkness unfold from the ground and snare the wolf, wrapping its legs like vines. It whimpers, struggling to get free, teeth bared and eyes rolled back, white half-moons of fear.

With another snarl, the monster pulls his hand back from the ground. The shadows evaporate in a rush, and the wolf, freed, falls down with a yelp. It scrabbles to right itself, paws carving the mud, then turns and runs swiftly back into the forest.

The monster watches it go before collapsing onto his knees with a groan. His head hangs forward, his face hidden behind his hair. He holds his arm against his chest.

Arien throws down the branch and runs over to me. "I went to find him. He came back for you—he wasn't going to, but we heard the wolf, and—"

I look quickly from the monster, slumped on the ground, to the forest, where a space has appeared between the trees. He won't catch us now if we run. We can leave him here. We can go.

But Arien's words are like a knife at my throat. *He came back for you.*

I take a halting step forward. "You saved me."

The monster's head snaps up. There's a smear of blood near his mouth. His sleeve is torn, and on his arm is a deep wound—from teeth or claws or both—that bleeds freshly crimson. We stare at each other as the truth of it settles. This monster, who claims there's darkness in my brother, who wanted to take Arien away and leave me behind, he came back for me.

I reach to my skirts, gather them up in my hands. The embroidered pattern I stitched at the hem is rough beneath my trembling fingers. It's the nicest of my two dresses, the one I save for best. I wrap the linen around my hands and pull, hard.

I tear once, twice, then a piece comes loose with a loud rip. I hold the length of cloth out between us. The monster doesn't move, but for just a breath his expression softens. It's like seeing a mask slip then quickly be put back into place.

I crouch down beside him. "I can help you."

He lets out a harsh laugh. "You've certainly helped quite well, so far."

But he sits still while I wipe the cloth over the cut. Blood spreads through the fabric and onto my fingers. I start to shake, overcome as I remember my own blood, too bright and too fast, as Arien helped me wrap my knees. The cloth slips from my trembling fingers. I try to catch it but instead put my hand clumsily on the monster's wrist.

He looks at me, startled.

"Sorry," I manage. "I—I just—"

"If you're going to be squeamish about blood, maybe *don't* run into the blighted woods next time."

"I didn't know they were blighted!"

Impatiently, he grabs the cloth and starts to bind his arm.

He moves deftly, not at all awkward, despite using only one hand. As though he's done this before.

Then I see another cut on his palm, visible through a slash in his glove. I peer closer. It looks different from the cut on his arm. The blood is darker.

When he notes me staring, he quickly folds his fingers closed over it.

I tear another strip from my dress and hold it out to him. He snatches it from me, turning his back as he wraps the cloth around his hand.

When he starts to get up, I reach out to help him, but he ignores me. He struggles to his feet, then stands for a moment, his hands against his temples as he gathers himself. He swallows heavily and takes a deep breath. "Ash *damn* it. You have both been one disaster after another."

Arien lifts the torch from the ground and holds it out. "Thank you for coming back."

"I'll not save your sister a second time. Don't run from me again, either of you." He takes the torch, relights the end with a sparklight from his pocket. Then he jerks his head toward the trees. "Come on, let's go."

Wordlessly, we go back through the forest. The monster ahead, Arien and me close behind. Florence meets us partway with a lantern. Her eyes widen at the sight of the monster with his bloodied face and bandages on his arm and hand.

"What happened?" She reaches out, but he pushes her away.

"Never mind that. There's a blighted grove." He points to

indicate the direction, then takes her lantern, giving her the torch in its place. "Go back and burn the trees. You'll need to watch the fire so it doesn't catch the whole forest."

Florence hesitates, her hand still stretched toward him. "Are you sure you're all right?"

He glares at her. "Yes."

She turns with a sigh and vanishes into the trees.

We walk the rest of the way in silence. When we reach the tree line, the monster motions for Arien to go on ahead and pulls me aside.

He puts his gloved hands around the tops of my arms and leans close. My gaze goes from his dark eyes to his bloodied mouth, and I'm filled with a strange, hot feeling that isn't quite fear. He slides his hands down my arms and holds my wrists loosely. He brushes his thumb against where my sleeve hides the bruises.

"Are you truly sorry I took you both from that cottage?" His eyes lower, and he goes on quietly. "I'm not going to hurt you."

The rest of it echoes, unspoken, made clear by the touch of his fingers on my wrist. *I won't hurt you, not like that.*

"And what about Arien? What do you have planned for him?"

He gives me a guarded look. "That's none of your concern."

"I don't care if you hurt me." My teeth clench tight at the thought of it, but I don't pull away. After all I've faced from Mother to keep Arien safe, I know I could bear it if the monster was cruel to me. *I could.* "Just leave him alone."

"You've heard enough about Lakesedge Estate to know I can't promise you safety."

He lets go of me and walks back into the wayside cottage without turning to see if Arien or I will follow.

He doesn't need to. He knows that we have nowhere else to go.

Chapter Five

Lakesedge Estate is a silhouette against the night sky. The road gives way to a graveled drive, arched by an intricate iron gateway. As we pass through the gate, Florence reaches out to collect an unlit lantern hooked on the post. She lights it with her sparklight. The colorless flame glimmers through the dark as we ride toward the house.

There are hills all around, thick with trees and studded with sharp granite outcrops. It's like a separate world, quiet and still under the secretive moonlight. I cling to the edge of the saddle as I look around, trying to see more. But it's too dark. Everything beyond Florence's lantern falls away to shadows.

The drive slopes downward; the house is at the very bottom. We stop, and the monster gets quickly down from our horse. He hasn't spoken a word to me the entire way. Now he very deliberately avoids making eye contact as he helps me dismount.

I climb inelegantly from the saddle, tripping over my feet when I step onto the ground. I'm sore from the days of riding, and I have to take a moment to breathe through the burn of my muscles, knotted into unfamiliar aches.

The monster pushes past me, leading his horse away into the darkness beyond the house.

"Wait," Florence calls after him. "Don't you want some light?"

She takes the reins of her horse and follows him with the lantern, leaving Arien and me alone in the quiet outside the front door.

I step closer to him, clutching my satchel against my chest. Almost my entire life is folded up inside: the itchy sweater I wear in the winter, a nightdress that's gotten thin at the elbows, a pair of stockings with mends across the toes. And a handful of stones, my treasures from the windowsill in our cottage bedroom.

"It's so big," Arien says as we stare up at the house. "It looks like something from one of your stories, Leta."

"It's . . ." I reach for the word, unsure. "It's beautiful."

All the rumors say Lakesedge is cursed. But none of them mention the faded, neglected beauty of it all. I thought it would be a place of spikes and shadows. But Arien is right—it's like a story.

Most of the windows are closed, and a thick tangle of ivy

winds between the wooden shutters. The front door is carved with a raised pattern. I trace my fingers across it, over vines and leaves so delicate they could have been embroidered against the wood. The iron handle is carved, too. An enormous ring shaped like a wreath, furled with leaves and bellflowers. When I put my hand against it, the cold press of iron makes me shiver. But slowly, it begins to warm beneath my palm.

A strange emotion threads around me like the vines woven across the shutters. There's something so sad about this poor, solemn house, with its windows like closed-over eyes and a ring of cold iron at the door. It's like something kept under a spell, too long asleep. I put my hand against the stone wall. Close my eyes. There's a stirring beneath my fingertips. Like the house is breathing, deep and slow.

Then a sharp cry echoes from the slope above the house. I snatch back my hand. A feathered shape swoops away into the night. Arien and I grab for each other. My heart begins to pound urgently, flurried as whatever bird was just disturbed.

The door opens, and a girl stands there. Small and plump, she's my age or younger. Her white skin is sprinkled with coppery freckles, and her chestnut hair is pulled into a five-strand braid that almost reaches her waist.

"Hello." She blinks at us from behind her large, round-framed glasses and smiles hesitantly. "I'm Clover Aensland."

She steps back to let us pass through the door. The entrance hall is easily the biggest space I've ever been in. It's overlooked by an arched window set high in the wall above the upstairs landing. Through the glass I can see handfuls of stars. It's late, the dim space before new morning.

Clover laughs good-naturedly as I stare at the room. "I know. My mother's whole cottage would fit in this hall."

Arien looks around, wide eyed. "It's all so empty."

It *is* empty. I can hear voices from the depths of the house—the measured notes of Florence, the deeper tones of the monster, but the entrance hall is quiet and still. There's hardly any furniture, and the walls are bare. There's no light except for a single candle. A lamp hangs in the gloom above, but it's unlit, threaded all over with cobwebs. Beneath the dust, the glass shades gleam like gemstones.

We follow Clover across the hall and down a long corridor.

"Have you been here very long?" I ask her.

"About a year. It's my first job, my first time away from home." She tugs at the end of her braid and smiles, shyly proud. "I'm the alchemist for Lakesedge Estate."

I look at her with surprise. I've heard of how alchemists sometimes leave the Maylands—their commune near the far-off capital—to live at an estate and help the lord. It's said they can do wondrous things. Heal beyond the power of village herbalists. Make crops grow from drought-ruined fields. But the materials used in their magic are rare and expensive, so most places like Greymere only have a healer.

"Oh," Arien says, his face alight with a peculiar longing. "Can I see your spells?"

Clover laughs and rolls back her sleeve to show us her arm. Her skin is inked all over with tiny, detailed marks. Circles and sharp-cornered lines all connected together. Arien leans in to take a closer look. "They're beautiful, Clover."

I wish I could share his awe. The symbols *are* beautiful, but the thought of having spells woven into me, marked forever on my body, is unsettling.

Clover leads us into a large kitchen. There's a table at the center and the cast-iron stove has just been lit. The new fire sends a flickering, orange glow into the room. Clover moves around busily, setting the table for tea. While Arien helps her, I go over to look out the window. Behind the house is an overgrown garden, silent in the moonlight.

The monster comes into the room. He ignores us, pausing by the altar on the opposite wall to light the candles. He takes one from the shelf and sets it into a jar, which he puts down carefully on the table beside the teacups that Clover laid out.

He's no longer wearing his cloak, and he looks younger without the weight of it around his shoulders. If I didn't know any better, he might just be a boy, with his hair knotted from the wind and tired lines beneath his dark eyes.

I start to walk toward him. I don't know what spurs me forward. Some reckless impulse. Like throwing a stone into the well just to hear it splash. Or maybe I want to prove to myself that I don't have to be afraid.

I swallow past the tightness in my throat. "Lord Sylvanan?"

His head snaps up. "Don't call me that. I don't use my title."

"Well then . . . *do* you have a name?"

He stares at me like it's the most ridiculous question. I move closer still. The candlelight turns our shadows to ghosts on the floor. Up close, I can pick out tiny details of him that I hadn't noticed before. His hair isn't black but dark, dark brown. Both of his ears are pierced with rows of slender, silver rings.

Finally, he sighs. "Rowan."

"Rowan." The shape of it lingers after I speak it aloud. A monster. A boy. A boy with a name that I can feel on my tongue. Darkly sweet, like honeyed tea. Heat starts to creep across my face. I laugh, nervous. "I suppose you're a little too young to be a real lord."

The monster—*Rowan*—scowls. "I'm older than you." When I raise a brow, he goes on. "I'm nineteen."

"Two whole years? Oh yes, an eternity."

"Wait," Clover says. "Rowan, what's wrong with your arm? Why didn't you tell me you were hurt? This looks awful!"

She reaches out to the bloodied cloth wrapped over his sleeve, then tries to touch his hand, where he's tied a fresh bandage over his torn glove. But just like he did with Florence, he pushes her away. "It's nothing. I'm fine."

She sighs, irritated, but doesn't argue. The kettle starts to boil, and Arien takes it from the heat. Clover goes back to the table and starts to make tea. While it steeps, she takes out a small glass vial from her pocket. The liquid inside is a virulent green. She pours the tea then uncaps the vial; a curl of steam hisses out as she tips the strange potion into each cup.

Arien reaches for his cup, but I put my hand on his wrist to stop him. "What is this for?"

"Just to help you sleep," Clover says lightly. "So you won't dream."

Rowan drinks his own dosed tea without hesitation, then looks from me to my untouched cup. "Do you think she means to poison you?"

His gaze is all challenge. My eyes fixed to his, I lift my cup and take a tentative sip. The tea smells of summer: leaves and flowers and a bright, cloudless sky. But it tastes terrible, worse than any draft from the herbalist.

Arien drinks, too. He cringes at the taste and swallows with difficulty.

Clover holds up a jar. "Did you want some honey?"

"Um." He drinks more, struggling not to cough. "No thank you."

Our eyes meet, and his mouth twitches into a smile. My brother makes a face at me, and I make one back. I force myself to drink another mouthful of the tea, then put my cup back down on the table.

Rowan sighs tiredly. He runs his hand over his hair, then tightens the cord that ties it back. "Arien, there's a room you can have, upstairs at the top of the landing." He frowns, then looks at me. "I suppose I'll need to put you somewhere, too. Try the door opposite; it should be unlocked."

"Yes, well, thank you for finding space for us." I glance down the hallway of abandoned rooms.

"See that you don't make me regret it." Rowan picks up the candle jar and holds it out. "Before you go, we need to discuss some rules." Though he's ostensibly speaking to Arien as well, he's focused on me. "Don't wander around. Don't touch any-thing."

"Anything?" I look pointedly at the offered candle. "That's very . . . unspecific."

He shoves the jar into my hands, the flame stuttering with the sudden motion. "You know what I mean. I don't want a repeat of your foolish stunt from last night at the wayside. And make sure you stay away from the lake."

I wrap my hands tight around the hot glass until it almost burns my skin. It settles on me with a sudden, horrible realiza-tion that just outside, beyond the darkened garden, is the place where Rowan drowned his family.

He knows I'm afraid. I'm sure he's glad of it. But I won't give him the satisfaction of letting it show.

"I'll do my best to remember all of your *rules*." I cross the room, then stop in the doorway. "Good night, Rowan."

At the sound of his name, he pauses for a moment. In the changeable light from the candle flame, his expression fal-ters. There's a flicker of emotion in his eyes that I can't read.

He points dismissively toward the hallway. "Remember what I said."

Arien and I go upstairs in a haze of candlelight. We find two rooms opposite each other, the only opened doors in a hallway just as bare as the space below.

Arien's room has a patchwork quilt on the bed, and a tidy collection of furniture—dresser, desk, table. My room is an

63

afterthought. Dust is thick over the mantelpiece, and there's a pile of dead leaves in the hearth. The furniture is shrouded in linen cloths.

I stand in the hall, twisting the strap of my satchel. I can't seem to make myself take a step either way. The upstairs of Lakesedge Estate has the same faded prettiness as the rooms below. But the whole house is full of unfamiliar sounds. Wind creaks through the walls like a whisper. In the pale light, the flowers on the wallpaper look spiny and sharp.

Then something flutters, far away. A whisper that draws longer and lower than a rush of wind. It slithers along the corridor and through the air.

I put my hand on Arien's arm. "Did you hear that?"

He squints into the darkness, then shakes his head.

"I'm sure I heard a sound."

The small flame of my candle throws shadows onto the walls as I move hesitantly down the hallway. The sound of the wind is almost like words now. I go over to one of the other closed doors. Try the handle. It doesn't turn. The house is as hollow and empty as the chambers of a shell.

Arien watches me from his room as I pace back and forth. "You're going to wear a path in the floor."

He rifles through the bedside table, finds a sparklight, and touches it to the lamp next to his bed. Then he starts to unpack his bag. I can still hear the sound. I follow it into Arien's room, my candle held high as I strain to listen. It's louder. It's changed.

A wet hush. Like . . . water. Like there's water beneath the plaster of the walls, dripping down, and—

I put my hand on the wall, and it stops. "Did you just hear it that time?"

"Leta. I think you should go to bed. It's late." When I don't move, Arien gives me a gentle push. "Come on. You don't need to stalk around with that look on your face all night."

"What look?"

"Like you're imagining every single terrible thing that might happen to me."

"I'm sure there's a few things I haven't been able to think of yet." We go over to the bed and sit down together. I lean my chin against his shoulder. "What did Rowan say to you last night at the wayside cottage? What does he want from you?"

Arien bends down and unlaces his boots, then kicks them off. "He said he can help me. With my shadows. He can help me control them."

"But they're only—" My mouth tastes bitter and a fresh shiver runs over me. *Only dreams.*

"No." He stares ahead and refuses to meet my gaze. "No, they're not."

Night after night I watched his eyes turn dark. I felt the shadows prickle across my skin as they spilled from his hands. I told myself I wasn't afraid. That they wouldn't hurt me. *Only dreams.* They overcame him; they spilled through him. But they didn't *belong* to him.

I look down at the candle and watch the flame dance inside the jar. I breathe in the smell of honeyed wax. "Arien, do you really think you should trust him?"

65

He lies down with a sigh and turns his back to me. "I'm tired. I want to sleep."

"You know what happened to his family. What he did to them."

"Please, Leta." He burrows his face against the pillow. "Just go to bed. It's not like the Monster of Lakesedge is going to come up here tonight to devour us."

"He might."

"You'll be first. Because you've annoyed him so much."

"I'd like to see him try." I get to my feet and pick up the candle, then go across the hall and into my room.

It's stuffy with a scent of camphor and fireplace soot. Neglect fills the shadowed corners. I set down my candle, open the window to let in some fresh air. But outside is hot and still. The curtains drape around me in dust-filled wisps. I look out into the darkness, but there's nothing to see. Only the low slope of the hills, the silhouette of trees, and the star-specked sky above the darkened landscape.

If the lake is there, it's hidden by the night.

When I pull back the cloth that's draped over my bed, there's only a bare, unmade mattress. I drop my satchel onto the floor, then lie down, curled up on my side with my boots still on and my sore knees tucked up inside the hem of my dress. This is the first time I've slept alone, in my own space. Though the stretch of hall between Arien's room and mine isn't much larger than the distance between our beds in the cottage, it feels as vast as an ocean.

My eyes are heavy. I fight against it for a moment, but they dip closed. I'm so tired that my bones feel bruised, and the medicine Clover gave us has dulled everything to a blur. My vision starts to dim. My limbs go heavy. I'm laid out in a field, and vines have wrapped around my whole body and smothered me.

The candle gutters out.

I'm half-sunk in sleep when the cries come.

The sounds cut through the dark. Tangled, thorn-edged howls. I sit up and stare toward the open door. I can see the huddled shape of Arien, asleep in his own room. It isn't him.

I hold my breath and peer into the darkness, trying to make sense of the cries as they come again. At first, they're incoherent, mixed with the hollow thud of my pulse. Then they begin to shape themselves into words.

Elan ... Elan ... please ...

It isn't Arien. But this is the same sound. The same cries. It's the sound of nightmares. The word echoes over and again until it loses meaning. A name, a plea, a helpless prayer.

Elan ... please ...

The curtain is a ghostly smear across the window. Night is pressed against the glass. I reach for my satchel and shakily unbuckle the fastenings. Inside, beneath my sweater and my spare dress and my stones, is a small, solid shape. An icon.

Arien painted it for me. Mother never let us into her workshop, but she would sometimes give him scraps of wood or leftover daubs of paint. This one is the first he made. The strokes of color are broad and blurred, like a face seen in a dream. More a wash of color than actual features. The edges are worn smooth from the rub of my thumb, and the frame is shaped to fit neatly inside my hand with a curve that follows my palm.

I run my fingers along the wood. The shape of a chant forms in my mouth—a messier, more indistinct thing than any litany. *Keep us safe, keep us safe, let this not be a mistake* . . .

The air tastes of ash and smoke. An indistinct memory stirs up, of a moonlit forest, a winter night. Frost in the air and across my cheeks. A heavy weight in my arms. My breath a cloud of steam as I whisper into the dark. My hands spread open to the cold. *Please help us* . . .

I fold my arms tightly around myself as a shiver passes over me.

The cries dim, and the silence fills with a new sound. A hush. A sigh. The light in the room goes soft. The silver, moonlit darkness blackens, blink by blink.

Shadows begin to rise. *Shadows.* They creep from the corners, slow and languid, then rise like mist around the edges of my bed. *No no no* . . . A cold gust of air hisses through the room. The curtains billow out then sweep back against the window. All the cloths draped over the furniture snap and flutter like startled birds.

Shadows. The same shadows that unfurl from Arien's hands when he dreams.

I get to my feet and rush across the hall. His bed is empty. His room is empty.

I turn back to the doorway. It's gone. There's a solid sheet of darkness across the wall. The shadows creep toward me as I stagger back, cold with terror. The thought of that darkness touching me, of being lost beneath it, fills me with a desperate panic.

It moves forward, pushing me farther and farther into the room, until I'm scrambling back on Arien's bed. The hard plane of the headboard is behind me, solid against my spine, and the icon is a leaden weight in my hand. My heartbeat thunders panic in my ears and pulses hard at the edge of my throat.

I curl my fingers closed, remembering the cold iron of the front door, how it slowly warmed beneath my touch. This beautiful house, with its carved flowers and faded wallpaper and neglected ivy-wreathed loveliness, would it *hurt* me?

From above comes a rhythmic *drip drip drip*. I look up. The ceiling is ink black. Rivulets of thick, dark liquid ooze down from the cornices and streak across the walls. The floor ripples and the shadows become a pool of water. The new, wet darkness covers the floor.

The air in the room thickens, until everything sounds hollow and muted. It's like the damp stillness of the well house. That silent air above the water's surface. I am there, waiting in the breathless dark. I want to cry out, but all that comes is a whimper.

I think of Rowan, his hands on my arms as we stood beside the trees, the roughness of his voice when he said *I can't promise you safety*. My heart twists desperately in my chest. I'm not afraid. I'm *not*. It's just light, just the wind. It's a dream— surely. Arien's shadows never hurt me, and these won't, either. *Only dreams.*

But Arien's shadows aren't dreams. They're a darkness. A darkness that Rowan *wants* from him, and I—

Another wash of air stirs over me. The cold is a kiss against my cheeks. The water rises, higher and higher. I'm in the lake. Strands of sedge grass start to wrap around me, and I scrape my hands against my throat as they wind tighter and tighter, cutting into my skin. Water washes over my face, and the world turns to a blur of opaque ripples.

I open my mouth to scream, and the black, icy water fills my lungs.

Chapter Six

I wake up breathless, alone in Arien's room. Crimson sunset spills through the window; it's the next evening, almost an entire day has passed while I've slept. And the nightmare . . . I can still feel it. Still *see* it. The shadows that crept over my bed, the blackened water that dripped down the walls.

It was a dream, that's all it was. There are no shadows in the corners. The walls are smooth, faded paper, and the bare floorboards are dry.

I kick my way free of the tangled quilts and get out of bed. Arien has unpacked. The handful of things he brought from the cottage sit neatly on the dresser: his brushes, his paints, a roll of parchment paper. His shirt from yesterday is crumpled in the corner, the same careless way he always leaves his clothes.

I smooth down the wrinkled fabric of my dress and comb

71

my fingers through my snarled-up hair, trying to reason with myself. What must have happened was this: I had a nightmare, I slipped into Arien's room. I slept deeply while he woke up this morning and went off into the house. That's all.

When I step out into the hallway, everything feels just as empty as it did last night. No voices. No movement in any other rooms. The only sound is the echo of my footsteps. On the landing, the arched window is lit up brilliantly by the sunset. I'm so high up that when I look outside, I can see down over the entire estate.

The grounds are cleaved into a strangely narrow shape by an enormous, ivy-wrapped wall. The space is completely neglected, full of tangled weeds and flowers that have sprawled their way past once-tidy borders.

And beyond the wildflowers and the weeds . . . is the lake.

The water is black. Black as ink, *darker* than ink. It's the same. Exactly the same as the water that filled my room last night, in my dream.

The shore is black, too, and torn. A sharp-edged wound all along the ground. It makes me hurt to look at it. I feel like someone has cut my skin and left behind the same jagged scars on me as on the earth below. This is the glass in my knees, the bruises on my wrists, the shadows in the night.

And down at the lake, three figures move across the shore. Clover and Arien, with Rowan beside them. I watch as he puts his gloved hand on Arien's shoulder and leans close to speak to him. Then they all move forward to the edge of the blackened earth, the line where grass becomes mud, where mud becomes water.

No no no.

I shove myself back from the window. Rowan Sylvanan wants the darkness in Arien, wants his shadows that are more than dreams. And now he's taken my brother to the lake. The lake where he drowned his family one by one.

I run.

I run down the stairs, through the kitchen, where pots clatter and steam on the stovetop, boiling over, out of the back door, and into the garden.

The Summerbloom twilight is heavy, air that smells burned. As I run along the path, branches scrape my arms and tear my skirts. Gravel scatters. My knees burn with a bright pain, like there are coals under my skin. The cuts reopen; blood washes over my legs.

I run until the garden becomes a forest. Pale bark. Dead leaves crushed under my boots.

"Arien!" My voice is lost in the trees.

I reach the shore. Up close, the lake is so much worse. Dark water that swallows the remaining sunlight. When I step onto the mud, I feel the cold through my boots as if it's pressed against my bare skin. The darkness feels alive. It feels *hungry*.

My feet sink deeper with each step. My breath comes out in hard, short gasps as I fight my way across the mud toward my brother.

"Arien!"

Arien looks up, startled. His eyes are as black as the lake. I'm about to reach him when Rowan rounds on me and catches my arm. He wrenches me sharply backward. I fall against him with a thud that pushes out all my breath. He grips me tightly, his gloved hands around the tops of my arms, and pulls me away from the water. Away from Arien.

"Let me go, let me go!" I hit him. Scratch him. He hisses when my fingers scrape his throat.

"I *told* you!" His eyes are narrowed, his face flushed. He's *furious*. "I told you to stay away!"

He drags me back across the shore. I fight him and fight him. I'm strong, my strength built on buckets of well water, on baskets carried to the village, on the ax chopped into firewood. I'm strong, but Rowan is stronger. I may as well be fighting against the rocks or the trees.

At the edge of the forest, he stops. We're face-to-face for a moment; then he spins me around with a frustrated growl and pulls me tight against him. My back is pressed hard to his chest and I can feel his heartbeat; it's racing as fast as mine, perhaps faster.

His breath is rough and unsteady. "You shouldn't be here. I *told* you—"

"Get your hands off me!" I dig my fingers into Rowan's arms. I can't reach his skin because he's covered by his gloves and his cloak, so I drive my elbow sharp against his ribs.

"Stop clawing at me, you little beast!"

I twist against him. I have to get away; I have to get back to Arien. "Let me go!"

At the sound of my voice, Arien looks up. He wavers for a moment, biting his lip uncertainly. Then he squares his shoulders, and his face sets into a determined expression. "Leta, get away from here! Leave me alone!"

His voice carries clearly over the flat shore. The shock of his words takes all the fight from me, and I go still. He turns away and walks down to the water.

Clover gives me a sympathetic look; then she and Arien begin to move together with slow, ritualistic steps. Five paces—I count them. Their footsteps make a disjointed circle, which Clover connects into a single shape by dragging her fingers through the mud. She leads Arien into the center of the circle. They kneel together. Arien presses his hands against the ground.

I start to struggle against Rowan again, my stomach tight with fear. A terrified confusion of images rushes through my mind. The blackened lake, the dead bodies of his family. His voice, rough, when he spoke to me beside the forest. *I can't promise you safety.* "You told me you wouldn't hurt him!"

"I'm not trying to hurt him. He's *mending* it." Rowan makes a derisive sound. "Haven't you ever seen anyone use alchemy before?"

"Alchemy? But Arien, he isn't . . ."

I watch Arien as he goes very still and the air around him begins to darken. Shadows—*his shadows*—spill out from his hands like water poured from a rapid stream.

Clover rolls her sleeves back. The symbols on her arms are glowing, and light gleams from her palms. She touches the

75

sigil, and magic illuminates the carved lines in a wash of gold. Then she puts her hands over Arien's and pushes down, until the earth begins to close over their fingers.

"Now!" Her teeth are set into a determined grimace. She shoves his hands farther into the mud. "Now, Arien!"

"This is what you wanted?" My eyes start to blur, and I blink, hard. I refuse to cry. Not here, not in front of Rowan. I owe so many tears that if I start now, I won't be able to stop. "You wanted to use him against this—against this—"

"Corruption."

"Corruption?" The weight of the word stays in my mouth. He has a *name* for the darkness. When I swallow, I can taste it, heavy as the thickened air in the forest clearing, where the trees dripped shadows.

I shake my head, a disbelieving cry caught in my throat. "Arien isn't—he's not the same as this terrible darkness!"

Arien turns, and we look at each other across the shore. His face is filled with the same wide-eyed hurt as when Mother put his hands above the candles. His mouth opens, but he doesn't speak.

"Is that really what you think of him?" Rowan asks. His grip on my arms loosens, and he fixes me with a scathing look. "No wonder he's so afraid of his power, the way you made him lie and hide. How long were you going to pretend his magic was just bad dreams?"

I wrench free from Rowan's grasp and slap him, hard, across his face. He stumbles back, his hand to the brightening mark on his cheek. Before he can react, I shove past him and run toward the water. Clover and Arien are hidden now, circled by shadows. I take a breath and plunge into the darkness.

I fall to my knees, into the cold, black mud. Distantly I hear Rowan's angry voice as he calls for me. "Get back, damn you—get out of their way!"

I reach out and find Arien's hand.

"No, Leta!" He tries to shake himself loose. "You're going to mess everything up!"

A jolt slams through me, and heat sears across my skin. I feel as if all my bones are lit up. At the center of my chest, there's a swift, taut pull, and my fingers grip tight. The space between our hands hums and hums and *burns*. And the shadows—they calm. They soften.

The unruly cloud folds back on itself. The billows of dark narrow to focused strands that unfurl through our clasped fingers.

And Arien's darkness—*his shadows*—the strands curl and thread together with Clover's magic, neat as a row of stitches. Never before have they been like this. Within his control.

For a moment everything holds. A latticework of magic across the earth, perfectly controlled.

"It worked," Clover breathes. Then there's a tremor. The ground lurches beneath us. I lean against Arien, my shoulder on his shoulder, as I try to keep my balance. Clover looks over at Rowan searchingly, her forehead lined with worry. Another tremor rolls across the ground in an elongated shiver.

"Quick." She jumps to her feet, pulling at Arien's arm and reaching out for me. "Both of you, get up. We have to—"

The ground splits apart with an enormous heave that sends us all stumbling. The circle Clover carved in the mud is now an open wound.

Rowan strides toward us. He grabs my arm and starts to pull me back. I struggle against him. "You can't do this; you can't make him do this!"

He doesn't respond. His eyes are fixed on Clover, on Arien, on the shifting ground.

Threads of magic trail from their fingers. Clover pulls Arien closer to the newly torn wound. Her magic sparks around them as she tries to help him guide the shadows back into the earth.

"Arien!" I cry. "You have to stop!"

The lake churns, and a torrent of water spills over the tear in the ground. It cascades down through the darkness. Arien leans against Clover. Her hands cover his as they both press against the mud. And beneath them, the ground wrenches farther open, widening, widening.

I can't let them do this. It's like the—what did Rowan call it? *The Corruption?*—like it's fighting back. Like it wants to protect itself from whatever Clover and Arien are trying to do.

I stretch out my hand desperately to Arien, but Rowan's grip tightens on my arm; I can't get loose.

"No," he rasps, a harsh plea beneath his breath. "No, no, no."

My heart spikes sharp with terror as the mud rises up over Arien's hands. It covers his wrists, his forearms, rising until he's submerged to his elbows, his face only a kiss from the ground.

Blotches of shadows—of magic—shift and swirl under the surface of his skin. He grimaces, teeth bared in a snarl, the muscles cording in his neck with effort.

"Please!" I sob. "Please, it's going to *kill* him!"

Arien screams.

The sound comes from everywhere, all at once. This isn't his voice, not any sound I've ever heard him make, even when gripped by the worst of his nightmares. A scream, a roar, a howl, all tangled together. The cries fill my ears, my blood, the world.

Rowan shoves me away. He goes toward the wound, toward the torn-up mud. He grabs Arien roughly by the back of his shirt, pulls him to his feet and away from the water. I rush forward and catch Arien in my arms. My foot twists, and we fall down together, hard against the ground.

I hold him tight against me. He's stopped screaming now. His eyes are blank.

"I've got you." I brush his hair back from his sweat-damp cheeks, leaving dark streaks of mud on his skin. "I've got you."

Clover stands beside Rowan at the edge of the wound. "You'll have to . . ." She trails off, her face anguished.

Rowan takes off his cloak, dropping it heedlessly into the mud behind him. His hand goes to his wrist. His fingers hook under the edge of his sleeve. He pushes it up past his elbow, baring the skin above the black line of his glove.

He has a knife in his hand. Small and neat, the blade fitted into the handle. He unfolds it in a quick, practiced motion. The steel has a sharp, silvered edge that gleams as it catches the fading sunlight. My stomach twists, sickened by the horror of what is happening.

Rowan puts the blade to his wrist.

Everything happens so swiftly. The images separate into flashes.

His skin.

The knife.

A cut.

He carves into himself without any hesitation. That image—of everything—is what lingers when I finally wince my eyes shut. How steady his hand is when he drives the blade deep into his arm and slices himself open.

Rowan kneels in the mud and shoves his opened wrist against the ground. A coil of earth rises up and binds his arm, wrapping around him, climbing higher until it snares his throat. He stays terribly, terribly still, not even resisting as it starts to pull him downward. His arm—the one he cut—is now completely buried in the earth. His head bends, his mouth opens, and the strands of darkness slither *inside*.

"Rowan." I whisper his name, a sharp, hurt sound.

His head snaps up. Our eyes meet. His skin is veined with dark all along the sides of his neck. The thornlike scars that wreathe his throat stand out, angry and raised. His eyes are crimson, bloodshot, his pupils huge and black.

This is the darkness I glimpsed when I first saw him. The shadows that limned his edges, always just out of reach. Now it's here, laid bare. I watch as he changes, as his gaze turns cold, as he is overtaken by feral, cruel hunger.

He stares at me, unblinking.

"Violeta." It's the first time he's said my name. His voice is like the hiss of the waves against the shore. "Violeta, get away from here *right now*."

I let the whole world close down. I shut out the sound of the lake. The feel of the ground as it trembles. Clover's voice, frightened and urgent. I let it all fade away until there's only Arien's hand in mine—our skin gritted with mud, his fingers gone cold. I get to my feet. He moves like a sleepwalker as he follows me.

When we reach the place where the forest thins to the narrow garden, we almost collide with Florence, who is coming down from the house. I shove past her. She calls out to us, but I don't stop. I don't turn.

I grip Arien's hand tight, and I start to run.

Chapter Seven

Hand in hand, with the silent trees around us, it's like we're in the woods near the wayside again. Now that I know the truth, I wish I'd never turned back that night. When the wolf wounded Rowan, I should have left him there on his knees, taken Arien, and run far, far away.

I drag Arien into the overgrown, weed-tangled garden at the front of the house. I slump back against the wall, trying to catch my breath, as a plan takes shape in my mind. We'll run along the drive to where the arched iron gateway opens onto a road. If we follow it for long enough, we'll find the village we passed on the way here.

"We have to leave," I tell Arien.

"We can't."

"What do you mean?"

He looks at me sadly, then rolls back his sleeve. On his wrist is a fresh, raised mark, made of delicate lines, just like the sigils I saw on Clover's arms. He closes his fingers around it. "We can't. I can't. There's nowhere else for me to go."

"Arien." My voice wavers. "Arien, no."

"You saw it, Leta. You saw *me*." He gives me a desperate look. The black in his eyes has faded to silver, but his fingers are still dark. "All those nights, all those times that Mother said she needed to fix me. She hurt me. She hurt *you*. And I couldn't stop her. I couldn't do anything. But now I can. I want to stay. I want to learn how to use my magic. Clover's going to teach me."

"So this is the help Rowan promised." Anger laces my mouth with a taste more bitter than the virulent tea. "Clover will teach you alchemy, and in return all you have to do is risk your life. You saw what the Corruption did to Rowan." A fresh horror fills me when I picture his bloodied eyes, the way he sat so *still* and unresisting as the earth crept over him. "What if that had been you?"

"I don't care if it's dangerous. At least here no one is afraid of me." Arien looks away quickly, his cheeks flushed. It hangs between us, unspoken. *No one is afraid of me here— except for you.*

I didn't want him to know how I truly felt, but he did. Of course he did. And now he's come to a monster who will give him what I couldn't. Who looked on his shadows—his magic—and was never afraid.

The tears I held back before spill loose. "All I wanted was to keep you safe."

83

Arien puts his hand on my arm. He's about to speak when a sound cuts through the dark from behind the house. I tiptoe closer, staying near the wall, and watch Rowan make his way back inside. Florence is helping him, her arm around his waist. His head is down, his face hidden by his hair.

After they pass, there's a dark trail of blood left behind, dripped across the stones.

Clover follows them wearily, carrying the lantern. She's covered with mud. It's in the end of her braid, on her glasses, on her face. She looks up and notices me; I hear her murmur to the others, urging them ahead.

She skirts around the side of the house and comes toward us. She touches Arien's cheek, giving him a worried look. "Please, don't run away."

He smiles at her weakly. "We're not running."

I step between them. "Ash damn it, Arien. How can you act like Rowan gave you a choice in this, when he hunted you down—when he threatened you?"

"Violeta, it's not how it looks." Clover tugs at her braid, tangling it around her muddy fingers. "The ritual wasn't supposed to happen like that."

"Which part, exactly, wasn't supposed to happen? When the ground tore open, or when the Monster of Lakesedge cut himself to feed that *thing*?" I hiss out a sigh between my teeth. "I want to know what's going on. I want to know the truth."

"It's not so easy to explain."

"You're complicit in helping someone who murdered his

family. You forced my brother to work dark magic. Is that a good start?"

Arien glares at me. "Leta. It's not her fault."

I kick at the ground, annoyed, knowing I should apologize. But even though Arien is right, and what just happened wasn't truly Clover's fault, I'm still angry. With her, with everyone. "Can you at least *try* to tell me what you're doing here?"

"You're right, Violeta. You deserve to know. You've seen a blighted tree, haven't you?" Clover asks. "Rowan told me about what happened in the woods on your way here."

"Yes. And the almond grove near our village was blighted one Harvestfall. But the Corruption—you can't tell me that's the same as a poisoned *tree*."

"It is, and it isn't." She holds out both her hands and motions like she's weighing something in her cupped palms. "There's light, there's dark, and usually they balance. And when they fall *out* of balance, it's like a wound. The magic in this part of the world—in the ground near the lake—is poisoned. Rowan told me he sent Florence to burn the trees at the wayside. What did they do with the orchard near your village? The same?"

"Yes. The keeper ordered it burned."

"The Corruption isn't like that. There's no one piece to cut or raze. But in the Maylands, I studied blight and I made a spell that can mend it, so it doesn't need to be burned."

Thoughts close in—distant things that I have tried to forget. Midwinter. My parents laid out on the ground beside our cottage. A torch set to the walls. Firelight streaked in orange sparks against the cold night sky.

I shake my head, push the memory away.

"So you plan to get the Corruption out of Lakesedge with this spell of yours? And what about the blood?" I rub my wrist, thinking of how Rowan took out the knife. The hideous, resolute way he cut himself, like it didn't even hurt. "Is *that* part of your spell, too?"

"Yes. It responds to his blood, and I use his blood in my spell." Clover meets my gaze evenly as I swallow, feeling sick. *His blood.* "Every full moon, Rowan and I have tried to mend the Corruption. But so far it's never worked."

Arien steps forward and spreads out his hands. "Because there was something missing. Clover's magic is light, and mine is . . . dark. We balance each other."

Clover gives him a faint smile. "No other alchemist can work the kind of magic you have. This really is our only chance to mend it." She tilts her head back until it rests against the wall, and sighs a hot, tired breath into the hot, tired night. "I'm certain we can do this if we work together."

I remember how she looked during the ritual: teeth set, fingers tight around Arien's wrist. Then I'd thought her ruthless—but now she just looks worn out and small.

I think again of the blighted orchard in Greymere, how after the trees were burned and the ashes cooled, everyone gathered around the field. We lit candles. We put our hands into the charred ground and mixed the ashes into the earth as we chanted the autumn litany. Then, the next year, we planted more trees. They grew, and soon it was like there had never been any difference.

Could Arien do the same? Use his shadows to mend the Corruption, to turn the blackened shore and the ink-dark lake back to sand and clear water?

I turn to him and put my hand on his arm. "Arien. Please."

"I want to do this, Leta. I want to help." He softens his voice and looks at me solemnly. "Rowan saved you in the woods. He didn't have to go back for you, but he did."

I let out a sharp laugh. "He only saved me because he wanted you to help him."

"Is that really what you think?"

I close my eyes against the thought of Rowan, how he spoke to me at the edge of the trees. The way his thumb brushed over the bruises on my wrist. "He wanted us to feel indebted."

Arien sighs. "Or maybe he was *worried* about you."

"If we stay . . ." I pause, let the feel of the words settle in my mouth. "It will be for *you*, Arien. Because you want to be here, not because we owe him anything."

Arien lifts his chin. "I want to be here, Leta."

Clover's eyes are all hope. "Then you will come back into the house?"

I can't trust my voice. I swallow, hard. Taste salt and ash. "Yes."

We go toward the front door. Before we step inside, I look up at the house. It's all dark, except for one of the topmost windows, which is filled with diffuse light. The type of light that would come from an altar candle, almost burned down. I picture Rowan hidden away in his room. His arm torn open. Streaks of darkness fading from his skin.

The entrance hall is still and silent. It feels wrong that we're back here instead of on the road, going far away from the Monster of Lakesedge and his horrible, cursed estate.

Clover leads us past rows of closed doors. I fix my eyes on the vines carved into the wooden panels of the wall, the patterned paper. *This is your home now.*

I grit my teeth and try to reach for some of the awe and wonder I had last night when we arrived—before my dreams of ink-dark water and whispering voices. When I saw the faded loveliness of the house and felt like it might be a friend.

After the darkness of the hall, the lamplit kitchen is bright. I stand in the doorway and rest my shoulder against the wooden frame. Let my eyes adjust until everything turns to a muted orange glow.

The kitchen is filled with steam from the pots that simmered on the stove earlier. The table is covered with skeins of bandages. Beside them is an enamelware bowl. The bottom is splattered with inky, dark liquid. A bloodstained cloth is crumpled up in the shallow water. My stomach twists. I look away from it quickly.

Florence sweeps into the room. She's smeared with mud from where Rowan leaned against her, and there's a streak of blood across one shoulder of her dress. She looks us over, rakes a hand through the ends of her hair and sighs.

"Well." She sighs again. "You all need a bath, and dinner, and about ten years of sleep. Sit down."

She starts to clear off the table, going in and out of the room with a brush of skirts. She shoves the bandages back into a basket, then takes the bowl with its revolting contents and puts it outside. Arien sways beside me for a moment then staggers forward and slumps into a chair.

I sit down beside him. "This is a terrible idea."

"I don't know," Clover puts in. "I liked the part about dinner."

I close my eyes and circle my fingers against my temples. My head aches. My dress is stuck against my knees in two dark patches where the cuts have bled through.

All my fright and panic from before has faded into cold shock, and I've started to shiver. Everything I've seen tonight has the feel of a terrible dream. My rush to the lake, the blackened ground, the way it tore open to that horrible, depthless wound. It doesn't seem real.

It doesn't seem real that we're going to stay here, either. That we're going to help the monster as he fights the darkness.

The kettle begins to hum. Florence sets out a new bowl and gives us each a clean, folded cloth. She fills the bowl with hot water and tips in dried herbs, followed by a handful of salt. The water steams. Bitterness fills the air as the herbs steep and the salt dissolves.

Clover unbuttons the sleeves of her embroidered dress and rolls them back. Once the water has cooled enough, she takes a cloth, soaks it in the bowl, and starts to scrub away the mud. Then Arien folds back his sleeves and cleans his hands with a fresh cloth.

When he's finished, I soak my cloth in the water. I'm filthy, but I do my best to wash the mud from my hands and arms. Beneath, my skin is tender. Like a blister, a burn. I look at Arien. His hands are the same. Reddened and sore where the mud touched him.

I think of Rowan, bent low over the ground. The way the strands of darkness hungrily covered his arms, his face. If just these small traces of Corruption hurt us like this, then how did *he* feel? I grip the smooth edge of the kitchen table and try to hold back a shudder.

"How many more times will you have to do this?" I ask Arien. "Is all of this really worth it?"

Florence sets a plate in front of me. "Rowan isn't doing this for fun, Violeta. He isn't asking anyone to risk more than what he faces himself."

I sigh and pick up my fork. My stomach unknots long enough to grumble hungrily when I see the meal. Nettle greens and sugar peas, wild strawberries, tomatoes cut into crescents and sprinkled with salt. Summer food. We'd eat this in the cottage when it was too hot for a stove fire.

Then tea. Clover tips more vials of the green liquid into the cups. It hisses and steams.

"You know, that tastes disgusting," I tell her.

She looks offended. "It's medicine!"

Arien stifles a laugh with the edge of his wrist. "Leta's right. How can something that smells so nice taste so bad?"

"It's not *supposed* to taste good. Anyway, you won't need it for much longer. The more you use your magic, the more you learn to control it, the less you'll dream."

I turn the cup around in my hands. "Why did you give it to me, then? I don't have magic."

"It will still help you sleep. That's why Rowan drinks it."

"I don't think it works. I had terrible dreams last night." I drink the tea quickly, trying to ignore the bitter flavor. Arien swallows his with a grimace.

"The ritual will get easier," Clover offers. "We have until the next full moon before we can try again. We have time to prepare. This attempt—"

"Was a disaster."

"Leta, I don't want to argue about it." Arien picks at the edge of his shirt where his cuffs are caked with mud. "They need me."

"You should let Rowan fight his own darkness," I say.

Florence sits down and leans her elbows against the table. She gives me a level look. "Whatever you've heard about Rowan—those stories—they aren't true."

"You mean he *didn't* murder his whole family?"

Her mouth draws tight.

"He's not cruel, Violeta," Clover says quietly. "He wants to help your brother, not harm him. Yes, we need Arien's magic for my spell, but in return I'll teach him alchemy. Don't you want him to learn?"

A lump rises in my throat. I look down at Arien's fingers, stained dark from the shadows. The marks remind me of

91

when he was small and Mother gave us a scrap of dough to make into a tiny loaf of bread. I told Arien to watch the stove, then came back from the garden to find him *watching* it as smoke curled out from the drafts and the bread burned. We ate it anyway. Put honey over the blackened edges. It was sweet and wonderful.

That burned-black bread with drips of honey . . . Arien's gentle hands casting dark magic . . . All this time I've wanted to keep him safe from the darkness. But now it seems that the only way for him to be—if not safe, then happy—is to call the shadows in rather than chase them away.

"I'm sorry." I squeeze his hand. "I love you."

His eyes shimmer in the firelight, filled with tears. "I love you too, Leta. And I know you're worried about me, but I want to do this." He draws himself up. "If I can learn how to use the shadows, how to *control* them, I won't have to be afraid anymore. I want to learn how to be an alchemist."

Tiredly, I bend down to unlace my boots. My dress is ruined, the hem torn from where I ripped it in the woods, the rest of the fabric filthy with blackened mud. I fold back my skirts and peel down my stockings. The cloths tied around my knees have dried stiff and dark. My hands shake as I unwrap them. The cuts look terrible. My skin is angry red beneath the crusted blood.

Clover draws in a sharp breath when she sees, and exchanges a horrified look with Florence.

"I could—" Clover eyes me nervously. "I could mend them for you."

"Mend them?" I stare at her, confused. *Mend*. It's the same word she used to describe what they're trying to do with the Corruption. Strange to think that with magic, both the earth and my skin can be put back together like a torn sheet.

She goes into the stillroom beside the kitchen and comes back with a case made from pale wood. Deftly, she flips it open. There's a proud gleam in her eyes as she shows me the contents. The case is divided into compartments, treasures nestled inside each one. Rows of tiny stoppered jars, polished stones, a bundle of slender beeswax candles. Folded papers, a pearl-handled pen, a bottle of bright blue ink.

Arien peers at the case, eager and curious. His face reminds me of the way I'd feel in Greymere when I saw jars of sweets in the store window.

"Will you let her?" He looks up at me, teeth pressed into his lip.

This moment feels like a chance. A way for me to tell Arien all the things I can't find words for. *I'm sorry. I was afraid of your shadows—your magic—but never you.* I nod slowly. "You can mend me."

Clover crouches down on the floor. "I have to touch your skin to check what I'll need for the spell," she says softly. "May I?"

I nod again. She puts her hands against my knees. Closes her eyes. Then she sits back and touches her fingers together as she counts under her breath, like she's calculating a sum. "It will leave scars as payment."

I don't quite understand what she means. But she's gentle as she wets a cloth and washes away the blood. It stings. She takes a small jar from her case, filled with sweet-smelling salve, and wipes it over the cuts. With her pen she sketches a quick symbol on her wrist. Then she leans closer, her eyes focused with concentration. I watch, fascinated, as they change color. Not black like Arien's but pale gold. Her skin is hot when she puts her palms flat against my knees.

I wince at her touch, and my eyes scrunch closed.

A press, a whisper. My skin tingling warm. And then I am mended.

I open one eye slowly, then the other.

"What's the matter?" Clover raises a brow. "Worried I'd turn you into a frog?"

"Of course not."

She shows me her hand. On her open palm, like an offering, are tiny pieces of glass. They were still there, buried under my skin. The cuts bled as my body tried to heal around those hidden shards. I get up and take them from her. I open the stove and flick the pieces of glass into the coals.

Florence comes over to stand beside me and hesitantly puts her hand on my shoulder. I remember how Rowan turned away from her at the wayside. Maybe each time she reaches out, she expects to be refused. But I let her touch me. I let her comb her fingers gently through my hair.

"I'm glad you decided to stay, Violeta."

Her fingers work carefully, unfurling knots into curls. Her

touch, the firelight, the way the kitchen smells of stove ash and burned sugar—it pulls at me. For just a moment I could almost feel safe. But no amount of kindness will take away the reality of what lies outside, beyond the house.

Because the lake is there. Waiting and wanting.

Chapter Eight

I trail back upstairs to the room that is now mine. In the flicker of candlelight, it looks much the same as before. An unmade bed. Cloth-draped furniture. Dust and neglect and a window open to the hot summer night.

I pace a restless circle from bed to window to dresser. Wrench loose each cloth until they're all strewn across the floor and the air is a haze of motes. With everything uncovered, the room looks more alive, more awake, than it did last night. But it still doesn't feel like mine.

When I pictured where we might go, that day in the village when Arien said we should run away, it was never somewhere like this. Yet here we are, in this strange, haunted place. I turn the thought over as I move through the room. This *is* mine now. And Lakesedge will be my home.

There are folded sheets inside the dresser. They smell of

camphor, and creases lattice the fabric. I make the bed, then take off my torn, stained dress. I shove it into the hearth of the unlit fire, because I want it as far from me as possible.

I put on my nightdress and lie down on the fresh sheets.

My mouth tastes bitter, and I'm so tired that everything looks blurred, like I'm underwater. I trace my fingers back and forth over the creases in the quilt. Think of Arien, in his own room, already asleep. Tomorrow he'll begin to learn how to use his magic.

He's in my dreams when I drift slowly into a scattered, restless sleep. We're in the Vair Woods. Our family is dead, our village lost to fever, our cottage turned to flames. Trees rise around us like sentinels beneath the frost. My frightened breath makes clouds in the air. Arien is in my arms, and he's so heavy I can barely keep hold of him. We go deeper into the forest. Into the cold, still night. Shadows start to lengthen across the icy ground.

A voice calls out to me through the darkness.

The shadows creep toward us, closer and closer.

Then everything fades and shifts.

I'm back in my new room. The candle is burned down; silver light from the full moon shines brightly through the window. Wind stirs the lace curtains. They flutter back and forth like pale ghosts. Strange sounds come from outside. The rustle of leaves, the far-off cry of a night bird. Shakily, I untangle myself from my quilts and sit up.

The air begins to shimmer, the way light reflects over the surface of water. A droplet lands on my cheek. Then another on the back of my hand. A damp splotch, dark as ink. I look up, my heartbeat quickening. The ceiling is a shadowed pool, blurred and rippled, and *dripping*.

The air is cold, cold as a midwinter forest, cold as the Vair Woods.

My room is filled with water. It spills down over the walls and pools in the corners. It starts to spread across the floor. It rises and rises, until the cold, black waves wash against my bed. My breath catches, and a horrified sound escapes my throat. It's just like the water in the lake.

But this isn't real. It's just a dream. The same dream I had last night.

I close my eyes and fold myself down beneath the hem of my sodden quilt. Breathe in deep, until my lungs are filled with the scent of camphor and dust and rose petals. All I can hear is a *hush hush hush*, which might be the wind, might be the lake, might be my own erratic breathing.

Then another sound comes through the wall. It's soft at first, like the wind as it hisses and stirs through sedge grass. Then it twists and sharpens, skittering around me, until the whisper becomes a voice.

Tell me your name.

I curl up tighter and try not to listen. None of this is real. Not the darkness, or the voice, or the water on the walls.

The sound comes again, closer now. From between my ribs, I feel a sharp wrench. As though there's a thread knotted around my bones and it's been pulled.

Tell me your name.

"Violeta." It tumbles out, unbidden.

Open your eyes, Violeta.

I think of the maiden in the labyrinth. How she faced a monster with only a ball of twine held tight in her hands. I don't want to look. But I don't want to lie here cringing in the dark. So I open my eyes.

The room is empty. The corner is just a corner. Silver and shadowed. The floor is just a floor. Bare, dry boards covered with a patina of dust. I peel back the quilt, stretch out a hand, and touch the wall. There's no water. Just faded paper, rough beneath my fingertips.

There are monsters in the woods, in the world. There's a monster in the shadows, and now it knows my name.

I slump back down on the bed. I can't stop shivering. Because the real horrors of Lakesedge aren't in this room. They're on the blackened shore of an endless lake, where a monster fed the ground with his blood. Where my brother will go, with magic and shadows, to try to mend it all.

I'm woken by a heavy knock on the door. I sit up to a room flooded bright. Golden daylight streams through the window. I scrub my wrist across my face and look around the room. Everything is as it was before I fell asleep, the room untouched by water, the floor strewn with the cloths I drew back from the furniture.

The knock comes again, rapid and impatient. Disoriented, I clamber out of bed and cross the room.

The monster is outside my door.

When he sees me, he takes a step back. He glances at me, then quickly turns away. "You were asleep."

I cross my arms over my chest. I'm in my nightdress—faded cotton, a badly stitched mend across one shoulder. My hair is snarled into an enormous tangle. "I *was* asleep."

"It's afternoon."

"It's been a tiring few days."

He raises a brow. Then his mouth lifts into the barest smile. "A slight understatement."

I search his face for hints of what I saw last night at the ritual. The creature he became when he was cut and snared and consumed by the blackened earth. My eyes go from the scars on his face to the ones on his throat. I know it's there, the darkness, the wrongness.

But in the daylight, it's easy to think that Rowan Sylvanan is only a boy with a sharp, handsome face and shadows of fatigue beneath his eyes.

He matches my gaze evenly. He doesn't speak, but he doesn't move away.

"Did you wake me up for a reason, or . . . ?"

"Oh. Yes. I've brought something."

He goes back into the hallway. There's a sound, the scrape of wood over wood, then he returns with a large trunk. As he carries it into my room, his sleeve rides up. He's still wearing gloves, the same as always. But between the cuff of his shirt and the edge of his glove, there's a fresh linen bandage wrapped around his wrist.

I think of the way he shoved the knife into his arm. The coldness in his voice when he spoke my name. *Get away from here.*

He puts the trunk down at the end of my bed. When he notices my eyes on his bandage, he pulls his sleeve back down.

"Clover told me she uses your blood in the rituals." Even as I say it, my stomach tightens at the thought. "Do you have to cut yourself like that every time?"

Ignoring my question, he tips his chin toward the trunk. "Go ahead, open it."

I crouch down and run my fingers over the lid. The polished wood smells like beeswax. The clasp is tarnished, but it opens smoothly when I unfasten it. Inside, carefully folded together, are clothes. Enough for a whole summertime wardrobe, packed with paper like wrapped sweets in a jar. Nightdresses and camisoles and pinafores and ribbon-topped socks. And dresses. So many dresses. I trace my fingers over the folds of paper.

"Whose are these?"

Rowan gives me the same look he did when I asked his name, as if the answer should be obvious. "Yours."

"But I have clothes."

He looks at the fireplace, where my stained dress is still in the hearth. "I never said you didn't."

I close the lid of the trunk and go over to the hearth to pick up my dress. I run my fingers over the torn hem, then trace over the embroidery I stitched around the neckline and cuffs. I was so proud when I made it. The dark green linen sash, the embroidered details. But now all I can see is the uneven hem, the snags and frays where the thread tangled.

"I don't want anything from you. Except for you to promise that Arien will be safe, and I know you won't do that."

Rowan rakes a hand through his hair and sighs. "I meant what I said when I came to your cottage. I'm going to help him. He and Clover have already begun their lessons in the library."

I think of Arien, how his face lit with longing, with hope, when Rowan made his offer. Then the fear that crowded in when he told Arien what he'd do, if he didn't go to Lakesedge. "That was a cruel trick, you know. How you threatened him so he'd be forced to come with you."

"I needed him here before the full moon. There wasn't enough time to explain the truth of it."

"And you think that excuses what you did?"

He steps closer and softens his voice. "He doesn't have to hide who he is now."

I press my nails so hard against my palms that they dig crescents into my skin. "Don't act like this is some benevolent gift you're giving him. If you truly cared about Arien, you'd fight your own Corruption."

Slowly, Rowan reaches for his sleeve. He pushes it back until it's past his elbow, and shows me his bared arm. The skin around the pale linen bandage is scarred, old wounds that are torn and ruined and badly healed.

"I *have* fought it, Violeta." He says my name quietly, like a word from a spell. "I am still fighting it. And if I had any other choice, a way to do this without your brother, I would take it."

I can't look away from his outstretched arm. The scars, the cuts. Before I can stop myself, I reach toward him, the movement almost unconscious. My hand brushes over his skin. He flinches, but lets me touch him.

"How many times have you done this?"

"Clover came here about a year ago with her spell for the ritual. She and I have worked together for twelve moons, more or less."

"More or less?"

"Before she came, I tried on my own."

I picture the same ruthless motion from the ritual—knife, skin, cut—made over and over again, moon by moon. So many times that he's lost count. "How did all of this even start?"

His eyes lower, his lashes veiling his gaze. He stays quiet for a long time. "It started because I did something terrible."

"Do you mean what happened to your family?"

"Yes." There's no apology in his voice, none at all. "That, and many other things besides."

"You really drowned them, didn't you?"

"I told you already. Everything they say about me is true."

My heart starts to beat faster. I blink, and all I can see is dark water. The water at the lake, the water that filled my room when I dreamed. The lake claimed their lives, and now the water, the shore, the earth is poisoned and ruined.

"So this is all your fault. And now you want Arien to fix it."

"Yes."

My hand is still on his arm. I press my fingers tighter, fixing my gaze on the scar just above his wrist, long healed and faded pale. He takes a sharp breath.

"You may have spent twelve moons and more hurting yourself this way"—I lift my eyes to his—"but I won't let you do the same to him."

A strange expression crosses Rowan's face. It's the same way he looked in the woods, when he was wounded and I was about to run away. The same way he looked in the firelight, when I caught him listening to my story.

"Arien wants to stay, and he wants to help. But—" I pull my hand away. "Don't ever threaten him again. If you want something else from Arien, you'll make time to tell the truth."

"I will."

I go back toward the trunk, kneel down, and open the lid. Part of me still wants to refuse Rowan's gift, but my hand reaches inside, unbidden, to unfold the scraps of tissue paper. Silk and cotton and ribbons dance under my fingertips.

The dresses are finer than anything I've ever owned. Than I've ever touched. They're the colors of sky, of sunset: peach and sage and lilac. Skirts full of lace. Sleeves lined with delicate embroidery.

And I want them. I want them so badly that when I touch them, I half expect the feverish longing in my hands to scorch through the fabric. I take out a dress. Pale cream cotton with a pattern of tiny crescent moons embroidered around the collar.

I hold it against my chest and stroke the delicate fabric. "Thank you," I say quietly.

Rowan turns, his hand on the door, about to leave. He looks from the dress to me. "You're welcome."

"Will you wait?" He stops, startled. "I need to get dressed, but I want you to show me to the library after I'm done. I'll never find it otherwise. Your wretched house is too big."

He raises a brow. "Did you want me to draw you a map?"

"Here, I'll start one for you." I sketch out an imagined shape in the air, then point at the spaces to indicate rooms. "Locked, locked, locked, library."

He smiles faintly and shakes his head at me. "I'll wait outside your room."

We've spent almost a week together. I know what he is and now I know for sure what he's done. And it feels strange, to tease him like this. More strange for how easily it comes.

I collect a few more things from the trunk—a camisole, lace-hemmed undergarments, and a handful of hairpins— then walk to the corner, where a screen divides the washstand from the rest of the room. I hold my new dress up before the window. Light shimmers over it, and the gossamer layers of fabric glow as they catch the sun. It's beautiful.

I undress quickly, feeling embarrassed to be doing this while Rowan is just outside the room, even though he can't see me. I'm embarrassed, too, when I put on the new undergarments, knowing that they were a gift. I scowl at my flushed cheeks in the mirror above the washstand, then slip the dress over my head.

There's a long, ribboned sash at the waist. A row of tiny, pearlescent buttons all along the back. I knot the sash. The buttons are awkward to reach, but I manage to fasten most of them. Then I sweep my hair into a haphazard braid and wind it into a crown, pinned around my head. My feet are bare, since I left my mud-caked boots down in the kitchen. The skirts wash about my legs like mist.

I feel like some made-up, dewdrop-fine creature from a story. I can't stop running my fingers along the sash and over the embroidery that edges the sleeves.

When I step out of the room, Rowan looks me over, from my pinned braids to the fall of the skirts. His mouth tilts slightly when he notices my bare feet.

"Come on, then." He turns and moves farther into the hall-way, waiting for me to follow him.

We go across the landing. The air is dim, lit by only the faintest drifts of afternoon light. My bare feet leave prints on the dusty floor. He walks behind me, deliberately measuring his pace so we don't walk side by side. At the top of the stairs, Rowan puts his hand on my shoulder. "Violeta. You— your . . ." He trails off.

I turn around to look at him, confused. "What?"

He motions awkwardly to the back of my dress. "You missed some buttons."

I reach my arm to my back. Bare skin, the lace band of my camisole, then a row of empty buttonholes. *Oh.* Heat creeps over my face as I twist around, trying to fasten them, but they're too small, and they slip away from my fingers.

Hesitantly, I turn my back to him. "I can't reach them. Can you, please?"

He doesn't move. I wait, feeling exposed with the buttons undone and him just *standing* there.

Eventually, with a rough sigh, Rowan reaches out and tries to catch hold of the buttons without touching me, but he can't. He pauses, takes off his gloves, then tries again. His fingers brush over my skin. Without the gloves, his hands are warm, his fingertips rasped by calluses.

"*Ash.*" His hands drop. "Sorry, I—"

He takes hold of the dress with another muttered curse. I feel the shift and tug of fabric and pearl. Sparks of heat dance through my fingers. At the center of my chest I feel a strange pull, as though a thread has been knotted up inside me.

At last he fastens the final button and rests his hand, flat, over the nape of my neck. I step away from him.

"Thank you." The words are half-stuck in my throat.

He walks forward briskly, forcing me to catch up. "The library is this way."

As I follow him down the stairs, my hand drifts up to curl over the back of my neck. I press down on the memory of his touch on my skin.

Chapter Nine

The library is sunlight and polished wood, a row of windows that reveals a sky hazed with summer clouds. The walls are lined with shelves, shrouded in dust cloths. At the center of the room, Arien and Clover sit together at a large table that's cluttered with papers and books and ink pots and pens.

Arien gets to his feet when he sees Rowan and me come in.

"Come and see what I've done!" He takes hold of my hand, his face alight with a pleased smile, as he pulls me farther into the room. "Clover taught me how to draw sigils. She's so clever."

Clover laughs. "Arien, you're delightful. It helps that you are a very good student."

Arien rifles through the piles of papers on the table. He finds a notebook and pushes it eagerly into my hands. I leaf carefully through the pages. The book is filled with intricate, beautiful illustrations drawn in delicate ink. I recognize the same interconnected symbols as the ones marked on Arien's wrist and on Clover's arms.

"Look." He touches his fingers to the edge of a shape. "That's iron, and this is gold, and this is salt . . ."

"All these elements are part of the magic that makes the world. The Lady's light, separated into individual pieces," Clover explains. "Every spell we cast draws on different elements. The more difficult the spell, the more elements you need, and the more complicated the sigil becomes."

"And that's how you channel the magic?" I ask. "You combine the elements to make a sigil?"

"That's right." Her eyes drop to her wrist, and she brushes her fingers idly over the markings. "And it's forever marked onto your skin after."

It makes a grim sense—the permanence of the sigils. Alchemy is so wondrous, so terrible. The enormity of that magic *should* leave a scar. Arien touches his wrist in an echo of Clover's gesture, then turns back to the notebook and points to a new page. "And this one is my favorite . . ."

Neither of us knows how to write more than our names. Mother never showed us, though she taught us to read, so we could learn the litanies. But Arien has always loved to draw. He sketched patterns on fogged-over windows or in the dust between rows of the garden. He hoarded scraps of paper and the slate pencils Mother used to mark down invoices. Kept the leftover wood and remnants of paints she rarely gave to us, and guarded them like treasure.

He made pictures to match the stories I told him. Leaves and flowers and birds. Girls in silver-hued dresses with gossamer wings. Boys with long-lashed eyes, crowns on their waved hair. Now he shows me his notebook full of alchemical sigils with the same shy, proud expression.

"They're beautiful, Arien."

And they are. But as I look over the pages, a heavy ache settles in my chest. Because these sigils are another irrefutable marker of his new life and what awaits him.

Rowan is still standing in the doorway. Arien smiles at him. "Did you want to see?"

"Oh." He hesitates a moment. "Yes, of course." He walks slowly toward the table and sits down. Arien sits beside him and smooths the notebook open.

Rowan leans close, listening intently as Arien tells him about the symbols and reads their names. At one point, he rests his hand on Arien's shoulder. As though he truly cares. I thought these lessons were only to serve his own means. That Rowan only wants Arien to be trained so they can use his magic. But there's no artifice in the way he listens. His expression, softened from his usual scowl, is gentle and . . . *sad*.

Clover notices me watching them. With a smile, she comes over to show me her own notebook. She opens the pages to display a larger, more complex version of the spell on her wrist. "This is the spell we'll use at the next ritual."

"But it didn't work last time."

"It did work. It's just that Arien couldn't hold the magic long enough for it to mend." She looks at him and goes on hurriedly, her voice reassuring. "Of course, that doesn't matter! We have a whole moon left to prepare. I'll draw samples from the lake, we'll practice the spell, and next time he'll be perfect."

Arien pages through his notebook, his enthusiasm fading. "I'm sorry I couldn't do it before."

"You have nothing to be sorry about. Especially when you had no warning of what was asked of you." I look pointedly at Rowan, but he avoids my gaze, his eyes fixed on Arien's book.

"Don't be hard on yourself, Arien," Clover says. "In the Maylands we train almost constantly to learn how to cast these types of spells. And you've only just begun."

"The Maylands?" Arien's face lights up, his eyes full of interest. "What's it like there?"

"It's beautiful. The houses are all built in a circle, with a meadow at the center full of herbs and flowers. This time of year, it stays light until almost midnight, and when the wind blows from the coast, you can smell the sea."

"That does sound beautiful," he sighs wistfully. I think of him gone to the commune where all the alchemists live and train. A life full of books and ink and arcane knowledge. A life far beyond anything I could imagine. "Did you love it there?"

"Well . . . I was *good* at what I did there. My research." Clover pulls at the end of her braid, chews her lip. "But I never fit in. It's not a popular occupation, in the Maylands, to be a family alchemist. To live at an estate and help the village healers and tend the gardens. There's no glory in this." She blushes and darts a glance at Rowan. "But it's what I wanted. I'm not ruthless enough to succeed in the Maylands. But here, I can make a difference."

"You've certainly made a difference in the amount of peculiar teas I'm forced to drink." Rowan laughs, then grows serious. "Of course I'm glad for your help, Clover."

"I told you to put honey in the tea. But anyway, thank you." She grins, pleased; then she turns back to me. "It's strange that you don't have magic, too, Violeta. Generally it runs in families. But you don't?"

"No. I don't."

I go over to the window and look down at the grounds. There's the narrow space of the garden, the wall covered in vines, the other side hidden by trees. Far in the distance I can see the black line of the shore and how far the Corruption extends beyond the lake. There's a gray expanse of skeletal branches woven through the forest beside the water. As though the poison has trickled in and devoured some of the trees.

A shiver goes through me. The room is warm—lit by hot, afternoon sunlight. But I suddenly feel cold.

I turn away from the windows and the view of the lake and start to inspect the bookshelves. A swirl of dust fills the air when I pull the nearest cloth loose. The shelf, unveiled, is empty. I move on to the next one. Then the next. I take down each cloth until the air is a haze of motes that sparkle, amber in the sunlight.

I run my fingers through the dust on the shelves and laugh in disbelief. "Why doesn't your library have any books?"

Rowan shrugs. "I packed them away."

He turns back to Arien and the notebooks, ignoring me.

I walk around the room, past shelf after shelf. They're all bare, and it looks so forlorn. We had no books in the cottage aside from a small, well-worn collection of litany chants. All of the stories I've told Arien were ones I've held in my memory, told to me by our parents. And now that I'm faced with this stripped-bare library, I'm full of longing. The same eagerness that lit my hands when I looked into the trunk of dresses.

There's one final cloth that I haven't taken down. I grab hold of the edge. Rowan looks up suddenly as I pull the cloth.

"No!" He starts to get up from his chair. "Not that one."

But the cloth has already fallen free. And instead of another bank of empty shelves, there's a portrait set high on the wall in an ornate golden frame.

Rowan stands, wordless, frozen in place with his eyes fixed on the portrait.

It shows a family. Two boys, young, just tracing the last edges of childhood. They both have the same tanned skin and wavy hair, much less unruly than my own curls. The taller of the two, the elder, has a serious expression that I recognize instantly.

"Oh, this is—*you*." I take a step back. "This is your family."

His father. Lord Sylvanan, who smiled at me and Arien on that long-ago tithe day. Tall and handsome, with tawny skin and neat, dark hair.

His mother. Small and willowy, with white skin and large brown eyes—the same color as Rowan's. And her dress . . . It's pale and delicate, with gossamer skirts and a ribboned sash and

113

crescent moons embroidered on the collar. It's my dress, the one I'm wearing now.

Rowan didn't even want me here, but he gave me all of his mother's beautiful clothes.

I look over to him, expecting that he'll be angry at me. But he isn't. His expression is one of clear, raw shame. I twist the dust cloth between my hands, wanting more than anything to undo this moment. "I didn't mean . . ."

He rakes his hand through his hair and heaves out a tense breath. I take a step toward him, but he storms out of the room.

I throw down the cloth and run after him. The corridor is empty, dark and quiet. I go past the closed doors, back toward the staircase. He's there, on the landing, framed by the carved balustrade. One arm braced against the wall, his head slumped forward, face hidden by the fall of his hair. Florence is beside him, a tray of tea things balanced on her hip.

When she puts her hand on his shoulder, a memory rises, dim and blurred. My mother and me curled into a single chair beside the fire. It rocked, that chair, and she hummed as it swayed back and forth. Her fingers combed through my curls. Gentle, gentle.

Florence puts her hand on Rowan with that same kind of gentleness and leans closer to him, speaking softly. Rowan shakes her off. He looks up, and our eyes meet. His face is stricken, flushed and tear streaked. Everything goes still for one awful, endless moment until he turns away.

He pushes past Florence and goes down the stairs. She sighs. "I don't suppose you'll tell me what that was about?"

"He didn't say?"

"No."

I listen to the sound of Rowan's retreating footsteps, trying to make sense of what just happened. "I upset him."

"That much is obvious." Florence sighs again, then continues along the hall with the tray balanced carefully.

I follow her, and we fall into step as we walk. Once we're inside the library, she looks from me—in my new dress—to the unveiled shelves. Then she sees the portrait.

"Well." She sets the tray on the table. Her expression is stern, but there's a flicker of sadness in her flinty eyes. "No wonder he was upset."

"But why was he upset? Does he regret what he did?"

Florence gives me a sharp look. "What he did?"

I gesture toward the window. Outside, the lake lies far in the distance, a shimmer of sunlit water beside the black expanse of the shore. "He told me that the rumors were true."

"Listen to me, Violeta. He is no murderer." She curls her fingers around the keys on her necklace, sliding them back and forth restlessly on the silver chain. "The stories people tell about Lakesedge have a lot of fear and very little truth."

"But he *admitted* they were true. He said . . ." A sliver of doubt begins to prickle at me. There's another truth, hidden between his words. His scars, his desperation to mend the Corruption. His reaction when I uncovered the portrait.

His family—could it be possible for him both to have killed them and mourn them?

"I've been here since before he was born," Florence says.

"His mother, Marian, and I grew up together. When she was handfasted, I came with her to be the keeper of Lakesedge Estate. We were friends."

Were. The word hangs, loaded and low. "How did she die?"

"She was the second to drown. Kaede, Lord Sylvanan, was the first. They found him dead on the shore the morning after Rowan's thirteenth birthday. Marian died the year after. And then, last year . . . Elan."

Her eyes go to the portrait. Rowan's brother has a sweet smile and rounded cheeks. I can so easily picture Arien at that same age. His scraped knees. His demands for stories. The elaborate plans he made for a playhouse we could build in the orchard.

Elan. I've heard his name before.

The cries in the dark, on my first night here. It was Rowan. Clover told me he drinks the sedative-dosed tea *to help him sleep*. The sounds I heard that night, echoing through the halls, tangled and tortured . . . It was him, calling out for his brother.

"I know Rowan," Florence goes on. "And I know he isn't capable of such a terrible thing. Whatever happened, it was an accident."

"Three members of his family all drowned in the exact same place."

"Four," Clover murmurs.

Florence turns to her abruptly. "He told you about that?"

"Not exactly. But . . . people sometimes get conversational once you've given them a sedative."

"What do you mean, four?" My pulse starts to beat a hard, panicked rhythm.

"When Rowan was five years old, he vanished for an entire day. At sunset we found him in the water. And at first we thought he was dead, but then he opened his eyes." Florence pauses as she gathers herself, her face toward the window. The afternoon light streaks gold through her pale hair. "And when he did, the lake turned black. That was the start of the Corruption."

I sit down heavily, landing in a chair before my knees give out.

When we were small—when Arien's dreams brought their first wisps of shadows—Mother warned us about the Lord Under. *If you step too close to the darkness, then he can touch you. Touch you, and send you back into the world, corrupted.* I didn't want to believe it. But it made sense, in a terrible way.

He's the lord of the dead. He comes at the end of our lives and guides us into the world Below. And if he came to you, if he left you alive . . . then all the years you lived, marked by his touch, would bring him so much more power than a simple death.

"He—he was dead," I stammer out. "Rowan was dead, and the Lord Under—"

Arien takes my hand, his brow notched with concern.

"Leta, he didn't die. I mean, obviously. He's still here." He gives my shoulder a little shake, trying to tease me. "Or maybe you've spent all this time arguing with a ghost."

"The Lord Under tends the souls in the world Below," Florence says. "He doesn't bring them back. I'd have thought you'd know not to believe that superstition."

But in spite of her words, she draws her fingers across her chest.

Clover pours out the tea and passes me a cup. I slump back in my chair and clasp my teacup tightly. Let my face be washed by the rise of bergamot-scented steam. All I can think of are the shadows in my room. The water that poured down and the whispers that spoke my name. Then a deeper memory pulls at me.

The Vair Woods in winter. The voice I heard as the darkness gathered between the trees.

What I saw, it wasn't real; but when my eyes shutter closed, I see Rowan, five years old and pale and still. Black water streaming from his mouth, his eyes, as the earth turned dark beneath him.

Could it have only been a dream, those things I saw in my room? The water on the walls, the whispers in the dark. Maybe my thoughts just tangled themselves into those hideous visions of voices and shadows. *Only dreams.*

It's like there are two stories about Rowan, about Lakesedge, written side by side in a single volume. The ink from one bleeding through to mar the words on the opposite page. A boy who almost died. A boy who *did* die. A boy who drowned in a lake and came back as a monster.

But which story is real, and which is just a ghostly specter of rumor and fear?

We finish our tea in silence. I help pack away the notebooks and the inkpots and pens. The sunlight fades, and we trail down the stairs to dinner. Outside the kitchen window the waning moon hangs luminous in the twilight sky.

It's an unavoidable reminder that soon Arien will have to go back to the lake and to the dark, hungry ground that tried to *consume* him. It's only a few weeks until the month of Midsummer and the next full moon, when they'll perform the ritual again.

But before then, I'm going to find out the truth about Rowan Sylvanan.

Chapter Ten

I t's late. In the starless dark, my eyes are heavy with fatigue. Everyone else is asleep, and the house is silent around me, where I sit in my room. The only light is from the candle beside my bed. In my hands are five vials of the sedative draft Clover puts in our tea. I stole them from her stillroom. The glass clinks together in my cupped palms.

I need sleep. Sleep that feels like being buried alive, that I can't escape. I need to sink so deep that when the dreams come, I won't be able to turn away.

I open the first vial. The glass is hot against my lips, heated by the warmth of my nervous hands. It's horribly bitter as it fills my mouth, so sharp and acrid that when I swallow, the whole world turns virulent green. The little wooden icon that Arien painted for me—set on my bedside table—wavers before my blurred vision.

For the past two weeks, I've watched Arien and Clover

prepare relentlessly for the next ritual. We've spent each day in the library, hemmed in by shelves filled with the jars of inky water and blackened mud they've dredged up from the lake. They work until sunset each day. Arien calls the shadows and weaves the magic around the jars of Corruption. Clover stands beside him and calls out instructions, trying not to be frustrated with him when he falters.

But no matter how hard they try, Arien can't control his magic enough to cast the spell.

"Again," she says when he slips, and the shadows dissipate into mist. "Again."

His hands shake. He scrunches them into fists, then grasps the jar. "I can do this. I know I can do this."

As much as Clover pushes him, Arien pushes himself harder. His arms are covered in sigils. His hands are smeared dark to the wrist with mud and magic and ink. The blackness never clears from his eyes. *Again again again.*

I've sat in the library and watched them and wished I could help. Watched the moon wane, a smaller crescent each night, and wished I could take Arien's place.

But I have no magic. All I can do is chase the shadows.

I need to dream again. I need to see the visions and hear the voice that knows my name. I've tried and tried. Sat awake, my eyes fixed on the corner of my room. Walked the halls and tried to open each locked door. Followed the path through the starlit garden, past overgrown weeds and flowers. I've even gone to the lake, watched the water lie inky and still beneath the slender moon.

But no matter how much I've watched or waited . . . nothing.

I open the second vial. Tip it into my mouth. The taste burns all the way down. Nausea rushes through me in a brutal, sudden wave. I curl forward as the world tilts unsteadily. My whole body goes leaden and sluggish, like my skin is full of stones.

All the remaining vials fall from my hands, the glass clinking as they spill onto the quilt. I stare out into the room, watching as the walls start to shiver and shift, as blotches of darkness bloom and fade over the floor.

Water begins to pool in the corners. I get to my feet; the bare boards are cold, like I've stepped into a forest of midwinter ice. The candle flame flutters like a frantic, luminescent moth.

The water deepens, rising over my feet. The walls are washed dark. I stretch out my hand. A cold, sharp hush of air kisses my fingertips, as though there's breath trapped beneath stone and plaster.

I put my palm against the wall. Taste bitter herbs. Taste ash and salt and blood. "I'm not afraid. Please. Tell me. Show me."

I can hear it—a sound, a whisper. I close my eyes and try, desperately, to *listen*. Then it comes. The voice. It speaks to me in a stir of night air. In a rustle of dry leaves.

Follow.

My eyes snap open. The room has gone. The house has gone. I'm outside beneath a lavender, dawn-lit sky. There's a forest behind me; susurrations of wind stir through the pale trees. There's a stretch of earth. Strands of tall, reedy sedge grass. And water. Endless water. Flat and smooth as mirror glass, it reflects the pastel clouds.

The lake.

I'm alone. I'm not alone. There's a presence—I'm sure there is—but when I turn, it slips away. I can't see it clearly no matter how hard I look. Only glimpses. Only pieces. Shadows and the steady *drip drip* of water. Always just to the side of me, here and not here. I can't see it, but I can feel it. It's watching me. It's . . . waiting.

Laid out along the shore are shapes. Shrouded in white like the dust cloths that covered the furniture in my new room. I take a halting step toward them. They're people. They lie still beneath the pale covers, without even a faint movement of breath. All four of them.

The wind rises, tangling my hair. It snatches at the cloth that covers the endmost shape. The hem peels back. I can't look. I can't *not* look. I kneel down slowly. The pebbles are sharp against my knees. Damp seeps up from the ground and over my skin. Waves *lap lap lap* against the shore.

I take hold of the cloth. Pull and pull until it's bundled up in my hands.

The boy lies beneath. His skin is pallid, his dark hair plastered in stripes across his face. He's smaller, younger, perhaps the same age I was when I wandered lost on the road at midwinter. Five-year-old Rowan Sylvanan—still and cold and dead.

He sits up. He *looks* at me. Streams of water pour from his mouth, his nose. His eyes roll back, pale and limpid. He coughs and chokes. The water starts to turn black. Oily strands drip over his skin. The lake begins to seethe and churn. Waves rush over the shore. Wash past him, past me.

The darkness—the same darkness that oozes from him—spreads across the lake.

The three bodies that remain on the shore are caught by the waves. One by one, they're pulled out, pulled down, deeper and deeper. His father, his mother, his brother all sink and vanish beneath the water.

The darkness rises like a mist. It closes in across the shore, the lake, the trees. I shut my eyes, frozen, despairing, trapped in the final moment before the darkness claims me.

Then I'm back in the house, on the landing beneath the arched windows. The glass is still warm with residual heat from the midsummer day. The sky beyond is lightless. A new moon, a dark moon, halfway to the next ritual.

I scrub my eyes. I'm awake—I'm awake—but I feel as though I'm still caught by the dream. Footsteps echo, and I look down over the carved balustrade to see Rowan in the entrance hall below. He's wrapped in his cloak, the hood pulled low over his hair. He has a candle in a jar. The shielded flame is as tiny as a faerie light as he moves through the house.

A few beats later, I hear the scrape of the kitchen door.

I go down the stairs. My nightdress trails around me, a

mothlike wisp in the dark. The kitchen is lit by stove coals and a dwindling altar candle. The door is still open.

It's hot out in the garden, and the heat on my face wakes me a little. The world comes into slightly sharper focus. I can just make out Rowan, far down along the path. I stagger after him in a wavery line, the gravel sharp under my unsteady feet.

I stumble into the overgrown grass and catch myself against the ivy-wreathed wall. I go along, leaning hard against it to keep myself upright. After a few paces, the shape of the wall changes beneath my hand and vines give way to iron. There's a gate hidden among the ivy. It's locked.

I peer through the curved rails. I see the dim outline of an orchard, the branches shaded indigo by the night, and a spill of wildflowers that's come loose from a wooden border.

A garden. There's another garden there, locked up behind the wall.

Farther ahead, Rowan's boots crush heavily over the graveled path. I keep following him. Past the gate, past the ivy, until the wall opens out to a familiar space.

The lake.

The water is a lightless whisper. I've been back here since the ritual, but never farther than this archway. I take a halting step out onto the blackened ground. I blink, and the earth seems to move. A shiver goes through me when I think of how it tore open. How it fought against Arien and Clover.

Rowan crosses to the place where they carved the sigil for

the last ritual. The lake begins to stir, as though the water is trying to draw him closer. His hood falls back as he steps onto the wet, dark mud. He drags a hand through his unbound hair and sighs heavily. Then he reaches into his pocket and takes out a knife.

Under my feet, the ground feels like it's breathing. It feels hungry.

No no no.

"Wait!" I run toward him. The mud sucks at my feet. Cold and hideous and *wrong*. "Wait, you can't!"

He turns, startled. I grab hold of his arm. His face, shrouded by the fall of his hair, is tense and grim. He shakes himself loose from my grasp. "Violeta, get away from me, now!"

Water rushes in around our feet, then recedes with a hollow hiss. "What is this? What are you doing?"

He struggles to speak but manages to choke out a single word. "Tithe."

It's almost lost to the sound of the waves. *Tithe.* I think of Greymere. The tables in the village square. Jars of sour cherries. Syrup and sweetness. I think of Rowan on the night of the ritual, crimson eyed and shadow stained. On his knees with the earth snared around him.

Tithe. It isn't just the rituals when he gives his blood to the ground and the spell. No wonder he couldn't tell me how many times he'd come here, to be cut and bled and *fed* to the Corruption.

Terror floods me, icy as the waves. "No, you can't do this."

He kneels down. His hands shake as he roughly unties the laces at his sleeve and bares the scarred stretch of his arm. His pupils are blown wide, irises dark as the night. "Violeta." He gasps out my name as the darkness spreads across his throat, spiraling out from the scars. "Please, just go."

He puts the blade to his wrist, and all I can think of is the way he looked at me when he gave me his mother's dresses. The grief in his eyes after he saw the portrait of his family. Whatever he's done, whatever he is, I can't turn away from him. I don't want to leave him alone.

I fall to my knees in the mud beside him.

He drives the knife into his arm. Wrist to elbow, a deep, vicious cut. Blood streams over his skin, over his gloves. It trails his palm, beads the tips of his fingers.

He shoves his hand against the earth, his fingers digging deep tracks through the ground.

The Corruption reacts instantly. Streaks of mud slice up and wrap around him. They curl hungrily around his wrist, his arm, higher. I snatch back my hand before it can touch me. It goes around his throat, over his jaw. His eyes close tightly. His dark brows knit into a determined, pained expression. His breath comes out in shudders.

Patches of mud flake loose from his mouth with each exhale. It slithers, re-forms, covers him again. It's inside him, in his mouth, his lungs, beneath his skin.

And then—the Corruption, it changes him. His gaze goes cold and feral; his teeth turn sharp. This isn't just a bloodletting.

He's lost to it, taken over. The darkness spreads and spreads through him, until he's barely Rowan at all, but some other creature made of mud and moonlight.

A monster.

I stare at him, feeling so helpless I'm near sobbing. I wish for power, for magic, for some way to fight the cruel hunger of the Corruption. But I have nothing. I can do nothing. Then I remember Arien, caught by the dreams that were never dreams. Lost and afraid as his shadows filled our room. How I'd hold him and think of warmth and try to pull him back from the dark.

I take hold of Rowan's wrist and push my other hand down against the earth. Usually when I touch the ground like this during observance, I feel the light of the world, feel it glow. But when I touch the Corruption, there's only cold and dark.

"Let him go." I work my fingers deeper into the mud. Think of summer nights. Of the banked kitchen stove. Of the locked-up garden, pale and beautiful in the moonlight. *Let him go, let him go, let him go.*

Heat rushes over my skin. A sharp warmth blooms at the center of my palm. I picture a thread, tied from Rowan to me, wrapped around my hand. I don't understand what this means. I'm not sure it's even real. But I can't bear to leave him like this, alone, devoured by the dark.

I close my fingers around the thread and pull.

The tendrils uncoil. The mud separates and falls away. A final tremor goes through the ground; then Rowan slumps back. With shaking hands he scrapes the mud away from where it covers his mouth.

He stares at me, shocked. "Violeta . . . what did you just do?"

I look down at my hands. I can still feel the residual heat pulsing through my fingers like an aftershock. Shakily, I put my hands back against the ground. I close my eyes and try to reach for that warmth, the thread, the feeling that the darkness heard me when I called out. But nothing happens. There's only cold mud and an empty quiet.

"I don't know. I don't know what I did. You looked so alone, and I . . ." Embarrassment prickles over my skin. "I just wanted to help you."

"I don't need your help. You shouldn't have stayed."

"Do you want me to leave now?"

His eyes shutter, and he turns away, his gaze fixed on the lake. Then softly, roughly, he whispers, "No."

We both get to our feet. Rowan wavers for a moment before falling against me. His skin is fever hot. I put my arm around his waist and he makes a sound, protesting, when I touch him, but then he leans against me with a sigh. Slowly, we start to walk back toward the house.

We stagger along the path, his boots dragging through the gravel. I hold him up best I can, but he's so heavy. My head barely reaches his shoulder, and I'm still numb and blurred from the sedatives. I stumble over my own feet and veer off the path onto the tangled lawn. Finally, we reach the house.

Once we're inside, he moves through the kitchen. I go along, pulled by his momentum. He opens a door to reveal a darkened space that might have been a parlor, once. It's less closed up than the rest of the rooms in the house. Sheets drape most of the furniture, but there's an uncovered sofa against one wall with a small table beside it. A window looks out over the front garden. The curtains are open, and an unlit lantern rests on the sill.

Rowan collapses onto the sofa with his knees drawn up and his hands shoved against his face.

"You can go now." He gestures roughly toward the doorway. Blood drips down his fingers onto the floor. "I'll be fine."

I grab hold of his arm and turn it upward, revealing a deep, rough-edged wound. "You are not fine. *This* is not fine."

He slumps forward, coughing wetly, then makes a choked sound. I dart into the kitchen and snatch up the tin bucket that Florence uses when she cleans out the stove ash. I run back to the parlor and shove it into his hands. He clutches it, white knuckled, and folds over farther. I hesitate, then put my hand on his back.

"Don't." Rowan's protest cuts to more rasped coughs. He begins to retch up mouthfuls of filthy, ink-dark water. My stomach twists. Revolted, I stare out of the window, so I don't have to watch him.

"The Corruption, it's *inside* you, isn't it?" I start to shiver uncontrollably. "It's poisoning you."

"Yes."

"You knew. All along, you knew, but you kept it from us. Was your family poisoned, too? Is that what killed them?" I turn on him. "If Arien gets hurt because of your secrets, I'll—"

"He won't." He coughs, choking out more black water. He spits, wipes his mouth on his sleeve. "It won't hurt him like it hurts me."

I take the bucket, go outside, and tip it out into the garden. Another wave of dizzy nausea washes over me. I swallow hard. Take a slow, deep breath of hot night air that smells of pollen and leaves.

When I go back into the parlor, Rowan has lit the lantern. The top drawer of the table beside the sofa is open. Inside are bandages, cloths, and a jar of the honey-sweet salve that Clover used on my knees. He's cleaned the cut and wrapped a neat length of linen around his arm. It's tidy and careful and practiced, just like when he tended his wounds at the wayside.

I sit down beside him. "Promise me—on your life—that Arien isn't going to end up like you."

"My life isn't worth that much." He sighs, adjusting the knot that holds the linen in place. "He won't be harmed. The Corruption only wants me."

"Let me see that." I look at his wrist. Blood has started to seep through the bandage. I take a cloth from the drawer and hold it against his arm. He tries to pull away, but I put my other hand on him until he stays.

"I'll get Clover. She can mend you."

"No. It doesn't work on this."

"What do you mean, it doesn't work?" I peel back the cloth. The bandage is stained. Not crimson, but black. And it's not like blood. It's darker. *Thicker.*

131

"Clover's magic doesn't work on me for the same reason it doesn't work on the Corruption."

I'm so horrified I can barely speak. I remember the water in his mouth, the hiss of his voice. "You don't just want to mend the lake—you want to mend yourself."

"They're one and the same. Clover believes that if they cast the spell at the place the blight began, on the shore, then it should mend the blight everywhere."

"Does she know you've been doing this between the rituals?

"She knows there's a connection between the Corruption and my blood. That it reacts to me. But I haven't told her or Florence about the tithes."

A laugh catches in my throat, threatening to become a sob. "Yes, it would be a shame for them to know. They might worry about you. *Ash*, Rowan. You can't hide this."

"Please." His face, for the first time, is open and sad and terribly earnest. "You can't tell them what you saw."

"You've let it take so many pieces of you. What happens when there's nothing left?"

"Eventually it will kill me." He's completely without self-pity. "I'm not afraid of that. There are worse things than death."

I think of shadows and whispers and deep, dark water. What I was searching for, when I reached out and put my hand against the wall in my room, when I listened to that strange voice. "I had a dream about you. No, not a dream. A vision. I saw you at the lake. I saw you drown when you were a child. I saw you come back."

"You saw me come back?" He looks at me intently; the expression in his dark eyes makes me shiver. "Why did you follow me tonight? You've been haunting my house like a little, prying ghost."

"I wanted to know the truth about you."

"What are you trying to ask? Go ahead. Say it."

"You drowned. You died; then you came back. And that's why you're like this."

"You truly think I faced the Lord Under, then walked away from death? That I came back poisoned? And that's why this is happening?"

The room tilts unsteadily. The lantern flares and flutters, though the air is still. I think of moonlight and frost and my hands outstretched into the darkness. The voice that called to me in the Vair Woods. "Yes."

"Do you think I'm a monster?"

"Yes."

His voice turns low and cold. "Are you afraid of me, Violeta?"

I don't flinch. I don't turn away. I see him, with his ruined arm and his beautiful face: the boy whose life was stolen by the lake, the boy who knows desperation and darkness. "No. I'm not afraid of you, Rowan Sylvanan. But you have to tell me the truth. All of it."

He looks at me solemnly from beneath his lashes, all

fierceness gone. "Each time I do this, it changes me. When the Corruption takes the tithe, I lose myself. It's getting harder and harder to come back from it. Sometimes I'm not even sure how much is me, and how much is the poison."

I reach out to him, then hesitate. "Will you take off your gloves?"

Warily, he removes the gloves and sets them aside. Even his fingers are scarred, and there's a mark on his heartline from where he cut his palm to fight the wolf. I take his hand between my own, and he goes very still. I wonder when anyone last touched him like this.

I squeeze his hand gently. "I won't let you be lost."

His mouth tilts into a faint smile. "Are you so unafraid of monsters?"

"Truly, the monsters should be afraid of me."

"Violeta, I'm sorry that I made Arien come here. I wish there was another way."

"So do I."

"Please don't tell anyone about the tithes. After the next ritual it won't . . . It won't matter, once the Corruption has been mended."

"Fine. I'll keep your secret until then. But . . ." I tap my finger against his chest. "It will cost you."

He laughs, surprised. "And what is the price of your silence?"

"I'd like a book. One of your packed-away books."

"Done."

We sit together, his hand in mine. This new closeness

between us feels strange; an easily broken thing that I'll have to treat with care. Lamplight dances over him: his fawn-gold skin, the silver rings in his ears, the waves of his dark hair. He looks so tired, with deep shadows cut beneath his eyes.

With a sigh, Rowan lets his head rest back against the wall. His eyes dip closed. His lashes are two dark crescents over his cheeks. His features relax for the barest moment, then he sits up with a start. It reminds me of Arien. How he'd fight against sleep when he was afraid of his dreams.

"I could—If you want to sleep, I'll wake you if you start to have a nightmare."

"You don't have to do that."

"I want to stay." My voice turns quiet; I feel shy, speaking it so plainly.

He frowns, but beneath his uncertainty, there's a flicker of longing. Slowly, he settles against me. I stroke my hand over his hair, thinking of the stories my mother told Arien and me, about how faeries would tie knots in our curls while we slept. After a long time, Rowan's breath goes heavy. He sinks closer. His forehead presses into the curve of my neck. When I next look at him, he's asleep. His hands, tensed, slowly loosen. He makes a sound. A murmur that might be a name.

"Elan." His fingers clench around mine. "Elan . . ."

I know I should be angry for how he's brought Arien into all of this. And my anger is still there, but I can't resent him for what he's done. Not right now, when he's here with poison in his veins and his dead brother's name on his lips.

I put out a tentative hand and brush my fingers gently over his cheek. He says more words that are lost in somnolent incoherence. Then he sleeps on. He doesn't dream. I feel the feverish heat of his skin against my neck, but I don't push him away.

Chapter Eleven

Rowan leaves in the faded dawnlight, when I'm still half-asleep. I stir enough to sit up, but he shakes his head before he gently lays me down. He takes off his cloak and drapes it over me. My last memory of the long, strange night is the brief touch of his hand on my shoulder, then his footsteps going quietly away, back up the stairs.

When I next open my eyes, afternoon light shines gold across the window. I'm curled on the sofa, alone. All that happened feels like a peculiar dream, except that I have the cloak, mud stained and still damp. It was real. The strange vision of Rowan's death. The voice that urged me to follow. The tithe.

And the truth that if Arien can't help mend the Corruption, Rowan will die.

I sit up and pull the cloak tightly around me, slip the hood over my hair, and fasten the clasp at my throat. It smells of burnt sugar, of boy, of silt and salt and sweat. I bury my nose against the collar and take a deep breath, then look around the room, blushing at my foolishness even though there's no one here to see me.

And then I notice that, tucked under the cloak, tucked close beside me, is a book.

I pick it up carefully and take it closer to the window. The cover is patterned with golden flowers, carefully stamped. The title is woven among them, as though each letter were a leaf or petal. *The Violet Woods.*

It's close enough to my name that it feels even more transient and magical. As though some strange alchemy took a part of me and transmuted it here. I am a girl. I am ink and paper.

I run my hands over the pages. There are pictures, too, each protected behind a transparent leaf. A princess, sleeping in a tower surrounded by blackberry thorns. A servant girl, wearing a magical dress of moonlight. A faerie queen with wings like mist, floating across a starry sky.

Inside the cover is a small square of card. Two lines, inscribed in neat ink.

You should be out by the orchard,
where violets secretly darken the earth.

The words—*violet, orchard, earth*—I like how they sound, all strung together. Some leaf-hued, secret place. Only flowers and sunlight. I hold the book close against my chest. My price, for a secret kept.

Now that it's day, I'm able to see the parlor more clearly. The wallpaper is patterned with curved vines. The sofa is embroidered with roses and bellflowers. And against the opposite wall, still half-hidden in shadows, is an altar.

I step across the room to look at it more closely. The altar is old, much older than the altar in Greymere. Framed in wood, with carved edges that have been weathered smooth. A bank of candles lines the shelf. They've been recently burned and are surrounded by rivulets of wax. And the icon itself . . . I've never seen anything like it.

There are *two* figures.

There's the Lady with her face upturned. Eyes closed, her hair encircled with rays of sunlight. Her gold-tipped fingers in the earth. And beneath her, painted in reverse . . .

The Lord Under.

He's little more than a silhouette. A featureless face, head crowned by a wreath of branches. His hands are raised, and his shadowed arms reach upward. His claw-sharp fingers join the Lady's hands at the center of the icon. And there are shadows—*shadows*—threaded around his palms.

Everything I've tried so hard to forget comes back, sweeping over me in a sudden, hideous rush. The Vair Woods. The frost on the ground and the ice in the air. The shadows that stretched toward me.

The voice.

The voice that spoke to me in the midwinter forest.

The voice that whispered through the walls in my room, that asked my name, that told me to follow and led me toward the truth.

It was him.

I stumble back from the altar, tripping over my own feet as I rush from the room. The kitchen is dim, stovelight and kettle steam and the sweet smell of almas cake in the oven. My chest feels tight, my throat closed up, my lungs full of a trapped, tangled scream. I can still see the shape of the Lord Under from the icon, see the shape of him as he appeared before me in the Vair Woods. The air is full of whispers and the too-loud echo of my heartbeat.

Violeta, Violeta, Violeta . . .

He came to me then, and he's come to me now.

This is impossible. He's the lord of the dead, and only those near to death can see him. When I met him on that long-ago night, death was close, circling me with want and hunger. But now . . .

What does he want from me this time?

The walls of the house seem to move closer and closer toward me. I cross the kitchen, throw open the back door, and rush into the garden.

I blink and blink, washed by sunlight, and draw in a deep, greedy breath. The air smells of pollen from the jacaranda tree. The altar beneath—where we will go, tonight, for midsummer observance—is dusted with lilac petals and fallen leaves. This icon is singular. Just the Lady, wreathed in flowers. But then the wind changes and a dark splotch of leaf shadow covers the bottom of the painting, a reminder of what I saw inside.

The Lord Under. I met him in the darkness. I sought him out. I spoke to him.

As my eyes adjust, I realize I'm not alone. Arien is on the lawn beside the tree. He's carved a sigil into the ground—a dark, muddy track that cuts between purple blossoms and dandelion leaves. At the center of the circle is a line of jars, each full of ink-dark water.

I draw up, startled by the sight of him. He's on his knees, hands grasped tight around the centermost jar. Shadows spill through his hands. From inside the glass, the water starts to churn. I hear the *splash splash splash* of it against the jar. It sounds like the water that dripped over my bedroom walls.

The Lord Under came to me. He called to me.

I watch as Arien tries desperately to wrestle control of his magic. His cheeks are reddened, his skin damp with sweat. Piece by piece, the mass of shadows begins to shift and change. It becomes smoother. No longer a cloud of dark, but neat strands of shadows. But then it all unfurls. The shadows dissipate into a cloud of opaque charcoal that wisps the air.

He slumps back and hits the ground hard, with a cry. "Damn it!"

Then he looks up and sees me. His teeth bite into his lip. I walk carefully around the sigil and sit down beside him. He rubs his wrist roughly across his face, leaves a streak of mud. He looks worn down, like a candle left alight too long, about to become nothing but a smear of smoke.

"Arien, my love. You don't have to do this."

"I *do.*"

"If you're not ready . . ." I trail off, looking down at the grass, the sigil, the Corruption-filled jars. The ritual is only two weeks away. The ground is poisoned, and the poison wants to devour Rowan piece by piece.

Rowan, who dreams of his dead brother. Rowan, who slept beside me in the parlor. Rowan, who gave me a trunk full of dresses and a faerie book. Who looked at me with such tender fear when he told me he is slowly losing himself to that hungry darkness.

I don't want Rowan to carve himself apart, to be devoured slowly. But Arien is his only hope of mending the Corruption. And he's going to push himself to the point of breaking.

Arien huffs out a despairing sigh. "Clover and Rowan went to the village. The tithe goods have come from Greymere. And I thought, while they were gone, I'd practice. I thought I could get it right—that I could surprise them—and—" He wrenches angrily at his sleeve. "If you're not going to *help* me, Leta, then just go away."

"Let me help you, then."

Arien stares at me, surprised. "You're not going to argue more?"

"Oh, I want to argue plenty. I'm saving it up for later."

"Can you just sit next to me?" He reaches out to adjust one of the jars. "I'm used to casting the spell with Clover. So it might help if you're there."

I step carefully over the edge of the sigil and kneel on the ground. Arien settles beside me. He takes a breath. Closes his eyes. Shadows fill the air, cold and smooth and slithery. I shift closer, so that we're pressed together, side by side.

For the barest moment, he controls the magic. The strands of darkness move, stitch by stitch, into a mesh-fine web wrapped around the jar. Arien's shoulders tense. His eyes scrunch closed. A vein throbs in his temple. His breath catches.

Then the shadows slip loose and cascade out into a thick, dark cloud. It unfurls around us in a rush. The cold is instant, chilling my skin. My lungs burn, and my mouth tastes of ash. The light blots out.

Arien sighs, dejected. "It's no good. I just can't do it."

I put my hand against the ground, remembering last night, how the heat sparked in me and made the ground change. The earth beneath my palm is quiet. There's no song or warmth under my skin. But doubt prickles me. When I held Rowan and tried to pull him back from the Corruption, something happened.

Slowly, I pick up the jar. "Arien, try the spell again."

Our hands, together, wrap around the glass. The shadows gather. I think of the cottage, our room at night, the village on tithe day. All the times I've tried—and failed—to keep him safe. How I've felt since we came here, so frustrated and powerless.

I reach desperately for whatever I felt in the darkness beside the lake. There's nothing and nothing, but then—a flicker of heat. It's small and swift and I can hardly see it, hardly understand. Then the light or power or *whatever this is* washes through me—from me—into Arien.

The shadows knit together. The strands wrap around the jars; neat, fine, controlled. The afternoon sunlight streams back in, the sudden brightness overwhelming. Arien looks at me, wide eyed with shock.

"It worked." He touches a shaking hand to the jar, now filled with clear water. He laughs. "I did it, I did it!"

The water is not just clear in the jar he held, but in all of them. And the sigil he carved is charred, as if something burned the ground. Arien stares down at it incredulously.

I get to my feet and start to back away, scattering gravel as I stumble toward the house. Arien calls after me, confused. "Leta, what's the matter?"

He doesn't realize. He doesn't know that I helped him, that it was because of me the spell worked and the Corruption mended.

"I'm sorry, I have to go." My mouth still tastes of ash. I can still *feel* it, that sudden heat that tore through me. I look down at the jars of now-cleared water and flex my hands as sparks of power burn under my skin.

I think of my desperate whisper into the shadows when Arien and I were lost in the Vair Woods. *Please help us.* And how the Lord Under replied from the darkness: *What will you give me, if I do?*

I have no magic. It can't be possible. *It can't.*

In the kitchen, Florence is at the table, dusted with flour as she kneads fresh bread dough. She looks at me and smiles, but I rush past and go down the hallway into the cool, dim dark, past the parlor and toward the stairs.

My room is full of afternoon sunlight. I turn a restless circle and scrunch my fingers into the folds of the cloak. The glass vials of sedatives are still on my quilt, scattered across the fabric like a handful of gemstones. I go from the window, to the corner, to the wall. Shakily, I rest my hand flat against the flower-patterned paper and take a deep breath.

"Why have you come back?"

At first there's only silence. Then a whisper echoes through the wall.

Not a voice. Just a hush, a hiss. A chill skitters across my back, like a finger scraped down my spine.

I follow the sound out of my room until I reach the end of the hall. Closed doors and locked doors and nowhere else to go.

From the corner of my vision, darkness rises. Water spreads slowly across the floor, a blackened pool under my feet. I wrap Rowan's cloak tighter around myself, but the cold goes right through it, through my nightdress and my underthings until it's right against my bare skin. The light turns darker. The whisper becomes louder, taking shape now, until it's a voice.

The Lord Under's voice.

The Violet Woods. Violet in the woods. Violeta in the Vair Woods.

"We made our bargain." I breathe out the word as a shiver, remembering the winter night, when I whispered a plea into the silent forest. "What do you want from me?"

What was it that you said to me? The air changes. A

sound—my voice—echoes through the shadows. *"Please, I'm not afraid, show me, tell me."*

Are you afraid now, Violeta?

Rowan had asked me the same question as we sat in the dark. *Are you afraid of me?* I answered truthfully when I said I wasn't.

But there's more than one kind of monster in the world. There's the Monster of Lakesedge. A boy with poison in his veins, leashed to the ruined magic in the ground. There's the Lord Under. Lord of the dead, of shadows and darkness. He's here. He's right behind me. He knows my name.

"I'm not afraid." The lie tastes as bitter as the stolen sedatives. "I'm not afraid of you."

I turn and I face him.

He is there. Shadows and shadows and dark. But I can't *see* him. I can make out his individual features. Sharp eyes, sharp teeth, sharp claws. I can see the shape of him—the same tall, jagged-edged creature who appeared in the Vair Woods. But though I look and look, I can't turn the pieces of him into a single *whole*. It's as if my eyes won't allow me to comprehend what he is.

Liar. He makes a harsh, hollow sound that might almost be a laugh. *You wear it well, the fear. But I won't hurt you.*

I press back against the wall. He moves forward. A shift and flicker, a *shape* that won't become quite real. Shadows wreathe me, and the air is cold cold cold. I think of the lake. The blackened water. The poisoned shore. How the wound

146

tore in the ground when the ritual failed. How the earth rose up and snared Rowan when he put his cut wrist to the mud.

I can't breathe.

You asked for my help. Did you find what you wanted? His voice is a kiss in the shell of my ear. *The boy, the monster, the truth.*

"I don't know." I don't know anything anymore. Only the bitten-down taste of my fear.

I think you do, Violet in the woods.

I hold out my hands. Upturned and empty. My skin is cold, but I can still feel the bloom of heat that gathered in my palms when Arien cast the spell. "My magic was gone. It's supposed to be gone."

But it isn't.

"Last night, when I touched the Corruption . . . it changed. Why is this happening?"

Let me show you.

The vision clouds over me, sudden and swift. I see the lake, black and endless. Twin moons, both full. One above in the night sky, one below, reflected on the water. There's a sigil carved into the ground. It's just like at the ritual, except I'm alone on the shore.

A rush of power sparks beneath my skin like a scatter of embers. Warm and bright and *mine*.

Magic trails through my fingers, but it's different from the magic I've seen Arien or Clover cast. It's dark; it's light. Shadowed and golden, it covers my skin with a mixture of intense

147

heat and painful cold. The same as the icon in the parlor, where the Lady and the Lord Under have their fingers entwined, light and dark, dark and light.

The rush of power floods through me until I'm sure my heart will stop. I'm in the lake, half beneath the surface. And the water is clear. The shore is smooth.

The vision ends. I am back in the hall.

"I have the power to mend it on my own?"

Not yet. But I could give it to you. You've accepted my help before, Violeta. Don't you want to be able to keep everyone safe?

I do. I do. I want this magic. I want the terrible, wonderful *force* of this power that would make it all stop. "But I don't understand. You made the Corruption, why can't you mend it?"

I can't. Not alone. It's grown beyond me now.

"If—If I agreed to this, what will happen?"

Why don't I show you what would happen if you don't?

The floor softens, turning to mud. My feet start to sink. Black water pours down, turning my whole body to ice. I'm pressed right against the door, carved wood and a cold handle behind me. The Lord Under moves closer.

What happens when Rowan Sylvanan can no longer pay his tithe?

"He will die." It's the first time I've said it aloud, and it hurts more than I thought it would to speak this truth. "He will die, and the Corruption will be gone."

Is that what you want?

He bends until his face is right beside mine. His impossible features shift and shiver as the light cuts through him. He's there and not there, real and not real. I tip my chin upward. I keep my eyes open, and I meet his darkness.

Do you want to watch it claim him? Take him apart, piece by piece, until there is nothing left? That's what will happen.

Will you let me help you?

A desperate *yes* clings to my tongue. But the Lord Under's help always comes at a cost; I know that all too well. I've bargained with him once and paid the price. I can't do it again.

"No. I don't want your help." I flex my hands open and closed. My fingers are wet and numb, but beneath the chill I can feel the faint warmth of power. "I can do this without you."

Do you think those scraps you have now will be enough? You know, Violeta, by rights that power belongs to me.

"You can't unmake our bargain." I tighten my grasp against the door. "You promised—"

He laughs, a sigh and a rush of waves all caught together. The water rises around me, until it's at my waist, then my throat, then pouring into my mouth. The world becomes darkness, and I'm lost at the bottom of the lake.

I'm lost, I'm lost . . . But then a sound cuts through the vision. A staccato *tap tap tap*, like the branches of the apple tree as they hit the glass of the kitchen window back at the cottage. I'm still holding the door handle. I tighten my grasp and let the hard edges bite into my palm. I hear the strange new sound. I tear myself loose from the dark.

The shadows are gone. The water is gone. The Lord Under is gone.

I spin around and press myself against the door with my cheek flat to the wood. My breath steams hot against the carved panels. The handle won't turn. I wrench it, hard, and it twists with a rusty scrape. I put my shoulder against the paneled wood and shove.

The door comes unstuck, falling open with a breathy whoosh.

I stumble inside, and I slam the door closed.

Chapter Twelve

The Lord Under has released me, but each word, each syllable, of what he said is lodged inside my chest. *I can help you.*

I wrap my arms around myself, shivering, and look around the room. It's as bare as a cell. Nothing but an unlit fire and a carved, upholstered sofa pushed up against the wall, flanked by two enormous windows. The vague shapes of furniture in the corners: a dresser, a desk, a chest of drawers. The only light is the outline of late afternoon sun around the heavy curtains.

From behind those curtains, the sound comes again. The frantic *tap tap tap* that pulled me free of the mud and the water and the dark. I draw in a breath. The room is dim, but these shadows are just shadows. There are no whispers, no presence at the corner of my vision. Slowly, I peel myself away from the door and move toward the window. My heart beats loud, in time with the sound. *Tap tap tap.*

My hand shakes as I reach for the curtain and draw it back. The room floods with sudden brightness. A glittering cloud of motes fills the air.

A bird.

There's a bird, trapped inside the room. It's small and delicate; frightened. The sound I heard was its wings against the glass. Smears of black stain its pale feathers. Maybe it flew down the chimney.

I reach past it to open the window, and the bird is so afraid it doesn't even move away. The more I watch it flutter, the calmer I feel. I was so helpless before, pressed back against the door as the black water rose around me. But here, I'm not.

I take hold of the window latch. It's stuck fast. I grit my teeth and lean in hard with my shoulder to the glass.

"You're safe, you're safe." I struggle against the window, the bird's soot-streaked wings brushing over my cheeks in a blur. "Let me get this open—then you'll be back outside."

Finally, the sash cord gives a high-pitched screech, and the window comes open in a rush. The bird flutters past me with a little chirp. I watch it disappear into the clear, hot sky. I'm breathless from the effort, and I lean out into the windswept sunlight, taking grateful gasps of the warm air.

I see something stuck in the gap between window and sill. I slide my fingers down and work it loose. It's a heavy key, as large as my hand, engraved with a pattern of twined leaves that reminds me of the carvings on the front door of the house.

I curl my fingers around it. I don't know what this key might open, there are so many locked doors here. A long length of ribbon is threaded through the key bow. I knot it at one end to make a loop, then slip it over my head.

The door creaks open. I hurriedly tuck the key down beneath my nightdress so it's hidden. Footsteps come heavily across the floor. A hand reaches through the tangled curtains and grabs my shoulder. "What are you doing?"

I jolt upward. Hit my head—hard—against the edge of the open window. "Ouch! Ash *damn* it!"

I guiltily whisk the curtains closed over the opened window and turn to face Rowan Sylvanan, his brows knotted into a scowl, his gloves gone, and his shirt half unfastened.

My eyes drift, unbidden, toward his bared skin. The scars around his throat go farther down than I thought, crossing over his collarbones and onto his chest. Blood rushes into my cheeks. I look quickly away.

"Violeta." His scowl deepens, and he pulls awkwardly at his shirt, quickly tightening the laces. "Why are you in my bedroom?"

"Your bedroom?" I look around. The bare walls. The scant furniture. The sofa beneath the window. Now I realize there's a quilt spread neatly across it, a pillow at one end. "But it's so empty."

"I prefer it this way."

"You're the lord of an estate. Why do you sleep on a sofa?"

Rowan makes a sound halfway between a sigh and an incredulous cough. "It's a *chaise*." His eyes narrow as they trail over me. "Are you wearing my cloak?"

"I'm borrowing your cloak. You left it with me." I take it off quickly and hold it out. "You can have it back now."

He doesn't move. The bundled weight of his cloak slips from my hand to the floor. He watches it fall with his arms folded. "What, exactly, are you doing in here?"

"There was a bird."

"A what?"

"It was trapped in here. I had to open your window to let it free."

A sudden gust of wind whips through the room. The curtains snap back and forth with a cascade of dust. We both sneeze.

"*A bird?* That's why you came sneaking around?"

Rowan sneezes again, and I start to laugh at him when he scrunches up his face against the dust. He shoves his way through the curtains and pushes at the window, but it's just as stubborn to close as it was to open.

"It's stuck. Here, let me help." I take hold of the frame. My shoulder brushes against his, and our hands are so close together they almost touch. "And I wasn't sneaking. I have better things to do than poke around your bedroom."

"I've had a long enough day without your particular foolishness, Violeta."

He gives the sash another shove, and the window slams

shut, the impact rattling through the glass. We both jump. The curtains, stilled, flutter down and make a soft wall between us and the rest of the room. Unfiltered sunlight streams over us. I look at him, and I want to touch the scars that cross the side of his jaw, his mouth. I keep my hands at my sides to stop myself from reaching.

"Was it very awful in the village?"

"What do you think?" He sighs. "The latest rumor is that Clover and I are trying to perform some kind of blood sacrifice."

I glance toward his bandaged arm. "I mean, they're not *entirely* wrong."

He lets out a tired laugh, then starts to unfold his sleeves and smooth them back down. "I'm sure it delights you to know everyone shares your opinion that I'm a monster."

I pretend to study him. "You're not even a very good monster. Really, you need fangs."

"Fangs?"

"Or perhaps a tail. You could twitch it when you were angry."

"If I *did* have a tail, it would be twitching now."

I can't help but smile. He's a monster. He's a boy. Sad and cross. He parts the curtains and holds them open for me. I slip through the narrow space, and he steps out of my way, looking at my nightdress with a grimace.

"You're still covered in dirt from last night." He walks out after me. The room dims as the curtains fall shut behind him.

I look down at myself. My nightdress is filthy, and my hair

is tangled, with mud clotted at the ends of my curls. I start to laugh. "Have I infringed on your standards of cleanliness? I've not had time to change since we went to the lake."

"You might want a bath before dinner."

Unlike me, Rowan is neatly dressed. The bandage on his wrist is the only hint of disarray from last night. An irascible urge comes over me to loosen him. Make him untidy. To step dusty footprints onto his boots or untuck his shirt. Crumple him.

"What's the matter? Are you worried I'll ruin your nice clean shirt?"

I grab his sleeve and crush the fabric inside my fist. He catches my hand, horrified. "There's still blood under your fingernails!"

"It's your blood!" I fall against his chest, still laughing, warmed by the utter delight of teasing him.

He glares down at me. "You are a complete menace."

He's still holding my hand, and I lace my fingers through his. A spark flares through my whole body: chest to ribs to fingertips. Heat stirs beneath my skin, like there's a garden of bright flowers blossoming in my veins.

Light flickers between our joined hands.

Rowan flinches back, shocked. "You have magic." He's guarded, but there's a surety in his words. "That's what you did last night. You used your magic against the Corruption."

By rights that power belongs to me. I shiver, remembering the Lord Under's words. "I don't—"

Rowan lifts my hand and turns it palm up, then drags his

fingers roughly across my heartline. We both take a breath, and I watch as the darkness uncurls at his throat, along the scars. As the threads of poison lace over him, I feel an echoing pull far down within me.

And the power, the magic, my magic, sparks and burns and *burns*. Brightness fills the room like a scatter of coals fallen loose inside a stove. For a brief, brilliant moment before the power fades, my hands, my palms, my fingers . . . they glow.

Rowan clenches his teeth as the darkness spreads across his neck and over his jaw. He closes his eyes, and slowly the lines start to fade.

"Why didn't you tell Clover you had magic, when she asked you?" He stares down at my hands. "That day in your cottage, if I'd known about this, I would have—"

"You'd have known I was useful to you, just like Arien?"

"That isn't true. I don't want to *use* you, Violeta. I—" He lifts his hand, but I step back.

"Can we please just forget this?"

"I can understand you not confiding in me. But what about Arien? Why have you kept this from him?"

Because it never happened until now. My magic is a distant throb at the palms of my hands, but I can still feel the way it unspooled when Rowan touched me. The sparks that bloomed from my fingers. When I think of it, I want to shove him away—I want to pull him closer. Why has being at Lakesedge—being with him—made this strange, lost power stir within me?

"You can't tell anyone about my magic. Not Arien, not Clover. I don't want anyone to know."

"Why are you hiding this? It could help. *You* could help."

His words are an echo of what the Lord Under told me. I shake my head quickly as cold prickles over my skin. "No. You don't want my help."

"Violeta . . ." He bends down, until his face is even with mine. He reaches for me, eyes full of concern. This time I let him touch me.

His fingers gently trace my cheek, and for just a breath everything between us feels softer. I realize that Rowan may be the only other person who has seen what I've seen. The voice, the shadows, the darkness. The confession is an ache lodged in my chest, sharp against my ribs. I cast around, searching for how to tell him the truth. That the Lord Under offered me power. That I made a bargain with him on a moonlit night in the Vair Woods.

That I might still be in his debt.

"Rowan, what happened when the Lord Under saved you?"

"I told you already. I drowned. I came back. Everything was poisoned."

"But what did he ask from you in return for his help?"

There's a flash in his eyes that I can't read. A mask slip, there and gone. Then the earlier softness evaporates, and he gives me a hard, cold look. "That, Violeta Graceling, is none of your concern."

But my mind has started to turn, setting together the pieces of everything I've seen, and heard, and know. "You told me the

Corruption started because of a mistake. It was your family, wasn't it?"

"No. I am not talking about this—especially not with you."

"You gave them up in exchange for your life."

He pushes past me and flings open the door. "I think you should leave."

The horror of it sinks in. Everyone said that he killed his family, but the truth is far worse. Rowan cheated death, just like I did.

Rowan gave his family to the Lord Under, in exchange for his life.

"I don't understand. Florence told me your father died after your thirteenth birthday. But if you gave them up when you were a child, then why—?"

His expression darkens, raw and furious. "*Enough.* I'll not discuss this."

Desperation burns hot at the center of my chest. "Did the Lord Under come back to you?"

"He's the lord of the dead. Only the dead can see him." He glares at me, then tips his chin to the hallway. "Get out of my room, Violeta."

When I don't move, he comes toward me swiftly and grabs my wrist. Magic sparks from my hand as I twist against him.

As he looms over me, his bared teeth look sharp. "I told you to go."

I try to pull away. His fingers tighten around my arm. We're so close that when he exhales, I feel his breath, hot, on my skin. I taste ash and salt and blood, as though the poison inside him has spilled loose into the air. I'm not sure if it's a trick of the light, but the scars at his throat seem to blacken. They look wet, like he's been cut, like he's bleeding.

Last night I said I wasn't afraid of him, but right now I am. All I want to do is run. But instead, I stop struggling and put my hand over his.

"Rowan." I say his name, say it over and over until it sounds like a litany. "Rowan. *Rowan.*"

He growls, then shoves me roughly away. I stumble out of the room, turning back to catch a last glimpse of him—poisoned and shadowed and wrong—as he slams the door closed.

I scour myself in a hot bath until all the mud is gone from my skin. I put on another of the new dresses, this one rose-petal pink with leaves embroidered at the hem, then find a pair of ribboned socks to wear with my now-clean boots. I tuck the key, on its long ribbon, down inside my dress.

The house is quiet as the day stretches toward an indolent summer evening. There are no whispers or shifting shadows. I hold the little icon between my hands and feel the fit of it in my palm as I stare at the walls and floor and hope they won't change. They don't. But when I walk past the parlor on my way down to dinner, I pause by the closed door.

I can still feel the power that the Lord Under showed me. The way I was strong and sure, and how I kept everyone safe. A small, reckless part of me wonders what would happen if

I went inside the room right now. If I lit a candle and knelt down before that strange, sinister altar.

I go quickly toward the kitchen, trying to push away the *want* that sings in my fingertips. When I enter the room, Florence greets me with a stack of enamelware plates in her hands. She passes them to me, then balances a pile of folded linen napkins on the top.

"Here. You can set the table." As I lay out the plates, she looks expectantly into the empty hallway. "Where's Rowan, anyway? It's his turn for chores tonight."

I put down the last plate with a clatter. "I think he's staying upstairs."

I circle my hand around my wrist, feeling the place where Rowan's fingers dug in. He's losing himself to the Corruption. If the next ritual fails, it might just claim him entirely.

Florence frowns, concerned, but then she's distracted by Arien and Clover coming inside from the garden. They're both quiet, with worry lined deep around their eyes.

"I couldn't do it, Leta." Arien looks from me to the open doorway, where the sigil is still carved out on the lawn, the center lined with jars. "It worked, before, when you were there. But after you left, when I tried again, I couldn't—"

He goes to the washstand and scrubs and scrubs at his hands. He wipes them against a cloth, then comes to sit at the table opposite me.

"You still have time," I tell him.

He sighs crossly. "I don't."

"You do." Clover's smile doesn't quite reach her tired eyes.

"It's only just past the dark moon. We have time until the next full moon, the next ritual. From tomorrow, we'll practice harder."

Florence puts her hand on Arien's back. "I'm sure you can do this."

She sets a platter onto the table and begins to slice a loaf of sourdough bread. The food here is similar to our meals in the cottage. Wilted greens, nettle salad, sugar peas, and summer squash. There's a clay bowl on the table filled with pink salt, a tin pitcher beside it full of mint tea.

Usually, the evenings together in the kitchen feel like a golden pause. A place where we can sit and talk and forget about the lake. Forget to watch the moon as it moves from dark to half to full in the summer night sky. But tonight feels grim and tense, and we all eat in silence.

Rowan comes into the kitchen just as Florence has started to clear the table. I quickly turn to him, my whole body wound tight with apprehension. But there's no sign of how he looked before when he was changed.

"There you are," Florence says. "It's your turn to wash the dishes tonight. Don't forget." She goes over to the shelves to collect cutlery and another plate, which she fills from the covered dishes set aside by the stove.

Clover pours out more of the mint tea and passes it to him. "I was going to steal your share of dessert."

She gives his arm a playful shove, but he only glares at her. Sighing, she goes back to her chair as Rowan sits down beside me. Our knees touch beneath the table, and he moves quickly away. We're no closer together now than when we stood by the window earlier, but somehow, he *feels* closer.

I lower my voice, aware that everyone else can hear me. "Are you feeling better?"

"I'm fine." He puts something down on the table. A book. My book. *The Violet Woods.* "You left this in the pocket of my cloak."

Clover stares at the two of us curiously. "You *wore* his cloak?" she asks in a barely concealed whisper. She tries, and fails, to hide her smile.

Rowan ignores her and eats silently, his eyes fixed on his plate. When he's finished, Florence brings out dessert: sour cherry cake, the top dusted with sugar.

"Is that from the tithe?" I ask Clover.

"Yes." She makes a face. "I never want to lift another basket again. I love sour cherries, but I'm not sure it's worth a whole day in the village being bossed around by Keeper Harkness and his annoying daughter."

Florence starts to cut the cake into squares. "I thought you liked Thea?"

Clover tugs at the end of her braid, and doesn't answer. Now it's my turn to hide my smile.

"I think I made those cherries." I laugh softly as I reach over and pick up a square of cake, feeling bittersweet as I remember all the time I spent in the orchard picking fruit, the days at the stove, and the endless stirring.

But my laughter dims as I recall the night in the kitchen when the air smelled like syrup, when I knelt with the shards of glass in my knees. Then, all I wanted was to keep Arien safe no matter how much it might have hurt me.

I can still feel the faint tug from the thread of magic that was tied between us when he cast the spell today. I look across the table at him. He's been quiet for most of the meal.

He picks at his dessert, scatters crumbs across the table. "What happens if I can't control my magic by the full moon? What happens if I can't help Clover cast the spell?"

"Then you'll wait," Florence says gently. "You'll try again on the next moon."

I look at Rowan. He frowns, avoiding my gaze. My book sits on the table between us, the price that I teasingly demanded from him for my secrecy about the tithes. Clover and Florence don't know about how much it will cost him to wait all that time longer.

"If we could wait, I know I could do it!" Arien chews at his lip. His face is all hope and nervousness. "It worked today. Leta, you saw me! I could—"

"Tell them." Rowan looks at my hands. He means that I should tell them about my magic. I shake my head no. *Tell them.*

I can't accept the Lord Under's offer. I can't tell the truth about my magic. I can't let Arien go unprepared to the ritual, but we don't have more time. And then there's Rowan . . . it will cost him to wait. It will cost him to fail. It will cost *everything* with his death.

I'm here, fighting like I have a choice. None of us have a choice.

I shake my head again and whisper, "I can't."

Rowan gets abruptly to his feet. His chair bumps against the table, making all the plates and cutlery and cups of tea rattle. Florence looks at him, startled. "What's wrong?"

"Nothing." He shoves his plate and spoon roughly into the dishpan. "We need more wood for the stove."

He grabs the lantern, snatches up the kindling basket and disappears out into the garden. Silence passes. After a while, the steady, rhythmic thud of the ax echoes back from the woodshed behind the house.

"What did he mean?" Arien asks, confused. "*Tell them? Tell us what?*"

I shake my head. "It doesn't matter. We argued earlier, that's all."

"You really need to stop picking fights with him."

Clover laughs. "No, don't. It's very entertaining to watch. You've really gotten him worked up. I thought he was finally going to stand up and confess how ardently he *admires* you." She waves a hand in protest when Florence gives her a stern look. "You should be pleased! By the time he's finished out there, we'll have enough kindling to last until Summersend, at least."

Chapter Thirteen

After dinner, we go out into the garden for observance. The beginnings of the long midsummer sunset have bled through the sky in streaks of crimson. We walk to the altar, careful to step around the sigil on the lawn, and kneel down on the flower-stippled grass. Clover reaches to the candles on the shelf beneath the icon. She touches her fingers to the wick of each one, and they flare alight with her magic. I fold my own hands closed.

Tell them.

I close my eyes and breathe in the scent of smoke and wax and honey. This is the first observance since we've come to Lakesedge. The last, we were in Greymere on tithe day, when everything changed. I press my shaking hands against my knees. The smoke, the candlelight, the altar . . . It's all so *familiar*. These are the candles that Mother lit to burn Arien's hands. This is the scent that drifted over me as I knelt on the shards of glass.

A sound escapes me, anxious, wordless. Clover gives me a concerned look.

"I—It's just—" I blink hard. "I just—"

Arien stares at the candles fixedly, twisting his hands in the ends of his sleeves. Since we came here, I've seen him light candles at the kitchen altar and dip his fingers into the dish of salt, just like we did back in the cottage. But now, as we kneel in the candlelight, his face is set into a hard, determined expression. He reaches out and runs his blackened fingers through the bank of flames in a swift, abrupt motion.

"She wanted to raze me, like I was the blighted field." He bites his lip. "Like I was ruined. Like I needed to be mended."

I take his hand. His skin is still hot from the flames. "Well, you're not. And you don't."

"I know." He looks at the candles. "It's not the same, Leta. *It's not.*"

Florence comes across the lawn. She kneels down and puts her arm around Arien. "No one will hurt you here. Either of you."

I put my forehead against Arien's shoulder and take a slow breath. "I know it's not the same."

I can hear the rustle of leaves in the jacaranda tree. The far-off sound of Rowan in the woodshed, the steady rhythm of his ax biting into kindling wood. This isn't the Greymere altar, with Arien trying to hide his uncontrolled magic. This isn't the kitchen at our cottage, with Mother afraid and Arien hurt.

I place my hands against the ground, then work my fingers through the grass until I feel the sun-warmed earth below. Leaves and petals and dirt. We all begin to chant the summer litany. Our voices weave together like the strands of shadows that Arien has spent the past weeks trying so desperately to control.

As I fall into the rhythm of the song, I close my eyes and surrender to this moment of sound and voice and light. Even after everything—the cottage, Mother, the endless nights of fear and shadows and *only dreams*—this moment, this observance, is still so beautiful to me.

I can feel the hum and glow of the Lady's light woven through the world, woven through me.

I feel her magic.

I feel *my* magic.

Faint and small and so long buried. But *there*.

I think longingly of the Lord Under's offer. If I let him, he would help me. I could mend the Corruption all on my own. I could keep everyone safe. I could make sure that no one I love would ever be hurt again.

But what would it cost? Rowan had to give up his entire family. I can't begin to imagine what the Lord Under would demand from me in exchange for the terrible, wonderful power he offered me.

Bargaining with him isn't my only choice. I still have the magic that has inexplicably slept inside me all this time. It isn't enough to use alone. But I helped Rowan when he paid the tithe. I helped Arien control his magic when he cast the spell. I still did *something*.

I take a breath. The air is full of song. The earth is full of light. I feel the heat in my hands and let it unspool. The Lord Under has a claim on this power. What will he do to me, to Arien, if I refuse his help and use these bare traces of magic instead?

At the altar, the bank of candles glows. In the ground, a second light reflects. Gold and warm and *mine*. I let the magic come from my hands. I let it gleam through the earth.

Everyone's voices fall to silence. Arien stares at me wordlessly as Clover takes my hand and holds it gently between her own. Tears prickle at the corners of my eyes. The candles at the altar shift and blur.

"I can help you," I tell them. "I can help with the ritual."

Silence stretches as I search for how to explain what I've done. There's so much I've kept hidden that I can only think to go back to the very start of it. Before the dark water in my room, before the voice that asked my name.

"When our parents died of winter fever, the lord burned our house. He meant to burn everything the sickness had touched. I thought he would burn me, because I'd been in the house with the fever." I look at Arien. "I thought he would burn *you*."

Arien doesn't remember, I know. He was too small. But when I close my eyes, I'm back there again. Arien and me, lost in the mess and chaos of the epidemic that swept through our village. The lord with a cloth tied across his mouth and a torch in his hand.

Clover touches her fingers against my shoulder. "What did you do?"

"I took Arien and I ran away. We followed the road out of the village. We'd never been so far from home before. The farthest I'd walked was from our cottage to the village altar. When I turned back and looked behind us, I could see the light from the fires. I could smell the smoke."

It returns to me now. The ash in the air, how the flames painted the night sky in a wash of sickly orange. The weight of Arien in my arms—I'd had to carry him because he was too small to walk. I tried to put him on my back, tied up in my shawl, the way our mother had done.

"You must have been in Farrowfell," Florence says solemnly. "I remember hearing about that, how everyone died and they burned the village. You went into the woods, didn't you?"

I nod. Summer heat fills the twilight air, but I shiver, chilled by memories of an endless road beneath the winter moonlight. Of nowhere to go but deeper into the trees.

"It was so cold." I glance toward Arien. "And you were so heavy. I walked and walked, and the woods went on, and we were lost."

His expression darkens. "Then what happened?"

"The Lord Under." I look down at my hands. "He came for me."

Florence touches her fingertips to her heart and draws

170

them slowly across her chest. She shakes her head. Her eyes are fixed on the altar.

"I didn't know the name for him then. He was just a figure who appeared through the mist. All I wanted was for Arien and me to be back in our cottage, by the fireplace. I wanted my mother's honey tea. I wanted my patchwork quilt. I wanted to be home again. But our cottage was gone. Our family was gone." I take a breath and rub my hand across my face. "And so, I asked him to spare me. I asked him to show us the way out of the woods. He was silent for a long time. Then he asked, 'What would you give, to make it so?'"

Clover's eyes, behind her glasses, are bright. She looks at me with a shocked, protective fury. "What did you give to him?"

I hold out my shaking, earth-gritted hands to show them my upturned palms. "I gave him my magic."

Arien sucks in a breath. "But you don't—You said you didn't—"

"I didn't even *know* that I was an alchemist. I thought I had nothing." I had my cloak, and my shawl, and my boots. The meager sum of my small, untidy life. "But then the Lord Under told me to hold out my hands. When I did, he touched me, and the magic woke up."

At the memory, heat pools in my palms. I can feel how it once was, rather than the remnants I now have. When the Lord Under stroked my hands, the magic was sunlight under my skin.

"He took my hand, and together we walked through the

forest. After a long time we came out onto a road. The Lord Under laid Arien down at the edge of the trees. And then—"

"You were alive," Arien says. "And your magic was gone. Except—it's not."

"It was gone. I don't understand how, or why, it's still here. My magic belongs to him. What if using it again means I'm still indebted?"

"Well." Florence looks at the altar thoughtfully, where the icon is illuminated by candlelight. She runs her fingers over her heart again. "Your bargain had clear terms. You didn't deceive him; you gave your magic. But that power comes from the Lady. It's woven through everything. Maybe it was so woven through you that he couldn't take it all."

"That makes sense," Clover says. "We're all made by the Lady, and her magic is part of us, even people without the ability to use that power for alchemy. The Lord Under had to leave these traces behind, because otherwise you wouldn't even be alive." She touches her fingertips to my palm. A lopsided smile crosses her face. "I want to see."

She strokes across my heartline, the same way that Rowan did, but no light sparks.

"I don't really know how to control it," I say.

"What did you do before?"

"It just happened with Arien when he was casting the spell." I fold my hand closed. "And Rowan, when he touched me."

Clover arches a brow. "Was that before or after you wore his clothes?"

"It was a *cloak*. I borrowed it." Heat creeps over my face. "It's not like I undressed him."

Clover hums, thoughtful, and looks behind us at the row of jars still on the lawn from when she and Arien practiced earlier. She gets up and walks over to the edge of the sigil.

"Come over here. You too, Arien." She beckons to us. "Show me what you did."

Arien and I kneel down in front of the line of jars. He looks at me, then takes hold of the jar as the shadows gather at his palms.

I put my hands over his, then close my eyes and think of how it felt, that last time. It's harder now that I'm trying to call on my magic with purpose. When the power finally rises through me, it's just a brief flash of warmth, like I've passed beneath a shaded tree to an open clearing, then gone back into the dark again.

Clover puts her hand on my arm. Her eyes shimmer as she sends magic over our twined fingers, adding her own power to the spell. Arien tenses. I can feel the poison inside the glass, inside the water. Feel how it could be mended. *Almost. Almost.* I take a deep breath and try to draw out my magic. Try not to think how easy this would all be if I had the power the Lord Under offered.

The strands of Arien's magic draw tight for a moment before he falters. I sit back with a frustrated hiss as the shadows dissolve. Clover picks up one of the jars and squints at it. The water isn't clear, but it *has* changed; it's no longer inky black, but the gray of softened charcoal.

"It's not the same as your magic," I ask her, "is it?"

"No. I don't know what it was like before, but now your power is like . . . a leftover." She makes an apologetic face, then scrunches up her nose as she thinks. "Wait. I have an idea."

She jumps to her feet and runs back into the house. Lamplight flashes in the window of her stillroom; then she comes back with her basket full of the notebooks and pens she and Arien use at their lessons.

Clover opens one of the books to a blank page, and quickly sketches a sigil onto the paper. It's not like any of the symbols I've seen Arien draw, or any of the marks on his arms. It's small and curved, like the petals of a half-closed flower.

"When you touched Arien, it was like you made his power more concentrated. This is a channeling spell. It will help you focus more." She blows on the ink, to make it dry, then passes me the pen. "Practice on the paper first."

I lean over and set the pen awkwardly against the paper. I've practiced my letters, and I can write my name, barely. The pen feels unfamiliar in my hand. The ink spills out, turning what should be a neat line into a dark smear.

"Can you?" I try to give the pen back to Clover, but she shakes her head.

"You'll need to draw it, otherwise the spell won't work."

"Start with the smallest symbol, at the center," Arien says encouragingly. "Then work your way outward."

I pick up the book and try again. The second sigil I draw is even worse, a blur of unsteady lines marred by blotches of ink. I sigh and grip my fingers tightly around the pen.

There's a rustle from the garden, and I look up to see Rowan standing at the far edge of the lawn. I can tell by his expression that he must have heard my confession.

He comes over and sits down beside me. "You're going to snap the pen if you keep clutching it like that." He reaches for my hand. "Hold it more gently. Like this."

I loosen my grip as he curls his fingers around mine. "Like this?"

"That's right."

He puts his arm around me. Together, we press the pen back against the paper. He guides my hand, and while my lines are still smeared and clumsy, it's much more careful than I could do alone. We fill the page with sigils, each one neater than the last. As he helps me, I start to learn the rhythm of the spell, the sharp angles of the innermost symbol, the curved arc of the outer lines.

Finally, I'm done, with my last effort almost passably neat.

"There." Rowan rests his chin against my shoulder. "You did it."

I lean against him for a moment. My eyes close as a peculiar feeling stirs in my chest. Then Clover snorts back a laugh, which she turns to a cough when Arien elbows her. I move away from Rowan quickly and busy myself in tidying the pile of notebooks.

"Anyway . . ." Rowan gestures to the pen and makes a sketching motion with his fingers. "I'm sure you can manage from here."

"If our inscription lessons in the Maylands had a teacher

like you, I'd have learned much faster," Clover says. Arien elbows her again. "What? I was just admiring his technique!"

"Excuse me." Rowan gets to his feet and walks past the altar into the darkness of the garden.

"Don't you want to watch Violeta cast her very first spell?" Clover calls after him. When he doesn't respond, she frowns at me in pretend seriousness. "Do you think he's worried it will be bad luck if he sees you before the ritual?"

"This isn't a handfasting."

"At least you've just practiced your inking, if you want to write him a proposal."

Arien rolls his eyes. "If you're both finished, maybe Leta can try drawing the spell on her skin?"

I pick up the book and stare hard at the page until the sigils are an indistinct blur. Then I push back my sleeve to bare my wrist. I draw the sigil, still feeling the ghost of Rowan's hand against my own.

When I'm finished, I look down at the new mark. Once I've done this, I can't go back. The sigil will be marked on me forever. If this works, then I'll have committed Arien—and myself—to facing the Corruption at the next ritual. But if I refuse to help and the ritual fails, then Rowan will pay. First with his blood, and then with his life.

There is no other choice.

Arien reaches for the jar, and we take hold of it together. "First, close your eyes. Then you just . . . listen." He glances shyly at Clover. "Is that right?"

She smiles and places her hands over mine. "Yes. That's perfect."

"It's always there for me," Arien goes on. "But you might need to reach further. Feel it inside your chest, then picture it at your hands, and on your skin, making the shape of the spell."

An ache fills me as he proudly explains how to call on the power. It's such a reversal of those nights in the cottage when he was so uncertain and afraid. He's had to hide it for so long, but this magic has always been part of him.

"Okay." I close my eyes. "Teach me how to cast the spell."

Chapter Fourteen

I sit alone by the altar after everyone goes back to the house. I blow out the candles and watch as wax pools around the soot-smeared wicks. Smoke covers the icon like a veil.

The spell to focus my power worked. When Arien and Clover cast the spell they're going to use to mend the Corruption, the sigil burned on my wrist and power unthreaded from me. Still faint, still weak, but it was enough. With my help, Arien kept hold of his magic. His shadows wove neatly around the glass as light spilled from Clover's hands, and the water turned clear.

Afterward, Clover gave me the pen to keep. It's in my pocket, and the small weight of it feels like another marker of how irrevocably everything has changed.

Rowan has stood far back in the garden, beneath an arbor

of white-flowered elder trees, watching our practice without comment. Now he comes over to sit down beside me at the altar. Gently, he reaches for my arm. "Can I see?"

I nod, and push back my sleeve to show him the spell inscribed on my wrist. "What do you think? Have I done well, or will I need another writing lesson?"

He frowns at my teasing. Then he tentatively touches the mark. A few tiny sparks of magic scatter into the air between us. He watches them fade. "You're far beyond anything I could teach you, Violeta."

"Oh, I don't know about that. You might give me some advice on how to split kindling. You missed observance while you were cutting all that firewood."

Scowling, he turns to the altar. He touches the earth for the barest moment before he sits back, rubbing the dirt from his hands.

I laugh. "You know, you're supposed to chant."

"I don't like to sing when people can hear me." He picks up some fallen petals from the ground and drops them beneath the icon. His eyes are distant. "Anyway, my observance is different."

An image flashes through my mind. The altar in the parlor. Rowan kneeling with his palms to the bare floor as the dual icon looms over him. "You really worship the Lord Under?"

He arches a brow. "That icon has *two* figures. All the noble houses have one similar. My father, and every lord before him, they've all worshipped there." He picks up another handful of flowers. "That altar, it's a reminder for me: I'm bound to this

179

land and all within it, their lives and their deaths. I'm still their lord, even if they all think I'm a monster."

I have a sudden, destructive urge to tell him what the Lord Under has offered me. Because Rowan and I have looked into the same shadowed dark and made the same desperate choices. But I can't. No matter what I did in my past, no one can know about this.

All I can say is, "I think I understand. I wish the others did, too. Everyone is so busy fearing you that they don't see it—how much you care for them."

Slowly, Rowan reaches toward me. His fingers are smeared with pollen from the flowers. I hold my breath as he traces the line of my throat, a dozen images flickering through my mind of what he might do next—of what I might *want* him to do.

But then he hooks his fingers beneath the ribbon around my neck. He draws out the key and curls his fingers over it. I try to move back, but he tightens his grip and the ribbon snags. Laughing, he gives it a little pull, tugging me forward. "I knew you'd taken this. Violeta, you're such a thief."

I reach to my neck, trying to unfasten the knot. "Do you want it back?"

"No." He pulls on the ribbon again, then the key slips from his hand and thumps against my chest. The scrolled iron is warm from being against my skin. I can feel the thrum of my pulse in my throat, in the place where he touched me.

Rowan gets to his feet. He looks toward the path that curves away from the house. "Come with me. I have something to show you."

180

I stand up unsteadily and take his offered hand. He leads me farther into the garden. We push through a bank of grass, the seed-filled ends almost as tall as my head. Everything is dried out by the midsummer sun and heated air. We follow the path for a long time, and then we reach the wall. The gate, covered in vines.

When I was here last, when I followed him through the dark, the garden was all silver and shadow. Now it's lit faintly by the twilight, the air faded and otherworldly, like an illustration from the book he gave me.

"Go ahead," Rowan says softly. "Open it."

I carefully move the vines away from the handle and slip the key into the lock. The gate swings open without a sound. Together, we step into the garden.

The orchard trees have spread from their ordered rows, and the flower beds are only tangles of dry grass. An endless bramble winds through it all, a sharp snarl of vine and thorn, leafless and bare.

But as I look around, a warmth hums under my skin. I can see how it all must have been once. This secret, locked-up place that's been kept asleep. Fruit and herbs and flowers. The air all sugar and pollen and the drone of bees.

It's beautiful.

Rowan stays behind me as I walk along the path where weeds push up between the gravel stones. Quiet stretches between us. The only sound is our footsteps.

At the center of the orchard I pause and rest my hand against the trunk of an apple tree. He puts his hand just above mine. His eyes are distant, fixed on the curve of the path as it disappears into the garden.

"Elan and I used to play in here all the time."

"Really?" I'm still not sure why he's brought me here. But of everything I expected, it wasn't this confession. *Elan.* The sound of his name seems to stay in the air, a note, resonant with memory. "What was he like?"

Rowan laughs. "A perfect terror. Any trouble you could imagine, he'd find it. He'd either convince me to join in, or blame me if we got caught." He points toward the branches, where the leaves are colored by the diffuse, lilac light. "He used to climb up there and throw apples at me."

"You probably deserved it," I tease, and his mouth curves into an almost smile. "So why did you lock it all up?"

"After he died, I—I didn't want to remember anymore. I closed up all the rooms in the house. I locked the garden. It was the worst, here. Because it was where he'd been the happiest."

"You wanted to forget him?"

"Yes." His eyes are dark and sad and far away. "I wanted to forget everything."

"I know so little of my own family. I can't imagine ever wanting to give up what I *do* remember. No matter how much it might hurt." But then I think of the story I just told to Clover and Arien. How much I've still kept to myself, pushed down and buried and left unsaid. Maybe I do understand—just a little—why Rowan has closed up so much of his house, his life, and himself. "And did you? Did you manage to forget?"

"No." He tips his head back and looks into the leaves above.

He sighs. "It hurts to remember; it hurts to forget. And now everything here is dead, anyway."

I look around the garden. We've come to the end of the path. The scattered gravel curls around a space of weeds that must have once been a lawn, bordered by more of the leafless brambles.

"No, it's not. You locked it up. You left it. But it isn't dead."

I go over and kneel down close to the tangled curl of vines. I take hold of the bramble, careful of the thorns, and scrape my nails over the stem. The topmost layer of the plant peels back to reveal pale green, hidden beneath.

Rowan comes to stand beside me. "What are you doing?"

"It's alive. See?"

He leans down to touch his fingers to the new, green place on the vine. "How did you know to do that?"

"My father showed me."

I see my father, in the garden behind our cottage. A clear space of earth. A handful of stems, cut from another plant. One by one he placed them into the ground. He cupped his hands around them. Light flickered between his palms as he cast his magic. When he moved back, the stem had leaves and tiny flowers. It was alive.

I take out the pen and shakily trace over the sigil on my wrist. I've seen Arien and Clover do the same, retrace the same spell over a spent mark to rework it. Beneath the outline, my skin feels hot, like I have a fever.

I reach out to the vine again. Close my eyes and think of

power. My power. It's so *small*. I can barely grasp it. It's like a tiny golden thread that slips through my fingers.

I wrap my hands tight around the bramble. Thorns pierce my skin, and I clench my teeth together against the hurt. I think of how it felt, before, with Clover and Arien, how our magic intertwined as we cast the spell. I think of how my power sparked up when Rowan touched the heartline of my palm.

And then the memory of my father in the garden comes back, so vivid that I can feel him here, right beside me. His hands over mine, his voice gentle as he shows me how to work the magic. I think of light and heat and sun and seeds. Of things that were not quite dead, now come alive. The sigil *burns*. I reach again for the thread. It's about to slip. But I grasp hold, and I don't let go.

I open my eyes and see what I've done. Most of the bramble is the same, leafless and dried. But between my cupped palms, there's a small cluster of purple-dark berries. A handful of green, heart-shaped leaves.

Rowan kneels down and touches the plant. He smiles at me. It's the first time I've seen him smile like this, so unguarded. His mouth is tilted, lopsided and boyish. His front teeth are charmingly crooked.

"You were right," he says, awed. "It isn't dead."

It's the first magic I've worked from my own hands, alone. I stare down at the berries, the leaves. I feel wrung out, like I've used up all my strength for this single piece of magic. Can I truly protect Arien in the ritual, can I truly help, when this is all the power I have? And what if continuing to use it puts me back in the Lord Under's debt?

It has to be enough. It has to be worth the risk. *It has to.*

"I don't know that I'll be invited to the Maylands to show off my skills anytime soon. But there you are." I want to laugh, but tears sting my eyes and ache in my chest.

I clutch the pen tight in my hands for a moment, then throw it down against the leaves. My fingers are smeared with blood from the thorns. I close my eyes. I won't cry over this.

"Violeta." Rowan touches the newly leafed bramble again. He picks up the pen and tries to place it back in my hands. When I don't move, he clumsily folds my fingers around it. "It's beautiful. Your magic . . . it's *beautiful.*"

"No. No, it's not. I shouldn't even——" All I can think of is that long-ago winter. Arien's heavy weight in my arms. How the wind changed inside the woods and the air turned crystalline with ice and frost.

And then it tumbles out. "There's more to it, to the story I told the others. When the Lord Under came to us, it was Arien that he wanted."

Rowan's expression darkens. "It was *his* life you gave your magic for?"

I nod. I've kept this terrible secret for so long. It's almost a relief to have it finally revealed like this. "We were lost. It was so cold, and he was so heavy. He cried and cried, and it was awful. Then he stopped crying, and that was worse. That was when the Lord Under came for him."

Rowan looks down at his hands. At the scars that mark his palms and his fingers. "Did he hurt you?"

"No. He was kind. He told me Arien wasn't quite gone, but if we stayed in the cold for much longer, he would be. So I asked him to show us the way out of the forest. He picked up Arien and carried him, and he held my hand. He was . . . gentle. We walked for the whole night through the Vair Woods. Then, in the morning, we came to the road. He laid Arien down. He took my magic. And then—"

I blink hard against the burn and blur of tears as they rise. Rowan reaches out, his fingers brush over my wrist, and the sigil gives a single, muted throb. "You can tell me, Violeta."

"After the woods, my magic was gone, but that wasn't all. What I did that night, the bargain I made, it changed something in Arien. His magic. The darkness he has. What he is, and everything that happened to him afterward because of it— it's all my fault."

"You were a child." He hesitates, then goes on. "There's no *fault* in what you did when you were afraid."

A laugh catches in my throat. "If I'd not done it, then we'd never have been able to help you. But what if using my power now will bring the Lord Under back to take Arien away?"

"You made your bargain; you freely gave up your magic to him. I don't think that can be unmade. As for your help, do you really think that's all I care about?"

"Isn't it?"

"No." Rowan wipes his thumb across my cheek. "It isn't."

I shake myself free of his touch. "I wish Arien hadn't been the one to wear the wounds made by my choices."

"You were hurt by it, too."

He looks toward my arms, his eyes filled with emotion. I think of that day in the cottage when he saw my bruises. How his hands trembled above my wrists. The bruises are long healed now. But all I can think is that it wasn't enough. I couldn't keep Arien safe then, or now.

"It was my fault. All of it. Mother, however much she hurt me, I deserved it. It was my fault she was afraid of Arien."

"You did nothing wrong," Rowan says fiercely. He's angry—but not at me.

"I was afraid of him, too. Of the darkness and his shadows." Roughly, I grab the hem of my dress and pull it up. Between my crumpled skirts and my ribboned socks, my knees are bare. The scars where Clover healed me are snagged across my skin in fierce, deep lines. Rowan breathes in sharply when he sees them. *I deserved it.*

I didn't cry then, even as the glass cut deep. How could I cry when all of it—Mother's fear, Arien's dark-tinged power—was because of me? But now I let the tears come.

I curl forward, folding in on myself. Rowan puts his arms around me. "Violeta. You made a terrible, desperate choice. And you *never* deserved to be hurt like this."

I bury my face against his shoulder. Now that I've started to cry, I'm not sure I can ever stop. Sobs catch in my throat, and hot tears spill down my cheeks. He runs his hand over my hair, murmuring against my ear. "It wasn't your fault. It wasn't, it wasn't."

Then slowly, hesitantly, he touches the scars on my knees. He is so gentle. He doesn't say anything else. He just sits with me and lets me cry until, finally, I shudder into stillness.

The light begins to fade, and the garden turns to velvet in the dusk. Between the branches above there's a bare space of sky where a few bright stars encircle the new moon. The whole world is quiet.

I wipe my face with my sleeve. "Please don't tell Arien about what I did. He spent so much time thinking he was dark and ruined and wrong. He's only just begun to see that it's not true."

"I understand. Don't worry, I'll keep your secret. I won't even demand a book for my silence."

"You have enough books. But I could probably grow you some more blackberries."

He laughs, and I lean against his chest. His skin is warm beneath his shirt, and the fabric is stuck to him where he sweat from cutting the wood. And though he held me before, when I cried . . . this feels different. My magic starts to stir awake; I feel it spun loosely within me. I like the weight of him, close, and how my cheek fits against his shoulder.

"Leta." He speaks my name in a low, tender breath. "Leta."

His hands are still on my knees, stroking gently back and forth over my scars. I start to think of him moving higher, how it might feel if his fingers pressed into the backs of my thighs. A throb begins in my throat. It flutters alongside my pulse, then travels lower, through my chest to my stomach. Then lower still. Heat pools within me, aching and tender.

I reach up and trail my fingers along the line of his jaw. He tenses. I can hear the slither and hiss of the Corruption as he breathes. Rivulets of darkness vein the edges of his throat as the shadows uncoil beneath his skin. Magic rises from my hands in a faint, warm glow.

One breath passes, then another. My face is a pale heart reflected in the depths of his gaze. There is only the barest space between us. It would be so easy for me to lean forward, to close that distance.

Scars brush the side of his mouth. How would it feel, that place, if I kissed him?

Rough.

Soft.

Slowly, slowly, I lift my hand and trace across his lips with the edge of my thumb. Sparks light from my fingers, and the lines of poison spread farther, covering his throat and creeping up over his cheeks.

Rowan catches hold of my wrist. "Stop." His voice sounds like the wash of lake water. "Please, stop."

"I'm sorry." I pull away from him, and we both stand up quickly. I brush down my skirts until the gossamer layers of fabric cover my legs again.

"Don't be sorry." He's so quiet. I can barely hear him. "I can't, Leta. I just can't."

I nod, but I'm embarrassed. What right do I have to want

this? What right do I have to ask anything from him, when he has already given and lost so much?

I reach for the ribbon around my neck and slip the silken loop over my head. I draw out the key and offer it to him on the flat of my palm. "Thank you for showing me the garden, Rowan."

He doesn't move for a long time, only stares down at my outstretched hand. His fingers are pressed against his throat where the darkness is still fading back under his skin.

Then he says a single word. "*Anything.*"

I look at him, confused, as I realize what he means. "That was your trade? You offered the Lord Under anything in exchange for your life?"

"Yes."

The enormity of it sends a cold, terrible shiver through me. An offer like that would have meant the Lord Under could set his own terms. He could take whatever he wanted. "Oh, Rowan. I'm—"

"No." He stops me before I can finish what I meant to say. *I'm sorry.* Roughly, he folds my fingers closed around the key. "I want to give this to you."

"I don't understand."

"This." He gestures to the trees, the brambles, the tangled beds.

"You want to give the whole garden to me?"

I look all around us, at this beautiful, forgotten place. The trees and the brambles, the crooked orchard and the wild-flower lawn. The plants are half-dead and gone to seed, but it's so much grander and larger and *more* than anything I've ever had. *Mine*.

"Yes. It's yours."

It hangs between us, unspoken, that there might be a time beyond the mud and poison and darkness. That on the next full moon the Corruption could be mended. And after that, I'll have this piece of earth as my own. I'll plant seeds and pick flowers. Bring this whole locked-up, too-long-asleep place back to life.

My throat still burns with salt and tears. I close my eyes and feel the faint spark of my magic. *Traces. Leftover.*

For just this moment, I let myself believe that it will be enough.

Chapter Fifteen

The night of the second ritual arrives in a heat wave. The midsummer sunset turns the sky to blood. The air is so heavy I can hardly breathe; sweat beads my face and trickles down the back of my neck. We stand beside the lake, at the edge of the forest. Shadows stripe between the pale trees. Arien and Clover are on either side of me. Our skin is marked with spells. The sigil is carved into the shore. We are almost ready.

The past weeks have been a blur of lessons. Days spent in the library, the table cluttered with papers and pens and ink, as I've practiced drawing the symbols for the spell to focus my magic. Days spent outside, the three of us circled around the jars of inky water, the sigil on the lawn now permanent: a sooty, charred mark. We've worked the spell so much that each night I've dreamed of it. My hands, their hands. The draw of power, the weave of shadows. The Corrupted water cleared and mended.

And all the while, outside, beneath the growing moon, the lake has waited for us to cast our magic. I've not heard or seen the Lord Under since he offered his help, but part of me is still afraid that using my magic will call him back to me. But there's no other choice. It will work. It has to work.

Rowan comes down the path and through the garden archway. He has his cloak tucked over his arm. Florence walks behind him, carrying a lantern and a basket packed with bandages and folded cloths. When she puts the basket down beside our feet, I try not to look at it. Try to ignore the reminder that if the ritual fails, Rowan will have to cut himself and bleed into the ground, to let that angry darkness overtake him.

Florence gives us all a steady, flinty look. "You'll be safe." There's no lilt of a question in her voice.

"Of course we will," Clover says. She smiles, but the brightness doesn't quite reach her eyes. "Well, we'll try our best."

Rowan puts his hand on Arien's arm. There's a brief tenderness in his eyes as he looks at my brother. Then he steps back, his face as set and unreadable as a mask. "Are you all ready?"

Arien draws up his shoulders. "We're ready."

"Good." Clover and Arien start to walk toward the water, but when I move to follow them, Rowan touches my arm. "Wait. Violeta, I . . ."

I turn back. He trails off. We stare at each other, neither of us speaking. He's tied all of his hair back and his face looks so different without any of the loose, dark waves tangled around it. He keeps touching his fingers to his throat. Around the scars is a pale, indistinct shadow, traces of the poison beneath his skin.

"Aren't you going to wish me luck in my first ritual?"

"You don't need luck. I've watched you." Rowan fastens his cloak around his shoulders, then takes his gloves from the pocket and pulls them on brusquely. "I mean—you and Arien. You've done well. Both of you."

"I'm getting better at drawing sigils now. See?"

I show him my arm, and he huffs out a soft laugh. "Be safe, Leta."

"You too."

I walk down to the shore and take my place between Arien and Clover, stepping carefully over the sigil so my feet don't smudge the carved lines. Arien kneels down and presses his palms to the mud. Clover flexes her hands, and sparks scatter from her fingers.

I kneel down beside Arien. The ground is so cold, and the wet mud seeps through my skirts. Though the air is hot against my face, the chill sends shivers all across my skin. I swallow down my revulsion as I put my hands into the earth.

Arien smiles at me reassuringly. "It will be just like when we practiced."

Clover looks at us. Her eyes are gold, and magic dances over her outspread fingers. "You know what to do."

The shadows come from Arien's hands. With the first touch of his magic, the Corruption starts to shift and churn.

His first few gestures are tentative, but with each movement he becomes more and more confident.

Power sparks up beneath my skin and the sigil on my wrist burns. I think of a thread. See it unspool alongside the strands of darkness. I hold the shadows in place as Arien casts them out across the ground.

Already, this ritual is different from the first attempt. Arien—all the practice, the lessons, our *life* at Lakesedge—it's changed him. His blackened eyes, the cold of his magic, the salt-and-ash taste of it in the air—it's part of him. It *is* him. He's clever and strong, and he's not afraid.

My magic still feels too small and too faint. But it's *enough*. I can help him do this.

Clover murmurs encouragement to us both as she sends light into the spell. "Cast it farther. Tighten it more, over there. Keep going."

The shadows lattice across the ground. Together, Arien and I weave them into a taut, controlled net. It spreads farther and farther, until it covers the entire shore. Clover's magic twines through it, and the spell gleams like sunsparks across shallow water. Beneath it, the Corruption begins to glow and waver. Tremors undulate across the ground, from the lake to the edge of the trees. We can do this.

Our hands dig deeper into the mud. It's so *cold*. The Corruption shudders against my palms. It feels the same as it did the night Rowan paid the tithe: dark and endless and hungry. So empty of the light that runs through the world—the golden warmth of the Lady's magic.

I clench my teeth. Think of sun and seeds and flowers. Beside me, Arien is tensed. His muscles are drawn tight. But his magic holds. He keeps control. It doesn't falter.

We push and coax and *force* our magic into the earth. The ground moves in waves, like a tide pulled by the moon. The spell is working. Clover and Arien and I, with all of our magic laced together, are mending the Corruption.

The blackened ground begins to change. It softens, the mud turned back to sand. Strands of sedge grass push up from the earth. At our feet, the water ripples, the inky darkness now becoming clear.

For a breath, everything stills. Slowly, Arien draws the shadows back, and Clover lifts her hands from the ground. We sit, encircled by the still-glowing sigil and look around.

It's mended. It's all mended.

Then blotches of darkness start to spread across the shore. Arien and I look at each other nervously, then turn to Clover. She holds out a hand, magic sparking across her palm, brow furrowed.

"I don't understand." She takes a tentative step toward the water, toward the changing earth. "It shouldn't be doing this."

I look down to see the ground tear open. Clover cries out. We fall back heavily as the darkening shore splits into a deep wound. Arien's elbow strikes my cheek, and all I can see is stars. From far off, I hear Florence calling out, urgent, "Rowan! Get them back. This isn't—"

Rowan is beside us instantly. He grabs my arm, trying to drag me away.

"Leta—" His voice is choked.

The rift tears wider and wider. Then a shape rises up from the mud. One, then another, then another. They're tall. Too tall. Oily dark that seeps and drips. They have limbs without hands. Grotesque, faceless heads. They slither forward, and my breath comes out in a desperate gasp.

"No!" I look to Arien, who is wide eyed with shock. "What are they? What's happening?"

"Get back, both of you!" Clover cries. Her hands are blazing with light, which she casts at the creatures in a brutal slash. They flinch back and melt into the ground. But then the rift opens farther, and more of the creatures rise up.

They have claws. Sharp slices of stone, hooked and brutal. They have *mouths*. Round, studded with shards of broken shells. They surge from the earth in a torrent. I reach for Arien, but they're so fast—I have no time to move before they've washed over him.

His arm thrashes out, caught by coils of mud. His face is pale, terrified.

"Arien, hold on!" I lunge toward him as he vanishes beneath the creatures.

Rowan wrenches at my arm. "Leta, get *back*."

"No! Arien—"

I twist free of his grasp. But before I can do anything, Rowan shoves his hands into the writhing mass of earth. He doesn't even flinch. The way he moves—it's *practiced*. Like he's done this before, faced the Corruption, pulled someone free. Or tried.

I crush in close beside him, my shoulder hard against his. I plunge my hands into the mud, desperate and frightened as the creatures rush over me, as I feel the scrape of claws and teeth. I reach farther into the icy darkness, searching desperately, but Arien is gone. There's only mud and cold and the hungry creatures.

I could have stopped this. If I'd accepted the Lord Under's help, then none of this would have happened. I grasp for the strength he showed me, a force far beyond my magic. But there's only the faintest throb. A burn at my wrist, an ache in my chest.

I can't do this. Not alone.

"Please!" I call out to the shadows. To the monster who was kind, once. Who held my hand and led me through the woods. Who saved my brother. "Please, you said you would help me—"

Darkness clouds my vision, and the evening light is swept away. Water rushes over me, followed by a sound. A breath, a hiss, a sigh.

I search again for Arien, but my hands find nothing in the dark. My voice is an incoherent sob that echoes through the shadows. "Help me, help me, help me."

With a flare of silvered brightness, the Lord Under appears. Tall and sharp and jagged, like the upturned roots of a fallen tree. Streaks of wet, dark shadows trail around him, and there's a spill of black water as he moves forward. I can't see his face, but I know—somehow I know—that his eyes are fixed on me. He watches me silently for a very long time as the dark closes down around us. When he finally speaks, his voice is as cold as a midwinter night.

I offered my help already, Violeta. And you refused it.

He's going to let Arien die. He'll die, and it will be my fault. *No.* Indignant anger burns through me. I'll not beg for his help. I'll not cower here, small and afraid. I am light and heat and fire.

"You'll save him." I grit my teeth and glare at him as power sparks, blistering, from my fingers. "You *will*."

He doesn't move. He doesn't speak. Then he laughs, softly, softly.

You're so brave. Be a little afraid—it will hurt.

I reach out, and the darkness wavers. My fingers touch cloth and skin. Arien—his sleeve, his wrist. He takes a sharp breath. I pull him close. I wrap my arms around him. I don't let go. As the shadows thin, as the light brightens, I brace myself for the promised pain, but it doesn't come.

Then Arien screams. He screams and screams. We're back on the shore, released by the Corruption. I hold him in my arms. *He screams.* Clover and I drag him back from the lake, across the shore and toward the pale trees, where we fall to the ground. He's crying, his screams changed to ragged sobs.

"Arien?" His hands are stained dark all the way to his elbows, the skin ravaged and raw. They're charred, like something held too long in the fire, but when I touch his fingers, his skin is cold.

Clover lets out a hopeless, wounded sound. "Oh, Arien. Oh, what have you done?"

Her magic flickers as she runs her hands over him.

"I—I can't feel—" Tears streak across his face. He drags in a tattered breath. "They're all numb."

Arien cradles his ruined hands against his chest. I hold him tightly as he starts to cry again. He shivers and shivers. I want to make him warm, but I'm just as cold. "We need to get back to the house."

"We can't." Arien tries to push me away. "Those *things*—they're still there."

I look back toward the lake, horrified, to see that the creatures have begun to rise up again. And Rowan—he's *there*. He's taken off his cloak, and his knife gleams in his hand.

"We need to help him," Clover sobs, starting to get up from the ground.

The creatures close in around Rowan as he stands with his arms outspread.

"*We* are not going to do anything." I move Arien gently into Clover's arms. "Stay here."

I run back toward the heart of the Corruption. *It will hurt.* The sun has set behind the hills now, and everything is streaked in darkness. I stare out into the night sky above the lake. Black water, black sky, twin moons. I reach desperately for the burned-down scraps of power I have left, feel it heat my palms.

I run across the shore until I'm beside Rowan. He's cut his arms—both of them. Blood streams from his wrists. He turns to me, and his eyes are crimson, his throat snared with dark. "Get away from me."

His voice is *wrong*: low and terrible, like a clotted-over wound.

I kneel on the ground beside him. "No."

He holds out his hands, bloodied and trembling, as tendrils of earth rise up and tangle around him, gripping his throat until the darkness seems to sink into his flesh. He hisses through clenched teeth.

The creatures come toward him in a rush. One after another, they fall onto him. He chokes out a desperate, hurt cry, but he doesn't fight, doesn't move. He lets them come. Their rounded, hungry mouths fasten at the wounds on his wrists. They tear into his skin. They bite at his arms, his chest, his throat. *It will hurt; it will hurt.*

Rowan sits with his arms flung wide, eyes closed, as the creatures writhe and feast. Cut and bled and devoured. I swallow down my cries, remembering how it was last time. When I put my hand to the earth and thought of warmth and made the Corruption leave him alone. I stretch my fingers toward the ground.

"No." He shakes his head. His voice is thick, water and mud and lake. "Let them."

I draw back and watch helplessly. There is more than one way for me to be hurt—how did I not understand this until now? I thought I could burn myself down to save the world. But I never thought of what to do if the world burned all around me instead.

After a long time, the creatures start to change. They soften, becoming more and more formless. Finally, finally, they let

Rowan go and seep back into the earth. He falls forward. The tendrils of Corruption unwind from him. The ground gives a final shudder, then goes still.

There's no sound but the *lap lap lap* of waves against the shore. The creatures are gone. The wound in the shore has closed. The ground is black, still poisoned.

"Rowan?" I crouch beside his collapsed body. His shirt is stained with blackened blood, and his face is ashen. I can't tell if he's breathing. I press my trembling fingers against his throat in search of a pulse.

His lashes flutter, then he stares up at me with bloodshot eyes. He tries to push me away, but he's overtaken by coughing. He curls up on his side, fighting for breath. He coughs and coughs, then chokes out mouthfuls of ink-dark water. He sits up, slowly, gasping for air. Spits out more of the oil-slick darkness and scrapes his wrist across his mouth.

"Arien." He scans the shore, then sees Arien and Clover huddled beside the trees. Florence is holding a cloth to Arien's arms; the contents of her basket are scattered across the ground. "Is he hurt?"

"Yes. I—" Tears fill my eyes. How can I tell Rowan—or anyone—the truth? "He was hurt, and it's all my fault."

Rowan's expression darkens. "Never again." He grips my arms with his bloodied fingers, fear and fury clear across his face. "Do you hear me? We are done with the rituals, with all of it."

"You can't give up. You know what will happen if it doesn't stop."

"Let it," he whispers roughly. "Let it kill me. I don't care. I'll not have you—or Arien, or anyone—hurt again."

He gets back to his feet, wrenching down his sleeves. More blood soaks through the cloth in dark streaks. He storms away, but when he reaches the gate, he falters and starts to stumble before catching himself against the scrolled iron arch. Florence goes to him quickly and wraps her arm around his waist. I watch him trying to shake her off as they disappear into the garden.

I go back to where Clover and Arien sit, and sink down beside them. I lean against one of the pale trees and press my face into my hands, breathing hard as I try to gather myself. The shore sprawls before us: cold and black and still. Clover rests her head on my shoulder and sighs. Arien stares out blankly toward the water. His hands are wrapped in a cloth, but he's bled through the pale linen.

I'm relieved to see that the stains are crimson, not black. But this small moment of relief is quickly swallowed by guilt. I wasn't strong enough. The wounds, the hurt, it's all because I gave in to the Lord Under. I called on the lord of the dead, and *this* is what he did.

I thought I could help, but all I did was make everything worse.

Chapter Sixteen

Night folds around me. I'm in the hall outside Rowan's room, a candle jar cupped tight between my hands. His door is closed.

A thread-thin gleam of light edges the frame. But when I knock, there's no response.

I close my eyes and lean my forehead against the paneled wood.

The house is silent and still. I feel as though I'm the only one awake—or alive—in the entire estate. After we came back from the lake, Clover mended Arien's arms, but his skin still looked charred and raw and ruined. She promised him it would be fine. She said it the same way Rowan did, after the tithe—*fine fine fine*. Hope knotted up in a lie.

While she worked, I lit candles, as many as I could find. In Arien's room, I lined the sills and the mantel and the bedside table with them, and set them on the floor in each corner. Never again would I let the darkness come for me or for Arien. When the wind stirred through the walls, when it sounded like my name, I refused to listen.

Florence came into the room and dragged a chair over to the bed. Sent Clover and me away and said she would watch over Arien. I left him shrouded in light, sound asleep. I went to my own room and tried to sleep, too. But when I closed my eyes, all I could see was the ritual. Images that came in swift, hideous flashes. The claws. The teeth. The sound of Arien's screams when the Lord Under hurt him.

And Rowan. Poisoned and wounded and full of hard, cold resignation. *Let it kill me.* He's lived for so long with that darkness inside him. Fought and fought, let it take him apart in a slow bloodletting to delay the inevitable. It makes me think of a dry well: the widening space between surface and water, the scrape of the bucket across the stones. He'll give up, give in, and I'll have to watch the Corruption slowly ruin him, piece by piece, before it destroys him entirely.

I care for him. But I still don't know him.

We've hidden so much of the truth from each other. I have to know what happened to him in the past. What *really* happened when Rowan was saved by the Lord Under.

I knock on his door again, harder this time. The sound echoes through the hallway.

I try the handle. The door opens. I go inside.

His room is just as bare as the last time I was here. The curtains are flung wide, the hot night air drifting through the open window with the scent of leaves and earth. Everything is so still, so silent. But then I see him, curled beneath the quilt on his narrow, makeshift bed. He turns toward me as I cross the room, but his eyes are closed. He's asleep.

His arm lashes out. His wrists are bandaged—he must have done it himself—and thick, black Corrupted blood has seeped through the cloth.

"Elan," he calls out, pained. "Elan, please . . ."

A nightmare. He's having another nightmare.

I tiptoe closer and set my candle on the floor near the bed, beside a tray bearing a half-drunk cup of tea. Three glass vials lie next to the cup. Empty, except for a few drops of the bitter sedative. My small light gleams weakly out into the rest of the room. In the corner, the shadows are heavy. I turn my face away from the darkness.

I lean over Rowan and put my hands on his shoulders. At my touch, he snaps awake, sits up and shakes himself free. "Violeta? What are you doing in here?"

His eyes are dark—pupils blown wide, sclera bloodshot. The scars at his throat are latticed dark, a tracery that spreads upward across his jaw, down over his chest. He isn't wearing a shirt, and in the candlelight I can see his broad shoulders, his lean muscles, the scars all over his skin. A strange yearning fills me.

His hair is tangled from sleep and still damp from when he washed out the mud. A loose strand hangs over his face, the dark line crossing out his features. I reach to brush it back. "You had a nightmare."

He catches my hand before I can touch him. *"Don't."*

"You had a nightmare, but it's over now." There's a cloth, folded up on the tray beneath the teapot. I pick it up. "Your arms . . . Here, let me help you."

He looks down and sees that the cuts have bled through the bandages. Sighing, he holds out his arms to me. I start to unwind the strips of linen. I shudder when I see the wounds, unable to stop picturing sharp teeth and hooked claws. I try not to touch the blood, but I can't avoid it; when it smears my fingers, it's thick and strangely cool.

Rowan takes the cloth from my hands. "There are bandages in the dresser. The top drawer. And—" He looks down, embarrassed. "And maybe a shirt, from the drawer beneath."

I open the dresser and take out a roll of bandages, then search through his neatly folded shirts until I find the softest one. I take everything back over to the bed, then sit down carefully on the floor and start to unwind the bandages.

Rowan sits very still as I wrap his arms. After I'm done, I lean against the edge of the chaise. "You told me the Corruption wouldn't hurt anyone except you. You swore it. But I saw how you looked when you fought to save Arien. It wasn't the first time you've done that—tried to pull someone else back."

He lowers his eyes as he roughly pulls on the shirt. "No. It wasn't."

"Tell me." I put my hand on his arm so he can't turn farther away. "Rowan, what happened when the Lord Under saved you? What really happened to your family? I want to know the truth."

He hesitates a moment, then he sighs. "It was as I said, before. I died. I came back. I was poisoned." His gaze drifts toward the open window, and his voice sounds far away. "I was maybe five years old. I went to play near the lake and fell into the water. It was so cold, and I couldn't breathe—then all at once everything changed. I wasn't in the water anymore; I was in a forest. It wasn't like anything I'd ever seen. It was dark, and there was no sky. I was there for what felt like a long time. Until he spoke to me."

"The Lord Under."

"Yes. What did you say about him? *He was kind.* I was frightened, like you. But he held my hand and told me that he could save me. When he asked what I would give in exchange for my life, I said *anything*. I suppose it's a pity I didn't have any magic to offer him." Rowan laughs darkly, then his expression turns solemn. "When I woke up on the shore, the water had turned black, and I thought that had been the price. My parents were so angry and worried that I couldn't bring myself to tell them what had really happened."

"So you pushed it down." It's hard to speak, remembering how I felt when I was in his place, how hard I tried to forget what I'd done in the Vair Woods. "And after a while it felt almost like it hadn't been real."

"Strange to think we have such a thing in common, isn't it?" He reaches out and traces over the sigil on my wrist. The gentle touch of his roughened fingers on my skin is like an offer, a question. I lean toward him, and he lifts his other hand to touch my face. "Leta," he murmurs. "Leta, I—"

But then he starts to cough. He closes his eyes, fighting against it, as darkness spreads across his throat.

Light glows from my hand, drawn out by the surge of shadows within him. I put my fingers over his heart and try to focus. The blackened tendrils start to shimmer, just like the lakeshore did earlier today at the ritual. I think of a garden, my father with his hands in the dirt as he turned stems to flowers. His magic is my magic. Petals and seeds, leaves and pollen.

My power is a thread, tied to Rowan. What I have is only a single flower, the smallest candle flame. I wish so terribly that I were strong enough to mend him entirely. All I can do is picture my magic unspun inside him, a brief flare of warmth against the cold, poisoned darkness.

Slowly, the Corruption fades back to pale shadows.

"Thank you." He holds my hand tightly for a moment, then moves aside to make space on the chaise. "Sit down with me. I'll tell you how it happened."

I glance at his makeshift bed, which is ridiculously neat, the linen sheets crisp and freshly ironed. But his hair is tangled, and there are creases on his face from where he's lain against the pillow. He's more undone than I've ever seen him.

I sit down next to him, close but not quite touching. I can feel the warmth, left behind from while he slept.

He stares pensively out into the room. "When I turned thirteen, my parents threw an enormous party. All their friends from other estates, from as far as Anglria, brought their children. I danced all night, trying to work up the courage to kiss Linden Hawke before he went home."

I give him a little shove. "Who knew you had such a wild youth?"

He laughs softly, embarrassed. "Elan told me I had to choose whoever had the prettiest brother, then we'd all live together in a tree house in the garden."

"That might have been a little chilly in winter."

They're bittersweet, these memories. Rowan and I exchange a small smile, and he continues.

"We made ourselves sick drinking spiced wine. Elan stole my cake from the kitchen table. We ate half of it together. Florence was furious, but Mother just laughed. She iced it again and told everyone it was supposed to be shaped like a moon."

Arien and I never celebrate our birthdays; we don't even know when they are. Each new year as the world turns, we just add another year of our own. When Rowan danced and Elan plotted their future house among the trees, I was eleven. I scrubbed floors and chopped kindling. I made up stories and sat, watchful, beside Arien in the dark.

I picture Rowan surrounded by his family. Loved and happy. I can see it so clearly: the now-empty house full of light and voices, lanterns strung along the drive, candles that shimmer over a crescent of freshly iced cake.

I know how it ended, but still, it fills me with a cold flare of envy. "It sounds wonderful."

His smile fades. "At the end of the night, my father put his arm around my shoulders. He told me I was a man now. And then . . ." Rowan presses his hands to his mouth for a moment. When he goes on, his voice is muffled inside his palms. "The

210

whole room went dark, like someone had blown out all the lights. The Lord Under, he came back for me. *You've had your childhood*, he said, *the rest of your life is mine*. That was his *anything*. He let me live; then he returned to claim me. It was the only other time I've seen him, aside from when I was saved. And that first time, he was kind. But this time . . ."

Rowan's fingers clench over the space he can't fill with words. But I've seen that same darkness. *This will hurt*. The Lord Under can be kind, but he can also be so terribly cruel. I shiver and pull the quilts higher around me.

"He meant to take me to the world Below, but I . . . I refused." His eyes shutter closed, and he shakes his head. He's not frightened by this memory, I realize. He's ashamed. "I don't know what I expected. Maybe that he would argue, that he would ask me to bargain again. But he only laughed. Then he went away."

Rowan tries to steady his words. This was what I wanted, wasn't it? The whole story. The truth. I could stop him now. Put out my hand and whisper *enough*. But I have to hear him tell it. I'm terrible and greedy and afraid. I *need* to know what happened to him.

"My father was dead the next morning." He looks at me for a heartbeat, then turns away, going on quickly, like he's afraid if he stops, he won't be able to speak again. "They found him in the water. All of the guests left, terrified. That's when the rumors started about the estate. How something dark had come into the house, and then my father had drowned in the cursed, black lake. Only I knew it was my

211

fault. The Lord Under took my father's life because I refused to give up mine."

"Oh, Rowan." I shift closer to him. He goes still at my touch but doesn't move to widen the distance between us. "You didn't tell anyone?"

"No. My mother, after it all happened, she was changed. It was like she didn't know who she was without my father. How could I tell her that he was dead because of me? And so I tried to forget."

I think of how I kept my own secrets locked up so tightly. How I'd tried so desperately to pretend that Arien's dark magic was only dreams, because it was easier than facing the truth. "I understand."

"I was the lord now. I had to do all the things my father once did. I went to the village. I collected the tithe. I made observance at the altar you saw." He sighs heavily. "I didn't know the Lord Under would come back, but then my mother heard a voice at night, in her room."

"He spoke to her." I recall the whispers I heard in the dark. How the Lord Under drew me out through the halls. *Follow.*

"She thought it was a nightmare. She'd had so many of those since my father died. But the next day, I found her at the lake. Drowned. And the darkness that had been in the water had spread onto the shore beneath her. In the village, everyone said I had killed her. That I had killed them both."

"If he had the power to take their lives, then why didn't he just claim you, instead?" My stomach sinks as I understand the reason. "He took them to punish you."

Rowan nods. Even after what happened with Arien today, it still shocks me to realize the depths of the Lord Under's ruthlessness.

"And then Elan began to hear the same voice. The Lord Under meant to take him, too. I'd promised him *anything*, after all. Once I knew what was happening, I was desperate. I had to find a way to protect Elan, to keep him safe. I'd heard stories of people who used an offering of blood to call on the Lord Under. So I tried to summon him."

"What did you do?"

"I went to our altar in the parlor. I lit the candles. I cut my hands and let my blood fall on the floor. But he never came. I stayed with Elan in his room every night, and tried to hear the voice, but only Elan could hear it. He told me it wanted him to go to the lake. So *I* went there. I went to the place where my parents had been found, the same place they had found *me*, all that time ago. I cut my arms this time and bled into the ground. When that didn't work, I . . ."

He raises his hand to his throat and traces his fingers across the scars.

"You cut—You tried to—" I fall silent, struck cold by the horror of what he did.

"Yes, I meant to end my life." He looks at me, his face shocked, as though he didn't mean to speak so plainly. "I didn't want to die and leave Elan alone. But I knew if the Lord Under didn't take me, then Elan would be lost." He shakes his head. "But when my blood touched the Corruption, it changed. It was like it woke up. It started to spread. It was hungry. I could feel it, what it wanted, and I knew it would spread to the house, to claim Elan. I had to stop it. I put my hands into the earth, like I was at observance, and the darkness went inside *me* instead. Afterward, I was like this." He motions to the darkness around his scars, the poison beneath his skin. "And when Elan told me the voice had gone quiet, I thought I'd saved him."

"But if it worked"—I feel terrible even asking, but I have to know—"what happened to Elan? How did he die?"

"To keep him safe, I had to keep going back to the lake. The Corruption would stir, and the poison inside me would call, and I knew if I didn't let the Corruption claim more from me, it would spread, and it would hurt Elan. But each time I gave my tithe, I took on more of the darkness. I wrote to the Maylands for an alchemist, to see if there was anything else that could be done. They sent Clover, but before she arrived . . ." Rowan closes his eyes as tears trail a slow path down his cheeks. "One night when I went to the lake, Elan followed me. He saw what I was doing and tried to stop me. And when he stepped onto the shore, it was like he was entranced. He started to walk into the water, and I tried to pull him back. Then the darkness changed me. I was still there, but alongside me was this other *thing*. I couldn't do anything to stop him. I didn't *want* to stop him. I watched him drown, and that terrible, poisoned part of me was pleased."

He's crying in earnest now, though he fights to hold it back. I reach out to him, feeling sick, thinking of the cold, lightless silence at the bottom of the lake.

"Rowan." I wrap my arms around him. "It wasn't your fault."

He struggles for a moment, trying to move away, then he relents and leans against me. "I was ready to die for Elan," he says, the words ragged between sobs. "But in the end I just let him go."

His hand goes to my waist and he pulls me closer, his fingers clutched into the fabric of my nightdress. He presses his face into my shoulder, and I rest my cheek against his hair. I'm almost certain he's never let anyone comfort him like this before. His shame, his grief, is like an open wound, and I know there's nothing I can say that will take away the hurt. So I just hold him. I hold him, and I let him cry, like he did with me in the garden.

We stay like that a long time, then he takes a deep breath and roughly wipes his eyes with his sleeve. "It wasn't a lie when I said everything you've heard about me is true. My family, they're all dead because of me. Even if it wasn't by my hand, I still killed them."

"No. You made a mistake, a terrible mistake."

"How can you be so kind after what I've done, Violeta? When I'm to blame for the Corruption?"

"That night in the garden, when I told you how I'd traded my magic for Arien, you understood me immediately." I remember his words. *There's no fault in what you did.* "You were afraid. You wanted to protect your brother. I would have done exactly the same."

Rowan is a monster. He's put all of us, especially Arien, in terrible danger. But I can't hate him for it. Because when I look at him, all I can see are my own choices. I have been in those same shadows. I have faced that same darkness.

And I would go there again if it meant everyone I care about would be safe.

I brush back a loose fall of hair from his tear-streaked face, then run my fingers across his scars. His brow, his jaw, the edge of his mouth. He leans his cheek against my palm. The gesture calls to something buried far within me. Hurt and want, all mixed together. I can feel my heart pressed hard against the inside of my chest.

"I'm sorry." His voice is a newly tender bruise. "I'm sorry for everything."

"I'm sorry, too."

He lies back onto the bed. He looks up at me, sad and shy, a hesitant invitation in his silence. I stretch out beside him and he tucks the quilts over me as we settle together. Neither of us move for a long, drawn-out moment.

"Leta." He breathes my name and reaches to me. He takes my hand. He bends to my wrist, to the place where I'm marked by the sigil. Then—so slowly that it aches—he brushes a kiss across my skin. It's the barest touch, but it echoes through me with liquid heat.

I gasp. A soft note that turns to a whimper. I'm pleading, though I don't know for what.

I've never wanted this before, to be so close to another person. Sometimes, in the cottage, in the dark, I'd curl up far down beneath my quilts and trace my fingers against my skin.

But I never pictured, never *wanted* someone else there. Following the paths I made in the hidden corners of my body.

And now, here with Rowan, I'm not sure how to find words for what I want from him. He lost his parents to the cruelty of the Lord Under, then stood powerless as his brother died. How can I ask him for this, to care for me, to let me in?

I reach out, tentative, uncertain, and draw him closer. He starts to stroke my hair, following the length of it down to the curve of my shoulder. His fingers are hot on the bare skin above the ribboned collar of my nightdress. My breath comes loose in a desperate sigh. Sparks of magic light from my hands. They drift upward and glimmer over us for a heartbeat, gone by the time I've blinked.

He leans over me. His skin smells of the same lavender soap that I use. And something else. Spice and honey. Burnt sugar. Black tea.

I put my hand on his chest, above the unlaced collar of his shirt, then trail my fingers upward. I touch the scars on his throat, the same way I did in the garden. He shivers, but doesn't pull away.

Everything between us feels strange and new and fragile. But I know with absolute surety that I want to protect him, whatever it takes.

I want to mend the Corruption on my own.

I want to be strong enough to ensure no one I love is hurt, ever again.

"Rowan." I whisper his name against his cheek. "I'm going to find a way to fix all of this."

He draws back from me warily. "What do you mean?"

I realize I've slipped and said *I* will mend things, rather than *we*.

"What are you going to do?" He takes my face between his hands so he can look into my eyes. "Leta. Whatever you're thinking—*don't*."

With my face cupped by his scarred, rough palms, I can think of countless foolish things I want to do. In the end, I do the most terrible of them all. I lie.

"I won't. I promise."

Chapter Seventeen

In the garden, everything has gone to seed and flower. The stems of plants are crisped to air-light dryness. I move through the tangled orchard, a basket in my arms.

Trees and brambles make a screen behind me as I follow the path, and soon I'm alone. It's quiet, with no sound except for my footsteps crunching over the gravel, then soft over bare earth.

At the very end of the path, the leafless, skeletal remains of two trees weave together into a bower, perhaps the tree house where Elan once daydreamed he and Rowan would live. I duck beneath the arch of branches. Inside, it's cooler, and the latticework of wood shades me from the early sun. I sit down on the ground, the dry earth covered by a scatter of grass and twigs, and curl my hands around the nearest trunk.

I reach for my power, trying to picture the magic coiled in my chest and strung across my skin. It's still a fight to draw it out. It feels as though I've put my hands into a dense fog to search for a single tiny seed. It slips and slips and slips, always just past my outstretched fingers. A metallic taste fills my mouth, and sweat streaks my temples.

I remember my father in our garden, the sparks of his magic over stems and leaves and flowers. I try to let that same bright warmth bloom from my own fingers.

I open my eyes to a world blotched white, with spots of color that dance and shift as I try to steady myself. I wipe the sweat from my face.

My power is still faint, but it was enough. For this, it was enough.

The bower above me is now verdant with delicate leaves. The branches hang low, heavy with fruit: round, ripe pomegranates. I reach for one large enough to fill my cupped palms and trace my fingers over the smooth, taut surface. When I tap the crimson-colored skin, a hollow softness resounds from inside.

I put the pomegranate gently into my basket, then reach for another. One by one, each fruit I've picked marks a beat of time. The morning sun tracks slowly across the sky. A sharp, needle-fine twig scrapes against the inside of my wrist. I rub my fingers against the welt and think of the promise I made to Rowan in the darkness. *I'll fix this.*

We spent the whole night together, curled up into a crescent. His arm around my waist, his breath against my cheek. I slipped from his room early while all the house was still asleep and went back to my room to change. I put on a new lace dress and pinned up my hair, and then, before I came here, I looked in on Arien.

He was in bed, sleeping fitfully, his wounded arms tucked close against him. With his eyes closed he looked small and young and soft. And whatever hesitation I'd had until then about my plan, it was all gone in that moment.

Back inside, I tiptoe through the kitchen and find the sharp knife that Florence keeps on the topmost shelf of the pantry. I leave my basket on the table, take one pomegranate, and slip it into the pocket of my dress. The weight of the fruit bumps against me through my skirts, and I feel . . . anchored.

In the parlor, the air is dim. A sliver of light cuts through the drawn curtains. The air smells of wax and dust and candle smoke. It's the first time I've been back since the night I was here with Rowan, the first time I've come past the closed door and not turned my face away.

I go over to the altar and look at the dual icon. The Lady, outlined in gold. The Lord Under, a darkened silhouette. I touch a sparklight to the bank of candles, one by one. Soon the room glows with golden light, and the flames paint movement on the lower half of the icon. On the floor beneath, there's a faint, faded mark where Rowan once pressed his bloodied palms.

After what he told me, I should be afraid. But somehow—I think this is different. What passed between the Lord Under and me, that night in the woods at midwinter, it's left a bond between us. I tried to forget him. I tried not to know him. I walked far from the border of death, and yet something drew

221

him back to me when I came to Lakesedge. I am alive, but I can see him and speak with him.

And I think I can *summon* him.

I kneel down before the altar.

I take out the knife.

It's precarious, to cut the pomegranate. The skin is hard. The knife slips before it slices through with a swift, wet sound. The fruit cleaves open. Two neat halves. Inside it glistens red and bright, like a heart filled with seeds. There's a mark on the floorboards from the blade. I lick my thumb and scrub at it, but it can't be wiped away.

I set the opened halves of the carved-up fruit on the altar.

And then I put the knife against my palm. My fingers shake. The blade scrapes my skin, but it's not enough to draw blood. I close my eyes, picturing how easily Rowan cuts himself, without any hesitation. I tighten my grip on the handle, take a breath, and drive the blade deep. The pain sears through me; blood wells in my hand like it's been poured there.

I turn my hand and press it against the floor.

The air shivers, and the honey-warm haze of the room turns to ice. From far off comes a steady *drip drip drip*. I look up, my heartbeat spiking, as water beads across the ceiling and begins to trickle over the walls. Slow at first, the droplets fine as mist. Then it changes, becoming swifter, darker. I back away as the oily, ink-black liquid pours down. It covers the floor in an opaque wash that spills across my feet. I flinch. The cold of it runs all through my body.

And then I hear a familiar whisper.

Violeta.

The water begins to ripple. A shape rises from the center of the darkness. I'm frozen in place as the Lord Under steps out of the shadows and comes toward me.

The light goes through him until he shimmers, a pale smear against the gloom. He's cloaked in a heavy robe that hangs loosely over his dark, close-fitting clothes. His shirt is fastened with silver buckles from his throat to his waist. A crown of driftwood circles his long, pale hair. At the floor, his form dissipates, the robe becoming shapeless mist, another part of the water.

At first his features blur and fracture. His mouth splits as he smiles until there are two sets of sharp teeth, one interlaid with the other. Slashes in the sides of his throat open and close in time with his breath.

I want to look away, but I can't. I'm pinned by the horror of him. He's terrible and beautiful and otherworldly. He is something I am not meant to see.

Then—it all settles. The cuts on his throat close over into thin, translucent lines; his mouth becomes one mouth, still curved into a smile.

He is here. Truly *here*.

"Hello, Violeta." Even his voice is stronger, more real. He looks at the altar, at the offering, then at the floor, smeared with my blood. "So, you've called me."

He is all I feared. He's *worse*, because while I expected the fear, the horror, I didn't expect his cold, stark beauty. The Lord Under is more than an opposite half to the Lady's golden brilliance. He's the silver of a sharp-edged crescent moon.

I am lost in the cold of him.

He looks at me. He sees me. He *knows* me. His smile widens and turns sharp at the edges. He makes a low sound. A pleased, satisfied hum. "I almost thought you had forgotten me."

All my apprehension, and all I'd meant to say to him, is washed away. Replaced by a single endless shiver, strong enough that I feel it over my tongue, my teeth, down the sides of my ribs.

"No. I didn't forget you."

"My little Violet, lost in the forest." He holds out his own hands to me, the candlelight dancing across his opalescent claws. Warmth throbs at my palms, like a faint, far-off heartbeat.

"Our bargain changed Arien. *You* changed Arien." Memories nettle at me, all we faced after the Vair Woods. "And at the ritual, I asked you to save him, but instead you hurt him."

"I had to hurt him in order to save him. My help always comes with a price. What is it they say . . . *Once saved from death?* It leaves a mark, that brush with death. Even I can't undo that." He laughs coldly. "A blackened lake, a poisoned magic, a wound, a curse . . . a girl who can speak to a god."

"Is that why I can see you now?"

"Yes," he says. "We are connected. We always have been, since that midnight in the woods."

I look at his beautiful, inhuman face, and the wrongness of it fills me with a bitten-back panic. *You shouldn't do this. You shouldn't be* able *to do this.*

His features are clear to me now, but around the edges of

his expression—a blink, a smile, a furrowed brow—is something else. Something decidedly *other* is still there, beyond the pale gleam of his eyes, the curve of his smile, the sharp glint of his teeth.

He is an eternal, terrible creature. And he is connected to me.

It's confirmation of what I already guessed. But to hear him speak it leaves me cold. "Why me? Of all those you've saved or bargained with, why me?"

"You were so brave when you faced me. You gave up your magic so willingly to save your brother. I suspect if I'd asked your life in exchange for his, you'd have given that, too." He touches the tips of his claws against his chin, smiling. "It made an impression, your selflessness. Your magic warmed me for a long while."

"What about all those times when I was hurt and scared and alone? If we're so *connected*, where were you then? Why did you only seek me out now?"

The Lord Under narrows the distance between us slightly. His smile is still there, still sharp and hard. For just a beat, I remember the feel of his hand on mine. How he was gentle as he led me through the woods.

"I couldn't, until now," he explains. "I've a strength here, at Lakesedge. All the lords of this estate have known me. Some have loved me, some have feared me, and every candle they've lit at the altar, every observance they've made has tended me well. When you arrived here, I was able to reach you in a way I could not before."

"If that's true, then why didn't you help Rowan when he

called on you? He's been just as close to the world Below as I have. Closer. He's lit the candles and made observance. He's *tended* you with his fear."

"I needed him in a different way than I need you."

"What do you mean?"

His eyes narrow at me impatiently. "What is it you want, Violeta? Why did you decide to finally summon me?"

"I—You told me once that I could mend the Corruption. I came to ask you how."

"No." He moves closer toward me. Another wash of water trickles down from the walls. "No, that's not what you *want*."

Want. It pulls at me, that word. My eyes flutter closed. I picture myself and Arien before the night in the woods, when we had our family, when we were *home*. I don't want to go back, but I want to feel that way again. Loved and warm and safe.

"I want the power you showed me." Each word to him feels like a risk. The truth is a weight in my chest, heavy as stone. "I want enough power to keep everyone safe."

"You have a soft heart, my Violet in the woods."

"Better a soft heart than no heart at all."

He smiles unkindly, not at all wounded by my words. "You want power. So do I. And there has been so much power in the fear and hurt and blood that Rowan Sylvanan has given me."

I stare at him, numbed by horror. He's a thing cleaved into halves. The relentless, cold creature who delights in cruelty and pain, who feeds on it. And the creature who held my hand, who cradled Arien tenderly in his arms as he showed us the way out of the dark.

"So if you want to hurt Rowan, then why did you offer to help me mend the Corruption?"

"Because," he says simply, "I want it gone."

"But you *made* it. Why can't you just unmake it?"

"*I* made it?" He gives me a hard, searching look. "Has Rowan not told you the truth yet?"

"He told me everything, including what you did to him. But it's *your* magic. *Your* darkness. You could call it back."

"It was my magic, once. The Corruption began as a mark—the blackened lake—left from when I saved Rowan from the world Below. But *he* was the one who fed it blood and desperation. It's changed, gone beyond my control. And his tithes of blood and hurt and fear are the only thing holding it back. For now."

"You mean if he dies—"

"As things stand, it's not a case of *if,* Violeta, but *when.*"

"When—" My voice catches. I can hardly say these terrible words. "When Rowan dies, the Corruption won't be gone?"

"No. It will continue to spread, and it will consume your world."

I put my hand against my mouth. A whole world like the blighted orchard near Greymere, or the grove in the wayside forest. Trees burned, the fields turned to ash, the air laced with wrongness. It's too immense for me to even comprehend, because at the center of it all lies the horrible fact that Rowan will be gone. That his ruin will only lead to more destruction.

"It will consume your world. And it will—" He hesitates, then goes on. "It will destroy *my* world, too."

A startled sound comes from me, not quite a laugh. "The Corruption is in the world Below?"

"Yes. So you see, I want it mended as much as you."

"In that case, maybe you shouldn't have murdered a family because a child broke a promise." I know I shouldn't fight him like this, but I can't hold back my anger. "You're the one who took it too far. So you should be the one to stop it."

When I'm met with silence, I realize I've grown used to my arguments with Rowan, that I've almost come to enjoy the swift exchange of words, our matched tempers. In contrast, the Lord Under is immovable. I wonder, for a breath, what I'd have to do to stir him to anger. If it would even be possible. I shake my head. *Why would I want to?*

"If I could stop it on my own, I would. I need your help, Violeta. You have magic, and you can see me as no other can, outside the borders of death. I can't ask this of any other alchemist. Not your friend, not your brother."

"No, you can't." I'd never let him go to Clover or Arien, draw them into the dark with his whispers and promises. "If you want help, then I will be the one to give it to you."

"Yes." He lifts his hand, and I go still, but his fingers pause over my cheek. The air stirs, cold, on my skin. "It has to be you. I need *you*."

"You need me," I repeat. In the shadows, with the candlelit altar and the smell of ash in the air, my words sound like a litany. "You need me."

It terrifies me, this truth, but buried beneath my fear is the glimmer of another, more hideous emotion. *We are connected.*

There's power in this. A wilder, more dangerous power than any magic.

"I do." The water rises and ripples, a blackened wave rushing across the floor. The room seems to fade as the Lord Under glows brighter. White as the moon. White as bones. "And you need me. You want power."

"I just want to keep everyone safe."

"And what do you think power is?" With a smile, the Lord Under holds out his hand, palm upturned. Magic sparks in my chest. It sings through me. The full force of what I could have. What I *will* have. My whole body hums and burns. "You feel it, Violeta."

I nod, overcome, and watch the light dance across my palms. The air *glows*. It reminds me—unsettlingly—of how my magic stirred that day when Rowan touched my hand.

"I'll grant you this power to use at the ritual, on the next full moon. You'll be able to cast the spell to mend the Corruption. Alone. Everyone will be safe."

"That only gives me a single night."

"That's all you'll need. Unless you desire more?" He grins, and I see the glint of too many teeth. There's a hunger to him, the same dark eagerness that I've felt from the Corruption.

"No. One night will serve." It's such a short time to wield this power, but if I can cast the spell on the next full moon, it will be enough.

"Then it's done," he says. "All you have to do is tell me what you will give up in exchange."

I look at him, startled by the sting of betrayal. A small,

foolish part of me thought he would give this to me freely, because we're connected, because I am special to him, because he just told me how much he needs me.

But I know, have always known, his help comes with a price. "What would you want from me?"

He laughs. "Do you really want me to set the terms? Go ahead. Promise that you'll give me *anything*."

"No," I say quickly. "I'll choose."

"Go on, then." His eyes flick to the altar. "I'll want more than blood and fruit."

I hesitate. What *can* I give him? As I search for my answer, he reaches for me, claws scraping past my cheek. My breath catches. I falter back, but he moves forward. The edge of the chaise hits the back of my knees. I collapse onto it.

The light from my magic dances over him. I can see tiny details that I missed before. The branches that wreathe his head are woven with strands of lake grass. He has delicate eyelashes, like a fringe of lichen over stone.

If he can speak to me now, really speak to me, instead of whispers in the dark, will he be able to touch me, too?

I force myself to meet his gaze. "I'm not afraid of you."

"A pity. I like your fear. It's very sweet." He smiles as he runs his tongue over the points of his teeth. His hand hovers just beside my jaw. "Now tell me your offer."

I tip back my face for one desperate moment. I feel like I'm at the lake's edge, the water before me—deep and dark and endless. With one word, I'll plunge beneath the surface.

When I speak, my voice is rough. "I need more time to decide."

His hand slips past me, only a stir of air, and my breath comes loose. He can't touch me.

Then the power that flooded me only moments ago turns dim. Back to the faint, small remnants that I had before. With the strength gone, I feel hollow. My heart gives a single, desperate thump against my ribs.

There's a sharpness in the Lord Under's eyes. He goes over toward the altar. Touches the pomegranate. The tips of his claws pass right through the fruit, but the inside turns black, the smooth skin charred.

"So. You want more time." He licks the juice from the edge of his thumb. "You may have until the night before the next full moon. Do you think we can come to an arrangement by then?"

I can't do this. And yet the answer that sticks against my tongue is a desperate *yes*. I swallow it back. Hardly even dare to think it. "I do."

"Very well." His eyes go to my hand, still smeared with blood. "Let me see your cut."

Shakily, I stretch out my hand to him. His claws scrape through the air above my bloodied palm. A cold shiver prickles over my skin. He makes a pleased sound as the wound closes into a dark crescent, then he touches his mouth. I look away quickly as I hear him swallow. I don't want to see it—the stains of my blood across his sharp teeth.

"Goodbye for now, Violeta." His mouth tilts into a smile that doesn't reach his eyes. "I hope Rowan will have enough strength to keep the Corruption quieted while you make up your mind."

The shadows around him start to clear from black to gray. His gaze is fixed to mine as a shaft of sun cuts through him. He hangs for a moment, suspended at the center of the paling dark.

His eyes are the last thing to fade. Hard as polished stones.

Chapter Eighteen

I crouch by the stove, the wood box pulled up close beside me. One by one, I feed pieces of kindling into the fire. They light slowly. Handfuls of smoke curl out before the flames lick up.

The new fire dances. I build it higher with more wood until there's a bank of orange coals and the air shimmers with warmth. I feel the glow of the firelight. I see the flames. But inside I am as endlessly cold as the depths of the lake.

I shut the drafts and put my hands against my face. The newly healed cut throbs. Can I really accept the help of such a creature as the Lord Under? I've made no promise to him—yet. But I can't forget how it felt, to have that power and know I could use it to end the Corruption.

The door from the hallway scrapes open. I get to my feet and brush the dust and ashes from my skirts. Rowan watches me from across the room. Light from the window streams in and turns him to amber and gold, his hair, his eyes, his skin. As always, his dark cloth shirt is without a single crease, and the firelight gleams over his polished boots. There's almost no sign of him as he was last night. Almost none, except for the way he smiles, hesitant and shy.

Then his eyes go to the table, where I've left the knife beside the basket of fruit. A wary confusion darkens his expression. The air still smells of wax and smoke, carried from the blown-out candles in the parlor.

He goes over and picks up the knife, cautiously running his finger along the side of the blade, which is still stained with ruby juice and the even deeper red of my blood. "Violeta Graceling. What have you done?"

I tuck my hand into my pocket, and for a brief moment, I think I'll tell him another lie. But I know I can't hide from this anymore. I show him the black crescent on my skin, delicate and beautiful and sinister.

"I've done something very foolish." The truth is inescapable, bitter. "I summoned the Lord Under."

He drops the knife back onto the table with a thud. He crosses the room and takes hold of my shoulders and grips tight. His expression is all raw betrayal.

"Tell me." His hands, circling my arms, have begun to tremble. His eyes are wide, full of desperate fear. "Tell me *exactly* what you mean."

I tell him everything. How the Lord Under spoke to me. How he saved Arien during the failed ritual. How I cut the fruit and myself to summon him. How he offered me the power to mend the Corruption. Me, alone.

"Leta, how could you keep such a secret?" Rowan stares at me as if he can puzzle the answer from my face. "Even after we—" His cheeks flush and he looks away. "You stayed with me when I gave my tithe to the Corruption. I told you about my family and all the terrible things I've done. Even after that, you didn't trust me enough to say anything?"

"I had to do this alone. It was the only way."

His head slumps forward and he sighs, frustrated. "How could you risk yourself like this?"

Guilt prickles at me, but I don't relent. "You've expected Arien and Clover to risk themselves for you. This is no different."

"It's completely different."

"No, it isn't. What would you have done, that day in Greymere, if it had been me you saw with magic, instead of Arien?"

He tries to turn away. I reach out, knot my fingers into his shirt, and pull him closer. "Tell me. If I'd had the magic you needed, what would you have done?"

Our eyes meet, and he tenses. I see him as he was when we first met. The Monster of Lakesedge who circled me with feral, watchful hunger in his eyes.

"I'd have gone to your cottage. I'd have asked you to come with me."

"You'd have offered to teach me to be an alchemist."

"Yes."

"You'd have threatened me."

"Yes." Darkness starts to spread in lines under his skin. At his throat, more slivers of poison shift alongside the scars, then slowly fade into shadow. "I'd have done whatever it took to have your help. But—" He touches my palm, following the curve of the crescent mark. "I'd never have asked *this*."

I curl my hand closed around his fingers. The mark on my palm gives a steady pulse. "You've not asked me to do anything. It was my choice to summon the Lord Under. And if I do work with him, that will be my choice, too."

"Leta, please." His voice lowers, rough and hurt. "Whatever price he'll ask of you will be too much. He'll take you apart, use you up until there's nothing left."

"He might. But he also needs me." I can't find how to put it into words: how I feel about the Lord Under, the fact that I alone was the one he sought out. That we're connected. "He needs me just as much as I need him."

"I know you want to protect Arien, but—"

"I want to protect *everyone*."

"Everyone, but what about you?" Gently, Rowan takes my face between his hands. He bends to me, until his forehead touches mine. "You fight so hard to keep everyone safe. But who is going to watch over you, when you go into the dark?"

The day when the Lord Under first asked for my help, I stood alone and afraid as the darkness overwhelmed me. For the first time, I imagine how it might feel to stare into the shadows with someone at my side.

I look up at Rowan. He's flushed from the heat of the kitchen

236

and the banked-up stove. I think of how undone he was when I went to his room. His bare skin. His tangled hair. The sparks of magic that scattered as he kissed the sigil on my wrist.

I've hated him. I've lied to him. I've seen him bled and wounded. I've bandaged those same wounds. I've heard truths from him that he's never told another person. And right now all I can think about is the two of us in my garden. The world turned to fire by crimson sunset. My skirts tucked back and my scars laid bare. His hands on my skin.

I slip my hand beneath his sleeve and touch the bandages I tied there last night. Then I reach up and run my fingers over the hollow of his throat.

"Rowan, I care for you. More than I've ever cared for anyone, except for Arien." The words are too raw, too tender, to speak louder than a whisper. "I don't want you to be hurt."

He reaches past me, enclosing me. I move back until I'm against the door with his arms braced on either side of me. He shoves the door, slams it all the way shut. We both jump—he's startled by his own action. Then he slides his hand into my hair. His fingers press into the nape of my neck. He moves slowly, and I realize he's giving me a chance to stop him if I don't want this.

But this is *all* I want.

I put my hands against the door, shift forward onto my tiptoes, and close the final distance between us. Rowan's breath catches in a strangled growl as my lips brush his. My first ever kiss. It's all so unexpected. How clumsy I feel, the rasp of his mouth on mine, the heat that unwinds all through me when he kisses me back.

At first, he's hesitant and soft, like he still wants to leave me space to change my mind. But at this moment, I don't want softness. I want fierceness and fire and incandescent surrender.

I catch hold of him, pull him toward me. He groans against my mouth and his fingers tighten and tangle through my hair. I kiss him more deeply, my tongue sweeping his. He tastes of burnt sugar and spiced tea. I can feel the place where the scars cross the edge of his mouth. Rough, it feels rough, and wonderful.

I let my head fall back, baring my throat. He kisses my neck. His teeth scrape sharply over my pulse. A tattered sound escapes me, and magic blossoms from my hands, heated and golden.

I'm overcome with a rush of desire that blisters, molten, through my whole body. We're pressed together. Heart to heart, hip to hip. His hand strokes down the curve of my waist, then lower. Through the thin gossamer fabric of my skirts, his fingers grip my thigh. He's so warm that it feels like he's touching my bare skin. I gasp, the sound loud in the quiet room. He sighs out a desperate breath that feathers hotly over my skin.

I start to pull at the laces on his shirt, but he catches my hands, stopping me. His thumb fits into the scar on my palm and he sighs again, softer. He bows his head and gently kisses the mark. "Leta, please don't summon the Lord Under again. Promise me that you won't."

His expression is so full of despair that I can hardly stand it. I press my lips together, tasting heat and honey. I wish for another choice. A way out of this where no one would be hurt. I wish I could lie to him, but instead I shake my head. "I'll not make a promise I can't keep."

He lets me go. "You say you don't want me to be hurt. Well *this* hurts, Leta."

I step away from him and cross to the table, to the basket full of the fruit I gathered. I take a pomegranate and slice it open, then scoop the seeds onto my fingertips. Small and bitter, they burst like bubbles over my tongue. Juice runs through my mouth, sharply sweet.

Rowan comes over and picks up a seed with careful fingers. We stand there, on opposite sides of the table, eyes on the opened fruit. Neither of us speaks. Slowly, we eat seed after seed, hesitating each time we reach to pick another. Making sure our hands never touch.

The door opens, sending a bright gleam of sunlight across the kitchen as Clover comes inside. She has a basket of herbs cut from the small patch in the garden; wild mint, nettles, feverfew. The scent of them fills the air. Sweet and bitter and freshly green.

"Whew, it's really hot in here." She runs her sleeve across her forehead and peers at the stove. "What have you done to the fire? You know Florence hates when we mess around with it." When neither of us replies, her mouth lifts into a curious smile as she takes in our stilted silence. "Did I interrupt something?"

I scrub my sticky hands against my skirts and step back

from the table. Rowan looks everywhere in the room except at me. "We didn't touch the fire."

Clover pushes her glasses up the bridge of her nose as she peers at him. "Are you sure? You look a little . . . overheated." She touches his forehead, then reaches to check his pulse. Her mouth twitches, as though she's trying very hard not to laugh. "Do you want some feverfew? I've picked plenty."

"It's nothing," he says tightly. "I'm fine."

As he pushes her hand away, his sleeve falls back. When Clover catches sight of the bandage, her face grows serious, and she reaches toward his arm. "May I see?"

"No, you may not."

"Clover, don't you want to put those herbs into the stillroom before they wilt?" I walk over and take the kettle down, fill it with water, and set it onto the stove with a loud clatter. "Arien is probably awake now. I'll make him some tea."

"Oh yes, the stillroom." She gives us both a pointed smile. "I'll leave the two of you alone."

She takes the basket into the small space beside the kitchen where she keeps her alchemy supplies. Through the half-closed door, I hear the rustle and scrape as she moves around. The snip of her scissors as she cuts twine to string up the fresh herbs. The kettle begins to hum, the water quickly boiled from the too-hot stove. I wrap a cloth around my hand and lift it away from the heat.

Clover comes back with a jar of dried flowers and a small handful of mint and feverfew. She takes down a tray and an enamelware cup, then fills the teapot with leaves and hot water and sifts in a spoonful of flowers.

"Don't forget," she says to Rowan, "you're supposed to go to the village later. Keeper Harkness wants to talk with you about the Summersend bonfire."

"Oh, *wonderful*." He rubs his forehead, scowling. "Exactly what I wanted to do today."

At the word—*Summersend*—I go still. The first night of Summersend is the time when the border between the worlds Above and Below is said to be the thinnest. Each village lights a bonfire, and everyone gathers to chant the litany as the wood and bundled greenery burns down to ashes.

It always filled me with equal parts fear and wonder. Some of the night was like a beautiful dream. The smell of woodsmoke and spiced cider, Arien and me amid the crowd with flowers worn in our hair, our hands sticky from marzipan cakes. But the crackle and spark of flames against the sky always drew out memories of an older, crueler fire I wanted to forget. Arien's dreams were always the worst on those nights.

And now Summersend carries a new kind of weight. The next full moon is the week after the bonfire.

"Do you have a white dress?" Clover asks me. I nod and she smiles, pleased. "I'll help you with the embroidery. And we can make wreaths!"

"We are not going," Rowan says.

"*You* have to go, since you're the lord. And it will be nice for all of us to do something fun." She twists the teapot back and forth to stir the leaves. Steam drifts from the spout. "Violeta, we can take this up to Arien now."

She sets the pot onto the tray beside the cup, while I fetch the jar of honey and a small wooden spoon. I follow her out of the room with everything balanced carefully. Rowan stays behind in the kitchen, but as I leave, he calls quietly after me. "Please, Leta, just . . . think on it, before you do anything else."

I close the door between us without replying. As Clover and I walk up the stairs, she arches a brow and looks meaningfully back toward the kitchen. "Didn't touch the fire, hm?"

I let out a breath, grateful for the cool air in the hallway, how it washes over me in place of the kitchen stove heat. "It's . . . complicated."

She snorts back a laugh. "Oh, I'm sure it is."

I want so much to join in her good-natured teasing, but the mark on my palm has begun to ache. My whole hand feels painfully numb, like frost has been stitched beneath my skin. It's an unavoidable reminder of what I've done, what I'm going to do.

Arien's room is filled with early sunlight, the window open to a stretch of cloudless sky. He's curled on his side, still half-asleep. Florence sits beside the bed, a spill of whitework embroidery on her lap. They both look up at us as we enter.

I wish I could preserve this moment, just stand here in the sunlit room and hold all my secrets close. I take a deep breath, searching for the right words to tell them everything. "I need to talk to you about the next ritual."

Arien sits up delicately, mindful of his arms, and reaches

242

for the tray with his bandaged hands. The confusion in his eyes shifts to wariness as he takes in my expression. "Leta, what's wrong?"

I lower myself onto the edge of the bed, careful not to tip the tray. "First, I have to explain what really happened in the Vair Woods."

He lifts the pot and pours tea into his cup. "You already told me about that."

"Not the whole truth. I did give up my magic. But it wasn't for myself, Arien. It was for you."

He clenches the honey jar in his hands, the motion so similar to the one he's made, repeatedly, during practice for the ritual. He puts it down, unopened. "You gave the Lord Under your magic to save me?"

I nod. "That's why your magic has changed. He told me it always leaves a mark, when he helps anyone. And that's why . . ." I swallow, steadying myself, then go on. "That's why you were hurt at the ritual. I asked him to save you then, too."

"You *asked* him?" Florence cuts in. She draws her fingers across her chest, her eyes widening. "Violeta, don't you realize how dangerous that was?"

"What else was she supposed to do, let Arien be eaten by those creatures?" Clover pulls restlessly at her braid, looking queasy. "No wonder your wounds were so hard to mend."

"Because I was hurt by the same magic that made the Corruption." Arien stares down at his hands, at the blackened tips of his fingers that show past the bandages. Then he turns back to me, his brow creased into a frown. "Why didn't you tell me sooner? And what does all this have to do with the next ritual?"

I hold out my hand and show him the new scar.

"Leta." Arien pales. "Leta, you didn't—"

"The Lord Under has offered me the power to mend the Corruption. Alone, on the next full moon."

"But only the dead can see him." He turns rapidly to Florence, then Clover, for confirmation. They both look as confused and shocked as Arien does. "You can speak to him, even now?"

"Not *right* now." I try to laugh, but his stricken expression silences me. "I summoned him, Arien. I cut my hand and gave him my blood, and I summoned him."

"Why would you do such a terrible thing?"

"Because I don't want you to be hurt ever again! Because the Corruption will destroy Rowan—and everything else, too—if we don't mend it!"

"So, it's better that you've done this?" He shoves the tray onto the bedside table. Tea splashes out of the cup, and the wooden honey spoon falls to the floor. "You didn't think to tell any of us about this connection before you called on him? You've seen what he can do." He thrusts his hands toward me angrily, showing me the bandages and his blackened fingers. "But you still went to him for help."

"I'm sorry. I wanted to tell you, I just—"

"You just wanted to do everything on your own, the way you always do." He draws up his knees and turns his eyes to the window. "Get out of my room, Leta."

"Arien." I try to touch him, but he pushes me away.

"Leave me alone."

Florence gets up slowly and comes to put her arm around my shoulders. "You must know you can't save anyone by working with the Lord Under. To even consider this is reckless."

She and Clover look at me the same way—desperate and concerned. Fearful. But I don't want them to be afraid. Like they think I'm not capable of this. Like they think I'll fail.

I shrug out from beneath her arm. "Everything we've been doing is reckless. Why is it suddenly a problem now that *I'm* the one with a solution?"

I go out across the hall and into my room, slamming the door behind me. I sit down on the floor, in the corner where I first heard the Lord Under's voice, and lean back to rest my head against the wall. I start to cry, hot, angry tears. There's a part of me that wants to apologize to Arien, to tell him we can find another way. But I don't.

This is my choice. To risk myself, to burn myself down, to face the darkness so they will all be safe.

Chapter Nineteen

Summersend arrives with a daylight moon, a neat, silvered shape in the still-bright sky. In my room, Clover helps me fasten the back of my dress. She stitched it for me, overworking the embroidered pattern with a new design. Tiny stars—white over white—endless, pale constellations. When she finishes the last button, she smiles at me, our faces reflected together in the mirror glass.

Distantly, I remember my mother dressing up for the bonfire, how I watched my father help her. He tied the sash at her waist, then leaned in to kiss her as she squirmed away, laughing. I touch my hair, then run my fingers lightly over the curve of my cheeks. Her hair was darker than mine, and straight, but sometimes when the light tilts against my face a certain way, I can see her eyes, the way her mouth went crooked when she smiled.

"There. You're perfect." Clover brushes her hands over my skirts, tidying them. "You know, the whole house has felt so different, so lived in, since you and Arien came here."

I turn to look around the room. The window is open, the lace curtains tied back. My collection of polished stones is on the mantel, next to a vase of wildflowers. The little icon Arien painted for me is propped beside my bed. "It certainly looks different."

Clover picks up the wreath I wove from the vines that grow near my garden. Carefully, she sets it on my unbound hair. She wears a similar one, and her hair, without the braid, falls down her back in golden-brown waves.

"Do you think Thea will be at the bonfire tonight?" she asks airily.

"Of course she will. Isn't her father the keeper?" I raise my brows at her, grinning. "You know, if you end up together in the bonfire line, you'll get to hold her hand."

"Violeta, you're such a schemer." Clover keeps her eyes fixed to the mirror, adjusting the wreath. A reluctant smile spreads over her face. "I like her. I really like her. But how can I ask anything from her, when I spend all my time here, doing this?"

She holds her arms wide, displaying the sigils on them.

"It might work in your favor. How many other girls will she meet who can cast magic and live beside a poisoned lake?"

"Oh?" She arches a brow at me. "Is that why you like Rowan so much?"

I laugh, but my cheeks feel hot. "I mean, he made such a good impression with all that scowling and threatening."

"You know what he called you when you first arrived?" Clover deepens her voice into an eerily accurate imitation of Rowan. "*That wretched little pest.* But he blushed whenever he said it."

"Truly what I've always dreamed of—a boy who blushes as he insults me."

"I'm glad you didn't run away that night after the first ritual." Clover puts her arm around my waist as her face settles into seriousness. "I'm glad you and Arien decided to stay here."

"I am, too."

"Despite the fact that there's a death god lurking around?"

"Despite everything," I say, smiling. She rests her chin against my shoulder for a breath. Then she reaches into her pocket, her face suddenly turned shy, and draws out a small, wrapped parcel. "Here. I made this for you."

I unfold the paper carefully. It's a ribboned bracelet, embroidered with leaves and tiny violet flowers. I run my fingers over the intricate pattern of her clever stitches. "Oh, Clover, it's beautiful."

"Don't cry," she says quickly. "Or I'll cry, too."

I hold out my wrist so she can tie it for me. "Thank you."

She picks up a lantern and lights it with a flare of magic, then takes my hand. Together, we go out of my room and down the stairs.

My skirts spill around me, a cascade of lace. My white dress is made of translucent layers that shift color in the light: cream, silver, pearl. We cross the entrance hall, then step out onto the drive. Arien is already outside. He wears a new shirt, the white linen decorated with a pattern of branches that curve sharply over his shoulders. He has a wreath set lopsidedly over his curls. He steps back to let us pass but avoids my eyes. He doesn't smile.

We've hardly spoken since the day I told him about my connection to the Lord Under. He and Clover have worked endlessly over the past few weeks, while Rowan has been in the village to prepare for the fire. They've filled countless notebooks with sigils and walked back and forth along the shore of the lake. Tried and failed and tried again to find another way—any way—that they can cast a different spell that will mend the Corruption at the next ritual.

I've helped by adding my own, faint magic to Arien's shadows when he practices one of the new spells. I've watched them grow tired and cross and more hopeless. And all the time, I've silently weighed and measured everything I have, wondering what I might offer to the Lord Under in exchange for his help.

Now, beside Arien in the drive with the ivy-wrapped house behind us, my chest aches with a heavy, uneasy feeling. The space between us feels like a wound that can't heal over.

"You both look perfect," Clover says. She smiles at me, then turns to adjust Arien's collar. "Look at you. You're like a prince from one of Violeta's stories."

She sets her lantern carefully onto the seat of the wagon that waits in the drive. Florence and Rowan already walked to the village earlier, to help with the preparations. Clover climbs into the wagon and takes the reins. The wagon bed is piled with branches and tangles of greenery that I've cut from the garden:

our contribution for the bonfire. The horses—the same ones we rode here, from our cottage—have more of the starry flowers braided into their manes.

I step toward the wagon. Arien catches hold of my arm and looks up at Clover. "You go ahead," he tells her. "Leta and I will walk."

She raises a brow. "Really?" Realization crosses her face as she looks between us. "Oh. Yes, of course."

She hums to the horses, and they start to trot. Arien and I watch the wagon grow smaller as it follows the drive away from the house. Once it is out of sight, we set off.

The now-empty house behind us feels hollowed out, with only a single lantern lit in the frontmost window. All around us, the tall, pale trees hush and whisper as the hot evening air stirs their leaves.

With all that's happened since our arrival, this will be the first time we've left the estate. We walk through the front garden, past where I took Arien after the first ritual. When I wanted to leave, and Arien insisted we stay. So much has changed since that night, and yet so much is the same. I'm still fighting to keep him safe.

We pass beneath the iron gateway, and the drive gives way to a path that widens slowly to a well-worn road. The land slopes upward, and the forest that surrounds the estate thins to fields: almond groves and apple orchards. We walk through stripes of faded shadow and pastel sunset, and I think of how beautiful it will look in Harvestfall, when the leaves turn to crimson.

Arien walks beside me. Neither of us speaks for a long time. Everything between us feels so tangled, but I don't know how to unknot it.

Finally, I reach out and take his hand. "Arien, I'm sorry."

"Sorry for what, exactly?" His fingers tighten around mine. He keeps his eyes fixed on the road. "The lies you told? The secrets you kept?"

"It does sound like a lot, when you put it like that." I try to smile, but he still won't look at me. "Yes, for the lies and for the secrets. I'm sorry for everything."

He huffs out a frustrated breath. "I know what you want to do. You *want* to make a bargain with the Lord Under."

"I want to make sure no one else will be hurt. And if he can help me, then—"

"You and Rowan are both so determined to throw your lives away. Look at what he's done, trying to fight the Corruption on his own. He's poisoned himself. He's made himself into a monster. And you—" Roughly, he turns my hand palm up. Bares the crescent mark on my skin. "You did *this*."

I snatch back my hand. "What else was I supposed to do?"

"You didn't even *think*, Leta. You act like my only choice is to stay back, that it doesn't matter if you're hurt because I'll be safe." He bites his lip. I can tell he's trying not to cry. "You're my sister. I want you to be safe, too."

"He's helped me before." I try not to look at Arien's hands. His arms. The thin, pale scars left from when Clover mended him are as delicate as embroidery. "He saved you."

"*You* saved me." Arien's mouth curves into a sad smile.

"What you did in the woods—what you asked the Lord Under, and how it changed me—I don't blame you, Leta. But this is different. He'll want more than your magic for this. You know that."

"No, he won't take my magic since he needs me to use it." I run my hand over my arm, trace the outlines of the marks on my skin. "Although . . . he might change his mind once he knows I draw messy sigils."

"You do realize you're not at all funny."

"Maybe he'll want my sense of humor. Then you won't have to listen to my jokes anymore."

"*Leta.*" Arien grabs hold of my hand again. "He took Rowan's whole family. What do you have to offer that can equal that?"

I glance back over my shoulder, to where the road stretches behind us. We've gone far from the estate now. All around us are only trees and fields and the darkening sky. I think again of what Arien said after the first failed ritual. When I tried to make him leave, and he insisted that we stay. When he showed me the sigil on his wrist and told me, *I couldn't do anything to help you before, but now I can.*

At the time, I hadn't understood how or why he'd want to use his magic in such a dangerous way. But now I've gotten that same chance. A way to make up for all the time I've spent powerless.

"I want to help." My voice goes out soft into the trees. "I want to do this."

Arien scrubs his wrist across his face, and his eyes fill with tears. "At least give us some time before you summon him again. We can still figure out another way. Please, just tell me you won't."

"I won't." I wrap my arms around him. The other words hang unspoken between us. *Not yet.* "I'm sorry."

"I'm still so mad at you." He takes a deep, unsteady breath to swallow back his tears. "Why do you have to be so—"

"Terrible, awful, the most foolish sister ever?" I hold Arien tighter and realize he's grown since we came to the estate. "Hey," I mutter against his chest. "Who said you were allowed to get so tall?"

I reach up and run my hand through his hair, knocking the wreath askew as I mess up his curls. He shoves me away, laughing. I trip over my feet, and he catches me before I can fall. I lean against him and laugh, too.

Things don't feel entirely mended between us, but they're a little softer. By the time we reach the village, the sun has set. The cottages around the square are black silhouettes, their windows lit by reflected lamplight. It looks much the same as when we passed through on our way to Lakesedge. Thatch-roofed cottages, a grove of trees, the altar at one side. The unlit bonfire is at the center of the square, the pile of branches and flowers and leaves circled by granite stones.

Everyone is dressed in white, hair unbound and wreathed with leaves or flowers. The crowd is a hum of voices—chatter, laughter, calls of greeting. It's the first time in months that we've been around so many people. It's dizzying to be among the noise of the crowd, after all the silence of the estate. My skin is warmer. My heart beats faster.

Arien and I pause beside the row of tables that border the square. They're laden with food. Marzipan cakes shaped like petals. Almond crescents dusted with frost-pale sugar. Enamelware pitchers of cider, spiced with peppercorn and cinnamon.

I take a cup of cider. Anise flowers float on the surface like fragrant stars. I sip. The sweetness of it spreads through me until the air wavers a little. I blink as the light shimmers. Then I see Rowan, half-hidden in the shadows beside the altar.

He looks so much like he did that day in our cottage. He's dressed all in black, with the hood of his cloak pulled low over his face. His gloved hands are clenched at his sides, and his eyes are fixed on the ground.

Then he looks up. Our eyes meet. He pushes back the hood of his cloak in an abrupt gesture. His hair is unadorned, the top half tied back into a knot. Light from the lanterns outlines him in gold. His mouth parts, as though he means to speak, but he only stares at me, wordless, as Arien and I move toward him.

"Leta." His voice goes soft. "You—you look—"

I reach and tuck back a strand of his hair that's come loose. "You forgot your wreath. Want me to make one for you? I can get some vines from the bonfire before it's alight."

"No."

"Don't think about it too hard," I tease. "You could at least say *No, thank you*."

His mouth tilts into a begrudging smile. He puts his hand lightly on my waist, drawing me closer, but then his face turns wary as he looks out into the crowd.

Florence walks toward us, followed by someone else—a tall, broad-shouldered man. After a few moments I realize I recognize him from Greymere. Keeper Harkness is even more serious than he was on the tithe day. He carries a basket of bundled pine-stem torches, each tied neatly at the end with twine, and passes them out as he moves through the square.

Thea and Clover trail behind, carrying another basket between themselves. In her long, pale dress, Thea is as beautiful as a crescent moon. Her curled black hair is crowned with summer roses, and her skirts are embroidered with a pattern of bellflowers. She and Clover both look shy and awkward, like they can't think of what to say to each other.

Keeper Harkness reaches us, and sets his basket down near the altar. He dips his fingers into the salt beneath the icon, then drops a handful of petals across the wooden shelf. He glances at Rowan. "Lord Sylvanan. We're almost ready."

Rowan nods, but he doesn't speak. Thea hands Arien a torch, then gives one to me with a confused, pleased smile. "Oh! I know you both from the tithe day! Whatever are you doing *here*?"

"They're guests at the estate." Clover adjusts her glasses and shakes back her hair. She gives Thea a proud look. "Arien and Violeta are my students."

"You're *all* alchemists?" Thea raises her eyebrows. She looks as though she can't quite decide if she's excited, or afraid. She bites her lip as her eyes drift toward Arien's gloved hands. "Why aren't you in the Maylands?"

"This is a special assignment." I lean close and whisper

conspiratorially, "Lord Sylvanan is going to use me for his next blood sacrifice."

Thea lets out a startled laugh and steps back. She looks warily at Rowan before she slips into the crowd. He glares at me murderously.

Florence gives us both a *look*. "Shall we begin?"

"Please, before Leta says another word and we're all chased out of here with pitchforks." Rowan pulls at the tie that fastens his hair, tightening the knot. Then he picks up a torch from the basket and steps forward.

Everyone goes still, and a nervous current ripples through the crowd. It's as though they had almost forgotten about him while he was in the shadows beside the altar. But now he's stepped out into the light.

The villagers here aren't as panicked as people were in Greymere. But the more I look around, the more I see signs of their fear. Garlands of rosemary and sage are strung protectively over windows, and there are scatters of salt across all the doorways. Every now and then, someone will raise their hands to their chest and draw their fingers across their heart.

The way they watch him, it's the same way I looked at him, once. It's strange now to see the fear I felt reflected on all those other faces.

And Rowan looks every part the monster they believe him to be.

He notes their fear, and he doesn't flinch from it. He meets it unrelentingly with a hard, cold stare. The scars on his brow and jaw and throat seem to glow, crimson and raised. And every now and then, so swift it could *almost* be a flicker of lamplight, shadows shift beneath his skin. Threads of darkness unfurl then soften back to faint, blurred marks. The monster, the boy, the monster.

I take hold of his hand. He tenses, but after a breath, his fingers weave through mine. I run my thumb across his gloved palm.

He leans down to murmur to me, his voice low. "Do you think to hold my hand and show them all they shouldn't be afraid of me?"

"Maybe." I rise up on tiptoe, so I can murmur back. "Maybe I just want to be the girl who held the hand of a monster."

He gives me a faint smile. He takes a torch and sets it to the altar candles. It springs alight with the sharp scent of pine. Then he moves out into the square. He doesn't let go of my hand, so I follow him.

Everyone draws back as we come toward them, the crowd parting into halves. Rowan strides down the path left at the center. His cloak is a spill of ink, his gaze is remote, almost otherworldly. I walk beside him, the skirts of my gemstone dress rustling around me. I feel like a faerie creature from one of my books. *Violet in the woods.* A tangle of whispers follows us, a sound that's half fear, half wonder.

Once we've reached the fire, there's a moment of stillness before everyone begins to move, until they've formed a single line that spirals around the granite stones. Rowan holds out his torch to me. I feel the heat of the flames as he lights the bundle of pine in my hand. I turn to Arien, who smiles at me as his torch comes alight.

One by one, torch by torch, the firelight spreads. We move forward to set our torches into the pile of branches and leaves. The fire is slow at first, all smoke and acrid, new-burned greenery, then the wind catches it. Sparks weave up hungrily through the bonfire, until it shimmers and dances against the sunset sky.

The silence draws out, longer and longer, broken only by a scatter of whispers. This is the part of the bonfire where we sing the litany. In Greymere, the keeper would lead the chant. But tonight, of course, it will be Rowan. He looks back to the altar, and I feel his hand flinch. His fingers tighten against mine.

I remember what he told me, at the Midsummer observance. *I don't like to sing when people can hear me.* And now there is a whole village ready to listen.

I lean over and whisper, "Should we do a blood sacrifice instead of the chant?"

He glares at me, but before he can speak, I start to sing. There's a puzzled mutter in the crowd, and no one joins in. An embarrassed heat prickles me, because I'm used to my voice being woven into the sound of others. Alone, it rings out off-key, a note stuck somewhere between head and chest. But as I finish the first stanza, a voice beside me picks up the chant. Arien. Then Clover, then Florence.

For a breath, it's just the four of us who sing. And I'm back in the garden, at the altar beneath the jacaranda tree. When I put my hands in the earth. When I let go of my magic and my truth, and light sparked through the ground. At the memory, a stillness comes over me. The crescent at my palm throbs. I picture a full moon. My magic kindled from a faint spark to a blaze as large as the Summersend fire. Light and heat and power.

More voices join the chant. The melody is discordant at first. But voice by voice, word by word, the litany weaves together like threads made into stitches. Soon the air is alight with song. The fire is on my cheeks, and petals wreathe my hair.

When my thoughts turn back to the night our cottage burned, I don't try to push them down. Instead, I let myself remember my parents. The garden my father made with his alchemy. The firelight across our hearth. My mother's voice, low and lulling, as she sang to Arien. How it felt to fall asleep beneath my patchwork quilt to the sound of my father's stories.

My family is smoke and ash, and their souls sleep far in the world Below, but these memories inside me are vivid. They will never be gone.

I think of the magic that turns the world. I think of everyone I love, home and safe, once the Corruption is mended.

As the litany ends, the line breaks apart, and the crowd drifts out into the square. Arien catches hold of my hand and pulls me toward the table of sweets. I turn to look for Rowan, but he's already gone back to the shadows beside the altar. Clover slips her arm around my waist. Thea is beside her, and she eyes me warily, as though she can't decide if she wants to move closer or run away. "You're . . . different, from when I saw you in Greymere."

"Different?" I brush my hand over my skirts and laugh. "I have nicer clothes now, I guess."

Clover shakes her head at the both of us. She looks at Thea and hesitates, then holds out her hand. "Come on, let's go before your father sees us and starts worrying you'll be Rowan's next victim."

Thea takes Clover's hand and goes with her, wide eyed. Arien and I follow, laughing. The night passes in a rush of sugar and firelight, beneath a sky filled with handfuls of stars. Bonfire smoke laces the air, turns the world to a haze.

I'm tired and breathless, and everything feels like a dream. I find myself alone in the crowd. Clover and Thea sit together near one of the cottages, a platter of marzipan cakes between them. Arien is curled up beside Florence, his head on her shoulder and his eyes half-closed. I go back to the altar, where Rowan stands against the trees. He steps into the light when he sees me approach. Wordlessly, he takes my hand and leads me away from the crowd.

We walk past the fire and out of the square, into the orchard that encircles the village. We follow the rows for a long while, then finally stop in a space between two tall apple trees. We let go of each other's hands and move apart. Rowan is still wrapped in his cloak, with the hood drawn down over his hair.

He picks a strand of leaves and starts to twist it through his fingers. "Thank you for singing instead of me."

"I'm glad I could help."

"I always wonder if it would be better for me to stay away." He gives the leaves a final twist then lets the strand drop. "I don't care that they whisper about me, or think I'm a monster. Really, it's better for them to fear me."

"Yes. It would be a shame to let anyone get *too* close. A terrible danger."

"Is this advice on being kind to strangers from the prickliest creature I know?" He arches a brow at me. "Perhaps you can skip the jokes about blood sacrifices next time."

"You have to admit it was a little funny."

He smiles faintly, then looks down as his expression turns serious again. "The least I can do is try to be a half-decent lord in my father's name. Even if they hate me or fear me. If I give up, then it feels like he died for nothing. A waste." He shakes his head. "I don't even know if that makes sense."

"No, it does." I run my hand over a nearby branch. The bark is rough beneath my fingers. "It's harder to stay, sometimes, even if that's the right thing."

"Yes."

"So how did you lead the chant before I was here?"

"Before?" His mouth lifts into a distant smile. "Elan led the chant. He liked to sing."

Oh. I move closer until our shoulders brush. "I hope he had a nicer voice than I do."

Rowan laughs softly. Moonlight filters between the trees and catches the lines of his face. Absently, he touches the scars that cross his jaw. "Sometimes I feel like he hasn't truly gone. I keep expecting to turn around and see him there."

"Or you hear a sound. And it's not a voice, but it almost could be." Memories of my family dance under my skin. They have their own kind of magic. I think of a garden, a cottage, stories told in the firelight. "I guess they're always *with* us, somehow. But it's not the same, is it?"

"Not the same, no. When I see you and Arien together— the way you play and tease and annoy each other—it makes me miss Elan even more."

"Hm." I squint at the branches above, then smile at him. "If you like, I could climb into one of these trees and throw apples at you. Would that help?"

"I'm not sure how I feel about your ideas of *help*." He says it lightly, but his eyes are sad, and soon the laughter is gone from his voice. "Everyone I care about has been hurt because of me. I don't want you to risk yourself because of my selfish mistakes."

"No one else will be hurt," I tell him. "I promise."

I step toward him, struck by how alone we are with the village far behind us. There's only the night sky and the quiet orchard and the scent of woodsmoke. When Rowan strokes his hand gently over my flower-threaded curls, the distance between us feels all at once too much and not enough.

His fingers trail over my cheek, down the line of my jaw. He's still wearing his gloves. He pauses, takes them off, then touches beneath my chin, tilting my face upward.

He kisses me, softly at first, then his hands find the curve of my waist, and he pulls me closer. A scatter of flowers spills down around us from my hair. "Rowan," I breathe, and he kisses his name from my mouth.

There's a wistfulness in his touch, as though he's trying to memorize each piece of this moment. Everything turns melted, slow, as his hands trace over me. Even the magic that lights my palms glimmers with an indolent warmth. I'm filled with an ache that is both painful and wonderful. It feels so good to be close to him like this. I wish we could stay here in the moonlight, among the trees, forever.

He cradles my face between his hands and presses his lips against my temple; a soft, tender motion that makes tears prickle at the corners of my eyes.

"Leta." His voice is a drift of sparks that rise into the moonlit air. "Leta, I don't want to lose you."

"You won't."

I lean my head against his chest. I can feel his heart, beating fast.

Once again I weigh and measure, wonder what I might give up to the Lord Under in exchange for one single night of power. I think of strength and magic and protection, of everything that I'd have if I made a bargain with him.

I can't do it. I know I can't accept his help. But oh, I wish I could.

Chapter Twenty

akesedge is silent when we return from the bonfire.
Arien sleeps beside me the whole ride home. I help
him stumble tiredly up to his room, my arm around his
waist, his head drowsing against my shoulder. When I reach
the top of the stairs, I look back at Rowan, who is still in the
entrance hall. "Good night."

He smiles at me. "Good night, Leta."

When I'm alone in my room, I lie on top of my quilts, still
in my bonfire dress. Petals scatter from my hair, and I breathe
in the scent of ash and pine and smoke. It's late, almost dawn,
but I can't fall asleep. When I close my eyes, all I see is the
house. How it looked when we passed beneath the iron arch
of the gateway. Wrapped with ivy, tucked between the hills,
one window aglow with lamplight, a curl of smoke from the
kitchen chimney.

Home. Lakesedge is my home. The thought rose, unbidden. And now it's taken root in me. Found a place between heart and rib. *Home.*

I want it safe. This beautiful, vine-wreathed house. My tangled, half-forgotten garden. My family. My friends. I want to protect it all.

I roll over restlessly, stretch out my hands, look down at my palms. One marked, the other plain. I have two choices, but either way I am damned. I'll be forced to watch the Corruption take everything away unless I make a terrible bargain with the lord of the dead. Maybe the only choice I have left is *how* I want the hurt to happen. My eyes drift to the corner of my room, to the place where the dark water first poured down.

"What would you ask?" My voice is a whisper, and each hesitant word feels more dangerous than the one before. As though the Lord Under might come to me, right at this moment. "How much would you want?"

A sound rustles inside the walls. I blink. A breeze blows soft through my open window. The corner darkens, for just a breath. I close my eyes. I think of his hand beside my cheek. How the air grew so cold as he moved closer to me. There's no voice, no darkness. But I already know the answer. He will take as much of me as I am willing to give. He would have me, entire.

But I don't want to be devoured.

What can I possibly offer him that will be enough, without destroying myself?

There's a knock on my door. I sit up and uncurl from the

bed, but when I open the door and look out, there's no one there. Arien's door, opposite mine, is still closed. I take a step forward, and my foot brushes against something. I bend down.

On the floor, at my feet, is a book. There's a thin length of ribbon tied around the cover, a square of card tucked beneath with only my name on it. I recognize the handwriting; it's the same as the inscription on *The Violet Woods*.

"Rowan?" I look down the hallway. Why did he leave this here instead of handing it to me? I take a few steps, then pause, resting my shoulder against the wall as I untie the ribbon. The book is small, with a paper cover, and the pages are soft and well worn. Some are creased; some have the corners folded over. It has clearly been read countless times. I leaf through it gently as my eyes scan the words.

It's not a story. The lines have a shape familiar to the written verses of litanies. But this—this is different.

> Place me like a seal over your heart,
> Like a seal on your arm;
> For love is as strong as death.
> Fair as the moon,
> bright as the sun,
> majestic as the stars.
> You are altogether beautiful, my darling;
> There is no flaw in you.

Heat washes through me. None of the stories I've told or read have made me feel like this. These words are a spell. Like

I have put my hands into the earth, felt the spark and burn of the magic that's woven through the world. This is the same thrill I felt at the Lord Under's words. *We are connected.* This is another connection, just as magic and powerful and frightening.

This light, this heat, this *love*—to see it all laid plain like this, in these beautiful words—it levels me. Is this how Rowan feels? When he looks at me, am I some faerie creature, all sun and moon and stars?

I close my eyes and picture the orchard, the way he kissed me in the moonlight. I want him. I want him in a way that I'd not expected to want anyone, ever. He's under my skin. In my blood. Tangled around my heart.

I close the book and hold it tightly against my chest. I take a few steps into the hall and peer onto the empty landing, where the arched windows show a bare space of pale sky. I want to call out into the silent house, call him back to me. But I don't.

How can we do this? How can we be together when the world is set to shatter around us?

In the kitchen, the stove is banked to a small fire, and there's a single candle lit at the altar. I touch my fingers to the salt, then look at the icon, watch the dance of the flame against the Lady. A door scrapes open, and Clover comes out of the stillroom.

"Oh!" She holds up a jar of dried chamomile and laughs. "You couldn't sleep, either? I never can, after the bonfire." She moves to the stove, sets the kettle over the fire. "You want some tea?"

When I don't answer, Clover puts down the jar and comes

closer, peering at me curiously. "Are you well? You look like you've seen a ghost." Her eyes dart nervously to the parlor doorway. "I mean, you haven't, have you?"

I shake my head. "This was outside my room."

I hold the book out to her. She flips it open and starts to read. Her brows rise higher with each line.

"Wait. Did *Rowan* give you this?" She sounds gleeful. "I knew there was something going on between you both!" She pushes her glasses up the bridge of her nose and leans closer to the book, as if she can divine secrets from the ink and paper. Her eyes widen as she turns through the pages. "Violeta, I feel like I need to sit by the altar after reading this."

"Oh, give it back!" I snatch the book out of her hands and shove it into my pocket. "It's not what you think."

"There's no use denying it. I saw you at the bonfire. The entire *village* saw you. They'll be telling stories about you for years." She pretends to be serious. "The maiden who tamed the monster . . ."

"Clover, this isn't funny."

At the look on my face, Clover quiets and puts her hand on my arm. "You know, it's all right if you're not interested in him like that. Not everyone wants a romance."

I touch my hand to my pocket and feel the crinkle of paper. "I don't know what I want."

"There's never been anyone who you liked before?" She nods to my pocket, where I hid the book. "Liked in *that* way?"

"You mean like you and Thea?"

She demurs, tugging at her braid. "If she writes me any poetry, you'll be the first to know about it."

"I never expected this." I close my eyes. Picture words from the poem strung one by one, like golden motes in the air. *Heart. Moon. Darling.* "I never thought I could have this."

"I expect Rowan feels much the same. He's not *let* anyone close since his family died, except for you." Clover's expression is serious for a moment, then she grins lasciviously. "If you want my advice, you should at least kiss him once. Anyone who reads that much romantic poetry *must* be worth kissing."

"Actually . . ." My eyes go past her, to the kitchen doorway. Warmth creeps through me as I remember the rasp of the wood under my hands. The feel of his scars—rough—against my mouth.

"Oh, you *didn't*." She claps her hands, pleased. "You did! Well, how was it?"

"It was a mistake. He and I, we absolutely can't do this."

"Why not?"

"Would you like me to compile a list?" I fold my arms. "In another week we'll have to go back and fight the Corruption. We barely have an idea of how to mend it. Unless . . ."

"Unless you do something ridiculously stupid, which you *aren't* going to do." She levels her gaze at me. "Right?"

"Right." I swallow hard. "And all of that danger aside, there's the fact that he's lost his whole family to the Lord Under, who I can summon. Who I'm connected to. I'll hurt him, Clover. If I let him love me, he'll only be hurt."

She comes over to stand beside me and slips her arm around my waist. "You and Rowan are perfectly suited. Completely stubborn and self-destructive." She squeezes me gently. "We're all in this together, you know that, don't you? We're going to figure this out. The ritual, I mean."

I nod. My throat feels tight, and I can't trust myself to speak.

"In the meantime, if you want help with the romance, I do have some contraceptive tea. It's on the top shelf." She nods to the stillroom, one brow raised. "Get him to drink it, too—it works better that way."

My face goes bright with a sudden blush. "I'll keep that in mind."

The room has begun to feel too small, too close. Everywhere I look is laden with a second meaning. The stillroom with the jar of tea. The door, the feel of the rough wood still tingling on my palms. The book with those words like a spell.

The kettle begins to hum. When Clover goes to take it from the stove, I slip outside quietly.

My skin burns with a restless heat as I walk along the path to the garden. I'm part magic, part fire, part wretched, wrung-out *want*.

I want so many things, all of them impossible.

I take a pen and trace the lines of ink on my wrist from long ago, a new sigil overlaid on the spent one. Magic sparks at my fingers. I pass a cluster of brambles and bend to them, wrapping my hands around the thorns. The sigil burns. I reach,

270

roughly, and drag out the weak threads of my power. When I'm done, I redraw the sigil, and reach again.

Again and again, each time I snag and pull at the faint, golden thread that's knotted through me. There is no easy flow of magic here, no light or wonder. None of the rightness I feel when I press my hands to the earth in observance. This is sheer fight and force. As though the power can feel my resentment. As though it wants to hide from me. I clutch it tight. Wrench it free. I make leaves and fruit and life.

By the end of it I'm breathless. My temples are streaked with sweat, and my hands won't stop shaking. There's a new clutch of wildflowers on the lawn, a bower of green overhead, and the brambles are heavy with syrupy fruit. My fingers are stained with blood and blackberry juice, and my bonfire dress has streaks of dirt around the hem.

I slump down at the center of the grass, lean my back against a tree, and put my head into my hands. It's only just morning, but the day is already hot. The air is like a stove that's burned and crumbled to heaped coals. Sweat beads up on my cheeks and in the hollow of my throat. I feel it trickle from my neck to my spine. I can still smell the bonfire smoke laced into my skirts and my hair.

I breathe out a slow, hot breath against my stained skin. All my magic, all I have, is faint, ineffectual scraps. And it's all the more frustrating now that I know how much *more* it could be. I think of what I could possibly trade to the Lord Under for that power. Weigh and measure, wonder which hurt would be the worst.

271

Footsteps crunch over the path. I see Rowan standing in the open gateway, at the very edge of the garden. The hood of his cloak is pulled up, and he's a silhouette against the early sunlight.

"Rowan." I look at him, shadowed and hidden and still, and touch my fingers to the book, the corner of it just outside my pocket. "We need to talk."

I wait for him to respond but he doesn't speak, doesn't move. My dress rustles as I get to my feet. I brush my hands over the layers of lace and silk. They shift, cream, silver, gold. "You saw my life, before I came here. There was no place in it for something like this. I never imagined that might change." I falter. He still hasn't moved, and his silence is unsettling. "I never thought I'd want to be close to anyone, until I got to know you."

I take a breath, trying to cool myself. I'm feverish all over. I tip back my head and sigh into the branches above. "I care for you. But we can't do this. We can't be together." I take a hesitant step closer, trying to see his face. "You have to realize it's impossible."

My voice cracks on the words. But it's the truth. There's no place for this, for us. Not here, not now. When I picture what I want, there are two images overlaid. There's Rowan and me in the orchard in the moonlight. He reaches to me, his fingers trail over my petaled hair, and I step into his arms.

And then there's me alone at the shore of the lake, my hands pressed to the earth, the ground mended, the poison gone, everyone safe.

I want them both, each as much as the other. But they don't fit together. Because in all the visions I have of myself where I'm strong and protective, I am alone.

Finally, Rowan crosses the path toward me, slow, and I brace myself for his response.

"I'm sorry," he says at last. His voice sounds strange. "It's too late now."

Then he pushes back the hood of his cloak. His hair is loosened; the dark waves spill around his shoulders. His face is expressionless. And his eyes—his eyes are bloodshot. Crimson. Beneath his boots, the ground is shadowed. No, not shadowed. Wet. *Corrupted.*

I stagger back and cling to the tree behind me, trying to steady myself.

"Rowan?" Our eyes meet, but he is not *there*. "Rowan, you have to make it stop."

He comes toward me, black water pooling beneath him, strands of darkness spilling across the lawn and through the brambles. Piece by piece the garden turns ruined. Leaves dissolve into dust; fruit withers. The air smells of ash and soursweet decay.

The ground begins to unpeel. A wound splits the center of the lawn. Beneath my palm, the bark turns rough. Charred.

All around, I hear the groan and sigh of the trees and plants being poisoned and destroyed. There's a heavy crash as a branch tumbles to the ground. Rowan watches it, blank and still and not *him*; it's not him anymore. I take a breath. I force myself to go forward. My boots sink into the mud, and it's so cold.

I close the distance between us and put my hands around his face so he is forced to look at me. I bite out each word, hard and clear. "Make. It. Stop."

He smiles at me, and his teeth are sharp. "No."

Threads of poison twine across his skin. The scars at his throat are raised and raw and dark. I think of what he told me—how he *made* the Corruption, how the darkness went inside him and poisoned him. All this time, I thought it would kill him. That the end point of this would be his death, and the volatile danger of this magic would spread unchecked.

But now as we stand on the blackened ground, his face in my hands, his eyes bright with blood, I realize the truth.

It's not going to kill him.

It's going to ruin him.

The Corruption wants to devour and devour and devour. It will take him over until all that I know and love of him is destroyed. He won't be dead, but he'll be consumed, entire. Unless I can draw him back.

I take hold of his shoulders and shake him, hard. He barely flinches.

"Fight it." I tell him. "You have to—"

I let out a cry as Rowan grabs a handful of my hair, winds it around his wrist, and pulls. The pain is sharp, awful; it steals my breath. I knot my hands into his cloak. At first I think I'll push him back, away from me. Instead, I drag him closer until his face is only a breath from mine.

I kiss him.

He tastes of the lake: silt and salt and the copper of old, dark

274

blood. Of water and leaves and stolen things. He kisses me as if he wants to devour me. I kiss him back. Fiercely, desperately, as if this could solve everything.

He makes a sharp, wretched sound against my mouth. The monster, the boy, the monster. My skin burns with magic and heat and longing. He drags his hand down my body, rib by rib, until he reaches my waist. Then his fingers dig hard against me, tight enough to bruise.

All around us the ground churns and splits as the poison spreads farther through the garden. I wrench myself free. Rowan's teeth cut against my lip as I pull back. I lick away the blood and we stare at each other, inches apart, our breaths stuttering. The taste of the lake is on my tongue, and my hair is still knotted around his clenched fist. Lines of poison wreathe his throat, there, gone, there again.

Rowan looks at me, and for a moment he's returned to himself. His gold-flecked eyes are full of tender heat. Wary and confused and afraid and *human*.

"Leta." Even now, tinged with ruin, my name from him is still like magic. "Leta, I—"

He blinks. Blackened water trails, like tears, from his eyes.

"Rowan." My heart beats out a sharp, frantic rhythm against my ribs. "Please."

He shakes his head. "I can't."

This has to stop. He has to stop.

I take hold of him and force him closer. He staggers forward. I kiss him again, swallowing down the taste of poison and blood and lake. And as he kisses me back, I run my hands

275

swiftly over him, searching through his cloak, his pockets, until I find his knife. The silver-sharp blade is tucked neatly into the handle.

His mouth moves from my cheek, to my ear, to my throat. I burn with waiting as I'm held captive by the path he traces, pinpoints on my skin. He pulls at the collar of my dress, baring the curve between my neck and my shoulder. He kisses me there roughly, and desire floods through me in a sudden rush. He's half-lost to the shadows; he's ruined and wrong. He's a monster, yet I want him still.

I have to make him stop.

I have the knife clutched in my hand. My fingers shake as I unfold it. Rowan sees the blade and makes a low, feral sound, too cruel to be a laugh. "Leta. It can't be stopped."

"It *can*." I wrench the laces at his cuff until they're undone, then push back his sleeve. Try not to think more than one step ahead. His skin. The blade. A cut.

I can't do this. I have to.

I grab his wrist tightly, but his skin, his arms, his *blood*—all of the cuts have reopened. And his blood is dark. Black as ink. Lake water streams from him, from his countless, impossible wounds.

Rowan has no blood left to pay the tithe to the Corruption.

He *is* the Corruption.

The knife slips from my fingers and lands dully on the softened ground. I reach for him, the crescent on my palm throbbing with pain, and put my hand against his cheek. His eyes flutter closed, and he leans into my touch, breathing out a long, pained breath. It sounds full of thorns.

I kiss him. The sigils on my wrist burn. I feel the flare of my faint, weak magic gather in my palms. I picture a thread, knotted around my ribs, tied to his heart. Think of warmth and summer and seeds and flowers. I search desperately for Rowan, for the boy imprisoned in this creature of mud and poison. I know he's still there beneath the darkness. I reach for him. And for the barest moment, I catch hold. But then I feel him slip and slip and slip.

I try to hold on, but he falls away.

Beneath us, the Corruption spreads. The brambles and flowers and trees are a blackened ruin. The mud slithers around my feet. It all feels so *hungry*.

"Rowan." I touch my fingers gently to his cheek. "It will hurt everyone. Florence, Clover, Arien. It will hurt me. You have to make it stop."

He regards me coldly with his crimson eyes, his skin laced with ever-moving shadows. When he speaks, his voice is the lake. A wash. A hiss. A rush of waves and tide.

"Let them all drown."

Chapter Twenty-One

my magic wasn't enough to free him. I raise my
hands, but only a few bare sparks rise from my
palms. The sigils on my arms are burned clear. I'm
a candle, guttered out.

Rowan comes toward me. I go still, but when he reaches me,
I shove him as hard as I can. Stunned, he staggers back against
the ruined tree. His shoulder hits against the trunk. A scatter
of ashen leaves shakes loose around us. I turn and I *run*.

"Leta." He calls after me with the voice that is no longer his
voice. It's a floodwater sound. Swift and brutal. "Leta, Leta,
Leta."

I hear the crush of his feet behind me. He doesn't run but
takes even, measured steps. He knows, and I know, there's no
way to stop this. Fast or slow, I'll still be overtaken.

I race across the lawn, trip my way up the kitchen steps,

and go back into the house. Clover is at the table, drinking her tea as she pages through her notebook, when I burst into the room, panting.

Her eyes widen. "What's wrong? What happened?"

"I—Rowan, he—" I fling my arm toward the still-open door. "He's *changed*."

Clover shoves back her chair and jumps to her feet. Her cup tips over, spilling chamomile tea across the floor. She looks past me, out into the garden, and sees the ground, the spread of darkness. She sees Rowan approaching, the Corruption spilled beneath him.

"No." Her face pales in horrified realization. "Oh no."

"Go and wake Arien," I tell her. "There must be some way to stop Rowan, or at least hold him back."

She nods, her mouth drawn into a resolute line. As she races past me, she gestures to my wrist. "The sigil, the one we used at the ritual."

I snatch up her pen from the tabletop, push back my sleeve, and hurriedly trace over the lines for the spell I used to help focus Arien's shadows. I blow a quick breath over the ink to help it dry. Outside, Rowan has reached the edge of the lawn, near the altar.

I hear the heavy thud of Clover's hurried footsteps in the hallway above. Her voice, raised, as she calls out for Arien to wake up. They come back down the stairs together, Arien barefoot with tangled hair, hurriedly tucking his shirt into his trousers.

"The Corruption—It wasn't supposed to do *this*," Arien says. He scrubs his face, then quickly rolls up his sleeves to inscribe his arms. He passes the pen to Clover so she can sketch a hasty sigil on her wrist.

Only a moment has passed, but I feel as though I've stood here forever with the taste of poison in my mouth and the throb of bruised, desperate kisses on my skin.

We rush outside. Rowan comes toward me—faster now, eager—his eyes intent. He raises a hand, and strands of oil-slick liquid drip from his palms. *Not blood.* Lake water pours from his opened scars. He's at the center of the lawn, at the center of the sigil we carved for practice. He crouches down and drags his fingers across the earth. It begins to split. The charred marks fill with mud. The ground slithers and writhes.

I see the next moments unfold before me, like a series of blinks. He'll close the distance between us. Wrap his hand over my mouth. He'll smear the poison across my skin. I'll swallow it down, and then he'll do the same to Arien and Clover. He'll take us all to the lake. And meanwhile the wound will open beneath us, spreading to the garden, the house, the village, beyond.

I run forward and throw myself against him with the full force of my desperate strength. He falls; we crash together onto the mud, he on his back and me sprawled over his chest. I hold him down, putting all of my weight onto him: my knees on his shoulders, my hands at his throat. His fingers grip into my thighs, sharp and relentless. He glares up at me. Dark and cold and *not him, not him at all anymore.*

"Keep him still!" Clover shouts. She and Arien kneel down swiftly beside us. Shadows fill the air, illuminated by bursts of golden light. Arien tries to steady his magic, but it spills loose, uncontrolled, stinging against my skin. But we've done this; we've done this before. We've faced the Corruption. Never mind that we haven't stopped it. Never mind that this is no poisoned ground but Rowan. This has to work, it has to— because if it doesn't, there's only one other choice.

I slip my hand free and wrap it around Arien's wrist. My power is faint and small and hard to grasp. It's not enough. It's never been enough. I bite my lip and suck in a pained breath. Finally, I manage to catch hold of my magic. It sparks, and Arien pulls the shadows taut. The cloud narrows into thread-fine strands lit by Clover's power. Together, we weave the spell into a latticework that unfolds around us.

Rowan snarls as the magic binds him. He fights me. I feel the grind of bone and muscle and tendon in his shoulders as I struggle to keep him still.

"Violeta." He hisses through clenched teeth. His mouth is black. Ink stained. "The lake will claim you. It will claim everyone."

"No," Arien snaps. He curls his fingers, and more strands of shadows draw across Rowan's throat. "It *won't*."

We fight him. Arien and Clover and me. Their power. My power. Light and dark and the scraps of my magic. Rowan is snared. The threads of shadow tighten and cut into his skin. He cries out, hurt and furious. And I realize, horrified, that maybe he's so far gone that destroying the Corruption will destroy him, too.

"You can't stop this," he snarls, as if he senses my thoughts. "It's too late."

Clover shoves her palms flat against his chest and unleashes a flare of light against him. He jolts, then his grip on my thighs slackens. He sinks back against the ground. His eyes close. Everything goes hauntingly still.

I shout in panic. "Is he—?"

"Of course not." Clover puts her fingers against his throat and checks his pulse. "He's not dead. Just unconscious."

I take hold of his hand, trembling. His fingers are blackened, the skin slick. At his wrist, the scars still bleed dark. I lower his arm against the ground, so the wound is on the earth. I wait for the Corruption to take its tithe from him, the same way it has, all the times before.

But it doesn't.

There's no movement. Everything is silent. Then the ground gives an abrupt, remorseless *heave*. From the gate of the garden, the ground splits open. It tears and tears, spreading across the lawn toward the tree. The Corruption reaches the altar, slithering over the candles and around the edges of the frame. The Lady is framed in poison, her golden brilliance hung at the center of the dark.

"He has no blood to pay it," I say numbly. "We can't make it stop."

I know now that the ritual will fail. There's only ever been one way to fix this. There's only ever been one choice.

"Can you hold him on your own?" I look at Arien. "Keep him bound?"

He shakes his head, his teeth dug hard into his lip as he

struggles to keep Rowan subdued. "I can't, not without your help. Leta, I *need* you. You know I can't do it alone."

"You have to." I squeeze his wrist. "You can do this; I know you can."

I slip my hand free, slowly, one finger at a time. When there's space between us, I feel my power unfasten from the strands of his magic. His brows knit and his teeth clench. The tightly woven strands begin to waver. Clover puts her hands down onto the ground. She sends a new wash of light beneath the shadows. They shiver, then tighten. "That's right, Arien. Hold it steady."

Arien nods, but all his effort is tensed toward the magic as he fights for control. It blurs and trembles for a moment, but then it holds.

I get to my feet, my heart pounding.

"Wait!" Clover cries. "Where are you going?"

"Just hold him." I call, already running toward the house.

I run through the kitchen. Snatch a pomegranate from my basket, still on the benchtop. Go to the pantry for the knife. Then I run to the parlor. It's dim, the curtains drawn, the scent of candle smoke still in the air. I kneel down at the altar, where the dual icon looms over me. I give one hard slice of the blade; it cuts through the fruit and into my flesh. Blood wells up, mingles with ruby nectar, and I smear my palm across the floor in a determined swipe.

I find a sparklight and click it against the candles. They flare, turning the room to honey. I press my hand against the floor, fresh blood over old blood.

I close my eyes and I call.

I could pretend I'm desperate and afraid, but I'm not. I feel the hollowed-out space where my small remnants of magic sleep. Picture it alight and brilliant. I'm not afraid at all.

If I think it hard enough—that I've been forced, that I had no choice—then I can push aside the terrible part of me that is glad to be here: my blood at the altar, a promise ready on my tongue. The part of me that has longed and hungered for this.

Please. Please. Please.

The air stays bright and silent. No shadows wash the room. No voice whispers my name.

I call, but the Lord Under doesn't answer me.

I bow forward until my forehead touches the floor and sigh out a hard breath. There's a faint tremble through the room. It rattles the window glass and resounds through the walls. Distantly, I can hear the groaning of the ground as the Corruption spreads.

"I have to make it stop," I whisper to the altar. "I need your help."

I look down at my hands. Mud smeared and bloodstained and empty. Beneath the icon, the cut pomegranate is a torn-open heart. The seeds gleam wetly in the candlelight. I remember the Lord Under's words to me when I last summoned him. *It will take more than blood and fruit.* I want him. I want his help. But he won't come unless I have something to offer him first.

All the bravery I felt a moment before melts away. I'm five years old again. Lost in the shadow-limned forest. And just like then, right now I want someone bigger than me, crueler and stronger. Someone to hold my hand and lead me through the dark. I think of how alone I felt. Those last desperate, impossible thoughts I had before the Lord Under appeared.

I want my quilt and honey tea and firelight. I want my mother.

The thought catches. Like a snagged thread that slowly begins to unravel. *My mother my mother my mother.* When I first told Arien my stories, it was her voice that I heard. When I first used my magic in the garden, it was my father's hands I felt. My mother, my father. All this time I've clung to my memories of them, comforted myself with the knowledge that while they were gone, they weren't lost. They've always been with me, within me.

I look up at the altar. The silhouette of the Lord Under is blurred by my tears.

"I know what I can give you." A sob thickens my voice, but I don't waver. I have no doubt in this. "I'm ready to make our exchange."

The air turns to mist. Droplets fall from the ceiling; then water streams down the walls and over the floor as the light starts to dim. There's a sound like a sigh, like the rise of a tide, and all other noise is closed out. I'm here, underwater, as the Lord Under comes through the dark.

I look up from where I'm kneeling on the floor. He stands over me, tall. The shrouded hem of his cloak spills into the darkness like a pool of ink. I know him now. His face, his voice, his pale hair, his pale eyes. His sharp teeth bared in an even sharper smile. It's still such a shock that I can see him in this way, that I can draw him out of the darkness to look on his face and *know* him. Lord of souls. Lord of the dead.

"Violeta." My name in his mouth is part threat, part caress. "What do you have for me?"

Once done, this can't be undone. Once I speak, there will be no way to turn back. I take a breath. Let the words fall before I can change my mind.

"My family." I close my eyes as the memories come. My mother. My father. Stories and firelight and our cottage surrounded by flowers. I've held them and held them. Given them strength each time I told Arien a story. Each time I felt the ghost of my mother's touch on my shoulder. Each time I cast a spell and saw my father with his hands in the earth. I kept them alight, kept them alive, all I have of the family who died and were burned to ash after the winter fever.

And now, I'll let them go.

"My memories of my family. I'll give them to you for the power to save Rowan now, and to mend the Corruption at the next ritual."

It has to be this. The Corruption began when Rowan lost his family. His family, my family, my power.

It has to be this. It could only ever be this.

The Lord Under lowers himself down, until he kneels before me. "This was more than we agreed upon. I offered my help—and your power—for the next ritual only."

"Rowan is going to hurt us, all of us." I pause, forcing myself not to beg, to plead. "It can't wait until the full moon."

"Then you'll need to give me something more."

My mind races as I stare up at him. What do I have that is *more* than the memories of my family that I've treasured all this time? I think of my parents, burned and gone—but not lost. The mourning litany speaks of how families will be reunited after death, and that's what I've always believed.

"What happens after death?" I ask the Lord Under. "My family—when I die, will I remember them and be with them in the world Below?"

His mouth curves into the barest hint of a smile. "You will."

"Then take that, too." I try to hold back my tears, but they spill free. "I'll give up my family to you forever. I'll forget them in my world and in yours. Even when I die, I won't remember them."

The Lord Under draws in a deep, slow breath as he considers my offer. He watches me with a gaze that is vast and endless and entirely inhuman. Did I expect him to look softer? To be sorry? There is none of that. Only a deep, endless *hunger*.

Finally, he nods. "I will give you a spell to cast on Rowan that will work only once. Your full power will come on the next moon, and it will last until sunrise touches the shore on the following day. In exchange, you'll forget your father and your mother. You'll be without them, always. Alone even in death."

"Yes. That's my trade."

He lifts a hand. "This will hurt. In more ways than one."

Each piece of me cries out to undo this, to run, but there is nowhere for me to go. I am right where I need to be.

His claws scrape through the air above my face. My eyes are still open, but everything turns dark. Water rushes down the walls, and the room fills with mud, with black water, with shadows that I feel, sharp, inside my lungs. His darkness tastes the same as Arien's magic. Salt and ash and smoke. It *hurts*.

As the Lord Under's shadows tear through me, he starts to whisper. "They will be gone, forever. And when the time comes, and Arien dies, he'll be lost to you, too. Your soul will sleep alone in the world Below."

A sob comes out of my mouth at his words, but I bite down on the sound, hold it back. I have to do this. I *choose* to do this.

His magic is cold, a steel-sharp swath that scrapes through my body. My heart. My bones. The inside of my skull. A swift, clean slice that severs everything. *Alone forever, even in death.* I see a single, final image: my father, the way he smiled as his magic filled the earth in our garden.

Then it's gone.

It's all gone.

Tears stain the corners of my eyes when I blink them open. In place of my memories there is only a blank space, a strange, hollow feeling. Like my hands were closed tenderly around some precious thing, and now I've found them empty. When I try to remember my family—the shape of their faces, their names—there's an absence, and it *aches*.

My heart is pounding, and my breath comes in short, sharp

288

gasps. "It still hurts. I've forgotten them. Why does it still hurt?"

The Lord Under touches his claws to his mouth. Swallows down my pain and my fear and my memories the way he once ate fruit and blood. "You've forgotten them, but the hurt won't go—it won't heal over."

Another tremor shakes the room, and I go tense and still, straining to hear the sounds outside.

I need to go back, but first I need to be sure of my power. "We have our trade. Say it."

"We have our trade. Hold out your hand."

I quickly reach my hand toward him. He leans forward, until there's almost no distance between us. The cold of his breath burns across my cheeks.

He traces his claws over my heartline.

Though I can't feel his touch, the power hits me all at once. Sudden and all encompassing, like a wave that's washed over me. It's cold. It's hot. My skin burns and turns to ice. The world evaporates into a heady rush of light and heat. I am magic. I am power. It's all I tasted before in those fleeting glimpses.

But better, but worse, because now it is *mine*.

Light blooms at my palms, and the room is illuminated in crystalline brilliance. Power. *My* power. The power I'll have on the next full moon. The Lord Under watches me, and the flare of magic dances in his pale eyes. For just one, ruinous moment, I wish he could touch me. I want to feel his cold, clawed hand on my cheek, on my hair.

I let the power burn through me. Let it burn away all the

helplessness and uncertainty in one last brilliant flare before it dims, settling back into the barest glimmer. I want to be safe at Lakesedge. I refuse to let the life I've found here be destroyed, not now. I won't let it be taken from me. With this bargain I can finally protect everyone—and everything—that I care about.

"Thank you."

"Thank *you*." His mouth curves into a hard, pleased smile. I'm not sure what pleases him most. My awe over the power or the hurt I've paid to gain it. I push away the thought. Stare at the light until my vision blurs and refuse to think of what it's cost me.

"Now." I shiver as aftershocks of the power flicker through my body. "Tell me what I need to do to save Rowan."

"You will need a spell. Listen carefully. Blood. Salt. Iron. Silt. Mud." He looks at my wrist, where the sigils are drawn. "Mark it on both of you. The same sigil. That will hold him until the full moon."

"And the rest . . . ?"

"Come to the lake for the ritual, as you did before. Your power will be enough to cast the spell." He flexes his fingers open and closed, mimicking the gestures that I've seen Clover make when she draws out her magic.

"You will give me enough power to mend it. Alone."

"Alone," he confirms. Then he looks to my hands. "Shall I heal your cuts?"

I scramble to my feet and scrub my bloodied palms against

my skirts. "No. Rowan needs me. And I can't afford any more of your help."

He smiles coldly. "Best of luck with your monster and your ritual, my Violet in the woods."

The shadows thin, and the light comes back into the room. This is the last time I'll see him. I'll have no need to summon him again. The realization comes with a tiny pang of sadness that I try very hard to ignore.

As soon as he fades, I run through the kitchen into the still-room. On a shelf beneath the jars of tea and garlands of dried flowers is a stack of notebooks. I grab the one I've used in lessons and flip through quickly, searching for the right symbols. But as I rifle through the pages, I realize I have no idea how to combine the symbols into a spell.

I hurriedly shove the notebook into my pocket and rush back outside to Arien and Clover. After the darkened house, the sunlight is disorienting. I blink and blink until my vision comes clear. Rowan is still trapped beneath the shadows. He's awake again, now, fighting against the magic as it cuts into his skin. The ground has torn open all around them.

Arien holds the shadows taut, his teeth set, his eyes closed in a grimace. When he hears me coming, he looks up. At first, the magic holds, and holds, but then it snaps. Rowan tears loose, reaching his hand out swiftly to grab Arien's throat. They fall down together into a tangle of magic and shadows.

"No!" I rush across the ruined lawn. "Rowan, don't hurt him!"

My boots sink into the churned mud. The blackened earth seethes and boils around us. It's angry. It's *hungry*. Clover casts a burst of light as Arien struggles against Rowan. Darkness spills from his palms, and they're lost in a cloud of uncontrolled magic.

I fall to my knees and grab for Arien's wrist. Send my power into him. The strands weave tight, and Rowan is caught again, writhing furiously beneath the snare of shadows. Roughly, I reach into my pocket, then shove the crumpled notebook into Clover's hands.

"Blood. Salt. Iron. Silt. Mud," I tell her. She looks at me, confused, but I keep repeating over and over the spell the Lord Under gave me, until the words lose meaning. "Show me how to mark it."

I bare my arm, but she shakes her head. "This isn't even a spell. These symbols don't mean anything. It makes no sense."

"You have no idea how little sense this makes. Please. It will work, I promise. Do it, Clover, or he'll be lost."

She sets her pen to the page and quickly sketches the spell. I copy it onto my wrist, the lines hurried and unsteady, then grasp Rowan's arm. He's caught so tightly in the magic that he can't move, but he glares at me, feral and vicious, when I shove back his sleeve. Tendrils of Corruption drip between his clenched fingers.

"Why are you marking him?" Clover looks at me, her face pale. "Where exactly did you get this spell?"

"Leta," Arien breathes, horrified. "You didn't."

"We can argue about this after—" I gesture to Rowan and the Corrupted ground. "After we're done with *this*."

Rowan snarls as I hastily write the spell on his wrist between the reopened scars. Then I take hold of his hand and press my palm to his palm, our skin slick with mud and blood. I weave my fingers through his. I close my eyes. I reach.

My power is a low simmer with the feel of a larger flame far beneath it, the strength that waits for the full moon. But when I call my magic, there's no light, or flowers, or warmth. There's an awful, hollow emptiness, a terrible feeling of absence. I'm all alone, on an ashen field. The thread of my power winds around me, and it's red, red as blood. I choke back a sob as the overwhelming loneliness rises up, aching, a wound.

My skin burns, and the sigil on my wrist ignites. The magic comes to me, swift and fast and strong. Sparks scatter through the air, the world turns to fire, but I am cold, so cold. It hurts so much, knowing what I've given up to do this, the price I've paid for this power.

I grip Rowan's hand. Put my other hand to the earth, the way I would for observance. But as my fingers sink into the softened mud, there's no light or glow, none of the warm current of magic that flows through the world. I feel the Corruption. The poison. The endless hunger. The wound, the imbalance that Clover spoke of all those nights ago. And I know I can't mend it—not here, not now.

But with this spell, I can make it quiet.

Magic fills me—my heart, my lungs, my skin. It hurts. I feel it blister at my palms, spark from my fingertips. I see myself, alone, only ash and decay and darkness all around me.

"Lie still," I tell it. "Be quiet."

The ground gives a final shudder. Arien and Clover watch, wide eyed, as the tremors stop.

"It *heard* you." Arien's whisper hangs between terror and awe.

I pull my hand from the mud and put it against Rowan's chest. He looks at me—crimson eyed and poisoned and gone—and draws in a sharp breath. I feel the tremor of his heartbeat. I lean close and bury my face into the curve of his neck. I'm shivering, feverish; my bones are *fire*. Light flares and everything glows. I try to push away the ache and emptiness, remember a time when my magic was gold and sun and wonder. Slowly, the thread unspools between us. I can do this. I can save him.

"Lie still," I breathe across his skin; the same words I used on the Corruption. "Be quiet."

Rowan flinches as the sigil flares like a sparklight set to lamp oil. The thread of my power is knotted around my ribs, my heart; the other end is tied to him. I take a breath. He takes a breath. He sighs it out. My own breath slows, matching his, as though the sigh has passed between us. He looks at me, and his eyes blink clear. Under my palm, I feel the air move through his lungs. There's no hiss or rush of lake water.

My temples thud with a headache, and my hands begin to tremble uncontrollably. A hot stripe of blood drips from my nose and across my mouth. I wipe it away quickly, but more comes.

I try to draw back the power. But instead it floods all around me. The thread between us winds tighter, tighter, until it *aches*. The sigil burns. My skin burns.

The world turns white.

I close my eyes and I let go.

Chapter Twenty-Two

I wake in the parlor, alone. My boots are gone, but I'm still in my mud-streaked bonfire dress. Someone has laid me on the chaise, tucked a blanket over me. The air smells of bitter herbs and honey salve. The curtains are drawn back, the walls turned amber by evening light. The altar looms over me from the opposite side of the room: the Lady all golden, the Lord Under darkly shadowed. The fruit I cut is still there, now dark and charred. The floor is still stained by my blood.

I get to my feet, the world tilting in a dizzying rush. I stagger out into the kitchen. Clover and Arien are at the table, while Florence stands beside the stove, feeding wood into the fire. Arien stays seated, his gaze fixed on the tabletop, but Clover stands up quickly and comes over to me. She takes my hands and peers into my face.

"You're awake." She brushes her fingers over the cut on my hand. "How do you feel?"

"Like I just fought off a monster." I scrub my wrist across my face, then look around the room. "Where's Rowan? Is he—? It didn't—when I stopped him, was he hurt?"

"He's in his room," Florence says. "He went upstairs after he helped you back inside."

I turn away from them and run up the stairs, stumbling slightly. The door to Rowan's room is half-open. I tiptoe inside. He's passed out on the bed, the quilts kicked into a pile beneath his muddied boots. I cross the room slowly, sadness rising in my chest. I kneel down on the floor beside the chaise, and put my hand against his cheek. His fawn skin is pale, and his brows knit into a frown when I touch him.

I close my eyes as, in a rush, it all comes back. I've done it. I've really done it. I bargained. I'm marked. I'm promised.

It's what I wanted, and I'm not sorry for what I've done. But the hollowed place left behind from where I gave up my memories is a constant ache. It feels painful and *wrong* to have this vacant, blank space where my family once was. To know that I'll never see them again, that when my soul passes to the world Below, I'll be alone, without even Arien there beside me.

I know I made the right choice. Still—it hurts.

I take Rowan's hand. The sigil on his wrist is a cluster of angled lines, like a sunburst. The identical mark on my own wrist pulses, as though there is still magic left inside it. For a breath I see flashes of color and catch a thread of emotions that don't seem quite mine. The same uneasy mix of relief and despair I felt earlier, interwoven with some darker thing. Anger. Guilt.

I let go of his hand, and the images fade.

Florence comes quietly into the room. She has a tray set with tea, and a vial of sedative. "Oh." She looks at him, smiling sadly. "He's gotten mud all over the sheets."

"Should we take off his boots?"

"No, let's not wake him." She sets down the tray and puts her hand against his forehead for a moment. "Come on, we'll leave him to rest."

We go back into the kitchen, where Clover sets a cup of tea onto the table for me beside a jar of honey. I sit down heavily. My whole body feels bruised. When I swallow the tea, I can still feel the grittiness in my mouth, like the mud is inside me. I scoop out a spoonful of honey and stir it into my cup. But even with the honey, the bitterness of the herbs stays on my tongue.

I look down at the tabletop strewn with notebooks. Each page filled with scrawled-out, rewritten, and half-drawn sigils. At the center of the mess is a cluster of jars, arranged in a circle. They're all full of ink-dark water, with a heavy paste of muddy sediment at the bottom.

I turn to Clover. "What is this? What are you doing?"

"We're—" She pulls at the end of her braid. "It's for the next ritual."

Arien folds the notebook closed and holds it to his chest protectively. "Clover and I are still trying to find another spell to use."

"Arien, you don't need it."

His mouth draws into a tight frown before I can finish.

"Arien. You *saw* me today. You saw what I can do now."

"Yes. We saw. You really summoned him, didn't you?" Clover looks toward the parlor with a shiver. "That icon is . . ." She waves a hand, unable to find words. Her eyes gleam with a mix of fear and fascination. "We were told in the Maylands that most estates have them, but I've never seen one before."

"You promised me, Leta," Arien says quietly.

"Do you think I *wanted* to do this?"

"Yes. I think you did." Beneath the hurt in his eyes is another emotion. Guilt. "We were going to work this through, together."

"We didn't exactly have another choice." I try to take his hand, but he moves back so I can't reach him. "I've made the bargain. I can't unmake it. *It's done.* I've saved Rowan, and now I can spare you all from this. You don't need to do the ritual. You don't need to face that danger again."

Arien picks up the jar with the lake water and turns it around between his palms. The sediment stirs up in a curl that makes smokelike patterns through the water. "What did you give him, Leta? What did he ask in exchange for this help?"

My throat tightens, and the words stick. I don't want to lie. But I know if I speak the truth of what I've done, the ache within me will hurt a thousand times worse. How can I tell him I gave up our family, in this world and the world Below?

How can I tell Arien I gave up *him*?

"I don't want to talk about it."

He puts down the jar and he looks at me, his anger softening into worry. "What was it, really?"

"Don't ask this of me, Arien. I can't tell you."

"If I'd been stronger . . . if my magic had worked, you wouldn't have done this."

"No." I reach out to him again. "I chose this. I wanted this. None of it was your fault."

"Leta, the magic he's given you, it's not safe."

I laugh darkly. "Arien, my love, *none* of this is safe. You know that."

"Whatever happens at the next ritual," Clover says carefully, "if it's us or you—"

"There's no *if*. It has to be me. On the next full moon, I'll cast the spell alone, and it will work. I have to do this on my own."

"No," Arien says. "You don't."

"They're right." Florence fixes us all with a long, hard stare. "Honestly. You've reached new heights for how much trouble you can get into on a single day."

She pulls out a chair and sits down beside me, putting her arm around my shoulders. Longing spreads through me at the gesture. It's like I've heard a sound echoed across a far distance. The shape of a caress that was once imprinted on my bones and is now gone. If I've ever felt this before—from my mother or father—that's one of the memories I've given up.

My eyes start to sting, and I blink very quickly.

"Listen." I roll back my sleeve and bare the new,

sunburst-shaped sigil. "The whole reason I bargained with the Lord Under is so that no one else need risk themselves."

Clover rolls her eyes. "You're even worse than Rowan."

"An even match, I think." Florence smiles sadly. She puts her hand over mine, covering the crescent scar. "I've watched him tear himself to pieces to protect everyone while he tried to mend this. I knew it was hurting him, but he wouldn't let me close. He kept it all to himself. I could have pushed him, but I—I didn't. I kept back. I let him stay alone. And I shouldn't have."

"It's not your fault," I tell her. "He doesn't exactly make it easy to help him."

Arien snorts out a derisive laugh. "Sounds familiar." He leans his elbows against the table and takes a measured breath. "Leta, just because you can do this alone doesn't mean you have to *be* alone when you do it."

"If you came with me, if anything happened . . ." I shake my head, remembering Arien caught and pulled beneath the earth at the last ritual. "I can keep you safe now. I've paid dearly for it. So please, just let me."

I get to my feet and go over to the door. It's closed, when usually we leave it open to let in the air. And the window is shuttered, too.

I go out into the yard, and as I stand on the path with the warmth of heated stone under my feet, I look out over the estate.

It's *ruined*.

The space beneath the jacaranda tree where we fought and

quieted the Corruption is torn through the center. There's a trench of blackened earth. Thick tendrils of mud snare around the trunk, and the branches are now bare of leaves. They twist against the sky like desperate, grasping hands.

The altar is all dark. The wooden frame is caked with earth. Swaths of black cover the icon, with only a slice of the Lady's upturned face visible between the darkness. Her single eye looks up at the skeletal branches above.

I take a halting step forward and go over to the charred remnants of the sigil. This isn't at all like the ink-dark lake or the blackened shore. This is a whole world made silent. Everything is cold and black and *still*. There's no wind. No sound of grass or leaves, no call of birds.

And this wasn't the only place touched by the Corruption.

I follow the curved path. The ground is still churned, cold and wet under my bare feet. I pick my way carefully across the uneven ground, through tall banks of overgrown grasses, now dead. When I reach my garden, I stop, put one hand on the cold iron of the gate, and look inside. I can't move any farther.

I made this locked-up place beautiful and alive with my magic. Grew fruit and leaves and flowers. It was never dead, only half-forgotten and half-asleep. But now the brambles are blackened tangles. A tree has fallen across the wildflower lawn, the roots upturned and sharp against the sky. The whole garden is gray and skeletal and empty. The leaves, the fruit, the flowers . . . they're all gone.

I sink down in the archway and lean against the ashen remnants of the star jasmine vines. I thought I knew the limits of the Corruption's horror. But this hits me with a visceral, bone-deep fear.

I put my hand against the ground, and the crescent mark on my palm throbs. I feel the poison that sleeps in the earth. It knows me now. It's waiting.

Magic stirs beneath my skin. I want to mend this. Make it all awake and alive and *safe* again. I close my eyes and picture myself on the shore of the lake. The full moon above. My hands in the ground. The whole world dead and silent around me. My power poured into the earth as I slowly bring it back to life.

A sudden rush of wind stirs across the ground. It rattles through the leaf-bare branches, and a sharp pain twinges in my chest. I get to my feet quickly as sparks of magic scatter from my fingers. I swallow, hard, tasting salt and silt and poison.

I will fight this. I will *mend* this.

I close the gate. I still have the key; I've worn it around my neck every day since I found it. I draw it out and slip it into the lock. The rasp turns with a final-sounding scrape. I wrap my hands around the iron rails and lean my face against the bars. I stare for a long time at the destroyed remains of my garden. Watch the shadows lengthen across the jagged ground and fallen trees. The blackened earth turns plum and lilac as the sunset envelops the sky.

When I go back into the house, Florence has set the table for dinner. Fresh bread, olive butter, and a dish of pink salt. Summer squash and sugar peas. And at the center is an enormous layer cake filled with almond cream and glazed with golden syrup.

"Rowan turned into a monster and nearly killed us all," I say. "The whole estate is Corrupted. I called the Lord Under into our parlor. And you . . . made a cake?"

"I cook when I'm stressed," Florence says primly. "It helps."

I close the door behind me. That, and the still-shuttered windows, gives the space an unfamiliar gloom. We all sit down at one end of the table, gathered close to the stove like we would in winter, though the air in the closed up kitchen is uncomfortably hot.

Arien puts his hand on my arm. "Leta, are you sure about this?"

In the dim light, his face is a pale wisp. His hands are mended now, but marked all over with fine scars that will never fade. In the lamplight, the tracery of slender lines looks like frost laced over a window on an icy morning.

"I'm sure."

He shifts closer and rests his face against my shoulder. "I don't want you to go. What if your magic doesn't work? What if it isn't enough? Please, let us help you."

I put my arms around him. He's grown so much since we came here. I've been so caught up in trying to protect him, that I forgot how much it meant to him: to learn how to use his magic, to help Rowan. That night after the first ritual, when he told me determinedly, *I want to do this* . . . All of this was a chance to prove himself, and now I've taken that away from him.

I imagine myself alone at the lake, with the Lord Under a pallid shadow above the water. My hands in the earth as I fight against the Corruption, the shadows gathered around me. Then I look at Arien and Clover, and remember the feeling of us all fighting together. What we did today—it wasn't me, alone. It was all of us.

Maybe they're right. Maybe in this, I don't need to be on my own.

"All right. On the full moon. All of us will go. We'll do this together."

Arien smiles, but his eyes are sad.

"Together," he says softly.

Chapter Twenty-Three

I go back to Rowan as the house rests in silvered silence. He's no longer asleep, and inside his room everything has been made tidy, the mud swept away, fresh sheets on the bed. He's changed his clothes—soft linen trousers and a shirt with the sleeves rolled back and the lacings at the collar loosened.

He sits on the chaise, curled up, his arms on the windowsill and his face turned toward the glass. Night has fallen, and the curtains are drawn back to reveal scattered stars in the sky above the granite-sloped hills.

He turns, startled, when he hears me close the door. I cross the room in a rustle of skirts until I'm before him. He grips the tangled blankets as he gazes up at me. His skin is marked with new, freshly healed scars. All of the cuts on his skin that bled that terrible lake-water blood have closed. There are bruises all over his throat, left from the magic Arien used to hold him still.

His eyes are clear, not crimson.

"When I said you weren't a proper monster because you had no fangs or claws, I didn't mean it as a challenge." I'm trying to tease him, but tears start to fall, hot, down my cheeks. "I thought you'd be lost. I'm so glad I could bring you back."

His fingers brush over my wrist, and he touches the new sigil. He's quiet for a long time; then he asks, "Is it gone?"

The tiny seed of hope in his voice almost undoes me. I stretch out a hand toward him and close my eyes. He breathes. I listen. It's a quiet, open sound, no rush or hiss of water. My magic stirs, a gentle curl of power that threads between us like a question. I feel him: burnt sugar and black tea and golden sunlight. I feel the Corruption: hunger and poison and darkness.

It's still there. Buried down farther than it was. Quieter. But there.

"No. It's not gone. But it will be soon."

Rowan takes my hand and holds it gently, stroking a circle against my palm with his thumb. "I know what you did to stop me. What did you give up to him, Leta?"

"It was—I—" But just like before, when Arien asked me, I can't put it into words. More tears fill my eyes. "It doesn't matter."

He leans closer, searching my face. "It matters to me."

"It was an equal trade. Nothing more than you gave," I manage. "And I gave it willingly."

His expression darkens. "Equal to *what*? What did you give that would match my life, and the lives of my family?" I don't answer, but after a moment passes, I see the realization settle on him. "Tell me the rest of the story from the night at the wayside cottage. You never did finish. I want to hear how it ends."

I swallow back a sob and shake my head. "No."

"Go on." His voice gentles, and he strokes my cheek, wiping away the tears. "Beyond seven forests, beyond seven lakes . . ."

"I can't." My voice cracks. "I don't remember. I don't remember anything of my family. I gave them up—now and forever."

For a moment Rowan hardly moves. Then his arms are around me, a sudden embrace. I sink against him, my ear over the rapid beat of his heart, and tuck my face into his shoulder. I start to cry harder. He rubs my back, strokes my hair, kisses away my tears. "I'm so sorry," he says. "So sorry that I've brought you into this."

He holds me for a long time, until I stop crying and the room is quiet, filled with just the sound of our twinned breath. We draw apart and look at each other. I wipe my face on my sleeve.

"I'm not." It's the first time I've spoken it aloud. The first time that I've realized it. He changed everything in my life, the day when he came to our cottage. And though at that moment I hated him and wanted him gone, now I find the memory is colored with tenderness. "I'm not sorry for anything. Not that I met you, or that I came here."

"Right. You nearly died. You've bound yourself to the Lord

Under. You gave up your family to stop me from destroying you."

"Actually, you wanted to destroy everyone. You were very ambitious." I press my fingers against the sigil on my wrist. Inside me, the magic stirs. The promise of power is right there, the magic like a flood, ready for me to unleash when the moon is full. "Do you remember what I said to you, that day in the kitchen after I first summoned the Lord Under?"

His mouth tips into a smile. "I'm sure it was something nonsensical, about wanting to risk yourself while we all stood back and watched you."

"Well, yes," I laugh. "I told you this was my choice. I've chosen this. My sacrifice, my promise, all of it."

"Leta." He catches my face between his hands. "I'd never have asked this of you. But now that you've done it, thank you. Thank you for stopping me. Thank you for saving me."

I run my fingers over the marks on his neck, the scars and the bruises left from the magic. Light flickers across my palms as I touch him. "Did you know this would happen? Did you know the Corruption would change you rather than kill you?"

His eyes shutter closed. "I wasn't certain, but I knew it was possible."

"So you let everyone fear you and call you a monster, because you wanted them to stay away."

"It's true enough, isn't it?"

"Is that why you didn't want me to come here?"

"That wasn't the only reason." He laughs, embarrassed.

"I've never—I never really wanted to be with anyone, to let them close. I knew it was impossible, that I couldn't ever ask someone to be part of this." He gestures to himself, to the landscape outside the window. An arc of his hand to summarize his entire life: the danger, the darkness, the Corruption.

"I'm not afraid, Rowan. You know that, don't you? Not even in the garden, when you were changed. When you fought me, when you kissed me. I'm not afraid of you."

"I know." He takes a slow breath. "When I first saw you, with your sunburned nose and tangled hair, with your poor, bruised arms . . . You looked as though you would tear me to pieces, but still, I was drawn to you. And I knew if I let myself care about you—if I let myself *want* you—it would be worse than leaving you behind in that awful cottage. You're right: I didn't want you to come with us. I needed to mend the Corruption. I didn't have time to worry about feelings. But even as I intended to leave you there, I still—I wanted—" He sighs. "I just want you to be safe."

"I am safe. And I am going to stay safe."

"I'm not sure *safe* is the word I'd use." Rowan looks down at the sigil on his arm. He touches it and frowns. "It hurt you, to use this magic. When you stopped me, it hurt you."

"Yes. But it was my choice."

"It's still *there*." He touches the sigil again, puzzled. "What have you done to me?"

He traces his fingers along the lines of the spell, and I shiver as the magic sparks, in response, across my own skin. I look down at my hand, marked with the blackened crescent. My wrist, marked with the sunburst spell. Then I place my fingers around the sigil. Rowan shivers as the spell sings between us. I catch the rush of emotions that are mine but not mine. A mess of heat and despair and want. *We are connected.*

"I'm bound to the Lord Under." I show him my palm, then I touch the sigil. "I'm bound to *you*."

He wraps his hand around his own wrist, frowning. Colors wash through my mind, rose, peach, gold. "Leta. Just because we're connected, doesn't mean you have to—" He lets his hand drop away, and the shift of colors fades into darkness. "You know how I feel about you."

"Do you mean the *fair as the moon* part, or the part where you wanted to drown me?" When his frown deepens, I laugh gently. "Yes, I know."

"You saved me. But that doesn't mean you owe me anything more. If you still feel this is impossible, tell me so, and I won't speak of it again, ever."

Slowly, I climb into his lap, my mud-stained skirts frothing around us in an opalescent cloud. I put my arms around his neck, and press my forehead to his. It steadies me, this closeness. My fingers in his hair, the prickle of his eyelashes against my cheek when he blinks. My heartbeat slows. Whatever hesitance I had before—the *want* and *can't* that I struggled against—it's gone.

"Everything about this is impossible," I murmur. "I can speak to the lord of the dead, and you are a monster."

I lean forward as he melts back, until I'm folded over him with my ear against his heart, my cheek against his rumpled shirt. He runs a tentative hand over my hair, and a tangle of dried leaves and wilting petals tumbles loose.

He catches one of the flowers as it falls, confused, then looks down incredulously at my still-filthy clothes. "You're all muddy. Why haven't you changed your dress?"

"Oh, I don't know. Maybe I was too worn out from saving your life." I push his hands away, laughing. "Do you want me to take it off?"

His eyes widen, then his expression turns heated. "Yes," he says, low. "I do."

My laughter changes into a shy smile. I'd only meant to tease him. But now it's said, all I can think of is that long-ago day when he helped with my buttons and I felt the roughness of his fingers against my bare skin.

"It unfastens at the back," I whisper into his ear. "You'll have to help me."

He gives me a careful look. "You're certain of this?"

"Yes." My hands have started to shake. But I know, undoubtedly, that I'm sure. "I'm certain."

"Turn around, then."

I turn. Rowan scrapes the weight of my hair from my neck and slips it forward over my shoulder. He reaches for the topmost button at the base of my neck. Each time he undoes a button he marks the newly bared place with a kiss, going all the way down my spine. My pulse beats hard in my throat, my chest, my stomach. With each button, with each kiss, I unravel further until I'm breathless and unsteady.

My dress slides away from my shoulders. The air is cold

against the heated flare of my skin. I slip free of the mud-stained tangle of my skirts, until I'm only in my undergarments and camisole, all lace and ribbon.

Rowan stares at me like I'm a poem, a wonder, a story. He puts a tentative hand on my waist. I shift toward him. Then his gaze lowers to my thighs, still marked by when he clawed me. "Leta," he says, stricken. "Leta, I'm sorry."

I take his hands, push back his sleeves, and kiss every mended cut on his arms. I unlace his shirt and gather the fabric into my fists, pulling until it untucks. He sits very still, letting me lift his shirt slowly over his head. His skin is warm, patterned with scars. It's so strange and precious to see him like this, bared and flushed and *mine*.

I slide my hands over his chest. His breath catches. He knots his fingers through my curls and pulls me gently toward him. Our faces are so close that when I speak, my words cast across his mouth. "Rowan, I love you." He makes a wretched, helpless noise and shoves me back against the tangled quilts. All breath is gone from my lungs in a single, sudden gasp. He pulls sharply on my hair and crushes his mouth against mine

His kiss is like fire. It burns through me until I am razed clear. There's none of the hesitation of when I kissed him that first time. This is rough, a mess of feverish heat. Magic sparks from my fingers. Desire spirals through me, coiling tight at my center where it becomes a persistent ache. I gasp and he kisses away the sound. He tastes of blood and silt and shadows.

His hands are all over me, tight against my waist, tangled in my hair. His teeth are at my throat. He bites down—softly, then less so. I dig my fingers into his shoulder, drag him closer. I want the space between us to become invisible. I kiss him, tracing a path down the line of his jaw to the side of his throat. I kiss his bruises and his scars. His heartbeat is a captured moth. His skin is honey and poison.

When I touch him, I feel the shift and shiver of darkness beneath his skin. Threads of black vein his neck, his chest, his arms. I don't know if I'm kissing the boy or the monster or both, and I don't much care.

He catches hold of my hips and lifts me against him. I put my hands over his and our fingers, together, press into my skin. He smothers my breathless moan with another endless kiss. Then he bends to the scars on my knees, kissing them tenderly as he strokes the fresh cuts on my thighs. He pauses and looks at me, a question in the heat of his gaze. A heartbeat passes before he asks quietly, "Can I touch you?"

A fervent shiver runs through me, right down to my toes. I bite my lip and breathe out, *"Yes."*

He slides his hands higher and higher still. Heat burns across my skin, lingering long after his touch passes. He's above me; I kiss the shadowed curve of his neck. He traces the edge of my undergarments, following the pattern of the lace. Then his fingertips graze over me.

"Oh—" It's a shock, at once bright hot and feather gentle. It feels like I've shared a secret. I've let him into these hidden corners of myself, where so far only my hands have been. Magic dances through my veins, and light glints across my palms. All my words are gone. I press my thighs together around his hand, dissolving into a warmth that spreads through my entire body. At my wrist, the sigil aches with power, and the tether strung between us begins to glow, turning to a bright golden thread.

I reach for him and hook my fingers into the waistband of his trousers. Then I stop and hold back, waiting. He looks at me, then to my hands. His eyes sink closed. He nods, once. There are so many buttons, and it takes me a long time to unfasten them. He rocks against me, impatient, and groans, "*Leta.*"

I laugh at him teasingly. I slide my hand lower and lower. His breath hitches as I finally touch him.

We lie facing each other, our legs tangled. At first we're both clumsy and unsure, all caught breath and tentative, searching touches. But it's still so right, so perfect. We soften into a steady rhythm. His hands on me, mine on him, the heavy cadence of our shared breath. Being close to each other like this is such a fragile, tender magic; its own kind of alchemy.

All that's ahead is a blank unknown. On the full moon, I'll go to the lake with the terrible, wonderful power granted to me. But for now, in this stolen moment, I try to forget. Forget the ruined ground and the ink-dark lake. The poison that waits to claim us all.

Now I am only little gasps, liquid fire. Melted candles. Sap dripped from a pale-trunked tree. I'm thorn and lichen, lace over stone. I'm an orphan with scars on her knees. A faerie creature in a gossamer dress. I am light and heat and power and magic.

Rowan circles his hand around my wrist. His thumb finds the raised edges of the sigil. He presses down against it. The world turns golden bright.

I let myself shatter. For just this moment, I forget it all.

Afterward, we're both breathless, perspiration like dew on our heated skin. I sit up and draw the curtains closed. They fall heavily across the window, and we're muffled in dark, with only an almost burned-down candle to light the room.

We curl up together. Rowan winds my hair into his hands, places a row of kisses against my neck. His breath is warm on my bare skin. "It was brave, what you did. Very, very foolish. But also brave."

I want to tell him I'm not afraid of the ritual. But I can't. It isn't the truth, and I've already told too many lies.

For a moment I let myself picture the shape of our lives, in the blurred space of *after*. We'll eat dinner together. Tell stories in the firelight. At the lake the water will be clear. The shore will be a harmless stretch of sand. There will be no more blood, no more payments. No more dangerous attempts at the rituals.

And Rowan—and I—

My future with him is such a dangerous hope. I can only allow myself the barest taste. Like picking up a final crumb. I turn over to put my arms around him, resting my head against his shoulder as I fold myself against him. He trails his fingers through my hair. Combs gently at the tangles, picks loose the scraps of leaves and tiny flowers still woven there.

I run my fingers lightly over the inside of his arm. He shivers when I touch the sigil. I feel the spell that's woven between us. A slender thread, delicate as filigree, but strong as steel.

"I'm so afraid," I tell him. "But I'm going to do this anyway."

Chapter Twenty-Four

The moon grows through the week until, on the night of the ritual, it's round and brilliant, crimson as a pomegranate.

As I walk down to the lake, the wind catches my skirts, and they drift out behind me. I'm all in black, a dress I found folded at the very depths of my trunk. It's dark and severe, cut low at the neck and high at the waist, unadorned except for a wide ribboned sash, embroidered all over in a pattern of thorn-sharp vines. The sleeves are sheer, folded back to bare my sigil-marked forearms.

Rowan and Florence are ahead on the path. Arien and Clover are by my side. We move in silence through the ruined grounds, past my locked-up garden. We pass beneath the arched gateway that opens to the shore, and pause at the fringes of the pale-trunked trees. The Corruption hasn't reached here—the grass still grows, and the branches still have leaves.

This is the last untouched place on the estate.

Beyond the blackened shore, the lake is eerily beautiful. There's a trace of haze in the air, the last heat of the day gathered above the water. A twinned moon is reflected, blurred by faint ripples. When I look out over the Corruption, something inside me gives a soft stir. I put my hand to my chest and swallow down the taste of blood that clings to the back of my throat. Soon all of this will be mended.

Arien and Clover pace back and forth with their eyes on the ground as they measure out the space for the sigil. We've agreed to perform the ritual as we did before, the same sigil on the ground, the same sigils on our wrists. But it will be me, alone, who touches the earth and casts magic. I curl my hands closed and run my fingers against the marks on my palms. Already I can feel the power awakening beneath my skin, like banked embers ready to flare alight.

"Here we are." I steady my voice. "I guess it's time."

Florence squeezes my shoulder reassuringly. "Good luck. Try not to do anything completely reckless."

I laugh. "I'll do my best."

She sits beneath the trees with her basket filled with blankets and bandages and a jar of Clover's bitter tea, waiting. I look at Rowan, who stands beside me. I want to say *something* to him before I go, but nothing fits. I take his hand, lean my head on his shoulder.

He twists his fingers against mine restlessly. "This is a terrible idea, you know. Of all the dangers you've gotten yourself into, this is by far the worst."

I cup my hands around his face and draw him down to me. I kiss him; his protests murmur to silence against my mouth.

"I can do this," I tell him. I try to smile, but I can't quite manage. "I *will* do this."

"What if your magic hurts you the way it did last time?" He rakes a hand through his hair. "What if it hurts you *worse*?"

I want to reassure him that all will be well, but I can't. My being hurt is the least of my fears. I'll only have this power for tonight; there won't be another chance to attempt this again. And if I fail, then Rowan will have to quiet it.

Even now, he's still pale and worn, his eyes bruised beneath with tiredness. Poison has clotted in dark stains under the skin of his throat and wrists. There's a halting unsteadiness to the way he moves, as though he's being very careful to keep himself here, held back and in control.

Though neither of us has said it aloud, we both know how much is at stake. Tonight will be the last time he can let the Corruption devour him. If he lets the darkness in, he will be lost. He will become that creature I fought in the garden. And if that happens, the only way to stop him will be with death.

I pull him closer and kiss him again. I don't want to think anymore, just be. I close my eyes and push away thoughts of him changed, or ruined, or *gone*. I think of how he ran his fingers over my bare skin. How my breath came out in gasps.

How the tether between us hummed and burned when we were together in his bed.

"You'll be with me." I touch my fingers to my wrist. The sigil throbs. He makes a soft noise, half sigh.

I slide my fingers beneath the loose edge of his sleeve and up along his arm, until the sigil is underneath my hand. It beats gently against my palm like a pulse. "You can feel it, can't you?"

Rowan wraps his hand over mine, against the spell. "Yes. I feel it."

I feel the magic shimmer through me. I can taste it: sweet and spiced, like almas cake and honey tea. I can feel *him*, the contradictions of his emotions. He's angry and frightened, angry *because* he's frightened. I know he wants the Corruption mended and he wants to keep me close, but he's afraid he can't have both.

It's strange, to feel his moods this way, like reading a page over his shoulder. Colors shift behind my closed lids, all laid one over another. First they're gray and grim and dark. Then I open my eyes and look at him, and everything softens to shades of peach and gold.

"We're bound together." I brush my fingers over the inked lines. "You'll be with me, no matter what."

"I'll be with you." Rowan kisses the corner of my mouth, the curve of my cheek. "Be safe, my love."

I push his hair back from his face and trace my fingertips around the delicate outsides of his ears. The silver rings pierced through his earlobes are warm under my touch. "You be safe, too."

We step apart slowly; I don't want to let him go. He sits down beneath the trees beside Florence, and when she puts her arm around his shoulders, he doesn't push her away. I give them one last look, then turn and walk down across the shore, my boots sinking into the mud.

When I reach the water, a cold wind blows across the surface. It's like frost against my skin. Icy sweat beads at my temples and drips down my neck.

I step over the outer lines of the sigil and stand very still as Arien and Clover circle around me. They mark shape after shape, until I am at the heart of the inscription they've drawn on the earth. Once they are finished, Arien smiles at me, uncertain and afraid. "Are you ready?"

I look out over the water. The lake ripples gently, and a wave breaks against the shore with a sound like a sigh. "I'm ready."

Arien grabs me swiftly, pulls me into a tight hug. I press my face against his shoulder, breathe in the paper-and-ink scent of him. He takes a deep breath, then bends down and cuts a line in the wet ground with his fingers. He draws his mud-caked hand across his chest, making the sign of the Lady.

Clover repeats the gesture. She wipes her muddied hand against her skirts and smiles at me. "Good luck, Violeta." She arches a brow and leans close to whisper. "By the way, you have an enormous kiss mark on your throat, did you know?"

I put my hand to my neck, my face full of heat, as she snorts back a laugh. I grin and shove her away, shaking my head. I inhale, then reach down to press my fingers into the earth.

Slowly, I draw my hand across my chest, leaving behind a streak of black over my heart.

Arien and Clover step back, careful not to blur the sigil with their feet. I kneel down slowly and put my hands flat against the ground.

The Corruption wakes up. A tendril of darkness uncoils and slithers across my fingertips. I stare at the lake, thinking of Rowan's family, all lost beneath that ink-dark water. Of Arien, caught by so many sharp-clawed hands. I let out a shuddering breath. *I'm so afraid.*

I look back over my shoulder. Arien and Clover stand together, just outside the sigil. Rowan and Florence wait beneath the trees.

I'm afraid. But I'm not alone.

Magic hums beneath my skin, and the sigil on my wrist begins to glow. As my power awakens, I'm filled again by an intense loneliness, a keen feeling of absence. The reminder that a part of me that was once here, burning bright alongside my magic, has been lost forever. When I close my eyes, I'm back on the ashen field where nothing grows, the thread of my power strung loosely around me.

I picture the thread knotted tighter and tighter. The new strength builds, and I feel it, hot and brutal, as it gathers in my hands.

I let it go.

Heat flares in my chest then spreads through my body in a feverish rush. I open my eyes and press my hands deep into the mud. Light blooms at my palms. I am the sun. I am a wildfire.

Around me, the lines of the sigil ignite into golden brilliance. It spreads along the shore until all the earth glows.

I can do this. I will do this. I'll send my magic into the darkness and mend it all.

The Corruption starts to writhe. I feel its fury, its hunger. It tries to fight me. I push; it pushes back. I dig my hands deeper into the ground. The power burns and burns and burns. The hollow, bereft feeling grows steadily, too, and the carved-out place within me fills with an unbearable ache. It *hurts*. I bite my lip, hard. My nose starts to bleed.

I can do this. I can do this.

The ground gives a hideous, endless shudder. Then all goes still. I turn around, a disbelieving laugh caught in my throat. Clover and Arien lift their hands from the sigil, smiling with hesitant relief. Beyond them, under the trees, Rowan and Florence have gotten to their feet. Hope fills me as I look back out across the shore.

It's mended.

The ground is smooth earth and scattered pebbles; the forest is pale, silken bark and new leaves fluttering against the star-specked sky. The water, rippling in the moonlight, is clear. I put a tentative hand back against the mended earth. *It's done.*

I want to sink to the ground and curl up and never move.

But then a strange, sharp *pull* jolts against my ribs. I stagger, nearly falling, as the earth turns darker and darker beneath my hand. Thin rivulets of shadow spread out around me, up toward the forest, and back down into the lake. There's a tremor, and then—a wound opens, tearing through the ground from my hands all the way to the edge of the water.

I hear Clover cry out, and Arien takes a step across the sigil. I throw out my hand to stop him. "No! Don't come close. It might—"

He stumbles back. I bend down and shove my hands into the ground. The Corruption rises quickly, wrapping around me until my wrists are snared. It tightens and tightens, a painful, crushing grip. The light of my magic flares up from beneath the mud. The sigil burns brightly, the intricate lines brilliant gold against the blackened earth.

I close my eyes and force all my weight against the ground. My heart beats desperately against my ribs. The world is too bright, too hot.

From far off comes the heavy sound of footsteps. Rowan runs to me, his boots smearing the sigil, fracturing the spell. Light scatters as the lines break apart. He grabs my shoulder. "Leta, you can't do this. You can't—"

He cuts off to a sudden, choked silence.

The ground shudders and he shudders. Blood stains the corners of his eyes. He blinks, and it spreads across his irises until they're crimson. At his throat the darkness writhes, the shadows unfold. I see him try to fight it: his teeth clenched, his breath fast. His scars tear open, and blackened water streams out from the wounds.

And then, just like in the garden, he's *gone*.

My hands are trapped by the earth, and I can't get free. I

hiss out a sharp, pained cry as he grabs my wrist. I try to pull loose, but he tightens his hold on me. "Rowan, *fight it*—"

But he can't; he's caught; he's lost. I close my eyes and try to feel the magic strung between us. I picture the thread of power held tight in my hands. I pull on the lingering magic and try to subdue him, just like I did before.

"Lie still, lie still." The words come out like a chant. "Quiet, stay quiet."

Blood runs from my nose as the crescent mark on my palm beats and beats. The whole world is heat and hurt and power. *My* power. The thread of magic wants to slip from my grasp. But I hold it tight.

I pull and pull and pull.

Rowan lets go of me and falls to his knees with a gasp. He has a hand at his throat. He takes another ragged breath. Then his eyes blink clear. "Leta, you have to stop the ritual."

"I can't." My voice sticks on the edge of a sob. "If I stop, it will only get worse."

He spits out a mouthful of ink-dark water. "Let it claim me—I don't care. I won't let you be hurt."

I shake my head, tears spilling from my eyes. I can't let go. The Corruption is quiet; I have it held, have Rowan held. But the poison isn't gone. I look down into the open ground, that endless, depthless dark. I was supposed to be able to mend it.

Then I understand.

This darkness before me isn't a wound. It's a path.

And I have to follow.

I'm so afraid. I'm so afraid. I don't want to do this. But I have to.

"Rowan." All I can see is that *path*, waiting to lead me into the lake. "I can't mend the Corruption here. I have to mend it in the world Below."

As soon as I've spoken, the earth that's trapped my wrists uncoils.

Rowan looks at me, his expression raw and wounded. "Leta, *no*."

"I have to," I tell him. "I have to do this, or it will never stop. It will spread; it will claim you; it will claim everything."

Arien comes over and puts his hands on my shoulders. Although his cheeks are tear stained, he looks at me evenly. "I'll hold it back for you while you're gone. Clover and I both will, just like in the garden."

His jaw is set, and his shoulders are squared. He has the same expression he wore the night after the first ritual, when he wasn't afraid of his power anymore. "I can do this, Leta. *We* can do this."

I pull him close and hold him tightly. I can feel the frightened beat of his heart against my chest. He grasps me back, just as tight, then lets me go.

I turn to Rowan and catch his face in my mud-streaked hands. "I'll come back." I kiss him, hard. "I promise I'll come back to you."

Silence closes out the world until there's only me and the

mud and the opened path. Then I see him, way out beyond the shore, a sliver of pale mist against the dark.

The Lord Under. He stretches out a hand as he waits for me. He knew—he knew all along that I'd have to do this.

I wish I could refuse him. Forfeit our bargain and tell him that I'll never, ever help. But there's no other choice. The Corruption is laced through the whole world—earth, blood, heart, skin. It's everywhere. And we will never be free—or safe—unless I mend it.

I get to my feet.

I go toward the lake.

I walk into the darkness.

Chapter Twenty-Five

I'm in the lake. One step and I'm past my knees. Another, and I'm sunk to my waist. The water takes hold of me. It's cold and cold and cold. Waves wash at my throat, then higher. The mud beneath my feet dissolves and the water closes over me, an icy shock. I'm pulled beneath the surface.

I want to go back to the shore and my garden. Back to the moment of moonlight where Rowan held me and I let myself forget the rest of the world.

I want to go back, but I can't.

The Lord Under is suddenly beside me, a smear of mist and shadows in the water. He speaks to me, his voice soothing. *Don't fight it.*

The lake floods my mouth, tasting of dead leaves and bitter tea. The pale glow of moonlight is gone. All is dark, even with my eyes open. Not the muted, marbled light of underwater but full dark. Fear closes in. My lungs burn and ache. I gasp, a rush of bubbles streaming from my mouth. Something brushes against my hair, my cheek. A tangle of lake grass, a piece of bone, the scrape of claws.

Don't fight it, Violeta. Let the water claim you.

Colors bloom across my blackening vision: blossom pink, rain-cloud silver. The tether is still there. Stretched from me to Rowan, from me to the world Above. No matter how far I go, how dark it gets, I'll always be tied to home.

I walked into the shadows. I came into the dark. I chose this, and I am not afraid.

I open my mouth. I let the water fill my lungs.

The world goes still. A terrible, lightless silence that seems to stretch forever. The mud is gone. The water is gone. I fall to the ground with a hard, bruising thud and curl over onto my side, coughing desperately as I drag in breath after breath of ice-laced air and ashen shadows. It's so dark that I can't see anything. I stretch out a hand and try to draw on my power. A faint heat flickers at my fingertips, but I'm too weak and numbed from my struggle against the Corruption.

I try again. Light flares, then scatters into sparks. Another light echoes in return, bright and brilliant. The Lord Under appears beside me. Shadows spill out around him, but at the center of the darkness he glows. Bone white, luminescent.

"Violeta." He speaks my name like it tastes of honey. "My Violet in the woods."

I try to get to my feet, struggling because my hair and dress and boots are heavy with water. I take a halting step, then stumble forward. I brace myself, expecting to fall past him—through him—but instead I land heavily against his chest. His arms go around me, startled. For a breath I'm held.

He's real. Solid and strong and *real*.

"Oh—!" I stagger back in shock.

His mouth tilts into a curious smile. "How . . . unexpected."

He closes the distance between us in a single stride and catches hold of my chin, tight. My breath comes loose in a gasp. *He can touch me now.*

His claws are cold and so very sharp. I try to shake myself free, but his claws dig in—not enough to pierce, but hard enough to pin me still, hard enough to drag a small, hurt whimper from my mouth. His eyes run over me, inspecting my knotted hair, my lake-drenched skirts. He scrapes his thumb against the blood beneath my nose, wiping it away.

Shadows—his shadows—rise around us.

I twist against his grip. I can feel the frostbitten burn of his touch as though his hands have traced all over my bare skin. My heartbeat echoes hollowly. The shadows spiral closer, winding around my ankles, my wrists, my throat.

"Let go of me!" I put my hands against his chest and shove him, hard.

He releases me and takes a smooth step back. I let my hands drop, then look down, realizing my hair and clothes are no longer wet. I touch my fingers to the streaks of now-dry mud on my skirts and try to shake off the rise of nausea and panic. I can still feel his magic slithering coldly through my entire body.

The Lord Under smiles at me, his expression one of studied

331

carelessness. "There's no harm done, my Violet. You're here, and safe, and now you can finish the spell."

"No harm done?" I whisper harshly. I look to the branches overhead. Somewhere above there's an open wound in the earth. Rowan, with his blood turned to poison. "You *lied* to me. Why didn't you tell me I'd have to come here to mend the Corruption?"

I try to keep the hurt out of my voice, but it creeps in. Even though I knew how cruel the Lord Under could be, I trusted him to be forthright, thought I'd be exempt from his tricks. Now, the realization that I am no different from anyone else he's lured into a bargain makes me feel angry—with him, and with myself.

He spreads his hands, as though in surrender. "Would you have agreed to help me if you'd known?"

I wrap my arms around my waist. I can still feel it, the determination that filled me as I made that first, terrible step into the darkness. I'd still have come here. Even if I'd known all along, I'd still have agreed.

I nod, avoiding his gaze, because I don't want him to see my face, the resignation in my eyes. "Yes, I'd have helped you no matter what. You didn't have to lie."

"I didn't lie." He is completely unrepentant. "You just didn't ask the right questions."

He means to trap me with whatever I've said, so what are the right words, the right questions? My thoughts tangle as I search for how to answer him. "Tell me why you need me here. Tell me what I'll have to do."

"The Corruption began from my magic, but it's slipped beyond my control. I can't call it back, can't mend it with my power. It needs an alchemist—an alchemist who can work not just in the world Above but here, too." He looks at me, smiling coldly. "Violeta, you're the only one who can see me and summon me outside the borders of death. The only one who can walk, alive, in the world Below. You're the only one who can cast this spell."

I look all around us: the mist, the trees, the watery, juniper light. Everything here is so quiet and still, so far removed from the torn ground, the blackened mud Above. It's hard to believe this place is under threat from the Corruption as well. "Where is it wounded?"

"I will show you." The Lord Under holds out his hand to me, but I don't move. His voice softens, both threatening and gentle all at once. "The moon is setting, Violeta. Come with me now."

His claws are smeared with my blood. His palm is crossed with lines, just as mine is. It feels strange to see a heartline on cold, inhuman skin. I don't want to trust him, but I've already wasted so much time. So I step forward and take his hand.

The sigil on my wrist pulses as he laces his fingers through mine. *Rowan.* The wash of colors is distant now, only the barest, pale echoes. But there. Still there. I think of everyone waiting for me Above. How close they are to safety. I hold the Lord Under's hand and let him lead me deeper into the world Below.

We walk quickly past rows and rows of trees. They're endlessly tall, their branches furred with slender leaves. In the litanies, the world Below is described as a forest where souls sleep. But this is not like any forest I've known. There is no sky, only branches and needle-sharp leaves, and crimson-red trunks.

Heartwoods, we call them in the mourning litany. And the deep red color of the bark is just like that. A bloodied, hidden heart.

We go farther and farther, our footsteps swift. The Lord Under grips my hand tightly. His gaze is set on the path ahead, his pale eyes distant and preoccupied. I turn the motions of the spell over in my mind, trying to prepare myself for what I'll face. Pretend this is no different from what I've just done Above at the lake.

Neither of us speaks. The only noise is from our hurried footsteps and the unsteadiness of my breath. The ground is covered with dark green moss, damp and cold beneath my boots. The path slopes down, the trees seeming to stretch taller as we move lower beneath them.

The enormity of it all—skyless, endless—is terrifying. But it's beautiful, too. An eerie, solemn beauty. And even though I'm wary of being led into this darkness, of where the Lord Under will take me and what I will do once we're there, I can't help but look at it with awe. It's a world. An entire world. Trees and trees and misted dark.

We move into a smaller, narrowed space. Here the lower-most branches are strung with tiny jars. Trapped inside are pale moths that dance and flutter against the glass, their wingbeats giving bright ghostlike flickers. The air is colder now, filled with dew that beads my skin and the ends of my lashes. Then the wind rustles the leaves with a susurration that—almost—sounds like a voice. As though the trees are whispering to one another.

I tilt my head, trying to listen; if I just concentrated a little harder, I'm sure I could make out words. When the Lord Under notices, an amused light sparks in his eyes. He pulls me to a stop beneath an arched bower of two enormous trees.

"Shouldn't we go?" It feels wrong to be still when I'm so aware of the moon fading above, of Clover and Arien holding back the darkness, of Rowan so close to being lost to the poison.

"A moment," the Lord Under says. "You have time for this."

He guides me to press my palm flat against the roughened bark of the closest tree. I feel a beat, steady and slow, then the sound becomes a voice. Many voices, solemn and musical.

"It's—" I look around wonderingly. "It's *alive*."

"You can hear them, can't you, Violeta?" He puts his hand beside mine and spreads his fingers. His face turns almost tender. "These are the voices of all my souls. My forest breathes and blinks and feels, just like you."

I lean closer to the heartwood, entranced by the sound of the interwoven voices. It's like a chant, a spell, a dream. Countless lives and deaths all *here* within the trees, whispering, whispering. "Why have you shown me this?"

"I wanted you to see my world. To know what it is that you'll be saving."

I let the weight of it settle over me. I am alive in a place where no one living should be. "I'd never thought about where our souls actually *go*," I tell him quietly. "The mourning litany sings about the forest, and the trees, but it's all so different from what I expected."

"And what did you expect?"

"We burn our dead." I imagine the scent of ash, the rush of sparks against a darkened sky. An ache fills me, and I know this is an echo of the memories I've given him. "The fire turns the body to holy ash. Sparks to the air, coals to the earth. I guess—" I glance at him, strangely embarrassed at how clumsy I sound, trying to explain. "I'd not thought about which part was left for you."

He peers down at me, his curious stare half-veiled by his pale lashes. "Which *part*? Well, you'll find out eventually, won't you?"

Shivering, I think of a pyre. In Greymere, they'd make the fires in a special field outside the village. We could see the smoke against the sky, and at night we could see the light of the flames. I picture the Lord Under standing in the field, his arms filled with a shrouded weight as he walks away into the darkness.

And then I imagine the weight in his arms is *me*.

I shake my head. "I'm not yours. Just because I'm here doesn't mean you have a claim on me."

"It doesn't?" His fingers hover just beneath my chin. I jerk my face away, and the points of his claws scrape through the air beside my throat. He lets his hand drop back, laughing. "No, you're not mine. At least . . . Not yet."

I suppress a shiver. I don't want to think about it, how my

soul will be here—and his—when I'm dead. "Take me to the Corruption. I want to mend it. Now."

The Lord Under brushes past me, the ends of his cloak stirring against my skirts. "Come on," he calls over his shoulder. "We're almost there."

We go farther into the forest, the trees lengthening as the path slopes deeper down. Soon the landscape begins to change, and there are stones among the trees. Tall, granite pillars covered with bright green moss. Mist traces through the air and over my skin.

The cold sinks into me, and everything is dark—there are none of the glass mothlights here. Each step we take stirs up grayish dust, like fireplace ash. It plumes into clouds that stick to my dress and my skin. The air—still cold—turns acrid. I cough and press my sleeve across my mouth. It hurts to breathe. "Where are you taking me?"

The Lord Under doesn't look back. "To the wound."

The path ends, and the forest thins into an open grove. At the edge are four trees, their crimson bark charred, most of their leaves burned away. They're *hurt*. I press my hand against one of the trunks, trying to feel the whisper of the soul beneath. It's different from the voice I heard from within the other tree. This one sounds faint and lost and frightened.

"What happened here?" I murmur beside the ruined trunk. "What happened to you?"

The Lord Under watches me with a curious expression. As though he's set me a test and now isn't sure if he wants me to succeed or fail.

I ignore him and press my cheek against the bark. I close my eyes as I strain to listen. The forest hums and pulses all around me, so full of power that it's impossible to comprehend. The soul speaks to me, but what I hear aren't words. There's a voice, intangible—alive and not alive. A heavy weight, a sense of *something* that I can barely shape in my mind, let alone name.

I press myself closer, the bark scratching my skin. And then I catch a flash of scattered, frantic images. A tree house beneath a pomegranate bower. A cake shaped like a crescent moon. A hand curled over a shoulder. Whispers in the dark. Confusion that gives way to slow, creeping dread.

Then blood and fear and water, endless water.

Everything sways dizzily. It's Elan I've heard, echoes from his soul.

"This is Rowan's family." The half-ruined trees. Four of them. Rowan's parents and his brother, and the last tree left empty and waiting. I scrub my hands against my face. Try to catch my breath.

"I told you my world was hurt, too." The Lord Under gestures to the ashen space where we stand. "Look around you, Violeta. This is what the Corruption has done."

My heart beats wildly, and I stumble forward, past the heartwoods that hold Rowan's family, into the grove. Here, the forest is blackened and bare. The trees are torn open, with leafless branches that stretch across the sky like desperate hands. I touch the nearest trunk. Beneath my palm, the bark is blistered, cracked, and rough. And it's *quiet*. There's no song, no pulse. "They're—"

"Gone. The souls within are destroyed, completely lost. And it will happen to the others, to the whole forest, if you don't mend it." He points upward. "You can see it, Violeta. You know what must be done."

I stare up in wordless horror. In the canopy above the clearing, the air is dark, full of heavy shadows that shift and churn between the branches. I've seen the darkness on the shore. I've seen the darkness turn Rowan into a monster. I've seen it fed and felt the endlessness of its hunger. And now I stand beneath its heart.

It seethes and writhes, an open, poisoned wound. It calls to me. A sound of despair and fury and depthless *want*. It knows me. Knows the taste of my power, the heat of my magic, the feel of my palms against the mud.

Darkness trails down over the trees, and I realize the Corruption has woken again on the shore above. I picture Arien with his hands sunk in the earth, fighting alongside Clover to hold it back. Rowan, poison filling his veins until there is only darkness left. This has to end now.

I rush toward the center of the clearing, where there's a circle of granite stones—like the stones that ringed the Summersend bonfire in the village. I slip as I scramble over, scrape one hand and both knees. Hurriedly, I sketch a sigil on the ground inside the stones, repeating the names of the symbols under my breath as I move across the ashen ground. When I'm done, the lines are blurred and unsteady, nowhere near as tidy as what Clover would mark.

I clean my hands against my skirts and step forward quickly

to stand at the center. But before I start to cast the spell, I glance back to the Lord Under. He waits outside the stones, back beneath the ruined trees. He's watching me intently.

"Go ahead," he says when I look at him. "Cast the spell like you did on the shore."

There's a desperate hunger in his face that reminds me so much of Rowan, that first day I saw him in the village. I dig my fingers into the crescent scar on my palm, trying to push down my wariness.

"That's all I need to do? Just cast the spell, and it will be mended?"

"Yes." The Lord Under smiles, and even his smile is hungry. "Don't be frightened. I'll be right here."

I remind myself that he has no reason to trick me again. All he's done—even the deception—has been for my benefit. I asked for his help, and so he's helped me. He's brought me here because this is where I need to mend the Corruption. And he wants it mended, too. The evidence of how much he has at stake is all around us in this ruined grove.

I force down the doubt that rises through me even as I ready the spell. Arien and Clover can't fight forever. I have to do this, and I have to do it now.

My magic has already started to build, rising in response to the churn of the Corruption. I feel the heat, the same heat that burned through me so fiercely before in the world Above. I flex my fingers open and closed, and light flares eagerly at my palm like a handful of bright petals.

Then I look at the Lord Under. His cold, cruel face and his sharp, pleased smile. I stretch out my hand to him, my palm upturned, the same way I did long ago in the midwinter forest.

"When I was on the shore, I wasn't alone." I reach toward him. "I want you to cast the spell with me."

Chapter Twenty-Six

The Lord Under looks at me so sharply that I'm certain he can see right down to my bones, my blood, my frantic heart. It takes everything within me to hold my face calm, keep my voice steady.

I don't move, and neither does he. I wait, daring him to call my challenge. If he means to harm me, if there is danger in this spell, then he won't step forward.

My hand, outstretched, begins to tremble. "I want you beside me. I've given up so much to be here. Surely you can grant me this. You need me, and I need you. We're connected."

At this, the hunger in his gaze intensifies, and he smiles, baring his too-sharp teeth. He crosses the stones easily and enters the circle. His cloak sweeps across the ground, stirring the dust as he steps carefully over the lines of the sigils.

He looks at my outstretched hand, then at me, and I can

342

see myself reflected in his eyes. The pale smear of my face, my bright hair like a captured flame.

"You know," he says, "you may not like the taste of my magic."

"I've cast with Arien before. I'm not afraid of shadows."

He laughs. "We'll see."

The Lord Under reaches to me, darkness already drifting from his hands. The frost of his skin is a shock against the heat of my magic, but I force myself to weave my fingers through his until our palms are pressed tightly together. We stand facing each other, his hands clasped around mine, his fingers over my fingers.

I take a deep breath. I thought I'd feel reassured with him close to me like this, but I'm still as uncertain as ever. A nervous laugh catches in my throat. "Aren't you going to wish me luck?"

He leans down until his mouth almost brushes my cheek. "Good luck, my Violet."

I close my eyes and think of gold and heat and sun. When I call on my power, the ache of absence quickly follows, the vision of myself bereft and alone in a blackened field. I push it away, pretend I am in the garden with my hands around the bramble vines. I see the thread of my magic strung loosely around me, feel the petals of heat bloom at my palms.

I reach for the spell, and the Lord Under's power is there alongside my own, another thread, one of sharp, spun steel. I clench my fingers closed, and his claws pierce my palms. I suck in a breath at the bright, sudden pain. The twinned threads of our magic snap tight, light pours through me, and our power ignites in a swift rush.

Shadows unfurl from his palms like silken ribbons. They weave around my wrists. His power is pale fire and new-moon shadows. It burns in me with a frostbitten ache. Apprehension rises through me but I force it down. I won't flinch from this. I've touched shadows and darkness before. I'm not afraid.

Instead, I let my own power—unsparing, brutal, granted for a single moon—blossom in my chest. I feed more of my magic into the spell, sparks blistering at my fingertips. The ground trembles as the lines of the sigil ignite.

And then, a sound starts up above.

The Corruption starts to *call*. At first it's soft and sibilant—like the wind. Then it turns sharper, harder. A plea, a snarl, a whine. It's familiar now, this voice, this song of want and hunger. I've felt it. I've spoken to it. I've kissed Rowan and tasted its poison in his mouth. *I know you.*

I open my hands and turn them up toward the sky. I let my magic answer the call. Light pours from me and spirals upward in thin, golden strands. The darkness in the sky churns and seethes. The air is alight with frost and sparks and ash.

The Lord Under sends more of his own magic into the spell. As we cast the spell together, I feel as though I'm undressed past clothes and skin. I've shown him some hidden piece of myself I didn't even know I had. His power on my power. His skin on my skin. His breath on my throat.

My power matches the cold slither of his shadows. At this moment, we are equal. *We are connected.*

I should be horrified. I've come to his world and seen things that aren't meant to be seen by anyone human, anyone alive. But buried further down—so far that I could almost pretend I didn't notice—is *pride*.

The Corruption writhes through the branches overhead. Water pours down over us, pooling within the circled stones. A cold, ink-dark wave washes over my feet. I send out more power into the seething darkness. Tendrils slither up from the earth, and I cry out, startled, as they snare my skin. Lines of darkness wind around my hands, my wrists. My mouth tastes of poison.

"Oh—!" I start to pull away from the Lord Under, but he tightens his hold on my hands. His eyes meet mine, and for one brief breath, his expression gentles. He blinks, slow, and his lashes fringe his frosted gaze. The darkness has spread over him, too, a tracery of thin, black lines beneath his bone-white skin.

"Violeta." He whispers my name, low and tense. "It will destroy both our worlds."

I know it will. I can't pull back. I have to keep going.

From above, more darkened water pours down. And then I can make out shapes. Slender arms and sightless faces and razored claws. The creatures that rose from the lake. Their hands reach out and tear through the branches of the trees. There's a pained, pitiful cry. Then another and another. They echo around us. The sound of souls turned *gone* as the trees are destroyed; devoured by the Corruption and absorbed to become part of the hunger.

I look back desperately toward the trees where the souls of Rowan's family sleep. They're untouched for now, but in no time at all, the darkness will be upon them. There are *lives* here, a whole forest of souls. I picture them all, enclosed in sap and bark, as mist trails through the branches. I picture Arien and Clover and Rowan, in the world Above, being overwhelmed by the creatures.

"No!" I feel the burn of my magic across my skin, my palms, my fingertips. "No. They are not yours to have. Come to me. *To me.*"

I remember what Rowan told me about the Corruption, how it first woke up and how he took the darkness inside himself to make it stop. I need to do the same. I need to let it in.

The dark lines on my skin snare tighter and spread farther, crossing my forearms and curving around my elbows. I cough, drag in a rasping breath. Blood streams from my nose and across my mouth. Even as the darkness covers me, I let the vicious brilliance of my magic burn through it all. The hurt, the fear, the darkness. I will fight this. I will *mend* this. I reach for my power. The threads of my magic, with the Lord Under's magic, are knotted around my hands. I pull on them, drawing them tighter and tighter. Light fills my palms. I let the brutal power gather, then send it up toward the sky.

At my wrist, the sigil hums, and when I close my eyes, I catch the far-off flicker of the world Above. It's the barest glow—rose and peach and gold—but it's there. I want to go back. To the shore, to my garden, to my home. But I can't. Not now.

I hope Rowan knows that I'm sorry. That I chose this, *all* of this. To fight with him and lie to him. To show him my scars. To make this terrible bargain. To fall in love.

I chose this.

I turn my face up to the wounded, ruinous heart of the Corruption.

"To me."

I let the darkness come.

The creatures fall—hungry, hungry. *Ravenous.* They've waited so long. They were so desperate, so *starved*, and now—and now—

A memory flashes. My hands grasped around the idol. I throw it hard against the floor. Shards burst like a fallen star beneath my feet. I'm on the ground, and there's glass in my knees. The shards are white hot. They cut me, but I don't cry out.

Claws rake across me. Sink into me, sink through me. They scrape deep into my arms, my chest, my wrists, my thighs. The Lord Under grips my hands as the creatures tear through my skin. I taste blood, I've bitten my tongue. I taste the cold, ashen burn of my magic.

The creatures cut me.

I'm carved up, spread open, ready to be devoured.

They cut *deep*.

I think of shards. I think of knives. I think of claws. I think of sharpened teeth.

The Lord Under is still beside me. He holds me close. "Don't be afraid."

I call to the darkness. *Come to me.* The sigil on my wrist beats out a rhythmic pulse. The earth will be mended. The poison will be gone. Arien will be safe. He'll turn fourteen at year's end, have a cake shaped like a crescent moon. Clover will give him alchemy lessons. He'll sit in the library and sketch patterns in his notebooks. He'll be *home*.

And Rowan—

And Rowan—and I—

I remember how it felt to lie beside him in his room, in the moonlight. How I pushed aside the uncertainty and the danger and tried to forget everything. For that brief moment, when I was curled against him, I was only Leta. Loved and warm and safe.

The darkness gathers from the sky, from the air, from the trees, from the pieces that have poisoned the Lord Under. The ground beneath my feet turns to softened moss. The frightened voices in the trees turn gentle. I hear them whisper. They tell me the trees are hungry, too. They tell me there's a hollow inside a new-grown heartwood, an empty space carved out for me.

But I'm not finished. I reach farther, *up*, beyond the world Below. I call to the poison that's tainted the lake and the shore. The poison that's infected Rowan. I call it down through the earth, through the worlds, and let it all in.

The darkness is inside me now. There's poison in my blood, my heart, my bones. I'm bitten and bled and devoured. Piece by piece I dissolve. I am consumed by the dark. I let it take me. I let it become me.

At my wrist, the sigil burns. *A seal on your heart, a seal on your arm.* I feel a wash of colors, of emotions. Fear and elation. Resignation and relief. I picture the world Above mended and protected and *safe*. Everyone at Lakesedge—Clover and Florence and Rowan and Arien—safe. Because of me.

The Lord Under catches hold of me and I sink against him. Gently, gently, he lays me down in the water that has collected at the center of the stones.

All I can feel and taste and see is hunger. Darkness above and darkness beneath and darkness within.

"Let me go home," I whisper. "Please."

He bends to me, presses his forehead to mine. "I will."

Chapter Twenty-Seven

The world is silent. A silence that swallows all sound. I'm adrift, far down beneath the water of the ink-dark lake. The waves rock me, soft and slow. They lift me up and up, until I break the surface.

It's dawn, but the moon still dips in and out of the clouds. Silver light traces the shore as I'm washed onto the darkened ground. The sigil on my wrist aches.

Far off, there's a faint light. A lantern flickers, a tiny flame that's almost burned down. Someone stands beside it. The ache in my wrist turns to a steady pulse.

Rowan is waiting for me. He touches the spell. I feel myself, held precious in his mind as colors wash over me, pearl and rose and gold. I picture an incandescent thread, knotted between our hearts.

Waves rush over his boots as he crosses the shore and

comes toward me. He bends to me, pulls me close. His breath is rough, unsteady. He's crying. His fingers touch my throat, searching for my pulse. He lets out a sigh, relieved, when he feels my heartbeat.

His arms tighten around me, and he lifts me from the lake. He carries me away from the water, back to the pale trees. "Leta," he whispers. "You're safe."

I try to respond but I can't move, I can't speak. I'm still lost in lightless silence. I lean against his chest, my head slumped heavily on his shoulder. I am a branch, a stone, a leaden weight. Behind us I can hear the lake, the hush and sigh of the waves. The sound softens as we reach the forest, replaced by the shiver of air through branches.

He lays me down beneath the trees. I look up at him—his eyes smudged with tired shadows, his throat marked by scars and bruises.

"Rowan." When I speak his name, the tether between us glimmers. *"Rowan."*

He leans close and brushes a kiss over my lips. At first, all I can taste is the lake. Beyond that, though, glows the tiniest ember, a little flare of remembered warmth. Honey, spice, molten heat. The two of us in the brilliant light beside the window.

The world comes awake, blink by blink, sound by sound. Someone takes my hand. Arien. He's crying, too. "I thought you were lost. I thought you'd be gone forever."

"No," I manage faintly. "Not forever."

I try to move, try to unfold. It takes a long time. I put a shaking hand against the ground and push myself upright.

Nausea surges through me. My lungs go tight. I can't breathe. I begin coughing, then can't stop, turning on my side as a wash of bitter, ink-dark water rushes from my mouth.

I can't—I can't—

All I can feel are claws, and teeth, and my skin being torn apart.

Rowan gently rubs my back as I struggle to catch my breath. I dig my fingers into the earth and curl forward as I choke and spit out the endless mouthfuls of poison. Finally, it stops. I try to scrub my mouth clean against my wrist, but I'm smeared all over with blood and dirt. I spit again, then slump down weakly, sprawled out with my back to the earth, my face to the sky.

Rowan folds his sleeve over his hand and wipes my face. Then he smooths back my hair and touches my sweat-damp cheek, looking at me as though he isn't sure I'm real. "Leta. You're home."

I try to smile up at him, but instead a sob slips out. My eyes blur, and I press my hands against my face. I feel like something broken that's been put back together imperfectly, the cracks sealed with gold paint. Mended, but changed. I can still feel the dark all over me. Inside me. The way the creatures tore me apart. The last terrible breath I took before I was devoured.

Florence tucks a blanket around my shoulders, and I curl into it gratefully. Clover kneels down beside me. She takes my hands between her own; her fingers alight with magic. Her power is warm against my skin, but the heat does nothing to cut through the chill that's overtaken me.

"You're safe," she says, her voice heavy with tears. "Oh, Violeta. I'm so glad you came back."

I slowly sit up. Rowan puts his arms around me and I rest against him, my fingers clutched weakly in a fold of his mud-stained cloak. I look out across the shore. The ground is still dark, the wound that opened and let me into the world Below still cuts through the earth. But everything is still. As though it's waiting.

I turn to Arien and Clover.

"You can mend it now." I don't have words, yet, for what I saw. For what I did. Perhaps I never will. "It's safe."

They exchange a look, then rise to their feet. I wait by the trees, just as I did on the night of the first ritual, and watch them walk down to the water. I can't stop shivering. Rowan holds me and strokes my hair, cards the tangles with his fingers. He murmurs to me as he picks loose leaves and bits of moss, all the pieces of forest and lake that are woven through my curls.

"You were brave." He whispers it over and over, and I let myself fall into the rhythm of his words. "You were brave, you were brave."

"I'm so cold."

He holds me tighter, close against his chest. "I'll keep you warm."

"Here." Florence takes another blanket from her basket and wraps it around both of us. She keeps her hand on my shoulder as we watch Arien and Clover work their magic on the shore.

Arien bends to the ground. Shadows unfurl from his hands, careful, controlled. They weave a delicate latticework across the mud as Clover presses her fingers to the earth. The web of shadows begins to glow as light streams from her palms.

The ground is still. No creatures rise. It won't fight them.

I think of that night, long ago, when Clover put her hands over my hurt knees. She and Arien touch the ground in the same way. Gentle, gentle. A press. A whisper. And it is mended.

Once again, the shore turns to smooth earth. In the pale forest, more new leaves unfurl from branches.

The blackness, the Corruption—it's all gone.

A thread of light glimmers over the horizon as the moon dips low in the sky. The clouds thicken, and raindrops start to settle on my skin and hair like a veil. A scatter of sparks drifts from my hands as the power granted to me by the Lord Under gives a final, bright shimmer. Then it goes dim. It's just my magic again now. Small and soft, the barest traces.

"It's done." My throat and chest and mouth feel scorched. "We've mended it."

Rowan takes my hand. "Yes, my love, it's done. We can go home."

Home. All I want is to go back to the house, scour myself clean, and sleep for a dozen nights while a fire burns in the hearth. Rowan helps me up. He puts his arm around my waist, holding me as we make our way back through the garden. The others follow; I hear their footsteps and the relieved murmur of their voices.

I wish I could share their relief. It's over, I'm safe, we're all safe. But a heaviness weights my chest, and I can't shake it off, no matter how hard I try.

The rain turns heavier, falling steadily through the leaves and over the lawn. I tilt my face to the sky, and the rain looks dark. Like shadows, like poisoned blood. My vision starts to blur. We reach the house, step into the kitchen. I take a single breath and let the scent of smoke, of spiced tea, of warmth ghost through my lungs.

Then the cold spreads over me.

I look down at my hands and touch the blackened crescent that scars my palm. It splits. Ink-dark water spills from the wound. There are cuts and cuts and cuts all over my arms and wrists and fingers. And my skin, beneath the wounds and the blood, is lined with darkness. Rowan gasps. "You're—you're—"

Poisoned.

"It can't be." I'm shivering so hard I can barely speak. "I mended it. It was gone."

But I can feel the Corruption uncurling beneath my skin. It has teeth and claws. It hungers.

Arien and Clover crowd through the doorway. Florence comes in behind them, the blankets still draped, forgotten, over her arm. Horror and despair fill their eyes.

"This was how I stopped the Corruption," I whisper. "I let it inside me. It's still there. It's *part* of me now. And I think it's going to destroy me."

Arien runs to me. I cling to him as he starts to cry. "You promised. You promised you'd be safe."

Clover throws her arms around me and presses her tear-streaked face against my shoulder. Florence touches my cheek with shaking fingers, her other hand pressed over her mouth. They encircle me, and for one single, perfect moment I am safe and I am home.

Then the darkness closes in. I take a struggling breath past the poison snared like thorns through my chest. My mouth is full of blood. My vision is blotched black.

Rowan pulls me close. His hand grips tightly at my waist, his shaking fingers knotted into my skirts. "Leta, *please*."

I wrap my arms around him and bury my face against his chest. His heartbeat is frantic beneath my ear. I know there's only one way this can end.

I look up at him, blurred by tears. "Take me to the altar."

"No." His voice turns fierce. *"No."*

I try to move forward on my own, but my legs give way. He catches me before I fall, and I sink against him.

Rowan looks at me with despair. "I can't do this, Leta. I can't give you to him."

"He's the only one who can help me."

His expression shutters. His arms tighten around me and he hesitates a moment. I think he'll refuse, that I'll be here in his arms until I'm lost to the shadows. But then he carries me into the parlor, with Arien, Florence, and Clover close behind us.

Rowan lowers me down beneath the icon. I clutch a handful of his shirt, drag him toward me. I start to kiss him, kisses that taste of bitter herbs, blood, and ash. "I love you."

He sighs a helpless, furious breath across my mouth, then he kisses me back. And in spite of all his fear and anger—he's gentle, so gentle, like I'm a fragile thing, made of glass.

I put my hand on the altar, smearing blood across the wooden frame. I find the dwindling thread of my magic and draw out just enough power to light a single candle. In the icon, the Lord Under is sharp-edged and dark, his fingers laced with shadows.

"What have you done?" I whisper, desperate. "What have you done to me?"

The world shifts and fractures. I see Rowan, with his dark cloak and long hair, haloed by the pale light from the window. I see the Lord Under, with the heartwood forest at his back, his hand outstretched, a sharp smile carved across his face.

Both come toward me. Both take my hand. Both whisper against my ear.

"Leta." Rowan sounds so far off, so far away. Like I am back in the lake, beneath the endless water. "Don't let it claim you."

"Violeta." The Lord Under runs his claws across the scar on my palm. "You did this to yourself, my Violet. You let it in. Our worlds are mended, but the Corruption isn't finished, not yet. It needs to devour you. Only then will it be completely gone."

I bite down hard into my lip until I taste blood and see stars. The pain steadies me, bringing the world back into focus. I reach for Rowan and cup my hands around his cheeks. I kiss him as the poison spreads through me, so strong and hungry and ruthless that I can barely fight it.

He strokes my face, his fingers trembling. "Stay with me, Leta. Please."

I think of an orchard beneath the moonlight, the whole world gone still. The two of us, alone among the trees. I rest my forehead against his and close my eyes. "I'm sorry."

Then I turn to Arien. He looks so hurt and wretched and angry that it almost breaks me. I put my arms around him as a sob catches in my throat. "I'm so proud of you, Arien. You were so brave at the ritual."

He presses his face into my neck and starts to cry. I hold him tightly and wish there was another choice, that I didn't need to leave him behind.

"You can't do this," he says. *"You can't."*

"Listen, my love." I put my hands on his shoulders and hold him still. "I need you to take care of everyone here. Take care of them for me."

He nods, his face streaked with tears. "I will."

I turn back toward the altar. Darkness gathers, and the air fills with mist. Waves of black water rush over the floor. Everything blurs and softens, until I'm shrouded in shadows. My heart starts to slow. I feel the Corruption in my blood, around my bones. I don't have long until I'm lost.

I see the Lord Under and the heartwood trees.

I get to my feet. It's almost impossible, the effort, but I don't falter. I stand before the Lord Under, meet the cold frost of his gaze as I turn to shadows and poison. "Take me back with you. Take me, alive, to the world Below."

He opens his arms to me. I step toward him. He enfolds me, as if with wings.

Then everything turns quiet, and I am gone.

Chapter Twenty-Eight

I'm curled on my side, in the center of the stones. Deep in my chest, the Corruption churns—it slithers and tangles, as though in response to my anger and despair. Threads of darkness vein my arms, my chest, and tighten against my throat.

Rowan lived for so long with this poison inside him. It hurt him and hurt him, before it almost claimed him entirely. And that was only a *part* of the Corruption. I have all of it within me now. All the darkness that poisoned the shore and the lake and the world Above. All the darkness that devoured the souls and the heartwoods and the world Below.

The Lord Under kneels down beside me. "Don't fight it." The same words he said after I'd walked into the lake. He leans over me, until all I can see is his beautiful, cruel face, and takes my hand.

My mouth fills with more of the ink-dark water. I shake

myself free of his touch, then gasp and choke and spit until I can finally take another labored breath. I put my hands against my face as I start to cry. I catch a muffled sob inside my palms, then swallow down my tears.

"You *knew*." I hate how betrayed I sound, that I can't hide how much he's upset me. "You knew all along that I'd end up this way."

His eyes narrow coldly. "Yes, I knew. I knew when you came to me that you would be able to do this. I needed your magic, but the spell wasn't all of it. More than anything, I needed your willingness to invite in the darkness, to offer yourself up, to let it in."

"You lied to me. You tricked me."

"Have you forgotten what you asked?" His words change until they match the cadence of my own voice. "*I just want to keep everyone safe. I have to make it stop. I need your help.* This— your sacrifice—was the only way."

"You know that isn't what I meant."

"I know what I promised." Angered, his features shift for a moment. Too many eyes, too many teeth, diagonal slashes opening at his neck. Then his face resettles. "They're safe. The Corruption is mended. I've never lied to you, Violeta."

I push back my sleeve. There's a deep, blood-slick cut through the center of the sigil on my wrist. I put my fingers against the mark and press down, feeling for the thread of magic that ties me to Rowan. A blur of emotions—mine and not mine—flutters through my mind. Faint and weak and far off, but still *there*.

"I just wanted to go home."

"And I took you home. I let you see everyone you loved, one last time." His implacable expression flickers, and for just a breath, he looks almost sorry. He tries to stroke my hair, but I push him away.

"Don't touch me."

The Lord Under takes a step back, then another, moving to the other side of the circled stones. "Don't fight it," he says again. "The darkness has to claim you. It will overtake you. You'll die and turn to ash, and your soul will sleep in a heartwood tree. Only then will the Corruption be gone."

As he speaks, I feel the poison snaring through me, tighter and tighter. It's harder to breathe, harder to speak, harder to see. I close my eyes and try to draw on my magic. It's past the full moon now, and my power is weak and small. Almost impossible to grasp. Every piece of me feels bruised by the effort, but finally, I catch hold.

Please. The Corruption writhes beneath my skin. My wrists, my throat, my heart, my lungs. *Lie still, stay quiet.*

At first, it fights. Pain sears through my bones, inside my chest. A flood of water fills my mouth. *Please.* I think of warmth and light. Of my skin, freckled and sunburned and unmarked by poison. I think of a deep, slow breath that doesn't taste of lake water. *Don't hurt me. Let me go.*

And then it all softens. The poison curls up, nestles between my ribs. The tightness in my throat and chest slackens. I take a desperate breath, run my hands over my skin to soothe the ache. But even though the Corruption has quieted, I can still feel its hunger. I know that soon it will reawaken, too strong for me to fight.

A drift of wind stirs through the needle-leafed branches. And the darkness whispers to me. *I won't hurt you. Let me claim you.*

I shake my head. *No.* I look at the Lord Under, who watches me in careful silence.

"Come here," I demand. My voice sounds like the lake. Deep, dark water that wants to drown the world.

He comes toward me, slowly, tensely, almost as if he's afraid of me. Maybe he never lied, but he never told the whole truth, either. And now I want to know. I'm not going quiet into the dark until I'm certain there's no other choice.

I meet his pale eyes with my own glare. "I'm going to ask you a question, and you will answer honestly."

He waits, expectantly. I consider each word, weigh it carefully before I go on. "Can your magic mend the Corruption, now that it's only inside me?"

He doesn't move. At first I think he will refuse to answer, but then his mouth curves very slightly into the barest hint of a smile. "Yes, it could."

"You could stop this?"

His smile widens until I can see the sharp points of his teeth. "That would depend on what you were willing to offer me."

I know I only have one chance at this. I think of how he swallowed my blood, my fear, my memories. Everything

I gave up to him at the altar. He could so easily let me be devoured. Whether he bargains with me now, or watches me die at his feet, either way he'll win. I need to make him realize that there is value in my safety. To make him *want* me, whole and alive.

In the Vair Woods, I was small and frightened and powerless, and I thought I had nothing to offer him. But now I have so much. I have family and love and a home. I have magic and strength.

I feel the shape of the word in my mouth. Let it sit on my tongue, until I can taste it. Then I tell him my offer. "Power."

He looks at me curiously. "Go on."

"You told me once there is power in fear. Well, I won't fear you. But if you can make me safe from the Corruption—take the poison from me—I will give you power." I press my lips together, holding myself steady, though inside I am alight with desperation. "I will love you. I will worship you. I will never forget you, even after I go home."

He steps closer, a pale glow against the quiet shadows of the darkened forest. His frosted-glass eyes, the fringe of his lashes, his hair like a veil of mist. Slowly, he lifts his hand and strokes my face. His claws are gentle as he traces the edge of my jaw. When he touches me, I remember how it felt when we cast the spell together. How raw and bared and *close* it all was. The cold burn of his shadows as they sang through me.

I lean my cheek against his palm for a moment. Then I put my hand over his and still his touch. "Will you accept?"

"I am considering it." He tips his chin toward the stones. "Sit."

My stomach twists into an anxious knot. *He hasn't refused. Not yet.* I ease myself back, until I'm sitting on one of the charred granite stones. He lowers himself to kneel at my feet. He looks down at my boots—sodden with inky water, clotted all over with mud from the churned ground.

"Do you think so highly of your company, my Violet in the woods?" He takes one of my boots in his hands and starts to untie the laces. "Perhaps I'd rather your soul. It would be much less trouble."

"But how much power is there in one soul?" When he doesn't reply, I go on. "Tell me, truly. Would I be worth as much to you if I was just another voice, whispering inside one of your trees?"

All I can hear is my heartbeat as I wait for him to answer. Finally, he laughs darkly and shakes his head. "No. Though I suspect you'd argue much less."

Relief sinks through me, and I force myself to smile at him. I fold back my skirts, so he can reach my feet more easily. "Oh, I don't know. I'm sure I'd find a way. As for my company? I'm the only person alive who can see you and summon you. I can touch you. I can walk in the land of the dead. I can hear the voices of your souls. So yes. I *do* think of myself that highly."

He looks up at me, and it's as though he's seen me anew. Like I'm a seed he planted here in this once-ruined earth, and now I've grown into an unexpected flower. He smiles at me, pleased.

He takes off my boots and sets them aside with the toes lined up. He takes off my ribbon-topped socks and tucks them into my boots. Then he looks down at my knees, and pauses when he sees my scars. He slowly lifts his hand, his claws hovering over the marks.

I start to think of Rowan, and even filled with poison—my heart aches. I remember how I felt when the two of us were in my garden on the night I told him about my magic. When he first touched my scars, his hands roughened and warm and gentle, that was the first time it woke up in me—my want for him, my unexpected longing.

"No." I grab the Lord Under's wrist. "Don't touch me."

Neither of us moves for a long time. I can hear his breath, feel the cold of him against my bare skin. I slowly release his wrist and unfold my mud-streaked skirts, smoothing them back down over my legs.

He gets to his feet and holds out his hand to me. His claws are blackened with dirt from my boots. "Come with me, then."

I look up, startled, then slowly stand and walk unsteadily toward him, hardly daring to believe I've convinced him. The ground is damp and very cold beneath my bare feet. I'm still shivering, and I can't stop. We stand, facing each other, the hem of his cloak brushing against my toes. He takes my hand, and his thumb strokes a crescent over my palm.

He leans down, until his mouth hovers just above mine. I

feel his breath on my lips as he whispers to me. "It will take time, and it won't be pleasant. You may come to wish you'd asked for the poison, Violeta."

Then he lifts me into his arms. I let him, though there's a part of me that feels I shouldn't. But I'm so hurt and sad and tired that I don't care.

He's too close, too real. Pale and cold and cruel. When I lean against his chest, there's no heartbeat. There's a wrongness to this. It's the same way I felt when I first listened to the voices of the souls. A sense that I have witnessed something incomprehensible. I shouldn't be able to see him or touch him or *be* here. And yet, now we're bound more inextricably than ever before.

He carries me through the forest, through the crimson heartwoods of the world Below. The path is bordered with luminous mushrooms that shimmer, ghostly, in the gloom. The branches overhead are strung with fluttering mothlights. They flicker, accompanied by a muted *plink plink*, the sound of wings against glass.

I reach to my wrist and touch the sigil, feel it pulse gently against my palm. I picture myself back at Lakesedge, in the kitchen, warm beside the stove. Florence with flour on her hands as she bakes a layer cake. Clover with her notebooks and bitter tea. And Arien. My brother, whose magic was strong enough to hold back the Corruption, to keep everyone safe while I went Below.

If I go back—*when* I go back—I'll tell him, *We did this together*.

There's a pull at the center of my chest, and I think of Rowan, the bright thread of magic knotted between our hearts. I imagine him touching the sigil on his arm, and the ache at my wrist responds with an answering heat. *I'll come back to you. I promise.*

Then I let my hand drop away. I curl up in the Lord Under's arms and put my head against his shoulder. Shadows and mist close in around us, turning the air to the color of storm-hued dusk. We go farther and farther, past groves filled with saplings, past dim hollows carpeted with ferns. Until, eventually, we reach a new part of the forest.

Everything looks different here. As we pass the trees, their bloodred bark starts to change. It's as though there are two forests, interlaid with each other. One is just trees and moss and mist, and the quiet murmur of souls. The other is . . . different.

The more I look, the farther we go, the more this second, hidden forest comes into clearer focus. It's like seeing ghosts of strange, half-faded human things that have found their way down from the world Above. On one tree there's an icon. Ancient, the paint weathered away to a blurred outline, the frame covered with lichen. A little farther along, there's a tumble of stones beyond the trees. Four walls, a space that might have been a window, once, and the tall shape of a chimney.

I don't know why, but I feel like the forest is changing for me. Making itself into a world that is more . . . familiar.

Finally, we reach a grove, where there's another path, lined by altar candles that flare alight as we pass, a haze of smoke and honey. The ground slopes upward. As we climb, a strange darkness starts to gather at the edges of the forest. There are shapes—tall and slender and almost *human*. I turn to get a closer look, but they fade, they slip, and no matter how hard I try to see them, they're always just outside my vision.

"You said there were no other people in the world Below."

The Lord Under looks at me curiously. "There aren't."

I blink and look again. The darkened shapes have vanished. There are only the trees and the spaces between them. Whatever I saw must have been a trick of the light, a dance of shadows across the mist-laced woods.

The ground levels out, and we enter a clear space lined with mothlights. Before us is an enormous tree. But it's not like the other heartwoods, with red bark and sharp, needle-fine leaves. This one is branchless and smooth and white, like it's been carved from bone. And as we draw closer, the bare, pale trunk begins to shift and change. The wood creaks and groans before peeling back to reveal the tender heart beneath.

Sap oozes down over the raw edges of the newly made arch. It smells fresh and sharp, like the bundled pine torches we burned at the Summersend fire. Inside, beyond the opening, there's a hollowed space that's all darkness. The Lord Under carries me toward the archway. He carries me *inside*.

I shiver and shiver and shiver. He puts his hand over my heart, and I flinch. "You're not frightened, are you, my Violet?" He smiles, amused. "After you promised not to fear me."

I swallow, with effort. "I'll never fear you. Never."

"I'll gladly accept your fear, should you change your mind. I told you before, you wear it well."

Inside the tree, the air is full of whispers, scented with petrichor and mist. I hear the voice of the Corruption; I hear the voices of other souls. The Lord Under still has his hand on my chest. And then, beneath his touch, at the center of my heart, I feel the darkness stir.

My magic stretches and unfolds as the darkness is pulled toward him. Sparks dance across my fingers. My power, his power, my Corruption, all begin to twine together. It *hurts*. I draw in a tangled breath.

I touch the sigil inscribed on my bloodstained arm. I am here. I have crossed between worlds. I have fought and bled and won. I have been poisoned. I have been taken into the dark. But I can still feel the throb and pull of the spell that ties me to the world Above. The magic is on my skin, inside my skin. Written on my bones, my heart, my soul. I promised to come back, and I will.

I will.

The Lord Under holds me close. We go farther inside the hollow heart of the bone white tree. We go deeper, into darkness stretching endlessly before us. I lift my head. "Where are you taking me?"

He's a silhouette, lit only by the silver mist that trails in from the forest. All I can see is the jagged-edged shape of the driftwood that wreathes his pale hair. The faintest outline of his face.

"I'm going to mend you." He looks down at me and smiles. "Then you'll go home."

The juniper light wavers. Everything fades.

Acknowledgments

The very first seeds of *Lakesedge* were planted many years ago, in a short story I wrote during my honors year at the University of Adelaide. Seeing that story transform into a published book has been such a wonderful process, and I am eternally thankful for all of the people who helped bring it to life.

Firstly I'd like to pay my respects to the Peramangk people, the traditional owners of the lands where I grew up, and which inspired so much of the environment in Lakesedge, and to the Kaurna people, the traditional owners of the lands where I live now.

To my agent, Jill Grinberg, thank you for falling in love with the early, untamed version of *Lakesedge* and for believing in me as we worked through so many rounds of revision. You've taken such great care with my book, and I couldn't have asked for a better advocate. Thank you as well to the entire team at Jill Grinberg Literary Management, especially Denise Page for your help and input, and Sam Farkas for your foreign rights magic.

To Tiff Liao, words cannot express how lucky I feel to have you as my editor. Your insightful advice has taught me so much about writing. I love how much you've always understood and celebrated the dark, romantic heart of my book. Thank you for indulging my enthusiasm for monster boyfriends and endless amounts of kissing scenes. I truly appreciate all your hard work and the time you've given to me and my story.

To the entire team at Henry Holt BYR and Mac Kids, I'm so grateful for all you've done to bring my book into the world. Rich Deas, thank you for creating the most gloriously gothic cover I've ever seen. I will forever be in love with your illustration of Leta! Brian Luster, your copyedits were a delight, and I am still smiling at how you pointed out the biggest flaw in the Lord Under's plan—if only *you* had been the one making a bargain . . . Mark Podesta, your eleventh-hour support has been wonderful. And to Morgan Rath, thank you so much for your publicity magic, and for helping *Lakesedge* reach the hands of readers. Thanks also go to Ann Marie Wong, Teresa Ferraiolo, and Mandy Veloso.

To the team at Pan Macmillan Australia, debuting in my home country is a dream come true! Thank you to Claire Craig, my wonderful editor, and to Brianne Collins, Candice Wyman, and Kate Butler, for all your work on the Australian edition of *Lakesedge*.

To Cat Camacho, Lydia Gittins, and the entire team at Titan UK, thank you for helping *Lakesedge* find such a perfect home in the UK. I'm so excited to be one of your spooky books!

To the booksellers and librarians who were my earliest readers—Cristina Maria Russell at Books & Books, Kiersten Frost at Brookline Booksmith, Kel Russell at Barnes & Noble

Indiana, Rachel Strolle at Glenside Public Library, Dymocks Adelaide and the YA circle—thank you for your incredible support. And to the authors who generously provided blurbs—Juliet Marillier, April Tucholke, Emily Lloyd-Jones, S.T. Gibson, and Dawn Kurtagich—I am so appreciative of your time, your advice, and your generosity in reading my book. You've all inspired me so much, and it was a privilege to share my writing with you.

To Kim Smejkal, thank you for guiding me through my very first revisions, and for being a grounding presence as I entered the chaotic world of publishing. You saw potential in the roughest, wildest draft of my book and I would not have made it this far without your help.

Life as a debut author can be such a storm of chaos, but I am so glad to have such wonderful friends to share this journey. Jess Rubinkowski, Cyla Panin, Jessica Olson, Lauren Blackwood, Ashley Shuttleworth, and everyone in the Monsters & Magic group—I am so glad to be here alongside you and your wonderful stories. Jenny Anderson, Kelly Andrew, Elora Cook, TJ Duckworth, Jo Fenning, Jordan Gray, Melissza Havas, Lillie Lainoff, Nat Lockett, Meryn Lobb, Leah Tesch, Emily Thiede, Ashley Schumacher, and Sarah Street—you were some of the earliest readers of *Lakesedge* and I can't thank you all enough for your enthusiasm and kindness.

Cass Francis, although you're an ocean away, in my heart we are sitting in a grungy Melbourne bar drinking gin cocktails. Cat Bakewell, cheerleader extraordinaire, you fill this world with joy and your wisdom has been so uplifting. Alex

Huffman, thank you for your art, for loving my book, and all your graphic design magic. Elizabeth Unseth, you are the best and I'm so glad we have shared our love of writing about terrible girls who want to kiss equally terrible villains. Saint Gibson, you are an inspiration and I adore you. Kit Mayquist, you have infused my life with magic. Ivelisse Housman, I am forever grateful for your enthusiasm, your kindness, and your gorgeous illustrations of Rowan and Leta.

To Katrine Williamson, Cait O'Callaghan, and Mhairi Tocher—your friendship over the past decade has meant everything. Thank you for your support, all the coffee dates, and for reminding me to come out into the real world every now and then.

To my family—I love you all so much. Barry, you've been here alongside me watching as I persisted in what often felt like an impossible dream. Thank you for giving me time to write, for understanding when I was a chaotic mess on deadline, and for always encouraging me to keep going. Felix and Orson, seeing how much you've grown to love writing your own stories fills my heart with joy. Kim, thank you for always supporting me to embrace my creativity. Mum, thank you for fostering my love of reading, for all of the bedtime stories and trips to the library. And thank you for all of your help babysitting while I worked—I couldn't have done this without your support.

And to Dad, thank you for a childhood where I could watch you work actual magic with plants. You inspired the alchemy in Leta's garden.